I0636930

REBECCA PATER

Falling Slowly

Falling Slowly

How do you forget your first love?

A Novel by Rebecca Pater

Ark House Press
arkhousepress.com

© 2024 Rebecca Pater

All rights reserved. Apart from any fair dealing for the purpose of study, research, criticism, or review, as permitted under the Copyright Act, no part may be reproduced by any process without written permission.

Cataloguing in Publication Data:
Title: Falling Slowly
ISBN: 9781763620179 (pbk)
Subjects: FIC042040 [FICTION / Christian / Romance / General]; FIC042000 [FICTION / Christian / General];

Design by initiateagency.com

Falling Slowly

How do you forget your first love?

A Novel by Rebecca Pater

Ark House Press
arkhousepress.com

© 2024 Rebecca Pater
All rights reserved. Apart from any fair dealing for the purpose of study, research, criticism, or review, as permitted under the Copyright Act, no part may be reproduced by any process without written permission.

Cataloguing in Publication Data:
Title: Falling Slowly
ISBN: 9781763620179 (pbk)
Subjects: FIC042040 [FICTION / Christian / Romance / General]; FIC042000 [FICTION / Christian / General];

Design by initiateagency.com

As always, thank you to Jason, who kept me sane in 2020.
Without you I think I would have fallen down a deep, dark hole.
I promise to always remember your advice.
Breathe all the way in and let it out slowly. And repeat.

Contents

Prologue
November 2006

"Sarah, Sarah," she heard in the background, but her focus was on something else – *someone* else. Someone far more interesting than the pile of Barbies Isabelle had laid neatly on the patio floor, along with the containers of clothes that each doll would wear for the big event. Today Michael – 'don't ever call him Mike', Mum had told them, because Aunt Caroline hated nicknames – was throwing the cricket ball to her brother Lochie. His dark curls were stuck to his forehead and after he'd bowled, he pushed them back from his eyes before jumping to catch the ball that Lochie hit with the bat. Missing, Michael turned to see where it had landed as Lochie started jumping in the air, screaming 'it's a six, it's a six', but Michael shook his head in disagreement and the boys fell into yet another argument about where the boundary was.

"Sarah," she heard again, and she reluctantly dragged her attention back to Isabelle. Today, like every time Sarah came to play – Ken and Barbie were getting married. Each guest had to be in their finest clothes and seated in the tiny chairs that formed a perfect semi-circle under the rose bush. She'd asked once if she could dress Barbie and Ken for their wedding, but Isabelle had said no. They were *her* dolls and only *she* could do it right.

It wasn't that Sarah disliked Isabelle. They had played together since they were babies, her Mum said. It's just that Sarah would have preferred to play something else once in a while. Maybe skipping rope or hide and seek. But Isabelle hated to get dirty and would probably say no like she always did.

Isabelle's new garden was so big and there were so many trees and bushes they could hide in. If they asked all the boys to play as well it could be really fun. Hiding quietly, waiting for someone to find her. But she already knew the answer she would get from Lochie. Like always he would say no and yell at her to go away 'cause nine-year-old boys didn't want to be anywhere near girls, especially their stupid sisters.' But Michael was always nice to her even though he was ten, which was a whole year older than Lochie. He was always kind to his sister Isabelle too and would play with her if she asked. Not dolls – boys didn't do that – but once he had come to one of her tea parties and he played snakes and ladders with her all the time according to Isabelle. Mum said it was because Aunt Caroline had made sure he had manners, and even though she'd tried with Lochie he was just too much of a boy. Sarah hadn't understood that because wasn't Michael just as much of a boy as all the rest of them.

Abandoning the make believe wedding, Sarah got up and brushed a few leaves from her jeans and pulled her sleeves down in an attempt to look tidy. Somehow, no matter how hard she tried she was always messy, her long brown hair always sliding out from the ponytail. Her Mum said it was the only way to stop her hair from looking like a bird's nest, but it never stayed in place more than a few hours, and they were always finding abandoned hair ties around the house. And forget about wearing dresses. Her knees were always scraped up from tripping and no matter how careful she tried to be when she was eating, at least some of her meal ended up down the front of her clothes. Mum had given up buying her pretty dresses with matching ribbons, like the kind Isabelle always wore, and now made her wear bright tee-shirts with lots of pictures on them so no one would notice the stains.

Heading over to the grass where the boy's disagreement had turned into a heated argument over which trees were the boundary for the cricket game, Sarah picked up the ball and took it over to Michael. She stretched her arm out to him, patiently waiting for him to notice her and take the ball. But instead of his usual smile, he turned to her with a frown and a growl in his voice she'd never heard before.

"What did you do that for? Now we'll never remember where it landed and if it was a six or not. Just go back and play with your dolls."

"I thought I could play with you. I'm good at cricket, and I don't have to bowl, I can just catch the ball when Lochie bats," Sarah whispered, her voice disappearing in embarrassment and confusion at his anger.

"We don't want you playing," Lochie piped in. "Nathan's the fielder for us."

"But he's only three. And he can't catch." Sarah looked over to see Nathan lying on the ground pulling up chunks of grass and throwing them into the breeze, completely unaware there was even a game of cricket taking place.

"So what?" Lochie spat at her. "A three-year-old boy is better than a six-year-old girl. Go away."

Looking to Michael for a smile of support, Sarah was surprised to see that he had turned away from her and thrown the ball to Lochie.

"Your turn to bowl. I'm batting, and the first lot of trees is the boundary," he bellowed, completely ignoring Sarah and moving to retrieve the cricket bat from where it had been thrown before their argument. Sarah, feeling like her heart at been scrunched up and thrown away, slowly made her way back to the wedding where the bride was eager to start the beginning of her new life.

Ken was waiting for her with a power ranger as his best man. Isabelle must have borrowed him from her brother's room. If Sarah had taken anything from Lochie he would have snatched it back and probably hit her, as long as Mum or Dad weren't around. But Michael never minded sharing with his sister. Well he didn't use to. Maybe he would now because today he was being just as mean as every other rotten boy she knew.

"Where have you been? We were about to start without you," Isabelle asked as Barbie glided down the aisle towards her dream man, perfect in a tuxedo. His face was plastered with a smile that would never change as he stood waiting for his bride, while Isabelle hummed the wedding song. Sarah, confused by the way Michael had dismissed her, held back her tears as she repeated Ken's vowels to Barbie, declaring he would love her until death they did part.

~~~

"That was a nice visit," Mum said as she pulled out of the longest driveway Sarah had ever seen. "I can't believe Caroline already has everything unpacked and the house looking so perfect. They've only been there for a week. And thankfully she didn't notice the patch Nathan made in the lawn. I would have never heard the end of it if she had seen him pulling up all that grass." Pulling out into the traffic she caught Lochie's eye in her rear view mirror.

"Did you have fun playing cricket?"

"Nope. Michael's getting as bossy as his sister, and stupid Sarah thought she could play with us."

"Sarah is not stupid Lochie, and if she wanted to play you should have let her. I don't want to hear you talking about any girl like that again. I'm a girl, do you think I'm stupid?"

"You're not a girl, you're just Mum," Lochie snorted.

"I am too a girl, and I intend on staying one until I'm old and grey," Mum replied.

"Well you look kinda old to me already Mum. Maybe you just used to be a girl."

"I'm going to pretend you didn't say that Lochie," she growled. Keeping her eyes on the road her attention turned to Sarah.

"And did you have a good time with Isabelle? I'll never understand how that girl stays so clean even when she plays outside. It looks like you've been rolling in the grass catching cricket balls all morning, even if you weren't. Next time if the boys say no just come and get me, and I'll make them let you play."

"No thanks Mum."

"*Okay*, not a fan of cricket anymore?" her Mum asked.

"No … just don't want to play with boys anymore. They're all mean, and I don't like them." Unable to hold it back any longer, one small tear rolled down her cheek and she was glad her Mum was busy looking at the road and couldn't see her in the back seat. Lochie had turned his attention to his Gameboy or he would have teased her for being a sook and Nate was asleep in his car seat. She didn't really know why she was crying; she just knew that she felt sad. But she did know she wasn't going to play Barbie weddings with Isabelle anymore. Because all the other times she had played she always pretended that Michael was Ken and that she was Barbie. But now he was just as mean as her brother.

Chapter One
Jillian
22 June 2018

Approved. They were finally approved.

It hadn't been an easy process, but finally they were coming out the other side. To begin with, there had been the initial interviews and the paperwork. They had laid their lives out for strangers to pick through, deciding if they were suitable to go to the next stage. Then had come the medical exams for both her and Matthew.

For two years Jill had been poked and prodded by different doctors and she'd sworn at the time she was never going to back to a hospital. But if she wanted to be a foster parent she had no choice. The agency insisted on making sure they were both in good health before they would take their application any further. She still couldn't decide whether that had been the worst part of the process or if the psyche eval had been the low point. Dredging up her history and having to explain why her first marriage had only lasted two years, and how all her recent medical procedures had affected her.

Matthew hadn't gotten off lightly either. He had been forced to recount how he had felt when his wife Amelia had been killed years ago, reliving the worst moments of his life, and the pain of trying to raise his baby daughter on his own, feeling inadequate and lonely.

In the end they were both declared sane by the psychologist, although Jill hadn't been sure she would stay that way before they made it through the ordeal. Even Zoe had been dragged into the application process, and at twelve she hadn't been that thrilled with the idea at first – especially having strangers asking her personal questions about herself and her parents. She was slowly come around though, and Jill couldn't wait to tell her that soon she wouldn't be the only child in the house.

This hadn't been the path Jill and Matthew had planned. Married a few months after her divorce was finalized, they knew they didn't have the luxury of time to start the getting pregnant process. And because she had been unable to fall pregnant during her first marriage, she had engaged the help of a fertility doctor immediately. At the time of their wedding she was already thirty-eight and didn't hold out much hope. But more than anything she wanted to be a mother and had been willing to do whatever it took.

Whatever it took turned out to be much worse than she could have imagined. Endless blood tests, humiliating examinations, injections that made her feel like a crazy woman (hormones, hormones, hormones) procedures for egg retrieval, and the waiting. Waiting to find out if there were any eggs, waiting to see if they fertilized, waiting to see if the fertilized eggs survived the first few days of their microscopic lives. And then after implantation there was the waiting to see if they took. With every unsuccessful implantation she had to wait two more months before she could start it all again.

The added layer of all these procedures was the feeling that as a woman she was a failure. Matthew could have married someone younger, someone who had a much better chance of giving him the other child he craved. Instead he'd chosen her, knowing that she hadn't been able to get pregnant even when she was younger. And despite the mood swings, the hysterical crying for no reason and the occasional rages that came out of nowhere that frightened her more than anything, he stood by her. He told her that even though he would love to have another child, nothing even came close to his love for her. She was enough for him.

Jill had one successful implantation and for eight glorious weeks she had been pregnant. She'd felt so feminine, part of that special group of women who could say, "I'm growing a human being. Inside of me. Can you believe it?" The miscarriage had almost undone her. Two years of constant disappointment followed by short bouts of hope, only to be crushed again had left her circling downward to a place she never thought someone like her, someone determined and strong would ever be. But even in the face of repeated failure she insisted she wanted to continue. In the end, it was Matthew who said it was time to stop. They had Zoe and Jill was her mother, even if she hadn't given birth to her. And they had other options. Weren't there babies all over the world who needed homes? Maybe they could adopt.

Unfortunately, adoption wasn't the easy process they had hoped for. It wasn't like a couple could just get on a plane to their country of choice and arrive at an orphanage and say, 'here we are. Come to save an adorable baby, only a few days old we hope, from a life of poverty. We're nice people we promise, and we'll give this perfectly healthy baby a wonderful life back in Australia.'

Babies, it turned out, were few and far between. The waiting list was long and getting longer as more countries closed their doors to international adoption. There were children that could be adopted but they were older, and more often than not they had health issues or were victims of abuse. Matthew and Jill felt they could love a damaged child, but they weren't sure they wanted to spend more years waiting. Waiting for the wheels of bureaucracy to turn, and not just dealing with one government, but two, both of which seemed to want to make the process as difficult as they could – just so one family could bring love and safety to a child.

It was her sister Beth who'd pointed out that Australia actually had plenty of their own damaged, neglected children who needed love and a safe home. Why didn't they find out if they really did have what it took to parent someone else's child. Agencies all over the country needed homes for children, some short term, some long term. And so began their journey towards fostering. Finally, after almost a year she'd received the call that they were deemed suitable.

A quick text to Matthew with only the two words 'we're in' was followed by a return text of a thumbs up from her husband but she hadn't expected anything else. His Friday afternoon staff meetings were sacred and anyone who expected to advance at Sustenance wasn't checking Facebook or answering their texts between three and five-thirty. Instead they were listening and contributing their ideas to one of the fastest growing companies in Australia's health food industry. So it wouldn't have looked good if the boss broke his own rule and sent his wife a lengthy message.

Jill was still astounded at the success Sustenance had become. It had been a gamble buying the run-down company two years ago. Matthew had been the accountant for the previous owners and when they decided it was time to sell up and see the world, Matthew leapt at the chance to buy them out. He had been banging his head against a brick wall for years, frustrated with the two aging hippies he worked for. They had never had any business sense and didn't think that using marketing was an ethical way to sell a product. Their philosophy was '*the food should just speak for itself.*' Which was fine if anyone had ever heard of them. The food line had been good, if a little limited, but the company just needed – well – Matthew.

His energy and passion for providing truly healthy food, along with his vision for Sustenance had been the perfect combination for success.

He'd surrounded himself with people just as passionate about healthy food as he was. Matthew wasn't hindered, as many bosses were by pride and the need to be right all the time. This meant his staff were free to come to him with their ideas and suggestions. They weren't always good ones, but they were always considered, and his team loved him for that. The result was that they finally had the right exposure in the small, but growing market and the team were adding new products all the time. The Australian public were becoming more aware that most of what they had been eating wasn't really food at all, and now Sustenance was having trouble keeping up with demand.

Jill was seriously considering making the move from her current law firm to becoming in-house counsel at Sustenance. The role would only be part-time and as the owner, she could choose her hours and work from home when necessary. With the extra little people that would be living in her house she didn't think it was a good idea to stay full-time where she was anyway. Especially when full-time meant late nights and weekends.

Jill knew she could contribute to the company they owned together. She didn't quite share Matthew's obsession with healthy eating, but it was growing on her. If only they could invent a chocolate that tasted exactly like a white Lindt ball but came under Matthew's exacting standards – no sugar, no dairy, no grains and especially no GMO's – she could totally get on board. And don't think that she hadn't made her request known to the staff at the last Christmas party. One grumpy nutritionist had pointed out that white chocolate had no health benefits at all and that they were working on a formula for healthy dark chocolate truffles. The rest of the staff had humoured her and promised at least to try. Jill didn't hold out much hope though and still had to resort to eating the real thing from the box she hid at the back of her desk draw at work where Matthew would never find them. But seriously, what harm could it do to have something a little bit naughty every once and a while? A girl had to live didn't she?

At least dinner tonight would be delicious. Caroline liked to keep it healthy too, but on special occasions she let her rules slide and cooked something special. And here they were, six years since Isabelle's death, and they were still having dinner together once a year. A night to remember Adam and Caroline's daughter who had been tragically killed when she was twelve by a car who was being driven by a elderly man having a heart attack. But it was also a night to catch up with each other and share all the important things that were happening in their lives. Tonight the timing couldn't have been better. Now she and Matthew could make their announcement. They were actually going to be foster parents.

And suddenly it hit her. Deep down in the pit of her stomach, and nausea washed over her like a tsunami. She was going to bring a stranger into her home. Probably, over time, many strangers. Kids who would come with emotional issues and could cause chaos. And what if they didn't like Zoe. Or she didn't like them. This could be an absolute disaster. What had they been thinking?

Chapter Two
Joan

She picked up the stick again. Nothing had changed since she saw the result an hour ago. Positive. Even though the situation wasn't. This was the last thing she needed, they needed. Another baby. Wrapping the pregnancy test in toilet paper, she shoved it to the bottom of the rubbish bin, not wanting to dwell on her dilemma anymore.

Bella had been an amazing surprise and Joan had sailed through her first pregnancy. She was never sick and didn't get tired until right at the end. She'd continued working with David, designing homes for their building company, and only stopped working when she was eight months pregnant. Other, younger woman had complained to Joan that it wasn't fair. She didn't gain too much weight and had bounced back within months to her former pre-baby weight once the baby was born. And Bella had been so sweet and easy. She slept through the night by eight weeks and hit every milestone on time or early.

Before Bella was one, David suggested they weren't getting any younger and thought they should try for another baby. It had taken longer to get pregnant this time, over a year. Probably because of the stress of trying and being that little bit older, Bella was already two and Joan was nearly forty-three when the stick finally said yes.

David and Joan had been thrilled when she finally did get pregnant again. She'd been warned there was a greater risk of miscarriage and abnormalities such as Downs Syndrome. Thankfully, all the tests came back normal, but that's where her good fortune ended. Her second pregnancy had been the complete opposite of her first. She was nauseous before she even knew she was pregnant, and once confirmed, the morning sickness followed quickly. For months she felt like she was being rung out. Nothing stayed down except fast food, which she hated, but without it she would have become a stick. The grease and the hormones made her skin breakout for the first time since she was fourteen and her hair hung limp around her exhausted face. And right on cue Bella decided to emerge from sweet baby-hood into a toddler. The terrible twos had come late, and she mistakenly thought they had avoided them. It was a shock to Joan who could barely get off the couch, let alone manage her daughter who had turned into a little monster.

David apologized repeatedly for wanting another baby and getting her into that state, but it didn't make anything better for Joan. She was the one who had to endure the constant tiredness and the rolling nausea that only ceased for an hour after she threw up, before returning full force. The first time she woke up feeling like herself she was already five months pregnant. For one blissful month she was able to enjoy being pregnant. The baby, a boy they were going to name Will, was growing and Joan began to gain some weight of her own.

When the doctor told Joan he was a little concerned about her blood pressure at twenty-eight weeks she promised to keep the stress to a minimum and watch her diet. With no previous health problems, he said it could be her age and weekly doctors' visits became mandatory. When her face started to swell along with her hands and ankles and her blood pressure rose above what was safe, she was admitted to hospital for monitoring and at thirty-six weeks Will was born by emergency caesarean section. She had been fine once the baby was delivered and Will only needed two weeks in the hospital NICU, and then he was able to go home. But the doctor had been very clear. No more babies.

Joan agreed with the doctor that two babies were plenty, and David promised to get a vasectomy. But in the time that had passed since Will had been born he hadn't quite gotten around to it.

The first time David cancelled the procedure was because his father suffered a mild heart attack. He was fine after a few days in hospital, but it took David another six months to pluck up the courage to go back to the doctor. The second time the procedure was cancelled, it had been the doctors fault. Suffering from the flu, he left a message asking David to call back and make another appointment for the following week.

Between having two kids, running their building company on his own while Joan was home with said children, and his secret fear of having someone actually perform such a barbaric operation on him, David had accidently, on purpose, forgotten to call back. And of course, the one time he and Joan had managed to get a night together with both children asleep at the same time (because Will was not the easy kid his sister had been) David had been a little too eager. Protection forgotten, here she was, pregnant again. Just like the first time. Not planned. But this time she knew what could happen and the risks were considerable. She was another two and a half years older, and with a history of high blood pressure this pregnancy, she thought, could end in disaster.

And it wasn't just her health that worried her. If she'd thought Bella had been naughty at three, Will was another matter. He hadn't even waited until his second birthday before the tantrums started. She tried everything, but he was impossible. Reasoning with him was useless – the professional who'd invented that strategy obviously didn't have kids. Smacking was out unless you wanted Social Services around, and he didn't respond to rewards or taking his toys away. How was she ever going to cope?

Leaning over the toilet she threw up for the second time today. The first time had been because of morning sickness. This time it was from fear. Washing her face under the cold water, she rinsed her mouth and then like a girl does, put on her lipstick. Tonight was not the night to dwell on this. It was her sixth wedding anniversary. And before dinner with David at their favourite French restaurant they'd agreed to drop in and have a drink with the others. Some years they stayed for dinner with everyone to celebrate Isabelle and commemorate her life, but Caroline completely understood that tonight David and Joan just needed a night alone.

Joan made a quick decision that she wouldn't tell David about the baby tonight. Tomorrow would be soon enough. Flicking off the bathroom light she walked through the master bedroom they had designed together and found David waiting for her while his mother fussed around her grand-children, probably with a pocketful of forbidden chocolates.

"You look beautiful my darling," David said holding a bunch of her favourite lilies. "You're glowing."

Joan smiled and thanked David for the flowers while thinking to herself, glowing, *David, you have no idea.*

Chapter Three
Beth

"Sarah. Come on. I'm sick of you making us late," Beth yelled down the hall hoping that her middle child could hear her over the music she was blasting in her bedroom. She turned to Nathan and pointed at the couch.

"Sit down and don't even think of disappearing," she ordered before striding down the hall towards her daughter's bedroom.

Still shocked and angry at Nates recent activities, she could hardly bear to look at him, let alone have a civil word at the moment. Banging on Sarah's bedroom door she only waited a second before opening it. The chaos was worse than usual. Clothes were strewn across the bed and drawers were half open with jeans hanging out. Her dressing table was littered with more tubes of lipstick than Beth had probably owned her whole life and yet again Sarah's hair straightener was left on. Afraid the house would burn down one day, Beth made it a habit to check all Sarah's hair straighteners, curlers and dryers were off and unplugged after she left for school every morning.

"Sarah, it's time to go. Grab your coat and get in the car please," Beth said as she leaned over and unplugged the straightener.

"Hey, I wasn't done yet."

"Your hair looks straight to me. Now let's go."

"I was going to curl it."

"With the straightener?"

"Yes mum. That's what you use," Sarah informed her as she rolled her eyes and slumped her shoulders in disbelief at her mother's stupidity. "How do you think it's done? With those old curling tongs you won't throw out."

"I like my tongs thank you. Although it was easier when a girl could get a spiral perm done."

"A *what*?" Sarah exclaimed.

"Never mind. You look fine so let's go. We're only going to Caroline's. I don't know why you care how you look; it's never bothered you before. And I'm surprised you're even coming. I've been waiting for your excuse to get out of dinner all week."

"I decided it would be fun to see everyone. Lochie's going to be there and we hardly ever see him since he moved out."

"Well he's only coming to see Michael so don't expect him to hang out with you all night."

"Chill mum. I promise not to be tragic. I just want to see my brother." She grabbed a lipstick, a much more muted colour than she normally chose, and applied it, smiling into her mirror. For the first time Beth noted that the usual torn jeans and singlet top were missing, and Sarah had replaced them with a pair of bootleg jeans in dark blue with a cream peasant style top with beading on the bodice and flared sleeves.

"You look pretty tonight," Beth observed, before the penny dropped. Michael was coming home today. Beth had hoped Sarah's little crush would disappear once he was out of the country, but evidently she was wrong. The muted makeup, the casual, but very flattering new clothes. She was hoping to impress Michael tonight.

"Thanks Mum. If I could just have an extra few minutes to put some waves through my hair?"

"No. We're leaving now. If you want to fiddle with your hair, then drive yourself."

"In this traffic. No thanks. I'll grab a ride with you. Maybe have a glass of wine with dinner." Sarah had turned eighteen two months ago and was enjoying the freedom having a licence bought, but she wasn't a fan of driving in the dark and at this time of the year the sun had already disappeared.

"You're not going to get drunk are you? I don't think I'm ready to see that."

"No Mum, I've got work tomorrow," Sarah sighed as she grabbed a band and in thirty seconds, she had pulled her hair into a flattering bun on the top of her head. *How did girls do that?* Beth wondered as she turned off the bedroom light and gently pushed Sarah towards the front door. Nate was still sitting on the couch as ordered, staring at his phone. Beth hated that phone, and after what Tom had told her last night she wished she could smash it with a hammer and then throw it off the roof or into the sea. Even a puddle would do. But Nate bought the phone with his own money after getting a part time job at Big W and constantly reminded them it was his and they couldn't touch it.

Tom was pulling into the driveway as Beth locked the front door. It was already five-thirty, but they were driving against the peak hour traffic so they wouldn't be too late. At least they didn't have to wait for Tom to shower and change after work anymore. When he'd worked as a plumber it had been a necessity after a day of fixing toilets and digging up old pipes. His work as a history teacher meant that he still looked good at the end of the day and he came home with a smile on his face, even after two years of full-time teaching. Beth had waited for the shine to wear off, but he loved the career change he'd made and insisted he enjoyed working with teenagers all day. She on the other hand loathed teaching and would be glad to walk away completely. With the news she'd received today she would be able to give it up for good.

"Hi Tom," she said, leaning over to kiss her husband hello as the kids strapped themselves into the back seat.

"Sorry I'm late. I just got so caught up in my prep for next term I lost track of time."

"You do know none of the other teachers go to school during the holidays don't you Dad?" Nathan said, "Isn't that the only reason to be a teacher? 'Cause of all the holidays."

"I happen to love teaching Nate, and for your information, I wasn't the only one there. Some of us care about your education."

"Yeah, yeah," Nate mumbled as he put his buds into his ears, conversation over.

"Did you say anything to him today?" Tom asked Beth quietly. She looked over her shoulder and saw that neither kid was paying them any attention. Sarah was texting or snapchatting or whatever the latest app was. And Nate barely acknowledged them these days unless he wanted something.

"No. And I don't think I'm the person for the job. You're his father," she whispered. "You need to be the one to talk to him. He'd be horrified if I brought it up, and to be honest, so would I."

"Fabulous," Tom muttered under his breath, but Beth heard him. Lochie had never given them this kind of trouble and until last night it never occurred to her that Nate would either. Teenagers. Every time you put out one fire another would ignite. And this one was a doozy. It wasn't just that it was disgusting. There were laws to take into account. The last thing they wanted was for the bad decisions he was making now to follow him into his adult years.

Chapter Four
Caroline

Caroline surveyed the dining room one last time. The table was set for the twelve she was now expecting for dinner. Michael had texted from Sydney asking her to set another place but hadn't given her any more information than that. Maybe he'd invited an old Uni friend for dinner.

Excited didn't even begin to explain how she felt. It was over a year since Michael had been home, having been away for a year studying medicine at Johns Hopkins University. With his high grades, Melbourne University had happily recommended him, and he had been accepted, to their international student program. Now that he was home, he would need to complete another eighteen months of study and then he would be able to start his hospital training. He had cut a semester off the time he needed to spend at Melbourne by studying during the American winter semester while Australian Universities were on holiday.

She was so proud of everything that Michael had achieved, especially after the death of his sister seven years ago today. Michael had just turned sixteen – a rough time for any kid – but the added grief of losing his only sibling and the near breakdown of his parents' marriage could have been too much. But instead of falling off the rails, he had focused solely on studying and was well on his way to becoming the doctor he had always dreamed he would be.

Caroline heard her phone ping from the kitchen and after retrieving it, saw there was a message from Adam.

Package collected but be prepared. He's not alone. Xx

I better check the guest bedroom, Caroline thought. *He must have a friend from the States tagging along for a holiday, and they might not have organised a place to sleep yet. A bit of notice would have been nice though.* Racing up the stairs she opened the window to let in some fresh air, even though it was winter, and freezing outside. They rarely had overnight guests, but the bed was always made, and the bathroom clean with fresh towels. Lighting a scented candle was a start but it wouldn't be enough she decided. She had put a fresh vase of roses in her bedroom this morning, but perhaps Michael's guest would appreciate them. She retrieved them from her dresser before she realised it was probably a waste of time. Most men didn't notice touches like that, but they were there now, and it gave the room a more welcoming feel. They smelled divine, which was rare for store-bought roses.

Seeing that it was already five o'clock, Caroline popped back into the kitchen and checked her list yet again. Dinner was right on schedule – she had been prepping most of the day – and Adam and Michael were due any time. They knew he would be exhausted after travelling from Maryland to Sydney which took more than a day. Then there had been a three hour wait at the Sydney airport. He could have got an earlier flight to Melbourne but when Caroline booked his flight she took into account that there was the possibility of his US flight being delayed. She hadn't wanted him waiting for hours hoping to find a spare seat. It was the weekend and flights were more often than not completely booked. Caroline didn't expect Michael to make it through dinner before crawling up the stairs to sleep, but there would be plenty of time to catch up in the next few weeks before his Uni semester started.

Hearing the crunch of tires on the gravel, Caroline threw her apron on the kitchen bench and made her way through the vast house, throwing open the front door. Adam was already at the boot of his Ranger Rover and was pulling bags out. Many more bags than Michael had taken with him, Caroline noticed. And expensive, she could see. Was that a Globe-Trotter trunk Adam was wrestling with? She'd spent hours looking for new suitcases to take with them last year when they'd visited Scotland and had stumbled across the Globe-Trotter brand which was very expensive and very British. Just one suitcase could set a person back nearly two thousand pounds. And that was *pounds*. Adam said he wasn't spending five thousand dollars on something he was going to stick his clothes in, and they found something nice and much more reasonably priced at Myer.

Michael leapt from the back seat and before he even acknowledged his mother, he made his way around to the other passenger door, opened it and reached in. From the dark of the car Caroline saw a slim hand, perfectly manicured, followed by tanned arms and then a flash of perfectly straight blonde hair. And like a movie star stepping on to the red carpet an immaculate girl emerged from the depths of the car. She was tall, maybe five-foot-eight, and beautifully slim. Her skin was perfect, but then she was probably only twenty-one or twenty-two. And she most certainly did not look like she had just been on a long-haul flight.

Beaming up at Caroline from the bottom step Michael put his arm around his companion. She shrugged him off, and straightened her hair, but this didn't seem to lessen Michael's smile.

"Mum, I would like you to meet Margaux. Margaux Thornton. Of the Baltimore Thornton's."

Caroline stepped down towards the pair, holding out her hand. Margaux took it, but there was no welcome in her grip and no warmth in her fleeting smile. Assuming she was tired, Caroline gave her cold greeting the benefit of the doubt and turned quickly towards her son, launching herself into his arms. Thankfully, Michael hugged her back and she felt all the anxiety she had been holding tight for a year slip away. He was home where he belonged, and hopefully he would never be away this long again.

After a minute of catching up, asking about the flight, and hugging him again, Caroline turned back towards Margaux, not wanting to be rude.

"Welcome to our home," she said. "I'm Caroline, Michael's mum. And you're a friend from, ahh, Baltimore I take it."

"Well, I'm a bit more than a friend. I told Michael to tell you I was coming, but he wanted it to be a surprise," she answered, her voice as polished as she was.

Michael looked at Caroline and then his father who had finally emptied the car. Three of the bags were Margaux's, so it was beginning to look like she was in Australia for a while.

"We've already told Dad," Michael grinned, "but we made him promise not to say anything. Margaux is much, much more than a friend Mum. She's my fiancé. We're getting married."

Chapter Five

“ So, tell me about yourself,” Caroline asked Margaux, taking a sip of her tea. After the news she'd just heard she could probably do with something stronger, but her guests would be arriving in an hour, and she still needed to finish cooking dinner. It was a rule of hers that she never drank and cooked. It was a great way to make sure dinner was either burned or came out half raw. She would have to wait to soothe her nerves.

“You said you're from the Baltimore Thornton's,” she continued, curious about Margaux's earlier comment. “What exactly does that mean?”

“Daddy's in finance,” she answered, sounding like she was already bored by the conversation. She held her hand out to check her perfect nails and then unconsciously straightened her hair for the third time since they had taken a seat in the formal lounge.

“His father was in finance too,” she continued. “We're a *very* well-known family.” Caroline felt like she was being told off – how dare she not know who the Thornton family was. “And Mummy was a British model in the eighties. Not a super-model, but still, a very recognisable face.”

“Lovely,” Caroline replied, thinking that explained the accent. More refined than the typical east-coaster. “Michael's dad is also in finance. He and your father probably have a lot in common.”

Margaux smirked as she looked around the room, a look of distain flickered across her face.

"Well maybe not. Adam probably isn't quite in the same league as Daddy."

"Adam's done very well over the years," Caroline defended her husband, beginning to feel a tug of dislike for Margaux. *What kind of woman in her twenties still calls her father Daddy? Yikes.*

"Oh, I'm sure he has," Margaux said, "but Daddy is very rich. *Very.*"

Well good for Daddy, Caroline thought, but kept it to herself. If Margaux was going to be her daughter-in-law, then she would need to tread lightly. The last thing she wanted to do was upset her and alienate Michael. Even if she was behaving like an entitled brat.

"Your house is very nice," Margaux said, looking around at what Caroline considered to be a very elegant sitting room. "Cosy. It reminds me of our holiday house in the Hamptons. Your house is smaller of course, but it has a similar feel. Thank you for letting me stay with you," she said, her manners finally kicking in, although cosy didn't feel like a compliment coming from this obviously spoilt girl.

"Our pleasure," Adam said as he rejoined them after dragging the suitcases up the stairs. No doubt Margaux's Daddy had staff for that.

"I've put your bags in the guest room. Turn right at the top of the stairs and it's the last door on the left. It also has an ensuite, so I'm sure you will be very comfortable," he continued. "Just wondering, how long are you staying in Australia?"

Before Margaux could answer Adam's question Michael shook his head in disbelief.

"Dad, Margaux isn't staying in the guest room. She's staying with me. In my room. We are engaged. And we are adults. "

"Sorry Michael. But we have always made it very clear. Girlfriends

26

don't stay over. These are unusual circumstances, and Margaux is very welcome to stay for a few days while she sorts out another arrangement, but our rules haven't changed. Until you are married, she will not be sleeping in your room. I don't care how old you are."

"Oh, come on Dad. You're being ridiculous. I've done the math's. We all know Mum was pregnant with me before you got married."

"That may be the case Michael, but that doesn't make it right. If you and Margaux want to find somewhere else to stay, that's up to the two of you. And no late-night visits. We aren't that stupid."

"Then I guess we'll start looking for somewhere to stay tomorrow," Michael sighed loudly, and Caroline caught him roll his eyes at Margaux.

"So Margaux," she asked, trying to rescue the situation before Adam and Michael started a full-fledged fight. "How did you two meet?"

"At a fundraiser. Daddy's company, Thornton and Holmes Capital always gives lots of money to Johns Hopkins University. Mummy couldn't make it that night, so I tagged along. I was home from school for the weekend and was at a loose end. The Dean likes to show off their success stories, so he invited Michael. The University was raising money for scholarships for disadvantaged students, and students from poor countries. Donors love giving to that sort of cause. They get their company's name in the newsletters and a plaque in the administration building if they make a large enough donation. It's good for the donor's image to be able to say they are educating students from poor countries who will go home and save people in their own little countries. Of course the fundraiser was the usual boring event, but then I saw Michael across the room and decided I wanted to meet him. The rest is history."

"Mmm. You do know Australia isn't a third world country. We have lots of brilliant scientists and Doctors here. People from all over the world come to our Universities to study," Caroline said thinking a week or two in an actual third world country would do Margaux some good.

"I know Australia isn't a third world country," Margaux replied. "But it's just so far away from America and Europe. It took us days to get here. Without first class I don't think I would have made it. The A380 is the only way to fly that far."

Adam turned to Michael with a questioning look on his face.

"I thought you were trying to save as much from Grandad's trust fund as possible. That must have set you back a bit. Paying for two first class tickets."

"Turned out I didn't have to," Michael answered. "I was all set with the economy ticket you bought me, but when I convinced Margaux to tag along so she could meet you, her father insisted on an upgrade. He said his girl couldn't travel with everyone else, and he wanted me to be with her. Make sure she got everything she needed. And because we were able to sleep, we're not exhausted and we can enjoy dinner with everyone tonight. Win, win."

"Win, win," Caroline repeated, but she and Adam glanced at each other, noting that the other seemed to feel the same. Margaux was going to be very high maintenance.

"Have you made any wedding plans yet?" Caroline asked, trying to make small talk. "Michael has eighteen months of study ahead of him, and then he has to do his internship which is another year. I guess twenty-four, twenty-five is a good age to get married, but that's a lot of travel back and forward from Australia to the U.S in the meantime. A lot of first class-tickets."

"The time will fly by. But I'm hoping to convince Michael to come back home and finish his degree there. Johns Hopkins would take him back in a heartbeat. I'll be here for three months because it's the summer holiday's at home and then I'll go back and finish my final year. I'm studying history and psychology at Sarah Lawrence. That's a College in New York. "

"And then you're planning on moving here after you get married?" Adam asked, knowing all about Sarah Lawrence. It cost over fifty thousand

US dollars a year to attend and students typically came out with a liberal degree that didn't guarantee them a job in the real world. "What job are you planning on doing when you finish school? Probably not a lot of call for a history teacher with an American degree at the state primary school down the road."

"Oh Adam," Margaux smiled. "I won't work. I'm going to be a wife. The wife of the most successful resident at Johns Hopkins."

"Mags," Michael warned.

"Don't be silly Michael, and please don't call me Mags," she said, her voice tight. "You know I don't like it. And they have to know some time." Margaux took Michael's hand, the first display of affection she had shown him since Adam had meet her. "Michael won't be doing his residency in Australia. Daddy already took care of everything. Michael can start as soon as he finishes school. In America. At Johns Hopkins Hospital." She laughed haughtily, the sound grating on Caroline's nerves, and patted Michael on the arm like he was her pet. "You didn't think we were going to live here did you?"

~~~

"Oh my gosh," Adam whispered as he closed the kitchen door behind them. After her grand announcement Margaux had declared that she needed to change before dinner and excused herself. Michael deciding he wanted a shower, followed Margaux upstairs. Caroline, needing to put the dinner in the oven, had asked Adam to join her in the kitchen, not because she needed help, but because if she was left to her own devices she might start crying.

"She's horrible. And spoilt. And horrible," Adam repeated, while trying to keep his voice down. "What is Michael thinking? He can't marry her."

"She wouldn't be my first choice for his wife, but there's nothing we can do. You need to keep your voice down. They might hear you."

"And what person that age calls their parents 'Mummy and Daddy'? She's an adult, not a six-year-old girl," he continued like he hadn't even heard her. "We have to put a stop to this."

"Adam we can't. We cannot interfere. It will only push him closer to her and further away from us."

"But she's so ... ahh," he yelled, unable to keep his voice quiet any longer.

"Yes, she is," Caroline agreed. "But do you remember how horrible your mother was to me? She hated me from the moment I met her. For crying out loud, she sobbed at our wedding. We don't want to do the same to our son. And once you tell him what you think there's no taking it back. We need to give her the benefit of the doubt. She's just got off a long plane ride and she's probably tired. Maybe she's just nervous about meeting her future in-laws for the first time."

"That girl hasn't been nervous a day in her life. She just wants us to know she's the one in charge. I've met people like her before," Adam said, "and I don't like them."

"It doesn't matter if we don't like her Adam. All that matters is what Michael thinks. He must love her if he asked her to marry him."

"He can't love her. There isn't anything loveable about Miss Thornton. She's using him, but I can't figure out why. She obviously thinks anyone from Australia is a hick, but he must have something she wants, or she wouldn't bother. It can't be his trust fund. He'll be comfortable for the rest of his life, but I don't think girls like that do comfortable."

"Adam now is not the time to deal with this. Everyone will be here soon, and let's not forget this day is to remember Isabelle. We can deal with Michael and Margaux tomorrow. It's not like the wedding is next week. A girl like that will need at least a year to plan the event of the decade. Let's just hope Daddy's paying for it, because apparently you aren't successful enough."

"What? I'm successful. Who said that?"

"Margaux implied that we weren't rich enough. Called the house 'cosy'."

"It is cosy," Adam said looking around the kitchen. "You've done an outstanding job. And I'm not the only one around here who has been a success. Events by Caroline has been a smash hit. How dare she try and make us feel inadequate. And anyway, money means nothing if you're a horrible human being."

"Thank you love," Caroline said as she put her arms around Adam's waist, attempting to calm him down. "I'm glad you love where we live as much as I do. Unfortunately, I think cosy might mean something different to Margaux than it does to us. The way she said it felt like a thinly veiled insult. Goodness knows what kind of house an heir of the Thornton family lives in."

"What was the name of her fathers' company again?" Adam asked as he pulled out his phone. He began taping his screen and bought up a page. Thornton and Holmes Capital's website appeared before him with a picture of the Chairman of the board, Emerson John Thornton. He looked exactly as expected. Probably in his late fifties, his hair was silver, and his eyes were a piercing blue. He was tall and slim, and the suit in the photo was elegant and paired with a red power tie. Reading quickly through their pages as Caroline busied herself with tonight's entrée's, Adam could see that yes Mags, as he was going to call her from now on, had a father that was probably *very* rich. His firm made loans to struggling companies, but upon further investigation on other websites, he learned that Emerson was ruthless. The minute you were late with a payment he took the struggling company, restructured it, and sold it off piece-meal, making a fortune and firing the staff, without benefits, if he could get away with it. There had been several investigations into him by the Securities Exchange Commission and the Department of Justice, but nothing had ever been proven, and there were rumours he bribed officials to make investigations disappear.

Not wanting to further distress Caroline tonight he kept what he had learnt to himself, but he fully intended to do a little more digging and see what he could find out. He knew a few people who might know something, or someone who did. Because the last thing he wanted was his son getting caught up with anything or anyone who was unethical or in a worst case scenario, someone who was breaking the law.

Chapter Six

Always the perfect host, no matter how she felt, and right now she felt devastated by the news that her only child was going to move away and marry someone they didn't even know, Caroline checked on her guests.

Beth and Tom were chatting with Jill and Matthew, sitting on the couches, where not more than an hour ago, she had been informed that her son was moving halfway across the world permanently. Joan was talking to Michael and Margaux who was showing off a ring Caroline hadn't noticed before. She could see it catch the light from the chandelier, highlighting its size. That must have cost him quite a chunk of change.

Michael's trust fund had become available to him when he turned twenty-one, but he always said he wanted to keep the money to buy a house when he finished University and moved out. Adam's father had provided well for both children – enough for anyone to buy a lovely home in Melbourne – and as he inherited Isabelle's trust when she died, he should have been set for life. But as generous as it was, Caroline doubted it would be enough to keep the beautiful, but so far very unpleasant, Margaux in the style she would expect. No doubt Daddy would have to kick in some dollars to make sure his daughter was provided for in the manner she appeared to be accustomed.

Joan didn't look well, Caroline noticed. Usually the most beautiful woman in any room, tonight she looked pale and tired. She was sipping on a glass of water, and twice in the last half hour she had excused herself and used the bathroom. Caroline hoped that whatever she had wasn't contagious. She didn't want her guests all getting a tummy bug. But then, it wouldn't be like Joan to come if she was infectious, so she was probably just tired. Bella was five and Will had turned two a few months ago. That was enough to make any mother look weary, but Joan was forty-six. And for the first time ever, she was actually looking her age. Perhaps David needed to whisk her off somewhere exotic for a week and give her a rest.

Caroline still couldn't believe that she now counted Joan as one of her dearest friends. They had hated each other when they were in school, and she had barely tolerated her for most of their adult years, only seeing her on the odd occasion when Beth insisted on bringing them together. But Joan was kind and funny and these days Caroline didn't know what she would do if she didn't have her in her life. And her beautiful Bella, who had been named after Isabelle, was just as sweet as her own daughter had been. It was a privilege to watch her grow up.

Tom, who usually preferred to fly under the radar, stood and called out, "Excuse me, can I have everyone's attention please." The chatter around the room ceased and Tom, seeing that he had everyone's attention, grabbed his wife's hand and pulled her up off the couch.

"I hope nobody minds me breaking up the fun, but my adorable wife got some wonderful news today. We know Joan and David need to leave early, so if it's alright, she's going to make a little announcement."

"I'm sure you all know just how much I love teaching," she laughed, and everyone joined her. Beth had hated her job for years. She had no passion for it and had been looking for something different to do but hadn't found the right fit. They didn't need her to work, but the idea of staying home all day horrified her. Cleaning and cooking were not her forte', and she left that sort of thing to Caroline, who did it perfectly. "Today I received notification that I have been accepted into The Southern School of Natural Therapies. It's a four-year course, and I'm much too old to do it, but I decided to take the plunge anyway. When I finish I will be a qualified naturopath and finally allowed to legally give you all the advice I've been giving out anyway for the past few years."

Congratulations were offered all around and Beth looked happier than she had in years. Caroline knew how unsatisfied she had been in her career. It had never suited her; it was something she fell into after high school when her exam results hadn't been what she had expected. But she'd wanted to go to Uni and settled for doing a teaching degree. As the years went on she had become more dissatisfied with her job but stuck with it because she didn't know what else to do. But as children became more and more disrespectful, every week she promised herself she would find somewhere else to work.

With the change in government several years ago she was now expected to teach things she didn't believe in. When several of the schools where she was an emergency teacher adopted the new 'Safe Schools' program, Beth had read through the curriculum and was disgusted at the indoctrination she could see was taking place, and she refused to teach it. She, like many parents, especially those who called themselves Christians, felt that there was no place for teaching children about sex in school, especially those in the very early grades. What they wanted her to tell children had no basis in science, and almost nothing to do with anti-bullying which was what parents were told their children were learning. Her refusal to instruct kids that there were more than two genders and that you could be whatever sex you wanted based on your feelings, meant that schools stopped calling her for emergency teaching unless they were desperate. But Beth upheld her principles and Caroline admired her for it.

"Well we might as well continue with the good news," Jillian said after congratulating her sister. "We have an announcement of our own. Today we received word that we have been accepted as foster parents. Matthew and I, along with Zoe, are delighted that we are going to be able to help children in need have somewhere safe to live."

"That's wonderful," Adam congratulated them both with a hug for Jill and one of those manly pats on the back for Matthew. He had written a personal reference for Jillian, having known her since school when they dated for a few months. It had nearly broken Caroline's heart at the time, but it had worked out for her and Adam in the end, and Caroline had no hard feelings. Jillian used to just be Beth's annoying little sister, but the two women had become friends years ago when Jill married an old friend of Adam's. The marriage hadn't survived after Chris cheated on her, but Caroline and Jill's friendship had continued. As if Beth would let them be anything but.

"And what about you David? Anything to announce before you head off to your romantic dinner?" Adam asked.

"Not from me. I have enough to contend with without a change in career, or more children in the house. Good luck with *that* you two. What about you Joni?" he said, calling his wife by his nickname for her. "Anything you want to share?"

"Nope. Nothing to report here," she lied, quite sure David was not going to take the news that she was pregnant again well. "But before we have to head off, I would love to offer up a toast to the girl who brings us together on this day every year." She looked over to Caroline for permission and with a smile and a nod, it was granted.

"To Isabelle. Who will always be missed and will always be loved." Glasses were raised all across the room and as one, the words "To Isabelle, who will always be missed and will always be loved," repeated around the room.

~~~

"Michael are you wanting to announce your engagement tonight? I see that Margaux's wearing an engagement ring," Adam asked as he poured a glass of wine for Caroline at the bar. She usually waited until dessert was served before she drank anything alcoholic when hosting, but today was stressful enough, and Michael's earlier announcement had made it all the more so. Adam thought she might want a small glass.

"Of course we want to tell everyone we're engaged. We would have done it earlier, but with so many other announcements tonight, I decided to wait so we could have our own moment. How about you do it between entrée's and the mains. We already told Joan because she was leaving, but I think people will start guessing soon anyway. That ring is kind of hard to miss."

"I'll say. I can't believe I didn't notice it earlier."

"We thought it was too valuable to have out on display with all the travelling, but we're home safe now, and I want everyone to know we're together. I can't believe I'm going to be married to such an amazing woman. She's just so beautiful and smart."

Adam looked over to Margaux who was talking to Beth's oldest son Lochie. As Michael continued to inform his father of all his fiancés special qualities, Adam noted how she was leaning in, touching Lochie's arm and showing more interest in what he had to say, than Adam had seen her show Michael in the short time since they had met her. Michael had always been a good-looking boy, and once he got through the teenage years of bad skin and limbs that always seemed too long to control, he filled out nicely and girls started to find him attractive. But he had always been more interested in books than the opposite sex, especially the popular girls, who he had always said weren't very nice. Adam always imagined his son marrying someone kind and pretty. Someone who would support him and his career.

Not in his wildest dreams did he think he would want to marry a socialite who had no problem flirting with one of his best friends right in front of him.

Dragging his eyes away from the pair Adam realised that Michael had stopped talking and was waiting for him to respond. What had he been saying? Beautiful, well there was no denying that. Smart, only time would tell. But clever he had seen on his own. Adam wasn't sure what she was up to yet, but he was suspicious of her and didn't trust her motives. But for now all he knew was he didn't see a girl who behaved like she was in love.

"Sure son. I'll make the announcement after the starters. Anything special you want me to say?"

"I'll leave that to you Dad. And by the way we want to have an engagement party here before Margaux has to fly back for school. We want to keep it small, just for friends and family, but I'm sure Mum can put something together. Margaux's mum is planning the real party for November. We can all fly over because I'll be finished school for the year, and that way you can meet the in-laws."

"Right. Well you might want to get the dates to us. Busy time for your Mum. All those Christmas parties to plan. And it's a long way to fly for one night."

"I know. But I'm your only son and I hear it's going to be quite a party. Oh, got to go Dad. Margaux looks like she needs another drink and Mum's just bought out the first course. And thanks for being so welcoming to my-wife-to-be. Make it a good introduction," he smiled.

After the first course, scallops in the shell on a bed of cauliflower puree and crispy prosciutto crumbs, Adam knew it was time to face the inevitable. Welcoming Mags to the family. He had given Caroline a heads up, and while it was clear she hadn't been thrilled with Michael's choice for a wife, she told him there was nothing they could do about it. She was adamant that they were not going to repeat his mother's mistake and write Margaux off before they had a chance to really get to know her, the way Adam's mother had written Caroline off. Adam's mother had doted on him, and nobody was ever going to be good enough for her son. Especially an ordinary girl from an ordinary family. Adam understood Caroline's feelings on the subject but wondered how long she would be able to stay quiet. It wasn't like her to hide how she felt.

Standing up at the head of the table, he took his fork and taped it against his wine glass. Too busy with their own conversations, nobody noticed him the first time and he banged the fork again, a little harder this time, earning him a glare from Caroline. She hated it when people banged the Baccarat crystal. He cleared his throat as the chatter quietened and Caroline came and stood beside him.

"Firstly, thank you everyone for coming tonight. It means so much to Caroline and me that you remember Izzie bee with us every year. She would be eighteen now if she had …" he stopped, his throat catching unexpectedly, "if she had lived, finishing off her final year of high school and probably driving us mad. We will always be sad that we don't get to go through that with her." He took Caroline's hand in his and turned to her. "Anything you want to add?" he asked.

"Just a thank you for helping us keep her memory alive. She was the best daughter a mother could ever ask for," she said as a single tear slipped down her cheek.

The heartbreak and the feelings of overwhelming grief had dulled over the years, but they were always there, lurking in the shadows. Hearing a song on the radio that Isabelle had liked or listening to Beth complain about Sarah could be enough to trigger a bad day, sometimes a bad week. But the people that loved her, and especially her newfound faith in God, always pulled her back from the brink. She had taken longer to accept that God was

39

real than Adam had, and even longer to understand that He loved her and had a plan for her life. Two years ago, when she asked Jesus to be Lord of her life she had been flooded with the joy and understanding that one day she would be reunited with her daughter. It might be decades away but knowing that kept her going and gave her hope.

Adam gave his wife's hand a loving squeeze, remembering how Isabelle's death had nearly ended their marriage. But they had prevailed, and they had never been stronger. Taking a deep breath in, he turned his attention to Michael.

"Tonight we have something to celebrate. As you can all see, Michael is back from his year away, and he hasn't come alone. And no sooner had he arrived home, did he announce to us that he was engaged. Of course we were surprised, but to us, Michael's happiness is the most important thing in the world. So as long as Margaux makes him happy, then that's good enough for us. So Margaux Thornton, welcome to the family."

As Adam and Caroline raised their glass to Michael and Margaux, congratulations could be heard around the table. Adam noticed a look of surprise on Lochie's face as he raised his glass. Caroline and Beth, both ignoring the happy couple, focused their attention on Sarah. Caroline had suspected for a long time that Sarah had a bit of a crush on Michael. She had been wrong. Sarah appeared to deflate right in front of her. Her head bowed, Caroline saw her wipe away a tear before she looked up and put on a fake smile. This was much more than a childhood crush.

Beth, guessing earlier today that Sarah's feelings for Michael hadn't gone away when he had, felt her heart break for her daughter. She hadn't understood how much Sarah had liked Michael until he left for America a year ago. Sarah had retreated to her room, talking only when necessary and had been emotional and almost impossible to live with. It had taken months before she had snapped out of her mood, and in the past few weeks she and

Tom had thought the worst of the teenage woes were over. She was eighteen and would soon be finished with high school. She was smart, and from what Beth had noticed tonight, was becoming more beautiful by the day. While he had been away she hadn't mentioned Michael to them once and had even gone on a few dates with boys from school. Beth had thought any feelings Sarah had were gone. But suddenly she could see she had been wildly wrong. All this time Sarah had just been waiting quietly for Michael to come home.

Chapter Seven

D r Clancy looked up from the computer where he had been reviewing Joan's records. He pulled his reading glasses off, laying them on his desk and then giving her his most 'I'm a professional, you can trust me stare' he said, "I strongly advise that you terminate this pregnancy. You're only about six weeks along. Because of your blood pressure issues I can't recommend RU486 so you will need to undergo a surgical procedure."

"I'm sorry Doctor. What's RU 4-2-6?" David asked.

"No, RU 4-8-6. It's two pills that are taken orally, two days apart. Very easy and a lot less traumatic for the patient. The first pill stops the hormone progesterone so the pregnancy can't progress any further. The second pill allows the body to expel the foetus. It has a ninety-nine percent success rate and recovery is quick and painless. But as I said, I can't recommend it in this case. But the procedure Joan needs is simple and in a few days she will be back up and about with her children. The closest clinic is in Hampton Park, and all you need is a referral from me to confirm the pregnancy. No counselling required. They will do an ultrasound to verify you're under twelve weeks, but with the dates you have given me that won't be a problem. Get an appointment as soon as you can. Best over and done with, and back on with life. No harm done, but David, you *have* to get that vasectomy sorted. I must say, I'm surprised you found yourself in this state at forty-six Mrs Saunders. Many women ten years younger have enormous difficulties getting pregnant."

"Thank you doctor. I'll make an appointment on the way out for the old snip-snip," David confirmed. "It won't be for a few weeks though. Let's get Joni back on her feet before we deal with me. Can't have us both down and out at the same time," David said as he reached for the letter of referral from Joan's GP.

"No." Both men looked over to the chair where Joan had been sitting, ignored for most of the appointment. "I'm sorry, but no. I will not be having an abortion." She'd wanted David to come in with her for moral support, but instead of listening to what she wanted, David had agreed to terminating her pregnancy without so much as a glance in her direction.

The doctor, in his mid-fifties, had seen it all. Pregnant teenagers who insisted on keeping their babies, and ones that couldn't wait to get rid of the problem. There were the women who waited for too long, thinking that they would be able to get pregnant when the timing suited them – usually after waiting for their careers to reach a certain point – or for Mr. Perfect to come along. There were the women who decided to go it alone and spent tens of thousands on treatments, which sometimes worked, but often not. What never seemed to be missing from any of these situations were the hormones. They made women illogical and emotional and some days he dreaded having to go to work and deal with them. He sighed loudly as he shook his head, preparing himself to explain yet again to Joan why she couldn't have this baby.

"Mrs. Saunders," he began in a tone that could only be considered condescending. "This is an extremely high-risk pregnancy. You have a history of pre-eclampsia and your second child had to be born by emergency caesarean. The chances of a repeat situation are very high, and now you are two years older. Your eggs are also two years older which increases the risk of chromosomal issues such as Down's Syndrome. We can test for this and if you have an abnormal result I hope *that* will be enough to convince you that it's a bad idea to try and take this pregnancy to term. And as I said, there is a very high risk of miscarriage. You don't want to have to go through that do you?"

"So you think it's better for me to go through the trauma and lifelong guilt of murdering my own baby, than to endure a miscarriage?"

"Mrs Saunders," Dr Clancy said, unable to conceal his frustration at this outdated argument. "Under no circumstances would this be murder. You are carrying a few cells that are about the size of a pea. Those cells don't have emotions and feel no pain. But they are a risk to your life. Do you want your children growing up without a mother because you refused sound medical advice? If you have had pre-eclampsia once, you could get it again."

"And what are the chances of that?"

"It varies. In the range of about twenty percent. It's really hard to say."

"I'm sorry Doctor, but that's not good enough for me. I will not be having an abortion, and I will not be having any test to find out if my baby has chromosomal issues because the outcome will not change my mind. I'll take my chances with nature and see how that goes."

"Then I can't treat you Mrs. Saunders," he said, leaning back into his chair. "I don't have the expertise to see you through this pregnancy."

"Don't worry Doctor. I'll find someone else. And if you don't have the expertise to help someone in my situation, might I suggest you stop handing out advice on something you know very little about."

Is this what doctors tell their patients who they think fall into the too hard basket, Joan wondered. *Get rid of your inconvenient baby and move on. How many women agree because they aren't strong enough to fight and how many babies are killed around the world every day because of their doctor's advice?* Joan picked up her handbag and taking the referral off a startled David, scrunched it up and threw it in the Doctor's rubbish bin.

~~~

"We talked about this Joan. I don't like the idea any more than you do, but I don't want to risk your life. I love you. The kids love you and they need you." They were sitting in the car, still in the Doctor's surgery parking lot. David hoped Joan would at least let him go back into the office and retrieve the referral. That way they could keep the door open on this option while he tried to convince her that this was the only thing they could do to save her life. "We have two wonderful children. We don't need another one. I agree with you, this is a terrible situation to be in. It's not something I ever saw myself agreeing to, but if I have to choose your life over the life of a baby I have never met, I choose you."

"David *we* didn't talk about this. You talked and gave me all the reasons why I should terminate the pregnancy. And then you agreed with the Doctor without even asking me how I felt. I know you think this is the right thing for me, but I don't. It's just wrong. Choosing one life over another. And you don't know. I could sail through this pregnancy like I did with Bella. And I promise to be very careful with my diet and my stress levels. I just need your help and support."

"Is this about Beth?" he blurted out, his frustration at her irrational stance growing. "She's been in your ear with all her *God* talk and her right-to-life agenda again, hasn't she? I know she's your best friend, but I wish sometimes that she would just butt out of our lives. I have no interest in her *God* and her moral judgements. This is *our* life, not *hers*."

"I haven't said a word to Beth," Joan defended herself, shocked at the anger David was expressing towards Beth. "She has no idea I'm even pregnant. The only person I've told was you and I won't be telling anyone else until I am through the first twelve weeks. I would have loved to talk this over with her, but I needed to make my decision without any outside pressure or opinions. I did however think that you would be on my side. And I have decided I'm continuing with this pregnancy until the baby is born, one way or another. And if you really believe what you say about 'it's a woman's body, so it's a woman's choice', then let me be very clear. I have made my choice and I will not be changing my mind. What you do with my decision and how you react is up to you."

~~~

"I'm just so devastated Abby," Joan said to her half-sister who was silently listening on the phone from her home in Ballarat. She had promised David she wouldn't tell anyone about the baby this early on, but after a few weeks of his moodiness and his constant sighing Joan had to tell someone or she would go crazy, and Abbey wouldn't say a word to anyone if Joan asked her not to. "He said he'd support me through the pregnancy and try to be happy about the baby, but I don't believe him. Every time I run to the loo to be sick he gives me this look of exasperation, like I deserve what I get. When I was sick with Will he used to hold my hair back and bring me a glass of water. But this time there's no care, just judgement. I feel so alone."

"Well that's one thing you're not. You have me, you have your kids and all your friends. And you have David. It might take a bit of time, but he will come around. Right now he's thinking he might lose you and that must terrify him."

"It doesn't help that I'm terrified too. What if I am making a mistake? The thought of an abortion is horrifying to me. I know not everyone agrees, but I believe it's murder. My mother was in a similar position with an unwanted pregnancy, and she could have chosen not to have me. Then Bella and Will wouldn't even exist. But I also have to come to terms with the facts. This is a high-risk pregnancy. What if something does go wrong? I could have a miscarriage, or the baby could have Down's Syndrome. And then there's the chance that I will have to have another emergency caesarean if I get pre-eclampsia again. I know it's rare, but it's still a risk." Tears started trickling down her face as she thought about having the baby too early and he or she struggling throughout life with learning or physical disabilities. Or they could even die if they were born too early.

"Joan, listen to me. What is the most important thing that the maternal-foetal medicine Doctor told you?"

"No stress."

"That's right. You need to stay calm. You need help at home with the kids and the house. What's your plan for that?"

"We hired a cleaner to come in once a week. David said I can use her for as long as I like, even after the baby's born. And Bella is at school during the day. But Will. He's two. Tantrums day and night. He won't sleep when I put him to bed and at the moment the only thing he wants to eat are fish fingers. David's mother gave them to him when she was babysitting last month. Seriously some days I just want to smack her. She never listens to me about what not to feed the kids, hypes them up with sugar and then sends them home."

Abby laughed, remembering what her mother-in-law had been like with her kids. Nobody knew what organic was back then, and she hadn't given too much thought to their diet as long as they were eating something, but sugar was sugar, and it had made children crazy twenty years ago too.

"What about putting him in childcare for a few hours a day? You could have a nap and he might be so tired from all the activity he'll sleep at night."

"You know how I feel about childcare. Why have children if you are going to palm them off for someone else to raise? Bella never spent a day in care."

"That might be the case, but right now you need some Joan care. Rest, peace, and a healthy diet. I could ask Paul to have a word with David. Tell him to man up and stop being such an idiot."

"Thanks, but David doesn't know I told you I'm pregnant. I was going to wait till I was three months, but I needed someone to talk to before I went out of my mind. So for at least a month I need you to keep this between us."

"Alright, but the minute I'm allowed to know, I'm coming down to see you. I'll take that little monster out for the day and you can get some rest."

"Oh no," Joan laughed, feeling the pressure lift after talking to her sister who always had great advice. "I've just had a terrible thought. What if this baby is a boy and he's just like Will. How will I survive this again?"

"I told you. Childcare. You have enough money. Use it."

Chapter Eight

Sarah had loved her job from the minute Caroline hired her. She was fifteen when Caroline rung her mum desperate, because two of her waiters had called in sick. Caroline begged her to let Sarah come and help. Sarah, who had half-heartedly applied to Maccas and KFC for a job, jumped at the chance. She didn't want to work at a fast-food restaurant, but she needed the money for a new phone. She'd been given her mum's old iPhone when she upgraded but the phone was a disgrace. All her friends had the new version and laughed at her when she pulled out her hand-me-down relic. So Sarah helped out that first night, and Caroline was so impressed with her, that she gave her a permanent job.

Caroline was bossy, and if everything wasn't perfect, then look out. Each waiter or waitress was checked over before they were allowed anywhere near the guests. Their white shirt had to be spotless and ironed properly. The only time one of her waiters turned up wrinkled, Caroline borrowed an iron from the client and made the waiter re-iron his shirt. When he couldn't get it right she did it herself, giving him a tutorial as she went. That was his first and last day working for Events by Caroline. The rules were clear. Girls needed to have their hair tied back if it was long and the boys had to have short back and sides. Caroline said if they didn't like it they could work somewhere else.

Makeup was to be subtle, no weird hair colours and no facial piercings. The staff weren't left wondering what was acceptable and what wasn't. It was right there in their employment contracts. They weren't there to make a personal statement with their appearance. They were there to serve the clients and their guests as unobtrusively as possible.

But Sarah didn't mind all the rules – she got to see beautiful people living in their beautiful houses. At first she couldn't believe the way some people existed, like humanity was there just to serve them. But she quickly got used to the huge houses with the sometimes bizarre artwork and the massive kitchens that looked like they had never been used. She also became accustomed to the clients who barely noticed the caterers until they wanted something. It didn't bother her that they were sometimes rude, if and when they finally noticed the staff. Caroline paid them well and when Sarah turned eighteen she'd been able to buy her van outright. Now she was saving for a house deposit. Her parents always drilled into her that the way to get ahead was by saving as much as she could while she lived at home, and she intended on getting ahead.

Working for Caroline had been an eye opening lesson in human nature. After three years working for Events she'd overheard many private conversations because most people didn't stop talking when a waiter brought them food or a drink. Men talked about work, stocks, and investments. Sometimes sport, but mostly money. Women talked about each other. Because her mum's friends were so nice and didn't talk behind each other's backs, Sarah hadn't realised that grown women could be just as mean as the girls at school. She'd always assumed things would get better with her friends as they got older, but she quickly realised she was wrong. People didn't really change on the inside no matter how old they got.

Now that she was close to finishing school, just four months till exams, she'd decided she wanted to stay in the catering business. Based on Caroline's advice, she chose business studies so she would know the basics about running a business. She also went to TAFE one day a week where she was learning commercial cooking. This was a much better use of her time; she was never going to need physics or chemistry. But Caroline made it very clear it was important that she could cook and cook well. Caroline didn't prepare the food for her parties herself, employing several cooks and a pastry chef who did that for her. But there were times she'd been let down and needed to jump into the kitchen and cook. She would never let something like a sick staff member ruin a party. Sarah had already applied to her TAFE to do a full-time course once year twelve was over and she did as many cooking classes as she could afford during the school holidays. She practiced on her family, cooking dinner when she had time and for the most part they were grateful. Even if a meal wasn't perfect everyone agreed, she was a much better cook than her mother.

But by far the biggest perk of working for Caroline had been seeing more of Michael. When Sarah started to show an interest in the business side of Events eighteen months ago, Caroline began to include her in some of the planning meetings. Before she got her license her mum would drive her, or she would catch a train and a tram to Kooyong, where Caroline lived. They would meet with clients in their homes and Caroline would ask them a list of questions so she could understand what they really wanted. She said they often thought they wanted one thing, but with a bit of digging she could figure out what they were actually expecting from their party or wedding.

Caroline introduced Sarah as her assistant, and she would sit quietly and take notes. She still wasn't brave enough to speak up in front of clients, but once the meeting was finished they would go back to Caroline's house and in her pretty study that looked out over the garden, they would plan. At first Sarah had very little to offer, but as she listened and learned her knowledge grew. Now Caroline took her suggestions seriously even though she was only eighteen, and she treated her like an equal. And if she was lucky, sometimes Michael was home from Uni and he would pop his head in and chat to them both. When he went to America she thought her heart would break. She counted down the days until the year was up, taking her misery out on her family, wishing she was older, hoping that when he came home he would notice her.

And then he did come home. With Margaux.

A month had gone by since he announced his engagement and every morning she woke up with a heavy heart. She was even dreaming about him and Margaux occasionally, the dream always ending with their perfect wedding. She couldn't even escape in her sleep. And now she had to help plan *their* engagement party. Caroline had asked her to take charge of the staff on the night and make sure everything went smoothly. She would be there if something came up, but she told Sarah, as the mother of the groom-to-be, she wanted to enjoy the evening, not be in the kitchen all night. And she thought this would be the perfect time to put Sarah's eighteen months of training to the test. Sarah, slightly ashamed of herself, daydreamed about ruining the party somehow, perhaps a laxative in Margaux's drink or simply tripping her over and making her look silly. But Sarah was too nice and well brought up, she could never harm someone on purpose, no matter how horrible she thought they were.

She was yet to find anyone who had a good word to say about Margaux. Lochie thought she was a bit of alright when he first met her, but that had been more about the way she looked than anything else. Then when Adam announced the engagement he quickly changed him mind. Margaux had been happily flirting with him, giving the impression that she and Michael were nothing more than friends. He'd been plucking up the courage to ask her out when they were called to dinner. He told Sarah he was so relieved he hadn't done it because if Michael found out it could have ruined their lifelong friendship. He'd gone out a few times to nightclubs with the pair, but when Margaux continued to flirt right in front of Michael, who seemed to have no idea about what she was up to, Lochie decided to avoid Michael until Margaux returned home.

Sarah only met her once, the night Michael returned home. Three days after she arrived in Australia Margaux took a suite at Crown Casino and spent very little time at the Anderson's house. Michael was still keeping up the pretence that he was living at home, but he spent most of his time when he wasn't at school with Margaux at her hotel. Caroline tried repeatedly to involve her daughter-in-law to be in the planning of the engagement party, but Margaux made it clear she wasn't interested. The real party would be in the States with all of *her* friends and family.

"Sarah, focus please," Caroline interrupted, pulling her back from her daydreams. "I don't know what's gotten into you lately." Not true, but Caroline had hoped that being faced with the reality of Michael's engagement, Sarah would see there was no point nurturing her feelings anymore and begin to move on. She was very young and being so pretty – she looked very much like her Aunt Jillian with her brunette locks and her tall, slim figure – she could have her pick of boys. It hurt Caroline that her little protégé was so upset, and that it was caused by her son, but he hadn't really done anything wrong, he didn't know how Sarah felt about him. And Sarah was so young. She would be better off with someone closer to her in age. Although Caroline would never dismiss the depth of Sarah's feelings just because of how old she was. She knew people could fall in love young and stay that way forever. That was her experience with Adam and she never found anyone to replace him in her affections all those years ago, even when he hadn't thought of her as anything more than a friend. Would she have married someone else if he hadn't come back into her life a few years after they finished school? Probably, but would she have loved them the same? Thankfully, she would never have to find out.

"Do you know what? The sun is out for a change. Why don't we wander down to Ebony's café and get a coffee? I need the fresh air. My shout."

"Sure," Sarah replied, not really caring. What she really wanted was to curl up on her bed and cry. Instead here she was ordering the peonies for the party. Even though they were out of season in Australia, Caroline's supplier could get her anything she wanted any time she wanted it.

"And grab your coat. It might be sunny, but it's freezing outside."

Once Caroline ordered a flat white for herself and Sarah's usual hot chocolate, she sat down at the table where Sarah was staring out on the street. Coffee shops like this were popping up all over inner-city suburbs, often in old, empty milk-bars that closed down because it was cheaper to get milk and lollies at the supermarket. Ebony's quickly become a favourite with the yummy mummy set, who liked to congregate together after dropping their children at school. Caroline preferred to come on the weekends when the mums were occupied with karate lessons or dance classes for their precious offspring. They were usually in too much of a hurry to linger on Saturday and after they had paid for their caffeine hit they were back in their Range Rovers off to another class that would hopefully distinguish their child from the rest of the pack. It was still early yet, but in the next hour or so the Saturday brunch crowd made up of baby boomers and millennials with money would arrive in droves for their avocado toast and their soy lattes, and Ebony's would be packed.

"Sarah, am I asking too much of you? If you don't want to plan Michael's engagement I completely understand. Most of the ordering is done, and I can ask Anita to run the evening. She's not nearly as good as you, but it's really just a big family party. No one will notice if it's not perfect." Sarah raised an eyebrow, and Caroline had the good grace to laugh.

"Ok. I'll notice. But I won't say anything. And you're part of the family. You should get to enjoy the evening, not be stuck in the kitchen counting out smoked salmon blini's and making sure under-age kids aren't sneaking in to steal the wine."

"Thanks Caroline. But I think it I prefer to work. It's such a fantastic opportunity you're giving me. I'll pop out and congratulate Michael and Margaux, but I doubt either of them would notice if I wasn't there."

"You're probably right about Margaux. She doesn't know you, doesn't know any of us really. But Michael will notice. You're like a sister to him."

"A sister," Sarah repeated under her breathe, and then the dam broke. For weeks she'd been holding back her tears, but the realisation that soon he would be married, and she would never have a chance with Michael, was finally sinking in. Caroline grabbed a bundle of napkins and handed them to Sarah, whose sobbing was becoming louder by the second. She was trying to control herself, but her pain ran so deep and she'd held it in so long, that she quickly began to lose control. The waitress, bringing over their drinks stopped midway, not sure what to do, but Caroline waved her over and then ordered a large piece of chocolate cake and two spoons.

"Sorry Sarah. I wasn't sure if I should say anything, but I could see that you were hurting."

"You knew?" Sarah wailed. "Does everybody know? Do you all talk about me when I'm not there?" she hiccupped between sobs, realising that her secret wasn't much of one after all.

"No lovely, of course not. Nobody has said a word. But I could see how you felt, and I feel devastated for you, and for myself a little too. He's my son and I adore him, but he clearly has terrible taste in women."

Sarah looked up, wiping her nose with the now saturated napkins. Caroline handed her a new one and pushed Sarah's hair that had become tangled by the wind earlier, away from her pretty, if very splotchy face.

"I'll deny it if you ever tell anyone I said this, but seriously, what is he thinking. She's rude, manipulative, flirts outrageously and is just awful."

"But she's beautiful and rich, and she has Michael," Sarah wailed, as she inhaled, tried to catch her breath.

"Yes she is, but beauty doesn't last, and who cares about money anyway? But you're right. She does have Michael and she's going to be my daughter in-law, so I am going to do my very best to love and accept her. So let's forget I ever said anything. I shouldn't have, but I've been holding it in for so long and I needed somebody to talk to, just like you did."

"Am I going to feel like this forever?" Sarah asked, relived that someone else could see what she saw in Margaux. "I've tried to forget about him, but it's just not working."

"I can't say. Everyone is different, some people move on quickly, some pine away for years. But if you decide you *want* to move on that would be a good start. And you're so pretty, and smart, and the best assistant I've ever had," Caroline encouraged with a smile. "You will meet someone one day who will love you the way you love them. And you're young. Michael's much too old for you. Four years is a big age difference. You're only eighteen. You don't need to be saddled with an old man like him."

"I've tried to move on. I want to. I get it. He's taken and that's not going to change. It's just been so long that I've felt this way, and I've known him my whole life. I never really even gave anyone else a chance."

"And I bet you get asked out all the time."

"Sometimes. I did go out a few times with a guy from school at the start of the year. He was nice, but I just didn't feel it. "

"Well just because it didn't work out with him, doesn't mean it won't work out with someone else. You're still young and you have years of meeting men ahead of you. There's no need to hurry, and you should finish school before you start anything serious. Go on a few dates and have some fun. I know that sounds weird coming from me. You probably look at me and think I've never had a fun day in my life, but I have."

"So just have fun. Don't be too serious. Ok, I can try that," Sarah decided.

"And I'm not kidding. You cannot repeat what I said about Margaux. It has to be our secret."

"I'll never say a word," Sarah promised.

Chapter Nine

I t had been six long weeks since Tom told Beth about what he'd discovered on Nathan's phone, and since that day she found it very hard to look at her son, let alone have a conversation with him.

Pornography. In *her* house. Even though Beth hadn't seen the images, taking Tom's advice not to look at what Nathan had been consuming, she still felt ashamed. As his mother she must have done something wrong, missed something. Both she and Tom had been careful about what movies and television their children watched and installed parental control blocks on all the computers in the house. They'd taken the time to talk to all three of the kids about computer safety and how children could be targeted by unsavoury people on the internet. Beth explained to Sarah how stupid it was to ever send photos of herself to anyone asking for them, and the laws dealing with the distribution of child pornography, even if it was a picture of herself. Tom did the same with both boys, making sure that they understood even forwarding inappropriate pictures could land you in serious trouble with the police. And he was very clear about the dangers of pornography. He wanted both of his sons to understand that viewing pornographic images changed the way men perceived woman, giving them a skewed idea of what real women looked like. He also told them the damage watching porn could do to their brains and how it could impact their future relationships. Lochie had listened to his father and taken his warning to heart. Apparently Nate hadn't.

When Tom discovered what his youngest son had been watching he'd been devastated. Nathan had left his phone on the dining table while he went to the kitchen for a glass of water. A notification popped up on the screen, and Tom saw it before it disappeared a few seconds later. It wasn't hard to figure out what it had been for, and when Nathan returned to the table Tom confronted him about it. Nathan denied any wrongdoing at first, saying his father must have misread or misunderstood what he'd seen. When Tom wouldn't back down, Nathan claimed he was being spied on, grabbed his phone and stormed out of the room.

Beth didn't know how to handle it – she was shocked and disappointed by his behaviour – and found herself ignoring Nathan rather than confronting the issue. She honestly didn't understand the appeal of pornography, especially the really awful stuff Tom told her their son was looking at. After weeks of discussion about how they should approach Nate, and who should do it, they agreed it would be better for Tom to talk to Nate one-on-one. Beth was too emotional and embarrassed by the subject and would probably do more harm than good. Tom had been doing his research and was finally ready to talk to Nate tonight.

When Tom finally crawled into bed at eleven later that evening Beth was still awake, waiting to hear how it had gone. She rolled over to face Tom, hoping that he had some good news.

"So, what did he say?" she asked.

"Well as you can imagine, it was all very awkward. He said if he promised not to look at that stuff anymore could we pretend this had never happened? I had to say no. There's no guarantee he would keep his word, and I wanted to understand what got him started down this path. Turns out a kid at school was sending around an image of his ex-girlfriend. Poor girl. She was from another school, so Nathan doesn't personally know her, but the image was sent to several of the boy's friends and was then passed around all over the place. Her classmates have seen it, so she's had to move schools. Nathan said that was the start for him. He swears he has never sent the image to anyone else, and he understands that if he did he could be charged with sharing child pornography. But it's what he's been watching now that is my real concern. Seems some of it's a bit violent. I don't want to go into details, but Beth, this has got him really messed up. He hates that he's been looking at it but didn't know how to stop. He feels ashamed of himself."

"Poor kid. I'm glad he understands how wrong this is, but what's the solution? We can't just take his word for it that he'll stop," Beth said, very close to crying, feeling like somehow she had failed as a parent.

"We came up with a plan. I don't know how successful it will be, but we have to start somewhere. He's agreed to give me the pin number of his phone. We talked about taking it off altogether, but that's a security risk. I checked and it's the right number. That means I can look at his phone anytime and see what he's been watching. That way it helps him to stay accountable.

"Okay. That's a good start. But what if he just finds other ways to watch porn, or clears his history? Kids can be devious."

"Honestly, Beth, he doesn't want to be looking at it so that's a great start. But he's going to need to be really careful. This has become an addiction, and something small could drag him back in. So for the foreseeable future we're going to spend a few hours together one-on-one, every week, and he can tell me anything. He asked that I promise not to share what he says with you, and I hope it's okay, but I said yes?"

"It's more than okay. I don't want to know. As long as he's comfortable talking to you then I'm happy. Do we get need to consider getting him some outside counselling?"

"I don't think so. If he finds talking to me isn't helping and he's still struggling then we can look into it. But for now I think we have a good plan. We also prayed together, and he asked God for forgiveness."

Listening to Tom, for the first time, Beth began to feel hopeful that there would be a good outcome to the situation. "You're a good dad Tom. Thanks for talking to him. I haven't known what to say. I can barely look at him."

"I know, but that has to stop Beth. He's horrified that you know anything about this. Right now he needs you to go back to being his mum and treating him how you used to. He will get through this, but if he feels judged by you it will compound the shame he's feeling right now."

"I know," Beth sighed. "I just keep seeing him as that adorable two-year-old, playing with his bucket in the sand pit. It's hard to accept he's on his way to being a man. When he was little I could protect him and make bad things go away. But here he is almost grown up and making mistakes I can't fix. Lochie's already left home and doesn't need us anymore, and Sarah's all heartbroken, and I don't know how to help her. Everything feels like it's outside my control, and I don't like it."

"Lochie's twenty-one and doing fine. He loves his job and he'll be finished his apprenticeship in another year. He's going to be a great electrician, and already talking about going out on his own once he gets his ticket. I have heaps of contacts in the building industry from my plumbing years and I don't have a problem introducing him to some builders. Sarah will be fine. She's excited about her life and her plans for next year. And when I popped my head in to say goodnight she was on the phone talking to someone called Noah, so maybe she's getting over her feelings for Michael. She's a sensible girl and must understand there's no hope. Sooner or later she'll move on with someone else. We aren't perfect parents Beth, but our kids are turning out alright. And we will get through this with Nathan.

"I suppose. And at least none of our kids have paired up with someone like that Margaux. I was talking to Caroline today, and she's beside herself. Margaux insinuated that if they ever wanted to see Michael it would be up to them to visit him in America. Seems she finds Australia boring.

"Poor Michael. Imagine being put in that situation where you can't see your parents when every you want and being at the mercy of someone spoilt like her."

"Poor Michael indeed. He's the one that picked her. Caroline said he only knew her a few months before he proposed. Serves him right for being so stupid," Beth said as she rolled over after kissing Tom goodnight.

~~~

Twenty kilometres away Michael was beginning to think the same thing. Had he made a mistake asking Margaux to marry him? Especially so early on in their relationship. When they met that night at the fundraiser, he'd been utterly mesmerised by her. He'd met beautiful women before, but Margaux had been so elegant, so sure of herself, and it was an intoxicating combination. When she asked him to join her at a nightclub after the University fundraiser he found himself saying yes immediately, even though clubbing wasn't his style. Since moving to America, he'd only gone out a handful of times and it had been for nothing more exciting than dinner with other students. Like him, they spent all their free hours studying and weren't interested in partying. But when Margaux asked him out he'd quickly blown off his plans to complete an assignment on infectious diseases, a special interest of his, due the following week.

After their first night out dancing till one in the morning, he was putty in her hands and continued seeing her whenever he could. On the weekends he would take the train up to New York to visit if she wasn't home in Baltimore, visiting with her parents.

Her Father sent a car to bring her home from New York whenever she wanted. Margaux was the youngest of four, with two older brothers and a sister. They were all married, and her oldest brother Henry had two children. Margaux's Father, Emerson, was very firmly in charge of the lives of his first three children, but Margaux, it seemed, was able to get away with anything. When Michael first met Emerson, he was intimidated, and rightfully so. The man exuded power and had buckets of money. Their home was a sprawling mansion situated on ten acres with its own private beach on the Choptank river. Built in the nineteen twenties by a Baltimore banker, he unfortunately made some very poor decisions in regard to the stock market. When Wall Street crashed in 1929, he lost everything, including his home. Margaux's great grandfather purchased the estate at a knock down price, renamed it Thornton Manor, and it had remained in the family ever since. Each generation added something of value to the property, Emerson's contribution being a private jetty where he moored his yacht and a boat house with all the creature comforts.

During the week, Emerson lived in the city at his condo in the Ritz Carlton, but on the weekend he was home, holding court, and the family was expected to join him and their Mother, Melody, for at least one dinner, if not the whole weekend. Melody was an older, but very well-preserved version of Margaux, and the friendliest member of the family. Michael got the impression her husband and children thought she wasn't very bright, and she was definitely under Emerson's thumb.

Michael had been more than a little worried that Emerson would try and put an end to the budding relationship with his daughter, as he didn't have the breeding and connections that the spouses of his other children did. Instead Emerson had pulled him aside on his first visit to the estate and told him he thought Michael was a calming influence on his youngest daughter and he was welcome anytime. It hadn't taken long for the subtle hints to begin dropping that Michael would be a perfect fit for the family. When Emerson asked him straight out what his intentions were, only two months after he had first met Margaux, he knew he had two choices. Either ask her to marry him or end the relationship. Emerson wasn't willing to wait until Michael felt ready – he made it clear he wanted Margaux settled once she finished college – and afraid of losing Emerson's support, he'd asked Margaux to marry him on their three month anniversary. She said yes immediately.

When Emerson gave the marriage his blessing it did not come without conditions. As soon as he finished his degree in Australia he was to return to Baltimore to do his residency. Emerson also made it clear that the couple and any future children they had would always reside in America. In exchange Emerson promised to take care of any visa and work permit issues and get him a much coveted residency at Johns Hopkins Hospital. How he could manage that, Michael had no idea, but he was under no illusion that his father-in-law-to be was going to be very much in control of his life. But he was so besotted with Margaux he decided that he didn't mind.

The first few weeks with Margaux in Australia had been bliss. They spent their nights together in her luxurious villa at the Crown Casino. Her father didn't bat an eye at the thousand dollar a night room, and she'd become very familiar with Melbourne's exclusive boutiques and restaurants. But in the last few weeks she decided she was bored, especially when Michael was in school. She refused to understand that he couldn't skip classes just because she was lonely and dismissed his suggestion to spend more time with his mother and help plan their engagement party. She started talking about going home early and he had to beg her to stay at least until their engagement party. Then out of the blue, two of her friends from school turned up in Australia and the real trouble began.

Margaux began clubbing all night with Pippa and George, short for Georgina, and sleeping most of the day. She wanted him to come with them, even though she knew Michael hated clubbing and always preferred a quiet dinner out with friends. He refused to go out during the week and Margaux had sulked at first, and then began ignoring him, not returning calls for hours and being rude when she finally decided to talk to him. Tonight he'd agreed to go out with the girls as it was a Friday and he didn't have classes the next day. He regretted his decision almost immediately. Margaux's behaviour tonight appalled him, and he didn't know how he could possibly marry someone as immature and wild as she was turning out to be.

The night had started out as expected. A few drinks at the hotel and then the girls dragged him to a nightclub they'd heard about from the owner of the café where they usually ended up after the night before, getting coffee and breakfast before they fell into bed. The club was new, and it was exclusive. The general public didn't know it existed and the three decided immediately that it was where they were going to spend their Friday night. From the moment they arrived Michael could see he was going to hate it. Margaux however, fitted in perfectly. The club was tucked away in an industrial part of Abbotsford which was deserted at night, and nowhere near a main road. This was definitely a word of mouth kind of place.

The club was in an old factory with no indication of what was going on inside except for the heavy bass beat that couldn't be muffled and a security guard that granted them entrance after they gave him a password. But inside it had been fitted out with a dance floor, lighting, bar, couches and tables. Michael didn't see how this could be legal and kept expecting the cops to descend on them at any moment. Margaux and her friends tried to entice Michael onto the dance floor, but when he refused, they shrugged their shoulders and went without him. It didn't take long before all three girls were dancing with other men, and Margaux seemed the most enthusiastic of them all. She was flirting and moving from dance partner to dance partner, glancing over at Michael every few minutes to make sure he was watching. If she was trying to make him jealous, it wasn't working. But he was angry. Her flirting with other men had become the norm, and it made Michael wonder if she loved him at all. When Margaux finally returned to the couch where Michael was sitting on his own, bored and wondering how long it would be before they could leave, she opened her purse and took out a small bag of pills. She swallowed one, chased down by a vodka martini, her drink of choice. Then she offered the bag to Michael.

"What's this … are you taking drugs?" Michael yelled over the music.

"Just a little biddy pill to relax me," Margaux said with a sloppy smile.

"Is this ecstasy?" Michael asked pulling one of the pills out of the bag.

"You should have one. You're so uptight. It'll make you feel better," Margaux answered loudly, trying to be heard over the thumping music.

"Are you insane? This could kill you," he replied, putting the bag in his pocket. He would be throwing them out as soon as he could find somewhere safe to dispose of them.

"Michael don't be boring," she slurred as she finished her third martini for the night. It was too soon for the drugs to have taken effect, but the drinks had. Michael decided he needed to get her back to the hotel as soon as possible. What if she'd bought a bad batch, if something went wrong an ambulance would find them easier at the hotel than in the factory district. He didn't even know the name of the street where they were, he'd just followed George's directions as he drove. Spotting the girls on the dance floor, he made his way through the throng of people and tapped Pippa on the shoulder. Unable to speak, the music was louder on the dance floor, he gestured that they were leaving. Both girls shook their head and

Michael shrugged his shoulders. If they wanted to stay it was up to them. Thankfully, Margaux was still where he left her, and he pulled her out of her seat. She stumbled a little and he grabbed her around the waist and guided her to the entrance of the club. She seemed unaware of what was happening, and when he got her back to his car, he belted her in and then locked the doors. The last thing he needed was her trying to get out while he was driving. His sat-nav directed him out of the industrial estate and with the roads being quiet at this time of night, he was back at the hotel within twenty minutes. The drugs had started taking their effect, Margaux turning up the radio and dancing in her seat, arms in the air, and moving with the beat.

When he arrived back at Crown he had to hand his car over to valet parking. It was a struggle getting Margaux out of the car, as she refused to leave, declaring the song on the radio was her favourite. The valet parking staff member waited patiently as Michael wrestled her from the car and ignored Margaux's drunk appearance. At this time of night the lobby was deserted so he was able to get her upstairs to her room without attracting attention. She headed for the mini bar, determined to have another vodka, but as this was the last thing she needed, he blocked her access to the fridge and convinced her to drink some water instead.

"You're so well behaved, aren't you Michael?" she mocked dancing around the room even though there was no music. "That's why Daddy likes you so much. You're such a good influence on me," she taunted, drawing out the word good. "Bet he wouldn't be so happy with you if he could see me now."

"I'm sure he wouldn't be very happy with *you* Margaux. I can tell you I'm not," Michael replied, his anger and disgust growing. He had never seen Margaux properly drunk, let alone drugged before. He hoped this wasn't how she behaved when he wasn't around, but it would explain the sleeping all day. All he wanted was to go home, but he couldn't leave in case something went wrong. Finally, she decided she was tired and sunk into the bed. He removed her shoes and pulled the covers over her. She was asleep within a minute and Michael went to the bathroom where he flushed the drugs. It wasn't ideal but he didn't know what else to do with them. There was no way he was going to throw them in the hotel bin where they could be seen by staff or found by Margaux. And taking them home wasn't an option. What if his parents found them? How would he explain that?

He settled himself in a comfortable chair where he could keep an eye on Margaux without having to sleep beside her. He had no idea what he was going to do about this, drug use had always been unacceptable to him. He had never heard even a whisper that Margaux took drugs before, and he hoped that she had only done it at the urging of her friends. The sooner they went home the better. She'd been different since they arrived in Australia.

He finally fell asleep at three o'clock. Margaux hadn't stirred for hours and he'd relaxed a little, thinking at least physically she was going to be alright. Whether *they* would be alright was another story.

Chapter Ten

Trying to balance work and fostering was about to become a bigger challenge than Jillian could ever have imagined. The agency had started them out slowly and Jill and Matthew were grateful for that. The first child that came to stay was a thirteen-year-old girl. Her mother had been in a car accident and required a few days recovery in hospital. With no family living in Victoria, the girl needed somewhere to stay until her mother was back home. Because her school was within walking distance of Jillian's house it turned out to be the perfect situation. Cassie had been lovely, quiet and barely caused a ripple in the Brookes household. After a few days, her mother was released from hospital with a broken leg and some bruising, but because Cassie was old enough to get herself to school, she was able to go home.

Jillian made the move from her city law firm to working at Sustenance as soon as they'd been approved as foster carers. Matthew, who always wanted Jill to join him in their business, came up with a plan to make work more flexible for her. The new role only required about twenty hours a week and was easily done from home. She oversaw new contracts and made sure they were complying with all the laws surrounding food manufacturing that changed constantly.

If they had any young charges who weren't attending school she would stay home and do what she could while caring for the child. If they were older she would work at the office during school hours. So far it had been the perfect solution and she didn't miss the long hours and juggling after school care for Zoe.

The second child that stayed with them had been completely different from Cassie. An eight-year-old boy – they made it very clear that they would not accept teenage boys into their home because of Zoe – named Mason, was moody and naughty. He refused to shower, left his clothes and shoes all over the house and wouldn't eat the food they served him. He asked for pizza and McDonalds at every meal and continually checked the cupboards for something that would appeal to his limited pallet. Packaged food didn't exist in the Brookes home, and eventually Mason was forced to eat what was put in front of him. But his table manners left a lot to be desired and Jillian was relieved when his grandmother was tracked down after two weeks and agreed to take him. Mason's mother had a habit of taking off a few times a year and leaving her son with his father. She always turned up eventually, either out of money or out of fun, but this time social services were notified of the situation. Mason's teacher called and alerted the department there was a problem when he turned up to school with bruising on his arms. The authorities decided to remove him until a relative who could take him was found, or at the very least his mother returned from her holiday.

There had been a few other children, usually staying for less than a week, and for the most part the Brookes family had enjoyed it. They were relieved they hadn't become attached to any of their guests as they liked to think of them but felt like they were doing something good. And it meant that Zoe could see how blessed her life was.

Today's phone call from Mandy, their liaison at the department had

been different. Jillian was busy sorting through an important negotiation with a new supplier that her husband had discovered. Matthew, who always used Australian grown ingredients unless there was no other option, discovered a new company selling coconut cream in Queensland. He needed someone who could supply them large quantities for a new product they were developing. It was important to Sustenance that the product was organic and ethically grown and harvested. This was hard to monitor as almost all the coconuts had to be imported from other countries, mainly Asia, before they were manufactured into the end product here.

Mandy was desperate. She had a brother and sister who urgently needed a home. She'd already been turned down by two families when they found out there would be two kids. Kelly was three and Sam was two. A neighbour found them alone in their home, with the body of their mother early this morning. Thankfully for the children the elderly neighbour had been concerned by what she saw going on at the house and had begun popping over with food a few times a week. When no one answered the door earlier, even though she could hear movement in the house and the television on, she decided to call the police. Kelly and Sam's mother had died of a suspected drug overdose and police believed that the children had been alone with her body overnight.

Jill agreed to take both children immediately. Separating them would be awful, and they had plenty of space. There were two bedrooms in their house for foster children. One for younger children who were still in a cot and one with a bed for older kids. After racing home from work to prepare, she decided that it would be better to put the siblings in the same room and pushed the cot into the larger bedroom. As always, she was fully stocked with nappies and spare clothes, because not every kid had turned up with a backpack containing everything they needed.

The doorbell rang a few hours later and Jillian was greeted by a very flustered looking Mandy. Jillian took the boy from her arms and Mandy came inside. Once they had a cup of tea in front of them, she gave Jill as many details as she could. The children's mother, Susan, did have a sister and they were hoping she could take the pair. But as yet she had not decided. She had two of her own and as they were living on government benefits and in a tiny, run down public housing unit, it wasn't the ideal situation. Kelly and Sam's aunt had been more interested in how much the government would give them if she took the kids than their welfare or even the death of her own sister.

Mandy took another sip of her tea before she continued to tell Jill about the family.

"I shouldn't say this, but I almost hope she says no. The house is a tip and her own kids aren't exactly living in a suitable environment. And they're teenagers, so they might not be welcoming to two toddlers."

"Well they'll be fine here. Zoe loves having little people around. Do you know how long they'll be staying?

"I'm sorry but at this point I can't give you a timeline on how long they'll be with you. We may need to find them a permanent home outside of family. Susan's sister said the father took off back to New Zealand six months ago. We'll work with the authorities there to see if we can find him, but he may not be any better than the sister. And it can be hard finding a family who is willing to take two kid's long term, but it would be a tragedy to separate them. "

Kelly was sitting on the couch in the family room with the television on low, and Jill was still holding Sam. He seemed happy enough sitting with her and would have no idea what had happened to his mum.

"We have plenty of space. And I can work from home for a few weeks if I need to. Don't stress. It's better to find them somewhere good instead of somewhere quick."

"I appreciate that," Mandy said with a tired smile. "You haven't changed your mind about offering permanent care, have you?" she asked as she rose from her chair.

"We're happy with things the way they are. Emergencies only," Jill told a disappointed Mandy. "Especially with Zoe turning thirteen soon. A few days here and there, or even a few weeks is fine. But permanent care," she shook her head. "We don't think we're ready for that yet."

"I understand," Mandy replied. "I'll be around tomorrow with the rest of their things. She gestured to the bag she had brought with her. "I couldn't find much in the way of clean clothes in the drawers, but there was stuff strewn all over the house, so I'll go through it and see what I can find. I would suggest you wash anything I bring you though. Just the smell of the place," she said wrinkling her nose in disgust. "I can't get back into the house until the police are finished but what I brought should do for now."

"We'll be fine. I have extra clothes. But maybe look for some soft toys that look well loved. It might help settle them in here."

"Good idea. I'll see what I can find. I don't know when the funeral will be, but I don't think the kids should attend unless the family insist. They're too young to understand and they don't need any more trauma right now."

"Agreed. I'll be here all day tomorrow, so bring whatever you can find, clothes and toys, even if they're dirty," she said as the two walked to the front door.

"Thanks Jill. Call me if you have any questions. They've eaten lunch so you should be right for a few hours. They will need a bath. From the look of them it's been awhile."

~~~

By the time Matthew arrived home after work the house was in chaos. Zoe had sent him a text begging him to come home, so he had moved a late afternoon meeting and missed some of the peak hour traffic. But it was still after five and the two new arrivals had been dropped off at two. Zoe, who came home via the bus, because Jill only had one car seat and needed to purchase another one, was playing with the girl in the family room quietly. Matthew could hear the screaming from outside, and as soon as he opened the front door, Jill who'd been waiting for him, handed off a little boy who was hysterical.

"I'm sorry. But I have to go to the toilet, and I can't take him with me. If I put him down it gets louder, and he starts pulling things off the tables and throwing them," Jill warned, running off in the direction of their bedroom. Matthew held the screaming two-year-old out in front of him to get a better look.

This wasn't Sam's finest moment. He had snot running down his face and he was bright red from all the crying. He was cute though. Blonde curls, that Matthew could see were replicated in his sister. She looked like she'd been crying at some point too, her eyes rimmed in red, but she was calm for the moment. It had been a long time since Zoe had been this little, but he remembered that at this age the best way to stop them from crying was to distract them with something new. He gave Zoe a wave hello and then looking around the room saw a figurine he and Jill had bought several years ago when they were holidaying in Chile. It was a tiny horse made of copper and would be the perfect size for the boy's hand to hold. Grabbing it and making, admittedly terrible neighing noises, he handed the little statue to Sam. Sam who was flailing about, trying to get away from Matthew, was not interested in his attempt at distracting him, grabbed the horse and smashed it into the side of his cheek. The pain was instant and excruciating.

"Son of a ..." he stopped himself before he said something not appropriate for little ears, but the kid was lucky Matthew hadn't accidently dropped him. Taking the figurine off him before he did more damage, Sam's screams ramped up another notch. Matthew, afraid the boy was going to wriggle out of his arms and hurt himself, encircled him tighter. Walking into the hallway he looked at his cheek in the mirror. A red mark was already forming, and he could see that by tomorrow he was going to have an impressive bruise. Returning to the kitchen he rummaged through the freezer looking for something to put on his face to bring down the swelling. Finally in the bottom draw he found a bag of pea's and when he pulled them out, he saw a box of magnums hiding underneath. Sam saw the box at the same, and it was obviously something he recognised because the crying instantly stopped, and he started reaching for the chocolate treat.

Whatever it takes, he thought and reached down for the box. There were three ice creams inside and he quickly opened one up for Sam who promptly put it in his mouth. Just managing to hold the bag of peas to his cheek, he took the other two ice creams to the family room and handed one to Kelly who was mesmerised by Zoe and looked happy playing with the Barbies Zoe had pulled out of the cupboard earlier. Zoe looked totally confused when he handed her an ice cream as well but took it. This was not the usual sugar free, dairy free, fake cream as she called it, that he let her have as an occasional treat. The only time she ever had real ice cream was when she stayed with her grandparents or visited Beth and Tom's house.

"All good?" he asked as she helped Kelly open the packet.

"Yep. Better now that the screaming had stopped. He's been doing that since I got home an hour ago. I wanted to pull my own ears off."

"He seems fine now," Matthew said has he dropped the bag of peas on the coffee table and pulled a tissue out of one of the many boxes Jill kept around the house. He did his best to wipe away the mess on Sam's face which was now beginning to merge with melted chocolate. "Thanks for playing with her. You probably have homework to do."

"That's okay. I can do it after dinner. Which we might want to get started on. I'm hungry, and Jill hasn't had a chance to cook anything."

"I will, I promise," Jill said as she returned from the bathroom. "How did you get him to stop crying?" she asked and then stopped when she saw all three children eating her stash of hidden ice creams. *Great*, she thought. *I've been looking forward to one of those all afternoon. I guess I won't be sneaking off later to have it now* "And what's with the bag of peas?" Matthew pulled the bag that he had retrieved from the table away from his now numb cheek and Jill saw the beginnings of a bruise.

"Horse injury," Matthew said as he handed a now very content Sam back to Jill, ignoring her look of confusion. "Don't worry about dinner. I'll get a pizza delivered." Jillian and Zoe exchanged glances at each other in shock. In all the years they'd been married, Matthew had never ordered takeaway. As he started looking through his phone for somewhere that would deliver, Jill asked Zoe under her breath, "How hard was he hit, because he appears to have lost his mind."

"I don't know," Zoe replied, "but I like it," she smiled.

Chapter Eleven

" No, not that one. That's for toasts later," Sarah pointed to a row of Champagne bottles. "The ones on the bottom row. You *do* know how to open it don't you?" Sarah questioned as Amy put the vintage champagne back into the huge wine fridge and grabbed a still, very nice bottle of Mumm. Amy who had been working casually for Caroline all through Uni knew exactly how to open a bottle of champagne without having it spill over or break a window with the cork. But she could see that Sarah was stressed, running her very first party, so decided to let the comment slide as she expertly opened the bottle.

The party had been going for about an hour, and the Anderson home was overflowing with guests. Michael had invited all his friends from Uni and school. Knowing that most people wouldn't make it to America for the wedding, he agreed to his parents inviting important business associates and many of their family friends. Margaux, not knowing anyone in Australia, hadn't invited a single guest. Even her parents decided not to attend tonight's engagement party, sighting the long flight as a reason. This didn't get Michael's parents out of attending the American party being held in two months though. Michael made it very clear they were expected to attend whether it was convenient or not. Emerson offered to pick up the bill for the flights, but Adam declined the offer, booking them himself. He sent Emerson a kind note thanking him for his generosity, but privately he said he wouldn't take a cent from the man he already disliked, even though they hadn't met yet.

The two cooks Caroline hired to cater all her parties were on top of everything, the strict running sheet was being followed to a tee, and the four waiters were busily taking out trays of tempting hors d'oeuvres to the guests. A marquee had been set up in the back yard with a dance floor and the DJ was pumping out a variety of hits from the last three decades. The neighbours were all here too, so there wouldn't be any complaints about the noise.

With everything running smoothly in the kitchen Sarah decided to pop out and make sure someone was picking up the empty glasses and used napkins that people seemed to leave in the oddest places. The house was almost empty now, most guest moving to the marquee, or outside in the beautifully lit garden. There were gas heaters dotted around where groups of people gravitated, chatting and catching up with each other. It would have been perfect to have the party later in the year when the weather was warmer, but Margaux was due back at school in two weeks and was flying home on Monday.

The enormous dining table had been used for the gifts. Many of them were wrapped in the signature black and white of David Jones where Margaux had registered. She'd wanted to register at Tiffany's, but it wasn't possible in Australia, and Caroline had been relieved. Expecting friends and family to fork out two hundred dollars for one crystal glass or a thousand dollars for a photo frame was ridiculous. Although when she checked the registry for Margaux and Michael online at DJ's, she saw that Margaux still managed to track down the most expensive brands. Caroline told people to feel free to shop wherever they wanted and changed the invitation without telling Margaux – who hadn't shown any other interest in the party, except what presents she would receive – to say that while gifts were welcome, they were not expected. Sarah had overheard her Mum complaining about the price of Margaux's choices and ended up buying some nice wine glasses from House. She said with a huff, if Margaux didn't like them, she could let the servants use them.

Gathering up several glasses that had been left on the dining room buffet, Sarah didn't notice Michael enter the room. Turning, she nearly crashed into him as he reached out to tap her on the shoulder. Pulling up, she started to apologise, but Michael waved his hand and then asked her to sit for a moment. When she said she should get back to the kitchen, he reminded her that it was his party and she was working for *him* tonight. Following orders she carefully put the glasses back down on the buffet and pulled out a dining chair.

"I know I'm very late saying this, but congratulations on your eighteenth," Michael apologised. "It would have been great to be at the party, but it just wasn't practical to fly home for it. I did see some photos on Facebook. It's looks like you all had a great time."

"Don't worry about it Michael," she said, her heart beating a mile a minute. She hadn't been this close to him in a long time. I know I sent you an invitation, but I never expected you to come home for one night, and especially just for my birthday. It was just … you know a courtesy. Mum thought you might feel left out if I didn't ask." Sarah neglected to mention how hurt she'd been when not only did Michael not bother to RSVP, but he didn't send a card or even a text saying happy birthday. She'd waited all day for some sort of communication from him, something to let her know that he was thinking of her, even if it wasn't in the way she wished he did, but it never came.

"Well. I still should have sent something. But I'd just met Margaux, and you know," he shrugged his shoulders as explanation. "I was blown away and I couldn't think of anything else but her." He pulled a small box out of his pocket. "I know it's six months late, but happy birthday." He held the gift out and placed it in her hand. "Go ahead, open it," he instructed, the excitement clear in his voice.

Sarah pulled the ribbon off the box and opened it, revealing a pair of earrings. Rubies, or what looked like rubies caught the light of the chandelier above, and Sarah gasped at the prettiness of them. Tear drops encircled by tiny diamonds, they were a little old fashioned, but classic. Sarah loved them immediately.

"Dad and I were going through our safety deposit box a few weeks ago and we found these earrings. They were my Grandmother's and she left them to Isabelle. It would have been a nice gesture for her to leave them to Mum, but Grandma hated her and left all her jewellery to Izzy. When she died it came to me."

"Then why are you giving them to me? They look expensive."

"They are. I mean, you won't be able to sell them and buy a car. But the rubies are real."

"Then you should give them to Margaux. She's going to be your wife."

"Don't worry," he smiled. "I have something beautiful to give her on our wedding day. And as pretty as these are, they wouldn't appeal to her."

Sarah raised her eyebrow and jokingly said, "So you're giving me something no one else wants?"

"No. That didn't come out right," he blurted. "It's just when I saw them, they didn't make me think of Margaux. They made me think of you. I don't know why, but I thought, Sarah would love these."

Sarah smiled, remembering why they probably reminded him of her. "Do you remember when I was eleven? I'd just had my ears pierced, and I bought those cheap earrings from the chemist with my pocket money. They looked a bit like these, but they were made of cheap red glass and fake gold.

I got that awful infection from them and Mum made me take them out and chucked them away. I was devastated."

"Oh yeah," he smiled. "I do remember. Lochie and I picked on you for weeks. That rash went down your neck and took ages to heal. We called you rashy face for weeks. Not exactly original." He shook his head and rolled his eyes. "I was such an idiot back then. I don't know why you put up with me."

"Probably because when Lochie wasn't around you were always nice to me," Sarah said, knowing she could never tell him the truth. "Thank you for the present. I love them. But are you sure your Dad was okay with you giving them to me? They were his Mother's."

"Not only did Dad not mind, he was thrilled for you to have them. And they belonged to Isabelle, so if you think about it, they come from both of us. And before you ask, I checked with Mum and she said she wouldn't wear and I quote, 'anything that the old bat had owned.'" So again, happy birthday, and congrats on getting your licence. You must be loving the freedom."

"Oh yeah. I'm never getting on another bus or train as long as I live. And thank you for the present. I can't wait to have somewhere fancy to wear them. And they are extra special coming from you and Isabelle." Without thinking she leaned over and kissed him on the cheek. Appalled at herself, she jumped up from the chair, and snapping the box shut, she put it in her pocket.

"I better get back to work, or your Mother will kill me," she said as she stood and picked up the glasses she had abandoned earlier. "And congratulations on your engagement. I hope you and Margaux will be very happy together," she said, meaning it. Well, not the Margaux bit, but she did want him to be happy. Her heart was on the mend, and she had even been out a few times with Noah from school, but seeing Michael in a tuxedo, looking more handsome than she had ever seen him would have been too much for any girl to ignore. And now he was giving her jewellery. He wasn't making it easy for her.

As Michael watched Sarah's retreating back, he thought about how natural their interaction had been. With most girls you had to be careful what you said in case they were offended, and Margaux was worse than most. *I guess it's different with people you've known most of your life*, he thought. There were so many shared memories and they understood you and where you've come from. As much as he loved her, he didn't have that with Margaux.

After the incident at the nightclub, Michael had been ready to end the relationship, but she begged and pleaded with him to give her another chance. She promised it was the first time she'd ever used drugs, and blamed Pippa and George for giving them to her. The two troublemakers returned to America a few days later, and since then Margaux had stopped partying. As Michael had never seen her so inebriated before, he chose to believe that night was just a one off. But while she was no longer out partying every night, she was still moody and difficult to deal with. She threw a tantrum every time he suggested they spend time with his parents, and then accused him of abandoning her whenever he slept at home. But sometimes he just needed a break from her. Studying was impossible in her hotel suite, and although he would never say it out loud, he was relieved she was going home in a few days. He needed to buckle down and prepare for his exams. It was next to impossible with her claiming every spare minute he had.

"There you are darling," Margaux exclaimed as she appeared at the dining room door. Everyone's been looking for you. Speech time." Michael looked at his finance'. There was no denying she was stunning tonight in a floor length gown, made of a pale coral silk, the tight embroidered bodice fell from her slim waste in layers. She was wearing the highest of heels which made her as tall as him, in a deeper coral. Her hair had been pulled into a classic French twist with diamante clips shimmering in the light, but on closer inspection he decided they were probably real diamonds. She was, as always, encircled by a cloud of her signature scent, Joy. It was the same one her mother wore and when he had thought to pick her up a bottle one day as a small gift he'd been shocked at the price. He sometimes wondered if he was ever going to get used to how much money her family had? He'd always thought he had lived a privileged life, but compared to Margaux, his upbringing had been rather ordinary.

"Coming," he said, standing and pushing the chair back in under the table. "I'm just going to pop into the kitchen and get Sarah. She should be there for the speeches."

"Who?"

"Sarah. My Mum's best friends' daughter. The person who has done most of the work for tonight and made sure everything has run smoothly."

"The girl who helps your mother with her little business. I'm sure she's busy washing dishes. Do leave it please. Everyone is waiting for you."

"But ..."

"Michael, seriously. Leave her where she belongs. In the kitchen."

"Alright," he capitulated, not wanting an argument. "Let's get this over and done with then. I hope Dad doesn't embarrass me too much." Clasping his hand, Margaux guided Michael through the door and outside to the marquee. Neither of them saw Sarah who'd returned from the kitchen to collect more glasses and had overheard their conversation.

What a horrible, nasty woman, Sarah thought. *And Michael couldn't even stand up for me, or himself for that matter. What a pathetic, weak joke he's become. He used to be self-assured and determined. He came out the other side of Isabelle's death, and hadn't let him change who he was. But six months with Margaux and he's become a door mat. How could I ever have thought I was in love with him*. Sarah continued to walk around the house collecting glasses, relieved she'd seen Michael for what he really was. At least he was going to make it easy for her to get over him. Sarah decided she done. She wasn't going to give him another thought.

Chapter Twelve

"You look so much better than the last time I saw you," Jill noted. When she'd last caught up with Joan, her pregnant friend had been a mess. Her hair was limp, and her skin had been greasy and pale. Now she looked like her old, beautiful self and her tummy was just beginning to show. "Pregnancy really does suit you."

When she first heard that Joan's third baby was on the way she felt that familiar pang of jealously. It was so easy for some women – women who weren't even trying – while others did everything they could, and it never happened for them. But jealousy had been quickly replaced with concern when she heard about the health issue's Joan might face. Now she was just happy that everything appeared to be going well.

"Twenty-one weeks and no problems. Let's hope it stays that way."

"And what does your doctor say. Is he, she, happy with how you're tracking?" Caroline asked.

"She is. I'm putting on the right amount of weight. The morning sickness has completely passed, and my blood pressure is where it should be. In three more months, if the baby was born early, the prognosis would be okay. Not that that's going to happen. I'm going all the way to the end with this kid. But that's it, this is definitely the last one," she insisted as she rubbed her hand over her belly.

"So has David had his little procedure then?" Beth asked, remembering back to the fuss Tom made at the time. The carry on about the pain had been epic, he acted like he'd lost a limb instead of a having a small snip, a few stitches and then all done. And under anaesthetic with pain killers to take home. She lost a little bit of respect for him that day.

"Yeah, all done. You would think he had saved the country or something. He was so proud of himself. Do these men have any idea what it feels like to give birth? I mean, they're right there in the room with us. Can't they see it's not a paper cut or a sprained ankle? It's torture," Joan shuddered, remember Bella's birth. It had been awful. And she was going to have to do it all again.

"It doesn't help that we keep doing it to ourselves," Caroline said. "So they must think it's not too bad and we're being dramatic at the time. I can guarantee you that if men had to give birth they would only have one each and we would halve the human population in a generation."

They paused their conversation as the waitress brought over the first of their meals. It had become a tradition for the girls to meet at a restaurant in Melbourne's famous Chadstone Shopping Centre for lunch, once a year, before the Christmas mayhem started. It had originally just been Caroline and Beth, but one year Jillian joined them and in the past few years Joan had been invited too. This year had been busier than most and all four were thrilled to be out of the house and spending some time with each other.

"How's your course going Beth?" Joan asked as she poured herself a glass of water. It was hard to even catch Beth on the phone these days.

"I love it. I'm mostly studying nutrition at the moment. I thought I knew a lot, but I'm learning that the right food really is medicine for the body. It's exciting, and I know I have years to go, but I can't wait to help other people improve their health when I've finished."

"Except you're no fun anymore. I used to be able to go to your place and eat yummy stuff without Matthew knowing. Now there's nowhere to hide," Jill said as she picked up a crispy chip off her plate. "What?" she asked, all eyes on her.

"It doesn't look like that lunch you're eating is exactly healthy," Caroline laughed.

"I only get to eat out a few times a year without Matthew, and when I do, I eat a yummy chicken schnitzel with chips, and I leave the salad. I'm even going to have cake after, so there," she childishly poked her tongue out.

"I'm just teasing Jill. I don't care what you eat. You stay slim no matter what."

"You're not exactly podgy yourself Caroline."

"I know," she sighed, "but I have to work at it these days," she said gesturing to her Caesar salad, no croutons and dressing on the side. "I'm completely over this 'getting old' business."

"Do we have to talk about food?" Joan groaned, "my doctor has me on a strict diet and right now I'd kill for a cup of coffee, a glass of wine and one of those chips you're eating Jill."

"What kind of diet restrictions has she put on you?" Beth asked, always wanting to learn.

"Reduced salt, but I don't have to completely cut it out. I'm allowed a pinch of that pink salt every day, but no regular table salt. She says there's not a huge amount of evidence that it will make a difference to my blood pressure, but just to be on the safe side I have to limit it. It gets so confusing trying to decide what's good and what's bad myself so now I just do what I'm told. I have to eat everything fresh, nothing pre-made from the supermarket, so I don't get a night off cooking anymore," she said missing the days when sometimes she cheated and ordered in, or grabbed a BBQ chicken and a ready-made coleslaw from the shops. "I'm supposed to eat fish, but not fish that could contain mercury like flake and some tunas. I can eat healthy fats, but not bad ones. I don't even know the difference. Isn't fat, just fat?"

"Afraid not. Some are good for you and too much of others can give you a heart attack. If you give me all your doctors recommendations, I can help you put together a food plan," Beth said.

"Okay. Like recipes?" Joan asked, a little sceptical. One thing Beth was not known for was her cooking.

"Nice," Beth retorted. "Try to do a girl a favour. Just give me the recommended food list and I'll get Sarah to put together some yummy ideas for you."

"That would be nice. Speaking of which, how is your lovely girl going? Last I heard she was dating someone from school. "

"She was, but that's over. He decided he didn't want to be in a serious relationship, which is ridiculous because she didn't want one either. She was sad for a few days, but I think the thing she's most upset about is that she paid for two tickets to go see a show with him next week and he's let her down."

"Can't someone else go with her? She must have a friend from school who wouldn't mind a free night out," Joan asked before spearing a slice of cucumber and looking at it like she wished it was one of Jills chips.

"It's not your usual musical. I think it's called *Once*. Supposed to be romantic. Not the kind of thing you take another girl to. Well not Sarah anyway."

"I've seen that movie. It *is* romantic. I thought the show had finished in Melbourne," Joan said."

"This isn't with the original cast. That cost a fortune to see. It's in a smaller theatre out in the suburbs, but it's still getting great reviews."

"Is that the movie with the song Falling Slowly?" Jill asked, still enjoying her lunch without a trace of guilt. "I love that song."

"I don't know?" Beth answered. "They all sound the same to me. I just hope she can find someone to go with, but she said she doesn't mind going alone. It's based on one of her favourite movies and she said she's not going to miss out because of some guy."

Good on her. If she can learn at this age she doesn't always have to have a man around to be happy, she'll make better decisions about men and especially when it comes to choosing a partner," Jill said. "Who hasn't made stupid choices at some point because they were afraid of ending up alone," she said, remembering her first disaster of a marriage. "Speaking of bad decisions, how are the plans for Michael's *real* engagement party going Caroline?"

"Don't let Michael hear you say that. He still thinks she's the most wonderful woman on planet Earth." Caroline hadn't been able to keep her feelings about Margaux from her best friends. Not that she was going around bad mouthing her, but it was clear to anyone who listened to Caroline talk about her future daughter-in-law for more than a minute that she wasn't the girl's biggest fan. And they were all aware of how Margaux treated Caroline. With complete contempt.

"As for the party, I have no idea," Caroline continued, as she, completely out of character, rolled her eyes. "We haven't been included in any of the planning and by we, I also mean Michael. We're expected to show up in our finest clothes and jewellery, and not do anything that will embarrass Michael's future in-laws in front of their rich friends. I just hope Adam doesn't get into it with Margaux's Father. He's been doing some digging online and asked some of his business contacts in the States about him, and it turns out Emerson has quite the reputation. Both with women and in business. Adam's so straight up and down, he hates the idea of someone who isn't, so I'm expecting some tension between them."

A phone started ringing and Jill, recognising that it was her ring tone for Matthew, answered it immediately, mouthing a silent apology. Nobody was supposed to answer their phone while the girls were out at their once a year lunch together.

"Hi Darl, what's up?' She listened for a minute before answering. "In the garage. Sorry they got dirty last time we were out, and I haven't had a chance to clean them." There was silence from her end and then she finished the conversation with an 'I love you' and 'see you later.'

"Sorry about that. Just had to solve the case of the missing gumboots. They weren't where they were meant to be."

"We heard," Beth chuckled. "It was riveting."

Jill light-heartedly wacked her sister on the arm. "I don't know why you're laughing. Your home is always in chaos."

"I'm just teasing. You seem to be enjoying the fostering thing. Have Kelly and Sam settled in yet?"

"I think so. Kelly has stopped asking for her mother, and Sam only did for a week or so. It was harder for Kelly. She was just that bit older. And now that she's four we need to start making some decisions about next year. She has to be enrolled for kinder soon because spots are filling up fast, but it's impossible to know where the kids will be living. If they're still with us at the start of the year, then there's a kinder a few kilometres down the road she can go to. But if a relative turns up, they could end up in another state, or even another country if their father shows up."

"But has no one agreed to take them yet?" Beth enquired. "I thought you were only interested in short term fostering. How long has it been?"

"Six weeks. Nobody wants them moved to another foster family unless they're willing to take them on permanently. Now that they're settled with us, moving them somewhere else for a few weeks and then moving them again would be awful. They're too little to keep making changes like that. And they both adore Zoe. So for now, we've agreed to keep them until a more permanent solution can be found. The police in New Zealand are still looking for their father, but since his arrival on an Australian passport into Auckland, nobody has heard from him. And their aunt decided she definitely didn't want the kids."

"I can't imagine refusing to take in any of *your* kids," Beth said looking at her best friends. "How do you abandon your own family?"

"Not everyone is as good as you lovely," Joan replied with a smile as she finished the last bite of her Thai fish cakes and salad. If David didn't have family who could step in if anything happened to the two of them, she would trust her kids with Beth and Tom in a heartbeat. "Now, I know I can't have a whole piece, but is someone willing to share a brownie with me?"

"What would your doctor say if she saw you eating that?" Beth asked raising her eyebrows.

"I don't see her here, and if you don't tell on me, she'll never know. And besides, I've spent the last four months throwing up. One small piece of something yummy isn't going to make that much difference to my figure."

"Well then," Beth agreed, "just to help you out, I'll have the other half."

"Oooh, should you do that Doctor Beth? I bet that's not medicine," Joan teased.

"Dark chocolate is bound to be the main ingredient, and everyone knows that's full of minerals and antioxidants," Beth argued as the others began to laugh as she blushed.

"Oh shut up the lot of you. And be nice Joan or I'll eat the whole thing myself."

"Well on your way then. It's faster if you order at the counter. And can you get me one too?" Caroline asked.

"And a piece of that mud cake for me," Jill added. "With cream and caramel sauce."

"Serves you right if you all get fat," Beth huffed as she pushed her chair back. "Anyone want anything else while I'm up?" she said over her shoulder as she made her way to the counter at the front of the restaurant. Ignoring them all as they threw out absurd suggestions at her of things they wanted, including a pony and a million dollars, Beth smiled to herself grateful that these women were in her life and knowing it would be impossible to live without them.

Chapter Thirteen

When Michael called a week ago asking Sarah if he could buy her spare ticket to *Once* she was horrified. Not at him, but at her reaction to him. She had been telling herself for months that she was over him, that she even hated him for the way he had let Margaux dismiss her like she was nothing. But the minute she heard his voice her heart had done a slow roll. When he asked to buy her ticket she said, without hesitation, that he could have it. And when he insisted on picking her up and taking her for an early dinner before the show to say thanks, instead of saying no, she'd agreed immediately. Instantly she was back to behaving like a lovesick teenager – which she was. Pathetic.

And even though she'd known it was a bad idea, she took herself off to the shops and bought a new dress to wear for the evening. She convinced herself she wasn't dressing up for Michael, she just wanted to look nice for her evening out. After hours going from store to store she finally found a dusky pink ankle length dress with a water colour style print of soft brown roses that looked perfect on her. It floated over her slim figure and with the caramel rattan strappy platforms she'd chosen, she looked soft and carefree. The very opposite of Margaux's designer chic dresses with stiletto heels.

Choosing muted colours for her makeup, and with loose curls that fell past her shoulders, she barely recognised the face staring back from the mirror. She'd always considered herself rather ordinary looking, Lochie had told her enough times she was ugly. But tonight, and maybe for the first time ever, she thought she looked … pretty.

She'd been avoiding her mum for the past few days after she offered to go with her to the musical, forcing Sarah to admit that she had was going with someone else. Her mum, as usual, probed, probably hoping that she had met someone new – and Sarah did consider telling a small fib – but in the end she knew she couldn't lie. Michael was coming to the house to pick her up and he was bound to come in to say 'hi.' And besides, Caroline and her mum told each other everything. She would find out one way or another that he was her date. Well not her date, but her escort for the evening. Mum gave her that look, that – "this is a terrible idea look' – that her Mother specialized in, but she didn't say anything. Just gave Sarah a 'hmmm.' But that said it all.

Sarah did one last twirl in front of her mirror and picked up a soft pink knitted shawl off her bed in case it got cold later. The weather in Melbourne could change in minutes, and October was a hard month to predict. She opened her bedroom door and nearly crashed into her Dad, his hand up ready to knock on her door.

"Mind if I come in for a sec Sarah?" he asked.

"Uh, sure I guess," she said stepping back to allow him to enter. Her Dad almost never came into her room anymore. Not since she turned twelve and said she was too old to be tucked in every night.

Tom surveyed the messy room, bed unmade, clothes hanging out of drawers and her study desk littered with schoolbooks that didn't look like they had been opened enough this year. Sarah was always messy as a child and Beth spent years trying to get her to keep her room tidy. She'd given up when Sarah was fifteen and said if she wanted to live in a pigsty then go ahead. Sarah had taken her at her word.

After moving a pile of clothes he sat on the end of her bed and took a deep breath in while his daughter gave him the 'what now old man' stare that all teenagers perfected over time. She wasn't going to make this easy for him.

"You look very nice tonight Sarah," he said noticing the difference from her usual uniform of black jeans and tee shirts. Beth had been saying for a while that Sarah was growing up and developing a style of her own. He'd chosen to ignore it, still thinking of Sarah as the little girl who wanted to muck in with the boys and didn't care if she was dirty or messy. But he could see that those days were long over, even if he wasn't ready for it.

"I'm sure you're going to ignore me and my advice, but I just wanted to have a quick word about tonight, and don't roll your eyes at me," he said as she did. "Just hear me out please. Your Mum and I are a bit concerned that you might misunderstand Michael's intensions for tonight. He's thinking he's taking an old friend out and nothing more. He's engaged."

"Really, I didn't know that Dad. Oh, hang on … I was there," she exaggerated to make the point. "*And* I seem to remember organising most of the engagement party. I'm not quite as stupid as you think."

"No love. I don't think you're stupid. But I am concerned that spending time alone with Michael might be a bad idea. He doesn't know you have a crush on him *and* – "

"Let me stop you right there Dad," she said raising her hand to stop him from continuing with his fatherly speech. "Had. *Had* a crush. As in, in the past. I didn't ask him to dinner, he asked me. And I know the only reason he even called was because he wanted to see *Once*, and I had a spare ticket. I know that this is not a date. He's getting married, and anyway, even if he wasn't, he's way too old for me. I understand all of that. And I get it that next year he'll be moving to America permanently, and there's a good chance we might never see him again. So you don't need to worry about me. I'm very aware of the situation and I'm totally fine with it. We're just friends, and that's all I want to be."

"Are you sure you don't feel anything for him? I would hate to see you with a broken heart."

"My heart is fine Dad. It's nice that you care, but I'm a big girl now and you don't need to worry."

"I'll always worry. When you're forty with kids of your own I'll still worry about you."

The shrill sound of the doorbell ringing broke the moment and Sarah picked up her handbag, popping her phone in. She smiled at her Dad and leaned over to where he was still sitting on the end of her bed and kissed him on the forehead.

"Love you Dad," she said and was out the door before she had a chance to hear him say "Love you too Sarah."

~~~

It took them over an hour to get to the restaurant that Michael chose for dinner on the Mornington Peninsula. Located in an old cool-store that was recently renovated, it housed a variety of businesses. Del's was a mixture of Italian classics like pizza and pasta, but there were also plenty of other choices. The community theatre *Once* was playing in was only a ten-minute drive away, but they would need to eat quickly if they wanted to be there on time. The traffic at that time of night was horrible, and it had taken longer to get there than Michael expected. He'd done most of the talking as he drove down the freeway away from the city, telling Sarah about his time living in America and she'd only added an odd comment here and there. She was too nervous to say much more and afraid if she started talking she would end up babbling like an idiot.

Once they were settled at their table, and chosen what they wanted for dinner, prawn risotto for Michael and her favourite, chicken fettuccine, Michael picked up his conversation from the car. He'd been telling her how he'd gone to Florida for spring break with a friend from college just to see what it was like. He said it made schoolies look tame, and asked Sarah if she had any plans to go away with her friends once her exams were over.

"No. I thought about going down to Lorne, that's where most of my friends are going, but I have no interest in getting drunk and sleeping in a tent at a caravan park for a week. None of us could afford to rent a house. And landlords want thousands of dollars for the bond for schoolie groups." Michael expressed his surprise by raising his eyebrows and rolling his eyes.

"I know right. Apparently we're going to leave their houses a disaster. I can't afford it, and neither can anyone I know. And your mum has me working long hours getting ready for all the Christmas parties we have booked anyway, so I had a great excuse to say no. If I get a day off I might drive up, but it's such a long way. Not sure I can be bothered."

"And you still like working for Mum?" he asked as their drinks were delivered to the table. Sarah had considered trying to be a little sophisticated and having a glass of wine, but as she hadn't taken up drinking as a sport the minute she turned eighteen like most of the kids at school, she decided tonight was probably not a good time to experiment with alcohol. What if she got drunk or worse, threw up? She wasn't trying to make a good impression on Michael, or that was the lie she was telling herself, but it would be humiliating if she made a fool of herself in front of him and opted for her usual diet coke.

"I love working for Events. I think it's the best thing that ever happened to me. I can't wait to be done with school and get on with real life."

"School's not real life?"

"Except for my classes at TAFE and Business Management, I feel like most of it's a waste of time. I don't want to be a doctor like you or an accountant or a lawyer. And I know it's not considered an important job, but I love turning someone's special occasion into something amazing. A night they will never forget. And your mum has taught me so much. Stuff I would never learn in school."

"If you love doing it then it is important. Don't let anyone tell you otherwise. Do you think you might even start your own catering company one day?"

"Maybe. I don't know," she said tipping her head from side to side. "It's a big risk and if there's a downturn in the economy people start planning their own parties to save money. I've thought about opening a store one day that sells really high-end decorations, with table rentals and quality ready-made food that can easily be re-heated. But that's years away. And lots of money I don't have."

"That's a great idea though. And a good reason to start saving," he suggested. "Look at you. You're not that annoying little girl who used to follow me and Lochie around anymore. You were such a pain in the neck," he remembered, "but here you are with a plan for your future and full of ambition. When I was your age most of the girls at school were only interested in partying and hoped they'd be discovered and end up as models or actresses. They didn't give their futures a second thought."

"I'd never thought of myself as having ambition before. I guess I do," she smiled as she tucked her hair behind her ear, her eyes holding his, and for the first time that evening, he looked at her properly.

"You're wearing the earrings I gave you. They look gorgeous," he said, his own smile growing as he responded to hers. And in that moment, unable to look away, he felt his heart shift. How had he never noticed how beautiful Sarah had become?

Shocked by his reaction to her, Michael, hoping for a distraction, picked up his phone and quickly checked an email he heard come through.

He'd barely noticed Sarah when he picked her up from her home tonight. Distracted by an earlier phone call from Margaux, he'd said a quick hello to Tom and Beth and told Sarah they needed to get going.

When Margaux called it had been about two-thirty in the morning in the States. Wondering why she was calling so late she admitted she had been out at yet another party. And she was slurring her words, so he guessed she was drunk – again. He didn't understand the way she lived, and it infuriated him to have to listen to her drunken ramblings. He didn't know if she was taking drugs, but sometimes when he called her on Skype there were times when she wasn't all there. She couldn't concentrate on what he was saying and on one occasion she had Pip and George over and they were all dancing in front of the camera with loud music blaring in the background. He had disconnected the call, not wanting to watch her behaviour. When she rang the next day she didn't even remember that they had spoken. He hoped once he was back living in Baltimore she would settle down. Because the last thing he wanted was a pill popping drunk for a wife.

They fell silent as he continued to read the email from one of his lecturers. He didn't say anything but sighed loudly and put his phone back down on the table. Sarah sensing a change in Michael's mood decided she needed to say something before the silence went on too long.

"Bad news?" she asked.

"Sorry?"

"Did you just get some bad news? You're frowning the way you used to when you didn't win at Monopoly."

"Sort of. I was hoping to do an accelerated class next year so I could move to America earlier. My lecturer has denied my request, saying the workload will be too much, which means I'm going to be away from Margaux for an extra two months."

For the last forty-five minutes Sarah had almost put Margaux out of her mind. Michael hadn't mentioned her once.

"And how is Margaux?" she asked, "It must be hard being away from her."

"It is. I'll be going to the U.S. once my exams are finished this year, and then spend Christmas and the first few months there until Uni starts again. I'll pop over for a few weeks after my semester one exams, but then we won't be able to see each other again until the end of the year. I'm trying to convince Margaux to visit, but she said she'll be too busy organising the wedding. So we won't get to see much of each other next year," he said looking sad.

"And then you're moving permanently to America?'

"I guess so."

"You don't seem that excited. Don't you want to live there?"

"I do. Margaux's there. But I'm going to miss my parents. And Australia. Life is so much more casual here. If I want to go to a café and get a coffee or just sit on the beach I can. In Margaux's world you don't do things like that. Every minute of every day is filled with lunches and appointments for manicures and meetings with personal shoppers, or whatever it is rich women do, and then at night there's always a dinner or a party. Staying in isn't done. No one puts on their pajamas, orders pizza and binge watches Netflix all night."

Shaking her head Sarah said, "Michael I think you'll find that's exactly what millions of Americans do every night. I don't think America is the problem. I think Margaux and her snooty friends with all their shopping and parties might be the problem." As soon as she said it Sarah felt absolutely appalled at herself and wished she could steal her words out of the air and stuff them back into her mouth. Over the course of the evening she had become too comfortable with him and she had just insulted the woman he was going to marry. *Stupid, stupid Sarah*, she thought.

"I'm so sorry. I shouldn't have said that. It was so inappropriate. And awful. I'm sure Margaux's friends aren't snooty at all," she apologized, unable to look at Michael. She focused on the dinner that had been placed in front of her, annoyed at herself.

"You know what, Sarah. You're right. They are snooty. I've never said it to anyone else before, but I really don't like her friends."

He remembered back to all the parties he had attended with Margaux. He usually spent most of the evening bored as they all talked about their trust funds and which exclusive resort they were all flying off to next. The males usually had some sort of future plans – they were expected to take over the family business at some point – while the girls did their degrees at an expensive school. But few of them had plans to do anything with their education. And not once had any of her friends made him feel welcome. They never once asked him about his life, and only talked about things he had no knowledge of. The private schools they'd attended and the trouble they had got themselves into, which they were all so proud of. There was no sense of responsibility from any of them and no appreciation for what they had. All they cared about was their self-indulgent lifestyles.

"Some days I wonder how I'm going to put up with them for the rest of my life," he continued. "But Margaux isn't always like that. She can be sweet and I'm sure once we have children she'll settle down. Her mother is lovely, and I expect Margaux will be like her."

"I'm still sorry. It was a terrible thing to say. I barely know her."

"Don't be. I've become aware that she didn't make a good impression when she was here. We just aren't her kind of people. Why she's settling for me I'll never know. I'm very different to the guys she dated in the past and I don't have the kind of money they do. They knew how to sail a yacht before they'd turned ten and they all have the same haircuts and go to the same type of schools. And seriously, you can't imagine how many of them have names like Thatcher or Bradley."

Sarah began to giggle, relieved he wasn't angry at her. "At least they aren't called River or Thorne."

"What about Romeo or Pike? And I'm not kidding," he was laughing now too. "There really was a guy in one of my classes called Pike. He was from California," he said, as if that explained everything. He took a bite of his garlic bread and then smiled at Sarah. "It's so good to laugh. My life is too serious these days. I'm either studying or hearing about the plans for this engagement party next month. I loved the first one that you organised, but," he sighed, "I have the feeling the next one might not be so much fun. It's all about being bigger and better than the last party 'everyone who's anyone' attended. Money's no problem so it's going to be 'amazing darling,'" he said, imitating Margaux's accent.

"Make sure you text me lots of photos then. I want to see how the rich and famous live."

"Promise. Now eat up. We have to be out of here in ten minutes or we'll be late."

"Yes sir," Sarah saluted, remembering how the boys used to play army when they were little. "Hey, I've been meaning to ask. How did you know I had a spare ticket for tonight?"

"I heard Mum and Dad talking about it. I loved the movie, but I never had the chance to see the play. Mum had a fit when I told her we were going together. Actually, it was really bizarre. She started ranting that Margaux wouldn't like it if I went out with you. I told her Margaux was fine with it, but then she started to say it was unkind of me, and then stopped and walked off. I didn't understand it at all. Why did you have a spare ticket anyway? Did you buy it for someone else?"

"An idiot called Noah," Sarah said, a little annoyed that Caroline had almost given her secret away. "We dated for a few weeks and he said he would love to come with me. But then he broke it off and started going out with Stacie with an 'i' from school."

Michael raised his eyebrow in question. "Alright, enlighten me. What does with an 'i' mean."

"It means she puts a little love heart above the i in her name instead of a dot, and she doesn't say no very often if you get my meaning."

"Right. I think I do. And you said no?"

"I did. And he said 'see ya,' and that was that."

"Then Noah is an idiot. I never understood why some guys do that. Pushing a girl into sleeping with them. We had guys like that at school. They were absolute jerks and usually dumped the girl once they got what they wanted. You, Sarah, are much better off without him and when you meet the right one, he will be the luckiest guy in the world," he said, unable to drag his eyes away from her lovely face.

Don't look at me like that, Sarah thought. *Don't say sweet things to me and make me fall in love with you all over again. I was nearly there. I was nearly free of you.*

"Come on," she said, looking at the time on her phone. "We don't want to be late."

Michael looked at his watch and realised how quickly the last hour had flown.

"Yep, let's get out of here," he said as he called the waiter over so he could pay. "I'm pretty excited about tonight. I know it's not a Broadway cast, but this should be fun. Come on, I've got a surprise for you in the car."

When Michael turned the car back on a few minutes later the sounds of the song, *If you want me*, from the soundtrack of tonight's musical flooded Sarah's ears. She knew then, as the familiar lyrics washed over her, that she was in trouble. This was one of the songs she'd played endlessly when

Michael moved away and hearing it now brought those feelings flooding back. Tonight had been a mistake. She'd tried to convince herself that she was over him and that spending time together would be fine. It turned out that she was wrong. She wasn't over him at all. When the track finished and her absolute favourite *Falling Slowly* began she could feel tears threatening.

"I wonder what that's like?" Michael mused as he drove towards the theatre. "Falling slowly. In love, I mean. Discovering that someone is the right person for you even though you didn't know it at first."

Sarah took a few seconds to compose herself before she responded. "I'm sure you have that with Margaux," she whispered, afraid her voice might crack.

"Not really," Michael answered. "It was fast and exhilarating, but it wasn't what I'd imagined. Like I expected love to be. I suppose I thought it would be more like what my parents have, or yours for that matter. Friends as well. Maybe that comes with time." Michael glanced over at Sarah as he drove. "Are you okay?" he asked, seeing her eyes shining with tears.

"Yeah. I'm fine," she lied. "It's this song. It gets me every time." And in that moment Sarah promised herself not to be alone again with Michael. It was too much. It hurt too completely. Because she had been falling for him – slowly – for most of her life. And it had to stop.

~~~

"He got home about five minutes ago," Caroline said into her phone quietly, not wanting to be overheard.

"And what did he say?" Beth asked.

"Not much. He said they had a lovely dinner and that the show was great. Did Sarah say anything to you?"

"She said the same thing. But then she said she had studying to do, and she went to her room. She didn't seem upset, but she's *never* studied without me nagging her."

"I shouldn't have let him go tonight. I tried to come up with something, some sort of excuse, but short of falling down and pretending I needed to go to the hospital, I had no ideas."

"What are you worried about. *I'm* the one who's going to have to deal with her broken heart – again."

"You're kidding right. This is all my fault. If I hadn't told Adam about the spare ticket, Michael wouldn't have overheard. And you know how I love Sarah. I don't want her hurt or sad."

"You should have seen her Caroline. She looked so beautiful tonight. I can't believe she's my daughter. So tall and slim, and I don't know … ethereal. I've never seen her look like that."

"Got to go," Caroline whispered. "He's coming down the stairs." She tapped 'end' on her phone and went back to the magazine she had been pretending to read while she waited for Michael to come home.

"Can I make you a cup of tea Michael?" she asked.

"Nah, I'm going to grab a glass of water and head off to bed," he replied.

"Well goodnight then."

"Night Mum," he said as he leaned down and kissed her on the cheek.

"Michael."

"Yes, Mum?"

"How was Sarah tonight?"

"She was great," he smiled. "I didn't realise how funny she was. And honest. What you see is what you get. Not many girls like that out there. She's going to make some guy very happy one day," he said as he headed for the kitchen.

If only there had been no Margaux, Caroline thought. *With time Sarah might have had a chance. But unfortunately for them all, and especially Michael, Margaux was in their lives for good.*

Chapter Fourteen

Although it had only been three months that Kelly and Sam had been with them, Jillian was already thinking of them as her own children. Kelly, who was enrolled at the local kindergarten for next year had started calling Jill 'Mum' because that's what Zoe called her, and Sam, mimicking his sister, followed quickly.

Matthew had floated the idea of becoming permanent care parents to the siblings a few weeks ago. That way Kelly and Sam would have a stable home and he and Jill would be able to start making decisions about their future without having to consult their case worker all the time. Adoption was another consideration, but it was rare, and with their father still missing, no permanent decisions could be made this early on.

When Mandy, their case-worker called earlier this morning and scheduled a meeting, Jill asked her the reason, but Mandy said she preferred to talk in person. Jill knew Mandy had been thrilled with how the children had settled in and agreed that in time, there was a very good chance they could be granted permanent-carer status if their father was deemed unfit or didn't want to take care of them, if he ever showed up at all. She just hoped Mandy wasn't coming to tell her that the children's Aunt had changed her mind and decided she wanted them after all. Jill understood that in a lot of cases it was best for children to live with family members. It gave them a better sense of who they were and where they had come from. But from what Mandy told her about the aunts situation, Kelly and Sam were much better off living with Matthew, Jill, and Zoe.

When the doorbell rang at twelve, as arranged, Jill let Mandy in and invited her into the kitchen where both kids were sitting at their art table. Jill often worked from the dining table instead of her study, it was the cosiest room in the house, and this way she could keep an eye on what the children were doing. Today Sam was stuffing play-doh into molds while Kelly coloured in the new book Jill bought her last week.

"Thanks for seeing me at such short notice," Mandy said after Jill put a cup of coffee in front of her and sat down with a cup of peppermint tea.

"We've had some news from New Zealand yesterday," she paused and lowered her voice so the children couldn't hear her, "Kelly and Sam's father has been located."

"Oh I see," Jill said, as her stomach dropped. "And what does that mean for us? And the kids?"

"He's arriving back in Australia in two days. He had no idea that his ex-partner had died. When he couldn't contact her he thought she must have not paid her phone bill and been cut off. He called her sister and that's when he found out what happened to her and the kids. He was due back in Australia next month, but he's moved his flight forward and will be taking custody of the kids as soon as possible. He's going to live with a friend who has space until he can find permanent accommodation."

"Can he just do that? Show up and take them. They probably won't even remember him. And he abandoned them. He can't be a very good father."

"But he *is* their father Jill. The New Zealand police confirmed his identification. And he hadn't run off. He was working. He was running a fishing charter boat for a friend who'd become ill. It meant he was out of phone range a lot of the time which is why he hadn't checked in for a while. He was being paid under the table, so there was no trail for him, which is why the police couldn't locate him. As soon as he heard what had happened he contacted us and said he absolutely wants custody. So he's back on Wednesday, but has asked if you can keep the kids until Thursday. That will give him a chance to set up a bedroom at his friend's place and get himself sorted out with Centrelink. He doesn't have a job yet because he wasn't expecting to return home so soon."

"So Thursday. Does he come here to collect them, or do we take them to him?"

"No Jill. I will pick them up from you in the afternoon and take them to their new home. It wouldn't be appropriate for you to meet him. I can't even give you his name for security reasons. Will you be okay to keep the kids here until Thursday? I understand that will make it more difficult for you, but I prefer, for their sake, not to have to move them again."

"Yes. Of course it'll be fine for them to stay for a few more days. We knew it was only temporary," she said, hoping she was hiding how utterly gutted she felt. "And they should be with their father. I'm glad you found him" Jill tried to swallow, but her throat was tight from holding back her tears. "I'll have everything packed and ready for you on Thursday."

"Thanks Jill," Mandy said as she stood up from the table. "Please don't say anything to the kids. They won't understand, and it's best coming from me. Just keep everything the same for the next few days and that will make the transition easier on them. No need to upset them before we have to."

"I'll need to tell Zoe. She can't come home from school on Thursday and find them gone without a word."

"I understand. But she has to keep it to herself. Kelly's old enough to notice a change in mood or any tension in the house. If she's already anxious it will make it harder when we have to hand them over. You don't want that, do you?"

"No, of course not. We won't tell Zoe until Wednesday night, and I'll insist she keeps the news to herself. That way she'll have a chance to get used to them leaving and hopefully she'll be able to say goodbye without becoming too emotional."

"Good. I'll be back at about three on Thursday. And thanks Jill. You and Matthew have done a brilliant job with these two. She went over to the craft table where Kelly and Sam had played quietly during the meeting.

"Bye kids. I'll see you later," she waved and then followed Jill to the front door. She never failed to feel guilty when she had to remove children from a good carer and return them to a parent when she wasn't sure it was the right thing. But their father had rights and they were his children. There was nothing else that could be done.

~~~

Jillian kept herself busy for the next few days making sure all the children's clothes were clean and packed, hoping they didn't notice what she was up to. Last night she and Matthew sat Zoe down and told her that Sam and Kelly would be going back to their father the next day. Predictably, Zoe had cried and begged them to do something to stop it. Jill felt devastated for her. Zoe had adored both children from the beginning, but especially loved spending hours playing with Kelly, or teaching her the alphabet and numbers. Zoe recently decided she wanted to be a schoolteacher, and she practiced on Kelly constantly. Thanks to Zoe, Kelly knew the alphabet song and could now count to ten.

She'd refused to go to school today and played with Kelly and Sam all morning instead. Matthew had even taken a rare afternoon off. He wanted to be there to say goodbye when Mandy took the children back to their father, but he also needed to be there for Jill. She hadn't cried or showed in any way that this was affecting her. She'd just got on with packing everything up, but Matthew was concerned that when they finally left she would fall apart.

When Mandy arrived at three o'clock they were ready. Matthew let her in and when Zoe saw her she began crying again. Earlier, Jill had asked her not to make a scene, so she gave each child a hug and said goodbye before she fled up the stairs to her bedroom.

Mandy sat down between the children who were sitting quietly on the couch hoping they would understand what she had to say.

"Kelly," she asked, "do you remember your dad?"

Nodding her head Kelly said "Sort of. But we haven't seen him for a long time. He went away."

"Yes he did. But he's back now and he wants you to come and live with him. He's waiting to see you. He missed you very much."

"But we live here."

"I know. And Matthew and Jillian took good care of you. But it's time to leave now."

Jillian felt her heart break as she saw Kelly's little face scrunch up and two tears welled in her eyes.

"Matthew, can you please bring the bags to the car?" Mandy asked. "Best to get this over with, and these two reunited with their father."

Matthew bent down and collected the suitcase full of clothes and toys Jill had lovingly bought for them. They had arrived two dirty little waifs, with plastic bags of filthy clothes, but now they were well fed and adorable in the matching overalls Jill hadn't been able to resist when she saw them in a little boutique in Brighton last month.

Mandy was about to scoop Sam up, but Jill beat her to it. She carried him out of the house as Mandy took Kelly's hand. It only took a minute to put them in their car seats. Jill kissed Sam's little cheek, and then made her way to the other side of the car. She gave Kelly a kiss too and then brushed her hair back from her face. The tears on the little girl's face said it all. She adored Jill just as much as Jill adored her. Not wanting to make this harder than it already was Jill gave her one last kiss and then said "Be good for Daddy, Kelly. He's very excited to see you." She closed the door gently and then stepped back from the car. Mandy put the car into reverse and pulled out of the driveway.

Matthew looked as forlorn as she felt. Both of them had fallen in love with those two little poppets and now they were gone. As the weeks went by and nobody claimed them she'd started to imagine that they would live with them forever. But not only had that not happened, she was left feeling like she had lost her own children. For the first time she was seriously beginning to question whether she wanted to continue fostering. She didn't know how she would be able to do this over and over. It was too heart wrenching. Perhaps they had made a mistake. How did other people do it for years?

"Come on love," Matthew said, holding out his hand. "Let's go inside before the neighbours start talking. You know what a bunch of gossips they are."

~~~

Jill made it through dinner, but when she was finally alone, soaking in the bath she gave in to the emptiness she was feeling and cried. Kelly's sad little face as they drove off, combined with Zoe's tears as she watched them leave from her window had been too much for the usually stoic Jillian. She didn't know if she was going to be willing to continue on as a foster parent, but if she did she was not going to find herself in a situation like this again. Short term only. She was there to provide a roof, meals, and safety. She wasn't going to let herself fall in love again with somebody else's child.

111

Chapter Fifteen

Caroline stood next to the open fire and surveyed the Great Room, as they called it. Even though it was an enormous space, it was cosy inside, while outside the weather was howling. Rain had been falling all day and put a stop to the outdoor bonfire and fireworks that had been planned for later tonight. Margaux, in typical form threw a tantrum and insisted that her engagement party be moved to another weekend. Even Emerson, who gave into almost every demand his daughter made, told her it was an impossible ask. To keep their guests warm during the short walk from their vehicles, the staff lined the portico with blazing fire pits and cars were to be parked away from the house by valets. Once inside, central heating warmed the house, and in every room a medieval sized fireplace was roaring.

Caroline and Adam both agreed this was the grandest house they'd ever been in. From the moment they stepped into the foyer yesterday and were given the grand tour by Melody, Margaux's mother, Caroline had been in awe. A circular staircase took them upstairs to the family bedrooms and Caroline was stunned at the vastness of each suite. She pointed out hers and Emerson's suite, but didn't take them inside, telling them it was the mirror image to the one at the other end of the long hallway that she did show them through. Double doors opened onto a seating area with a desk and a small bar. Through another set of doors was an enormous bedroom, featuring an elaborately carved timber bed with matching furniture that looked like it had been there since the house was built. But it was obvious the room had been recently redecorated, and exuded luxury. Soft light radiated from lamps strategically placed around the room, and the monochrome beige pallet was offset by cushions and throws in the softest sage green.

The bed looked so inviting, piled high with damask cushions, that Caroline, exhausted from the almost twenty-two-hour flight, wanted to crawl under the sheets and sleep for days. But the tour continued into the walk-in robes – his and hers – and the elaborate ensuite with an antique clawfoot bath and a rainfall shower that on its own was bigger than most people's bathrooms.

There were eight suites altogether upstairs, some bigger than others, but all with their own sitting room and ensuite. The view across the Choptank river was spectacular, and Caroline was sure she would appreciate it more after she had slept.

Downstairs there was a massive library with a competition-sized billiard table. The walls were lined with books, many that looked old, some behind glass doors to protect them from the environment. This was obviously Emerson's domain – there was nothing soft or feminine about it. Through the Great Room which opened off the foyer there was another space, less formal and much more conducive to relaxing with family and friends. It too was decorated in beiges, but this time with accents of pale greys. To the right was a huge formal dining room with a table that would easily seat twenty. To the left were double doors that lead into an honest-to-goodness ball room. The parquet flooring looked original and it was obvious that this was where tomorrow's dinner would be held. Tables were already set around the dance floor and looked like they were just waiting for the elaborate floral arrangements to be delivered. Floor to ceiling windows looked out over a tiered formal garden and beyond that was the river.

The kitchen was extensive with walls of cabinets and enough space to cook for three families. Staff bustled about, obviously preparing delicacies for tomorrow night's party. If Caroline hadn't been so exhausted she would have loved to watch the process of prepping for two hundred guests and maybe steal a recipe or two. Melody, who was obviously used to having staff do everything for her, barely gave them a glance. She invited Caroline and Adam into the morning room, and it was clear this too had recently been redecorated. A much more intimate room than the formal dining they had seen earlier, Caroline got the feeling that Melody spent a lot of her time here. The fire was lit, and coffee and tea were set out on a round table for eight. Silver frames with photos of her children at different ages were placed on every surface and jugs of flowers sat beside her memories. A pair of reading glasses was casually left on top of a planner and there was a half-drunk cup of tea and a plate of fruit beside it.

She'd offered Adam and Caroline refreshments, but they declined, claiming exhaustion, so Melody, the perfect host, took them to the guest house where they would be staying for the next three nights. Michael, who'd arrived the day before, was still sleeping off his jetlag in the second bedroom of the guest house. Melody left them, asking them to ring the house when they woke up. She would have dinner brought out to them whenever they were ready, assuming they would still be too tired to join the family for dinner tonight. Caroline barely noticed the luxurious surroundings as she kicked off her shoes and climbed into the bed. Adam didn't even have time to say goodnight before she fell into a deep sleep.

~~~

Tonight, refreshed from yesterday's sleep, and then staying in bed till lunchtime today, Caroline could finally appreciate how wealthy the Thornton family really were. Even before she'd seen the house she'd been concerned that Michael would find fitting in with such a grand family difficult, but now that she was here, she was terrified for him. He was never going to be able to provide for Margaux the way her father did, and although she had a trust fund that would make your eyes water, Michael was the kind of man who would want to be the provider. His own trust fund would make him a wealthy young man in Australia, and if he was prudent it would provide nicely for a family. But she doubted that the yearly income would be enough to keep Margaux in designer clothes and handbags, let alone pay for a house and the cars and servants that went along with the kind of substantial home Margaux was used to. Caroline could see trouble on the horizon.

Adam approached her, champagne in hand. He was still as handsome in his tuxedo as he had been when she met him all those years ago in high school. He was more pepper and salt these days, but it suited him.

"For you," he said, handing her the glass. Caroline took a sip and then felt guilty.

"You know I don't drink at parties. What if I forget to do something?"

"You, my dear, are a guest. There is nothing for you to do tonight, except continue looking as gorgeous as you do right now."

"You're not so bad yourself," she said, reaching up to straighten his bowtie. When the engraved invitation to the engagement party arrived it called for the men to be dressed in black tie and the women in winter white. Completely out of character, Caroline decided she wasn't going to go along with Margaux's request and ordered from her dress maker the slimmest of fitted gowns in a deep ruby red. It was accompanied by the teardrop diamond necklace Adam gave her for their tenth anniversary, and the

115

matching earrings he had given her for their twentieth. Her hair was pulled into a classic chignon and Melody had insisted on having a makeup artist come in to take care of her. Apparently Caroline was not to be trusted to do it herself. There were going to be professional photos taken during the evening and everyone had to look perfect. Six weeks ago Caroline put herself on a strict diet, but it had been worth it. She was thrilled with how she looked tonight.

"I'm starving," Adam proclaimed. "I hope they start serving food soon."

"I think it will be a while yet. Melody said they would wait until enough guests arrive before they started serving hors'doeuvre's. Apparently Margaux's friends are notoriously late, so let's hope Emerson and Melody's friends are more prompt."

"Mind if I join you two?" Michael asked as he made his way across the Great Room, after coming from upstairs.

"Not at all. Where have you been?" Caroline asked noting how handsome her son looked. His dark curls were a genetic throw back, taking after Caroline's mother. Both she and Adam were blond with fair skin. Michael had a much more olive complexion.

"Upstairs checking on Margaux. She's still upset about the weather, and worried that her friends will cancel."

"I'm sure they won't. Isn't this *the* party of the season? They won't want to miss out."

"Um, Mum."

"Yes, darling?"

"What are you wearing?"

"It's called a dress. I'm sure you've seen one before."

"It's red."

"It's ruby actually. Do you like it?"

"You look very nice. But Margaux is going to have a fit. She's wearing the same colour. You were supposed to be in white."

"Darling I look horrible in white. And I'm a grown woman. I decide what I wear."

"But it was on the invitation. It's what she wanted."

"I know that Michael. I can read, but I decided it was a ridiculous request. I can't imagine why she would want everyone to look the same."

"Of course you can. It was so she would stand out from everyone else. And don't look at me like that. I know it's a bit over the top, but she said this was her party and all eyes should be on her."

"It's your party too Michael. And ours and her parents party. Not everything needs to be about Margaux all of the time."

"Did you *bring* a white dress?"

"No. And even if I had I wouldn't change. "

"Well thanks Mum. I was hoping tonight would go off without any drama."

"Michael, it's just a dress. I didn't get drunk and start a fist fight. If Margaux gets that upset about such a trivial thing, she might want to take a look at herself. Where is she anyway? Shouldn't she be here to greet her guests?"

"She'll be down later. There's hardly anyone here yet."

"Ah. Planning on making a grand entrance is she?"

"Something like that," he mumbled. "I've gotta go. Emerson wants me to meet some of his business associates and he's calling me over. Wish me luck."

"You don't need luck. Just be yourself and they will love you."

He leaned over and kissed her on the cheek. "You do look nice Mum. And don't you know by now. No one here is allowed to just be themselves."

~~~

The party was in full swing before Margaux dramatically descended the stairs. She waited at the top until enough eyes were on her, and then floated down into the waiting arms of her father. They posed together for pictures, and then her mother joined them for another shot. But if Margaux, in her floor length, scarlet red gown, expected to be the only colour in a sea of black and white, she was going to be disappointed. Many of the older women had also chosen to come in colour, and it was only the younger crowd who'd obeyed Margaux's command. Caroline thought they were probably afraid to face her wrath. The matrons of society, it appeared, didn't care what Margaux thought of them.

~~~

Michael had been looking everywhere for Margaux. Emerson wanted the formal family photos taken now, to be followed by the late dinner that would be served to the two hundred guests. There hadn't been much in the way of dancing so far, people were still mingling in the Great Room and the only music was coming from a stringed quartet. After dinner and speeches an up and coming local DJ was going to entertain them for the rest of the night. Michael hadn't heard of her, but she was fast getting a reputation in the Baltimore club scene, and Margaux promised her she would make the society pages if she DJ'd the party. Odele had jumped at the chance.

After looking everywhere downstairs, Michael moved upstairs to see if he could find his fiancé. When he found her suite empty, he decided to check the other bedrooms as well. She wouldn't be outside – the rain hadn't let up even for a second – so she could only be in the house. After checking out that she wasn't in any of her sibling's bedrooms – they all still kept a suite at the Manor – he saw that the door on the guest suite at the end of the hall was ajar. He strode towards it, and lifted his hand to knock before entering, as he'd done before he entered any of the other bedrooms. He didn't expect to catch anyone fooling around up here, but it was always best to check to save embarrassment. But before he had a chance to knock he heard the familiar tinkle of laughter and sighed with relief. He'd found her.

Pushing the door open, he expected to find Margaux with one of her friends but found the sitting room empty. Voices were coming from the bedroom and when he heard murmurings that were definitely male he paused just before he was about to push the door open.

As they hadn't bothered to shut the bedroom door properly, leaving a gap of a few centimetres, Michael could see Margaux with a man he'd never met before. Her arms were wrapped around his neck as he whispered something in her ear. She laughed again, and then unwrapping herself from him, gently pushed him away.

"I told you this has to stop, James," Margaux whispered. "You shouldn't be here. If anyone see's you and my father finds out, he'll lose his mind."

James, Michael thought. *As in Margaux's high school boyfriend James?*

"But Maggie" – *Maggie?* – "you know how good we were together," James begged. "I just wanted to remind you of that before you make the biggest mistake of your life. I'm a reformed man, I promise."

"I am getting married James. And besides, Michael's going to be here for months, so this has to end tonight. I think he would notice me sneaking off all the time."

"Then dump him. I know you don't love him. What you ever saw in him in the first place I'll never understand."

"James, I told you. He's very good to me and Daddy approves. And I don't have to worry about him cheating on me the way you did."

"I promise you I'll be good this time." He leaned in, kissing Margaux and for a few seconds she kissed him back.

"No," she said, stepping back from him. "Last week was a mistake. It wasn't supposed to happen, and if I hadn't been drunk it wouldn't have."

"You know my theory. People do the things they want to do when they're drunk that they aren't brave enough to do when they're sober. And Maggie, you weren't that drunk. You knew exactly what you were doing."

"So what? I can't let it happen again. Michael wouldn't forgive me if he found out. He doesn't really understand the way we live. He has this ideal image of marriage, it's all love and commitment. If he knew about you he'd call off the wedding. And do you know what happens if we don't get married. Daddy is going to cut me off. I can't live on what I get from my trust fund. You know I don't have full access until I'm twenty-five"

"So you're going to marry someone for your father's money. If you feel that way, marry me for mine. I have an endless supply of the stuff."

"James, it's not just that. I like Michael – he's kind and we hardly ever fight. When you and I were together that's all we did. And it's important that Daddy approves of who I marry. We both know he thinks you're too much trouble to be part of the Thornton Family. He said you wouldn't be good for the family's image. With Michael I have stability, and he will be a wonderful father one day. Being with you is exhilarating and you know I find you irresistible, but …," she paused reaching up and stroking his face. As James leaned down to kiss her again, Michael turned away, unable to watch, not wanting to hear anymore. If he was a different kind of man he might have stormed into the room and punched James. Instead he realised he'd just done Michael a favour. He finally got it. As he left the suite he slammed the door behind him.

Adam had also been dispatched to find Margaux, but after going in the other direction to Michael he had ended up in Emerson's study, not caring if she was found or not. The door was shut, but not locked, and Adam needed a moment to himself. The party was in full swing now and he'd been introduced to the elite of Baltimore society, but he was yet to find someone he liked. Caroline, swooped up early by Melody, was being flirted with by some of the richest men they would ever meet. All this money, all this extravagance was too much for him. He settled himself into a wing chair made of the softest leather and taking a sip of the scotch he'd just poured himself – he didn't think Emerson would mind – he closed his eyes for a moment and enjoyed the quiet.

Less than a minute passed before the door to the study opened. He was alerted as the sound of the festivities crowded the previously quiet room, and then disappeared as the door was firmly closed. A light on the desk switched on but only gave off a faint glow that didn't reach past the billiard table to where Adam was sitting in the dark. Emerson was talking into his phone and he was not happy.

"I told you, I want that company!" he barked, obviously believing he was alone in the room. Adam knew he should announce himself, but Emerson had already been dismissive of him when they met yesterday, and might not be happy to find him in his study.

Emerson shook his head and then continued as he unlocked a draw in the desk, "We have the dirt on him. Make sure he understands his wife will be receiving those photo's if he doesn't sign the contract by the end of the week." He fell silent again for a minute as he pulled out a black ledger and a file from a drawer. Opening the file he started shuffling through the papers while he listened to the other half of the conversation.

"No I won't negotiate. Fifteen million. That's all we're paying. And you have the shop steward on board?" He paused his conversation and then answered, "Good. Those workers are being paid too much. We can replace the majority of them with migrant labour and pay them half as much." He listened to the other side of the conversation for a minute and then issued more orders. "I don't care if they hire illegals. I have someone on the books who will let me know if there's going to be a raid, and with the shop steward on our payroll, the unions will never know what we're up to. Get this done quick. I want to take over operations by the end of the year. And don't worry about threatening him. If he doesn't want his family to know what kind of person he really is then he shouldn't be hanging out in cheap hotels with working girls." Emerson laughed at something the person on the other end of the call said and then hung up. He put his phone back into his jacket pocket and turned to a page in the ledger. Nodding to himself he flipped the book shut and turning off the light, left the library.

Emerson had left the file and the ledger on the desk. A very stupid thing to do, as anyone could walk in and see it. But Emerson had been drinking steadily all evening and obviously wasn't thinking straight. Adam waited another minute to make sure Emerson didn't come back before he walked towards the desk. His heart was beating out of his chest, but he knew instinctively that he needed to get a look at that ledger. He opened the book and started taking pictures with his phone. It was pages and pages of names with dollar amounts beside them. He didn't have time to do more than give them a quick glance, but none of the names were familiar to him. When he was done he decided to take pictures of the file as well. It took him two minutes to photograph every page and then he placed the ledger and the file back where Emerson left them and quietly slipped out of the room.

~~~

Emerson and Melody were standing with Caroline in front of the fire with the photographer. Margaux's brothers and sister were waiting in the wings for the family picture, but the photographer wanted one of the parents and the betrothed first. Michael stepped off the last stair tread at the same time as his father quietly closed the door behind him, hoping nobody noticed him leaving the study. Caroline saw them both and called them over, puzzled at the equally furious look on their faces. They might have different colouring, but in this moment their features were mirrored in each other's face. Adam took his place next to his wife and Michael stood on the other side of her. Margaux, flying down the stairs called out to her parents that she was here, and the photographer positioned her between her mother and her fiancé.

Taking his place behind the tripod he called for everyone to smile. As he began clicking away Michael leaned closer to the woman he had thought he loved and whispered, "I've been looking everywhere for you … Maggie."

Chapter Sixteen

"Michael please let me explain. I don't know what you think you overheard, but you have it all wrong," she pleaded. Margaux didn't know how long Michael had been standing outside the bedroom door or how much he'd seen or heard. Until the sound of the door slamming shattered the romantic moment she was sharing with her old high school boyfriend, they had no idea that someone was outside listening, and would have seen her and James together. But when he called her Maggie, something he had never done before – and a name only James called her when they were alone – she knew it had been Michael and he had obviously heard more than enough.

After the photographer finished taking endless pictures of the family, Margaux told her father she needed a minute alone with her fiancé before dinner began and dragged Michael into the morning room where they wouldn't be overheard. He resisted at first, telling her they would discuss it later, but she begged him to let her explain. Recognising her body language, he could see she was close to a melt down and the last thing this evening needed was a scene that would be witnessed by Baltimore's elite. Reluctantly following her, he firmly shut the door behind them, and then fell into a wing chair, deciding he was going to take control of this conversation.

"What's to explain Mags?" he said using the name he knew she hated. "I know you think I'm just some hick from Australia, but it's not hard to understand what's been going on. You've been cheating on me with your ex-boyfriend, and you're only marrying me because your father was going to cut you off if you didn't settle down with someone he considers suitable. Did I get that right? I must have looked perfect to the both of you. I'm well behaved, I don't party, and when I moved here permanently I wouldn't have any friends or family so I would have to rely solely on yours. Your father must have thought I was a dream come true. Easy to control. And I was. But not anymore."

"If I ask Daddy to back off, can't we just forget what you heard?" Margaux begged. "I was breaking it off with James, I promise. I will never see him again."

"Don't be ridiculous. I'm not going to marry you. I don't deserve to be treated like this. You cheated on me."

"I know, and I'm sorry. I didn't plan to sleep with James, but I ran into him at a party and I was so lonely without you. But I'll come and visit you as much as you like in Australia, I could even rent a house and move there until you finish Uni, so we don't have to be apart anymore. But please don't call off the wedding."

"Are you delusional? You must really think I'm an idiot if you think I would marry you after this." Michael could see the anguish on Margaux's face, but guessed it wasn't because she was losing him. There was something else behind her distress.

"Answer me this Mags. Why did you father want you to settle down so quickly, and with me? I don't have that much money, and I don't have the family connections he got with your sibling's marriages. So why was he willing to marry you off to me, and more importantly, why did you agree to it?

"He liked you that's all. He thought we would be good together. And he was right. We are good together," she said, changing her tone to flirty as she reached out her hand to touch his arm.

Michael shifted his body to avoid her touch, his face flooded with contempt. "Stop lying to me Margaux. You can't change my mind about marrying you, but if you have even the slightest feelings for me, you owe me the truth."

Margaux sank into the opposite chair, the fight gone out of her. She hung her head, twisting her engagement ring round and round, realising nothing was going to change his mind.

"I was arrested. Just before we met. I was picked up for a DUI after I crashed into a parked car. I wasn't hurt because I was driving slowly. I knew I shouldn't be driving and was taking the back roads, but I was surprised by a cat running across the road. I swerved to avoid it and that's when I hit the car. The owner heard the crash and called the police. When they searched my car they found ecstasy."

"You were driving drunk, and high? You could have killed someone." Michael exclaimed, disgusted by her selfishness.

"I wasn't high, I promise. I'm not that stupid. I was going to take it when I got home. One of the police officers at the station recognised my name and called my father. He made the charges disappear. I don't know how; we don't ask those questions. He bought the guy whose car I hit a new one in exchange for his promise to not to go to the press and I thought I had gotten away with it."

"But your father had other plans?"

"He sat me down in his study and said that if I didn't sort myself out and stop using drugs he was going to send me to a private rehab. If I wanted to stay out of rehab I had to settle down, finish school and I had to stop hanging out with George and Pip. He has no idea they visited me in Australia.

Please don't tell him," she pleaded. "He said it was time to find myself a stable husband, one who wasn't into the party scene like most of the guys I grew up with, get married and be a wife and mother. And if I didn't he would send me away and cut off my money. You know my trust fund doesn't fully kick in until I'm twenty-five. At the moment he subsidizes me. I agreed, and then a week later I met you."

"So you used me to keep the money coming in? What kind of person are you?"

"I'm sorry, Michael. You don't understand the pressure I'm under. And I liked you so much."

"Nope," he said shaking his head. "If this was just about money, then James was right. He has plenty of it. You could marry him and be just fine. Why me?"

Margaux sighed out, knowing how pathetic her reasons would sound, but Michael was right. He deserved an explanation. "It's because you're respectable. Reputation is everything to Daddy. He never liked James or his family which is one of the reasons it didn't work out for us. Daddy said he would never give his blessing to our relationship. I know it shouldn't matter, but I've always been terrified of letting him down."

"You're an adult. Stop blaming your father for your behaviour."

"I know you don't understand, but I can't help it. He has this hold over us. He calls the shots and we do whatever he says. There is nothing worse than him telling you that you are a disappointment."

"You're right. I don't understand it. You should live your life how you want to, and marry the person you love, not someone who will look good in the society pages. Who cares what anyone else thinks?"

"I care. I know I shouldn't, but I do. If my DUI had made it into the papers it would have brought disrepute to the family. He has people whose job it is to make sure there is never a bad word spoken or written about any of us. He has his affairs with younger women and when he's done with them they're paid off to keep quiet. Mummy never says anything, she just goes along with it, and so do my brothers wives. It's just how it's done in our world. As long as we're discreet and stay out of the public eye he doesn't care what we get up to. But after my accident he said I couldn't be trusted. According to him I wasn't in control of myself and was a liability to the family. Apparently drugs are a no-no, and I crossed the line. So he gave me an ultimatum, settle down or basically be cut out. He wouldn't let me be part of the family anymore." Margaux wiped away a tear, her first for the evening, remembering how cruel her father had been when he threatened to disown her. She had always been his favourite and was spoiled from her first breath. Until the day after her accident her father never had an unkind word for her. It had come as a huge shock, and she agreed to do anything he asked. Michael was the perfect solution.

"Marriage means nothing to you people does it?" Michael spat at her, realising just how badly he'd been used. "There's no love, no caring for another person. You make a suitable match and then pretend to the rest of the world you have these perfect relationships while behaving appallingly in private. And you thought I would accept that way of life?" He shook his head in disbelief. "I wanted a life with you, I was willing to move away from my family and my home for you. And you didn't even love me a little, did you?"

"I wanted to love you. I hoped with time my feelings would grow."

"But you never loved me. I've been sitting here listening to you, trying to remember if you ever said it and I can't think of one occasion when you actually said the words. You would tell me I was handsome, or I was going to be the perfect husband, but not once did you say the words 'I love you Michael'. I suppose that was the one thing you didn't lie to me about."

Margaux continued to look down, ashamed of herself. She never intended to hurt Michael. But he was right. She didn't love him. She looked at her left hand and pulled off her engagement ring. "What happens now?" She asked as she held the ring out to him.

"I don't want to make a scene, Margaux. Put the ring back on and go upstairs and fix your makeup. And in five minutes you will meet me in the ballroom where we will eat dinner with our guests. We will listen to your father do his speech and pretend everything is fine. You should be good at that. It will take some work for me. And tomorrow my parents and I will leave, and I won't ever set eyes on you again. What you tell your friends and family is up to you."

"Thank you Michael. It means a lot to me that you won't embarrass the family."

"I'm not doing it for your family Margaux. I'm doing it for you. Regardless of how you felt about me I did love you. I don't anymore."

~~~

Michael's face hurt from forcing himself to smile. He sat through Emerson's speech, listening to him lie about what a wonderful couple he and Margaux were, and how proud he was of his daughter. The second surprise of the night was that Emerson had bought them a house and Margaux's job when she finished college would be to decorate it for them to move into together when they were married next year. Apparently a date had already been chosen for the wedding without his input or knowledge.

As expected the party went on into the early hours of the morning. Many of the older guests left after the buffet dinner was served, and when his parents asked if it was alright if they went to bed, he asked them to stay up for half an hour when he would join them in the guest house. He danced with Margaux once to keep up appearances, and then thanked her parents for the wonderful party and said goodnight to her family. He didn't have anything to say to her friends. He had never liked them, and they had never had any time for him. Thankfully, he didn't set eyes on James again and Margaux confirmed that he wasn't on the guest list and had snuck out after Michael discovered them together. Undoing his bowtie as he walked towards the back entrance of the manor that led to the guest house he saw that the last person he wanted to see was waiting for him. Leaning up against the wall she looked nervous and he almost felt sorry for her. Her life was probably about to come crashing down around her. But there was no way he was going to sacrifice his future and spend his life in a loveless marriage.

"Michael, I know this hasn't turned out the way we wanted," she said and then hesitated.

"No Margaux, it hasn't," he replied running his fingers though his hair as he sighed.

"I am truly sorry. I just … I didn't know what else to do."

Michael shook his head and looked at her for the first time since she had left him in the morning room. "I hope you learn something from this. You played with my life. What if we went through with it and had children? It would have been a disaster."

"I know," she said under her breath."

"Goodbye, Margaux."

"Goodbye, Michael," she said as she held out her hand. She dropped the ring into his hand, turned away, and walked back to her party.

Michael looked at the ring for a few seconds before sitting it on top of an occasional table before walking out the back door. He didn't want the ring back. He didn't want to find it accidently one day in the back of a drawer and be reminded of what a complete fool he had been.

~~~

As requested his parents were waiting up for him after changing out of their formal clothes and were in pajamas curled up on the couch with a cup of tea.

"Sorry to keep you," Michael said as he collapsed into a chair opposite them. "I needed to do the rounds before I could leave."

"I have to admit I'm a little surprised you didn't stay till the end of the party. Won't people think it's a little strange, leaving Margaux there on her own?"

"Frankly, I don't care what people think."

"Okay. You do look exhausted. Can I get you something? Maybe a cup of tea?"

"No, Dad. But if you open that cupboard over there you will find a fully stocked bar. Could you pour me a bourbon? On ice please."

Caroline and Adam exchanged a glance. This was not typical behaviour for Michael. He never went through a drinking phase when he was eighteen like most of his friends and was always the designated driver. Adam stood and walked across the room to the armoire Michael pointed to. Inside he found bottles of various spirits and a freezer with ice. He poured a *Makers Mark* for Michael and a *Ballantine's* for himself. After adding ice, and checking that Caroline didn't want anything, he gave Michael his drink and returned to his seat.

"Thanks so much for coming to the party. I know it was a long flight just for one night, but I'm so glad you were here."

"That's our pleasure darling," Caroline replied. "And just think. Next time we come and visit we'll be able to stay in your newly decorated house. Goodness knows what we'll be giving you as a wedding present, but we won't be able to compete with that."

"You don't need to worry about that Mum. We broke up this evening. I won't be marrying Margaux."

131

"What?" Caroline exclaimed, shocked.

"I see," Adam said, not as surprised by Michaels announcement as Caroline was. He'd noticed the tension between them throughout dinner, and Margaux hadn't looked how a happy bride-to-be normally would. "We understand if you don't want to tell us what happened, but it might help to talk about it."

"It was that old story Dad. She was cheating on me. Oh, and she didn't actually love me. She was using me to keep her father happy."

"Someone told you that she was cheating, at your engagement party. Not exactly the best timing."

"No Mum. No one told me. I saw her with my own eyes. Kissing her ex. When I confronted her she admitted she didn't love me. I got it from the horse's mouth."

"I'm so sorry love. I know how you felt about her. Are you … alright?"

"Am I alright? No. I'm not. But I will be. Right now I just want to go home to Australia where I belong and put this behind me."

"Right then. Well let's get our bags packed and I'll call a taxi," Adam said switching into problem solving mode. "There must be a hotel we can check into at the airport, and we'll catch the first flight out that has seats. It's time to go home."

Michael felt so grateful to his father for his support, and for a moment he thought he might cry. He hadn't cried since Isabelle died, but in this moment it felt perfectly justified.

"Dad let's just stay here tonight. If we leave now people will see us, and it's still raining. I don't want to be standing around in the cold waiting for a taxi. And I'm exhausted. All I want is a hot shower, and to go to sleep. In the morning we can leave. That lot won't be up for hours and no one will even know we're gone. But yes, then we can book into a hotel and get the first flight home."

"What are we going to say to Emerson and Melody?" Caroline asked. "We should at least thank them for their hospitality. None of this is their doing."

"No we don't," Adam growled, "That man is a disgrace. If you want to leave a nice note for Melody go ahead. But I won't be thanking Emerson Thornton for anything."

Both Caroline and Michael sat staring at Adam, surprised at his outburst.

"Is there something you want to tell us Dad?"

"I just don't like him that's all." Adam wasn't going to complicate things by telling them what he had overheard. And now he didn't need to warn Michael about how corrupt Emerson was. He wasn't going to be in their lives anymore. "Let's go to bed so we can get out of here in the morning. It's one o'clock, so up at seven and we can be gone by eight. We can catch up on sleep at the hotel while we wait for flights."

"Sounds like a plan," Caroline said, standing. "Michael are you sure you're alright? You seem so very calm about all this."

"It's a shock. But I should have seen the signs," he said shrugging his shoulders. "She never seemed to miss me the way I missed her when we were apart. And to answer your earlier question, I'm leaving it up to Margaux to tell her parents whatever she wants."

"But she might lie. I doubt she's going to admit she was cheating on you."

"Doesn't matter. That's on her conscience, not mine."

"Alright. If that's what you want." She leaned down and kissed Michael on the cheek, and then pulled him into a hug before heading to the bedroom. "Goodnight Michael, and don't stay up too long," she called from the doorway.

"Night Mum," he replied as she quietly closed the door behind her. He took another sip of his drink and sat, only illuminated by the glow of the lamp. The dark suited his mood as he replayed his conversation with Margaux over in his head. He knew calling off the wedding was the right decision, but that didn't take away the sense of loss he felt. Until today, he knew what the plan was for his life, but now he had no idea where he would end up. Obviously, he wasn't going to do his residency here and would need to find a placement in a Victorian hospital. The one thing he was sure of was that for now, romance was definitely off his radar.

He put his empty glass on the lamp table. He could have another, but what would that solve? He stood up and made his way to his bedroom, pulling off his jacket. Taking his phone out of his pocket to charge it, he saw that he had a message from Sarah. Before finding Margaux with James he had been sending her, as promised, photos all night. He tapped on her message to find a thumbs up. *That was it*, he thought. No funny comments about the picture of the man whose toupee' had been slipping that Michael sneakily captured a picture of, or the ostentatiousness of the flower arrangements that he thought had been garish. He'd even snuck into the kitchen before the party started and snapped a pic of the caterers, thinking she would appreciate seeing the huge kitchen full of people working.

Before the rain set in he'd sent her photos of the formal gardens, and of the view out over the river. All up he probably sent thirty to forty photos over the past two days. And all he got was a lousy thumbs up. As he pulled back the covers and climbed into bed, when he should have been thinking about his broken heart, he instead found himself worrying about Sarah. He hoped she was alright. That just wasn't like her. He would text her in the morning and see if she was okay.

~~~

When they got to the airport the next morning they discovered it was going to take them three days to get home. They couldn't catch a flight out of

Baltimore and instead took the train to New York. They were going to stay the night and take a flight home the next day. Michael, still concerned about her, texted Sarah to check if everything was alright, and after being reassured that, 'yes she was fine, just busy', he sent her photos of *The Sherry Netherland*, the boutique hotel they'd checked into for the night. It was beyond luxurious, but his Dad said they needed a treat before flying home. Located opposite Central Park, Michael wandered for hours, snapping pictures of police on horseback, joggers running around the paths and families out in the winter sun enjoying their day. She responded occasionally, but he was beginning to get the feeling that she wasn't as fine as she said. Perhaps she was more upset about her breakup with that boy Noah than she had let on, or maybe her exams hadn't gone well.

Adam waited until Caroline took a taxi to Bloomingdales for a little retail therapy before he downloaded the photos he'd taken of Emerson's ledger to his laptop. He had all the information about the deal that Emerson was working on, including a photo of the shop steward, details of the manufacturing plant he wanted to buy, and the owner he was blackmailing.

Adam skimmed the ledger, but still didn't recognise any of the names. He found the address he was looking for and then attached the file with the photos. He wrote a short message and then emailed his old university friend who worked for the Australian Federal Police. He'd done all that he could. He didn't know anyone in the FBI, and chances were no one would want to listen to an un known Australian anyway.

~~~

The next morning in Australia, Agent Patrick Wilson sat down to read his personal email before he started his shift. Most of it was the usual junk selling natural supplements or cheap accommodation. It didn't matter how many times he unsubscribed, he always ended up back on the list. He opened one from his old buddy Adam, wondering what he had to say. Maybe he wanted to meet up for a drink before Christmas. The subject line, please forward to the FBI, was intriguing and he glanced at the message.

Hey Mate,

Remember me asking about Emerson Thornton a few weeks ago? I'm in the U.S, and I just overheard him talking about a new business deal. It sounded like he's involved in some really shady stuff. I know I shouldn't have, but I took photos of a file and a ledger that he left lying out in plain sight. I was also an invited guest to the house if that helps with the legal side of things. I thought you might have a contact at the FBI who would be interested in the information.

Adam.

Patrick opened the file that contained pages of photos. The file seemed straight forward, and he would forward it to the white-collar crime division in New York. He didn't know anyone in the Baltimore office. He started looking through the ledger pages, guessing that these were payoffs to contacts and might be useful to the same division, even though none of the names meant anything to him. He gave each page a quick glance, but it was when he reached the tenth page that a name jumped out at him. He saw that the same name appeared three more times with fifty thousand recorded beside each entry. He quickly forwarded the email to his work address and forgetting the coffee he had been drinking, made a phone call.

"Boss," he said when his call was answered, unable to hide his excitement. "I think I've found it. The link we've been looking for."

Chapter Seventeen

"Looks good Beth. Need help with anything else?" Tom asked.

"I still need to get the kid's presents wrapped." she suggested hopefully.

"*Anything* else? You know I can't work the sticky tape."

"No, everything else is done," she sighed, looking at her tree discontentedly. It was the same every Christmas. She always had grand plans to colour coordinate the decorations with the wrapping paper and get the gifts under the tree early. She tried coming up with a theme this year and wandered from store to store hoping something would catch her attention. There were decorations everywhere, but they were mostly cheap, and even Myer had been a bust. So like every year, she pulled the boxes of old decorations out of the back shed and put them on the fake tree they'd bought when the kids were little. And instead of beautifully coordinated gift wrapping, the presents would be wrapped in whatever paper hadn't been used last year, along with whatever she picked up at Woolworths. They were spending Christmas day with Jill and Matthew at their house, along with their mum, so it didn't really matter what her tree looked like, but just once she wished she could compete with Caroline.

She wasn't jealous of her best friend, just in awe of the atmosphere she created in her home. They had been there for Christmas drinks on Monday night and everything was perfect. The seven-foot tree in the formal lounge was exquisite, the light from the chandelier reflecting off the hundreds of glass ornaments. Beneath the tree every present was wrapped in gold with a perfect red bow attached and gorgeous hand-made gift tags.

Adam and Caroline brought them up to date on their very short trip to America. They hadn't given any details – that was Michael's story to tell – but they had told them that the engagement was off. Adam didn't say anything about the information he'd come across in Emerson's study and how he had passed it to his mate at the AFP. He couldn't say he wasn't disappointed after receiving an email back from Patrick saying he had forwarded the info to the FBI, but they didn't think there was much they could do with it. Emerson was going to get away with his corruption again. It was like the man was made of Teflon. Nothing stuck.

"Stop it," Tom commanded, snapping Beth out of her daydream, "You're comparing our tree to Caroline's again, aren't you?"

"I can't help it. She does everything so perfectly."

"So what. Our tree is quirkier, filled with all the things the kids have made over the years. Sarah made that star, and look," he pointed, "Nathan made that little snowman in prep. Those are memories. Caroline's tree might look perfect, but it doesn't have the same *heart* as ours."

"You know you say that to me every year Tom Fraser," Beth smiled, appreciating how her husband always tried to make her feel better.

"And every year you ignore me. Now, I'm going to have a beer. Can I get you a glass of wine? You've worked hard today. Relax tonight, and tomorrow I promise to help you with the wrapping."

"Sure why not?" she agreed, tired from two hours of climbing up and down the ladder to hang up tinsel around the house. Beth rarely drank these days, but she still had the occasional glass of white wine. After Isabelle's death she began drinking more which contributed to her weight gain at the time, along with the years of poor eating and complete lack of exercise. She'd now successfully kept the weight off for years and learning about the power of good food had sparked her interest in more natural therapies and why healthy eating was important. It had changed her life and after finishing the first semester of her course last week she knew she'd made the right decision to give up teaching so she could study to be a Naturopath.

Tom returned from the kitchen a few minutes later with the drinks and they decided to take them outside to enjoy the sunset. It had been a lovely day and although it had cooled off a little, it was very pleasant sitting on the back deck with a cool drink.

They talked about Tom's job for a while and worried about Sarah's VCE results which were due in a few days. In the last month before her exams she'd knuckled down and studied which was completely unlike her. She even took a month off from her beloved job with Caroline to study. The change in their daughter had taken them by surprise, especially when she cleaned up her room, insisting it was easier to concentrate when she wasn't living in a mess. After talking it through they both agreed that they wouldn't tell Sarah about the broken engagement yet. She seemed to be getting over Michael, but if she found out he was single, it might give her false hope. The longer she spent thinking he was getting married, the better.

"Tom," Beth asked when the conversation lulled for a minute. "I know I'm not allowed to ask the details of your chats with Nathan, but can I at least ask if he's doing okay?"

"All I can say love is that he's making progress. He can go weeks without looking at anything he shouldn't, and then he has a slip. He's addicted, and that's a hard habit to break."

Beth shook her head. "I just don't understand it. Women all have the same," she breathed out, not sure how to put it, "features. Why do men want to look at pictures of pretty much the same thing over and over?"

Tom took a swig from the bottle while he pondered how to answer his wife's question. "I'll try and explain it as simply as I can. When a man sees an image of a woman that he finds attractive he gets a dopamine hit. It makes him feel good. And when you feel good you want to repeat the experience. So you look again. But after a while you don't get that same feeling. Think about it. If you have a glass of wine you feel good, relaxed. The next day you have another one. Same response. But by the time the week is out, that one glass is not having the same effect. So you have two. Until you're drinking the entire bottle to get that same feeling you used to get from one glass. Maybe you decide the wine isn't cutting it anymore because you've built up a tolerance. So you move to spirits, or maybe drugs for the same high. Pornography is no different. It's consumed through the eyes the same way alcohol is consumed through your mouth and both affect the brain. And when the images stop having the same effect, the consumer needs to look at something more graphic, maybe even violent. But be assured, Nathan is doing well. He's not cured, but he's working on it, and he's being surprisingly honest with me about it."

"Okay. That I understand. What if we hadn't discovered it when we did? It could have been a lot worse."

"It could have, but it was bad enough. I'm just grateful I realised what was going on before he got himself into real trouble." He took another swig from the bottle and found it empty. "I'm going in for another beer. You want a top up?" he asked.

"No," she said, thinking about what Tom had said about addiction. I think I'll just stick with the one glass".

~~~

Twenty-five kilometres away Sarah was not in a good mood. She was as worried about her exam results as her parents were, and the thought that she might fail had made her agitated for weeks. To make matters worse, the kitchen she was using tonight to prepare the food was hopeless, and to top it all off she had been lumbered with the useless Chad as one of her waiters. Penny, another waitress, had called in sick an hour before the event so she was a man down and Caroline hadn't been able to find a replacement yet. Tonight could be a disaster.

Taking a minute, she tried to calm herself. There was nothing she could do about her exam results. Worrying wouldn't make a difference, so 'stop thinking about them' she told herself. She now had the kitchen clean and they finally got the oven heating. Someone had turned the main power switch off and it had taken them half an hour to figure out the problem. Now her biggest issue was Chad. If he asked her if he could go out for a smoke break one more time she might just smack him.

This should have been an easy night. Christmas drinks and finger food for a firm of solicitors. She could do it in her sleep. But as they waited for the first trays of food to go out – delayed by the oven mishap – the office manager who'd organised the event had been into the kitchen twice already asking what the holdup was. Sarah tried to explain, but it fell on deaf ears. She said if food wasn't out in the next five minutes she would be calling Caroline to make a 'very serious complaint'.

Sarah took the first tray as soon as Alice had the spring rolls on it, instructing Chad not to move from his spot until the second tray was done and then get it out as soon as possible. She had barely left the kitchen before hungry people swamped her and the tray was empty in less than a minute. Chad passed her on the way back to the kitchen with a full tray and she breathed a sigh of relief. The food was finally going out, and Alice already had a tray of arancini balls waiting for her.

This was her third event this week. Once her exams were over she decided against taking some time to recover from year twelve like most kids she knew, instead wanting to make as much money as she could over the Christmas season. She would relax after Christmas when things settled down and there was less work.

It hadn't just been exam stress that had made the past two months hard. She'd avoided being at the Anderson house as much as possible so she wouldn't see Michael. It was easier now that she didn't have to worry about running into him anywhere. He would be in America for months. That should be more than enough time to get over him. He hadn't helped by sending her pictures of his party, and weirdly, New York – he must have taken a day trip – and making funny little observations about the things he had seen. He had asked how she was going, how she had done on her exams, and when she didn't answer him, if she was alright. He was finally paying her the attention she'd craved for years, but now she didn't want it. What she wanted was for him to go away and leave her alone.

Picking up the waiting tray of arancini balls, Sarah spun around and nearly crashed into someone who'd entered the kitchen without warning. Michael. What was he doing here? He gave her that gorgeous smile and grabbed the other side of the tray.

"Let me take these out and you help Alice. Mum said you were a bit behind."

Sarah stood still, staring at his retreating back. He was supposed to be in Baltimore with Margaux, not waiting on drunk Solicitors in Melbourne.

"Hey Sarah, can you pass me those gloves? I need to get the quiches out of the oven," Alice asked.

Snap out of it Sarah she thought and handed Alice the oven gloves. Together they filled the tray and when Chad returned she handed it off to him and got started on setting out more trays, her imagination going into overdrive as she tried to come up with a reason why Michael was back home.

An hour later they had caught up and the office manager even came back to the kitchen to compliment them on the food. The managing partner had been very impressed with the dumplings and wanted to know if he could get the recipe for his wife. Sarah made a note to ask Caroline if that was okay, but doubted it would be – Caroline was very secretive about her recipes – and then started taking the mini desserts out of the fridge to bring them to room temperature. Dessert would be served in about fifteen minutes and she needed all hands-on deck to pick up empty glasses and used napkins. It sounded like Benji had done an excellent job at the bar tonight as the sound of Christmas carols playing was drowned out by a room full of tipsy, rowdy solicitors.

Michael returned to the kitchen with a tray full of empty glasses and sidled up beside her at the bench. He was standing so close to her she could almost feel heat coming off him. Turning to face him, Sarah stepped back, needing some distance. "Do you know what Chad's up to? We need to get all these desserts on the platters and get the tea and coffee table set up, although from the sounds of it, nobody's going to want any."

"He went downstairs for a smoke. He said he'll be back in ten."

"He what?" she exclaimed. "He knows that's a no-no." She pulled out her phone and sent him a text telling him to get his butt back upstairs now.

"Can you do another sweep of the room, and then help me get these out?" Sarah asked Michael.

"Sure, but it's pretty clear out there. Chad did help before he went down for a break."

"I don't care. It's in his contract. No smoking while he's on the clock. Now he'll stink of cigarette smoke while he's handing out food."

"Hey, I'm just the messenger. You should see your face," he grinned. "You look just like Mum right now." Sarah glared at Michael, not amused at his gentle ribbing and he put his hands up in surrender and went out to do another sweep for abandoned glasses. When he walked back into the kitchen Chad had returned and Sarah was not happy.

"Go home Chad," she was saying. "I told you not to leave. This is only a four-hour shift and you don't get a break."

"You're sending me home? But we still have another hour. I need the money."

"Then you should have thought about that before you broke the rules and went out without permission."

"I'm calling Caroline. She's the boss, not you."

"Tonight, I am your boss – but please, go ahead – I'm sure she'd love to hear what you've been up to."

Chad gave Sarah a scathing stare, and then pulling his apron off and flinging it at her, he turned and stormed out of the kitchen. Alice silently continued to fill the platters with desserts as Michael stepped out of the doorway so Chad could pass.

"Wow, you're tough," he said, putting the glasses he had found on the bench.

"Had to be done. He's already had a warning from your mum for the same thing last week. Sorry, it does mean you might need to stay a bit longer to help with the cleanup."

"That's fine. I have nowhere else to be and nothing else to do."

Sarah opened a container of mini chocolate mud cakes and began arranging them on a platter. "I'll help you get these out and then we can get this lot of dishes finished while people are eating. Alice are you able to stay back for an extra half an hour to help with the cleanup?"

"Sorry love. I have to pick up Ellie from work. Her shift finishes at ten. I need to be gone by nine-thirty at the latest. And well done sending Chad home. He's a lazy one, always sneaking off for a smoke. I don't know why Caroline hired him."

"Looks like it's just you and me then, kid" Michael told her as he grabbed a pair of tongs and started plating.

"Yeah," Sarah replied as her heart sunk. "Great."

~~~

All the party goers had left except the Office Manager who was waiting for them to finish so she could lock up and make sure they didn't steal the computers. Everything was washed, and they were nearly finished packing up their equipment. Sarah estimated they would be about ten more minutes and then she could escape.

"I'm surprised you haven't asked me what I'm doing here," Michael asked, trying to fill the silence. Sarah had barely said a word to him all night, which was unusual. Usually she chattered away, although he'd noticed she wasn't herself lately. "You know I wasn't supposed to be back until the end of January."

Of course I want to know why you're here, the voice in Sarah's head screamed, but she shrugged her shoulders so he would think she wasn't that interested, and continued packing glasses.

"You're going to find out sooner or later. We broke up. Margaux and me. Didn't your mum tell you?"

"No, she didn't say a word," – *and a heads up would have been nice, thanks Mum.*

"Well we have. Completely over – hope I never see her as long as I live – over."

Sarah stood up from the crate she had been filling and looked properly at Michael for the first time that evening. She'd been avoiding eye contact, even though every time he was near her he tried to engage her with a joke or a comment about the solicitors who thought they were well above the serving staff.

"I had no idea. Are you alright?" she asked, her heart betraying her as it began to beat faster.

"I am. Turns out marrying her would have been the biggest mistake of my life. It's not a good idea to marry someone who was cheating on you *before* you get married. Can't imagine what she would have been up to after a few years and boredom had set in."

"Why would she cheat on *you*?" Sarah blurted before she had a chance to sensor her words. "You're perfect."

"Well thanks. But not according to Margaux. She admitted that she never loved me and was only marrying me to make her 'daddy' happy. Not how you want to start your life with someone."

Sarah – embarrassed by her 'you're perfect' outburst – busied herself shoving trays into crates completely out of order hoping that Michael didn't notice that she was blushing. Why couldn't she control her mouth around him. It felt like every time she spoke she ended up sounding like a silly kid.

"I definitely dodged a bullet there," Michael continued, "So while I should be sad, I'm really not. I guess I didn't really love her either. If I had I would be heartbroken. Instead I'm just relieved."

"Pass me those gloves?" Sarah asked grabbing anything left on the benches and putting it anywhere she could find a spot as quickly as possible. "I think we're done here," she said and started stacking crates on the trolley they used to move heavy items.

"Let me do that," Michael said, taking a particularly heavy crate and stacking it on before he secured it with an octopus strap. Obviously in the mood to share, Michael continued talking. "Do you remember when I said what Margaux and I had wasn't very deep? I didn't know how right I was. I won't be making that mistake again. Next time I commit It's going to be with someone real, and honest."

"Hmmm," Sarah said as she wiped down the last of the benches. "Well

I think we're all done here. I'll take the trolley," she said throwing the cloth in the top crate. Michael had already taken three loads down to her van earlier.

"Don't be silly. I'll take it to your van for you and help you load. Snazzy ride by the way. A white van for your first car," he grinned. "Your friends must be begging for rides."

"It's practical for work. And it's a tax deduction if you must know," she proclaimed as her face continued to blush.

The office manager, spying them as they walked to the lift, waved goodnight as she started turning of the lights.

"Do you want us to wait for you?" Michael called across the room.

"No, you go ahead. I'm in secure parking, but thanks," she answered as the lift opened for them. Michael wheeled the trolley in and hit the basement button.

"Thanks for coming tonight by the way. I would have been in a terrible mess if you hadn't showed up."

"No worries," Michael answered. "Mum tried everyone before she asked me to fill in tonight. I got a lecture about being professional and doing anything you asked. I think she's forgotten I used to help out all the time when she first started Events."

The lift opened to the basement and Michael began walking to Sarah's van. She hit the button to unlock the door and Michael loaded the last of the crates. He looked at his watch after he put the trolley in. "It's not too late and I don't want to go home yet. Any interest in going for a drink? If Mum's back from her own event she'll fuss over me, making sure I'm okay after, you know, the breakup. To be honest, she's driving me crazy."

"Sorry Michael. I'm exhausted and I have another one of these tomorrow night," Sarah said, knowing that there was nothing more she would like than to spend the rest of the evening with Michael. But she intended on sticking with her resolve. She wasn't going to spend any more time with him than necessary. "I need to get home and get some sleep."

"Okay then. Raincheck?"

"Sure, why not? Maybe after Christmas. When it's not so busy."

"Have I offended you?" Michael asked, finally picking up on Sarah's reluctance to engage with him. "You've been quiet all evening."

"No, of course not. It's just … weird being your boss tonight," she said, saying the first thing that popped into her head. "You can go home and report to your mum now about me. Just trying to keep it professional."

"Okay. Well I'm holding you to that drink after Christmas. And if I don't see you before, have a lovely one." He leaned in and kissed her on the cheek. "Merry Christmas Sarah."

As Michael walked over to his car Sarah slid in behind the driver's seat her hand momentarily reaching for her cheek where he had kissed her. She turned the key over, and the radio began blaring. Her favourite carol was playing – Mariah Carey's *All I want for Christmas* – which was absolutely *not* the right song to be hearing after spending the evening with Michael. She reached over and changed the station before pulling out the parking garage, her hands shaking as she relived how he had kissed her, even if it was only on her cheek. She was going to have to ask Caroline to not put him on the parties she was running. She needed all the distance she could get from Michael.

Michael followed her through the carpark, but they turned the opposite direction as they drove out of the building. *That was a fun night,* he thought. *I think I might ask Mum if I can do more parties with Sarah.*

Chapter Eighteen

"Thanks for agreeing to do this Jillian," Mandy said.

"I haven't said yes yet Mandy. Why don't you give me the details before I decide if I can help you out? Matthew has left the decision up to me."

The Brooks family had only taken in two foster children since Kelly and Sam left. Both had only been with them for a few days before they were placed with extended family. Mandy had rung this morning, sounding desperate. Jill agreed to hear her out, but if this was going to be a long term placement, she was prepared to say no. As much as she'd told herself she was fine with children coming and going when she first started fostering, she found the whole process unsettling, and was beginning to regret her decision to go down this path. She was a person who needed routine and having other people's children in the house hadn't suited her. It was also hard on Zoe. She was never sure what she was going to come home to, and Zoe was always going to be Jill and Matthew's top priority. Jill was ready to give the whole thing up and get on with her life. If she couldn't have children of her own then so be it, but fostering, it seemed, wasn't the answer to fill the gap in her life.

"Jayden is eight. His mum calls him Jay, so it's best to stick with that.

He's been in two homes since he was removed from his mother's care last month."

"That doesn't sound good. Is he causing trouble?" Jill asked, her decision already made. A difficult kid was the last thing they needed.

"No, not at all. Jay is one of the quietest children I have ever come across. Until a year ago his life was normal. He lived with his mum, went to school and his mum had a good job. Unfortunately, she suffered a brain injury after she fell during a hike. She broke a few ribs, but the knock to her head did a lot of damage. Once she left the hospital things seemed normal at first. But she started to forget to collect Jay from school, and then the outbursts started. Once her boss fired her, things really started to spiral down. His teacher called us in when she suspected neglect, and what we found at the house was appalling. There was very little food, the house was filthy and his mum, completely out of character had been having regular visits from different men. When we arrived there was a man in the house who was very clearly high. I had a word with the neighbours, and they reported seeing different men coming and going over the last two months. We don't know if there was an exchange of money, or she considered these men boyfriends, but Jay couldn't stay there."

"Okay, but if he's no trouble why keep moving him?" Jill asked.

"It's his mother who's causing the problems. When we first took him into care he remained at his school. He'd already suffered enough trauma and he liked his teacher. That was a mistake. His mother started showing up at the school, trying to take him home, and then she followed the foster parent to their house. Once she knew where he was living it became unsafe for the carer's and their own children. We moved him that day to another home and changed schools. It was a few suburbs over so we thought it would be fine. Unfortunately, an old friend of Jay's mum saw him at the shops out with the foster family. She rang Jay's mum to find out what was going on, not knowing about her friend's mental health issues. Once his mum knew approximately where Jay was living she made the rounds of the primary schools till she found him. His teacher alerted us before he was picked up from school – she made quite a scene – so we need to move him again, and fast."

"And you want him to come here? What's to stop his mum finding him again?"

"She lives on the other side of the city, in a working-class suburb, and this – she looked around Jillian's lovely home – is not. The chances of Jay's mum knowing anyone who lives in Brighton is negligible."

"Tell me what you expect from us then. You can't keep moving Jay. That's not fair to him."

"We have exhausted all other possibilities. His grandmother is dead, and his grandfather can't look after a child. He's in his seventies and not in good health. He said he would like to see Jay when possible, but even he understands Jay can't live with him. There's no father listed on the birth certificate so that avenue is closed. And he cannot stay in the home with his mother right now. Even if she takes the meds she needs, and apparently she isn't compliant at the moment, the doctors don't know if she will ever fully recover from her injury. It's one of the saddest stories I've come across because, before her accident, she was providing Jay with a good life."

"So you want him here long term? You know how we feel about that."

"You know I don't know what's going to happen. All I know is that right now a very sweet, very sad little boy urgently needs a home. And if I have to beg, I will." Mandy slipped a photo out of her file and slid it across the table. Jillian took in the dark circles around his eyes, and the tiny frame that looked like it hadn't been feed properly for months.

"You don't play fair, do you?" she said, as she picked up the photo.

"Thank you," Mandy smiled sensing victory. "Can you take him today?"

Jillian exhaled, before she told Mandy, "bring him today. I'll make sure I have his room ready."

~~~

Matthew called from the front door, "I'm home. And I could use some help please." Jillian ran to the door and grabbed her husbands' briefcase as he juggled it along with a large box.

"Is he here yet?" he asked as they walked together to the kitchen.

"No but it should be anytime. Zoe's just putting some finishing touches in his room to make him feel welcome. It's good that her school holidays have already started. She can help Jay get settled in. Mandy said we won't enrol him in the local primary for the rest of the year. They only have a few days of term left, and then it's six weeks off. That will give us a chance to figure out if this is going to work out."

"Why wouldn't it work out?"

"I'm concerned about his mother. She's caused trouble for his last two families. But she lives in the Western suburbs, so it's unlikely she will track him down here."

"Is she violent?" Matthew asked as he took a pair of scissors out of the draw and cut the tape on the box.

"Not so far. Just a bit stalkery. She tracked him down twice and tried to take him home." Jill hadn't had a chance to tell Matthew the whole story of Jay's mum, just the highlights, but he had agreed to come home early to meet him. "What's in the box?"

"Something that's going to make us rich, I hope. We've started taste testing the new yoghurt, and I was hoping you would give it a try?"

Matthew had been approached six months ago by a national chain of service stations looking to expand their product range. They sold the usual pies and donuts along with bad coffee and chocolate bars. But focus groups had alerted them that people want to be able to pick up something healthier from their stores when they filled up their car, especially for breakfast when they were on their way to work. Matthew's company had been working on a formula for a coconut yoghurt with a gluten free, sugar free granola topping in three different flavours. They had created a regular granola, a freeze-dried berry version, and a chocolate granola. They figured out a way to keep the granola from becoming soggy in the yogurt and now they were waiting on approval from the service station chain. They insisted on conducting their own taste testing before committing to stock the range. But Matthew was already sure what the outcome would be. The new product was healthy *and* delicious.

Jillian had been instrumental in putting together the contracts with the chain and the manufacturing plant that would fulfill the strict guidelines to make sure the product would not be contaminated with either gluten or dairy. If the yogurts were a success, Sustenance would expand the product line to include low carb, fresh muffins and the chain had expressed interest in stocking Sustenance's existing line of protein bars. If they could pull this off then their little company would officially be a success.

When the doorbell rang half an hour later all the flavours had been tested. Zoe declared the chocolate her favourite, and Jillian liked the berry the most. Not wanting to overwhelm Jay, Matthew and Zoe waited in the kitchen, while Jillian answered the door. Mandy was holding a suitcase and the hand of a very small Jay. Jillian immediately felt protective of the little boy waiting on her doorstep. He had mousy brown hair that hadn't seen a decent cut for a long time and his eyes were huge in his sunken face which needed fresh air and sunshine. His knobbly knees stuck out of his worn shorts and his tee-shirt was much too big for his tiny shoulders.

"Come in out of the heat you two," Jillian invited. "Let's leave your bag here for now and go through to the kitchen. We' re trying some new flavours of yoghurt and we need an expert opinion. Do you think you might help us out Jay?" Jillian held her hand out to Jay who obediently took it and followed beside her. Matthew hopped down from the stool he had been sitting on at the island bench and held out his hand to shake Jay's. Jay looked a little confused but reciprocated and as Matthew shook his hand he introduced himself.

"I'm Matthew, and this is Zoe. And you have already met Jill. We're very pleased to have you come and stay with us. "

"I was just asking Jay if he would mind trying some yoghurt for us. We can't decide which is the best and he can be the deciding vote," Jillian suggested as she opened three new tubs and tipped the toppings out of their recyclable sachet onto the yogurts. She handed him a spoon after Matthew had lifted him up onto the stool he had just abandoned.

"Jay, do you mind if Zoe keeps you company while Jill and I have a quick word with Mandy?" Matthew asked. Jay didn't answer but picking up the spoon started eating the berry flavour.

Mandy followed Jill and Matthew into the formal lounge. They kept the door open so they could keep an eye on the kitchen, but kept their voices down so they wouldn't be overheard.

"He doesn't look well Mandy. Has anyone taken him to the doctor?" Matthew asked.

"We did but they say they can't find anything wrong with him. He has a good appetite, but he doesn't seem to be putting on any weight. The doctor was at a loss. Jay's heart sounded fine and his bloodwork came back normal. He thinks it might be the stress of everything he's gone through. Give it a week or two and if nothing has changed after Christmas we can investigate further. I'll check in with you in a few days to see how everything is going."

"Does he talk at all?" Jill asked.

"Not much, but before his mother's accident he was doing great in school, so there's nothing wrong with him developmentally. He's just very shy and very traumatized. You should take it slow with him," Mandy suggested.

Mandy returned to the kitchen to say goodbye to Jay and then she left. Jillian saw her out and then decided to put in a call to her sister. If what Mandy said was right, and it appeared to be as Jay had eaten all three tubs of yoghurt, then there had to be a reason why he was so thin and sickly looking.

"Hey Jill," Beth greeted as she picked up after the third ring.

"Beth, can I pick your brain?" Jill asked. "Jay, our new foster kid has arrived, and he doesn't look well. He's really thin, even though I have just witnessed him eating three tubs of yoghurt, and Mandy said he has a good appetite. Any ideas what could be causing his low weight? The doctor who checked him out couldn't find anything wrong. Does he need vitamins or something?"

"I wouldn't bother with vitamins. They probably won't help. Unless you know exactly what he's deficient in there's not much point." Beth thought for a minute and then she had an idea. "He might have worms. They steal the nutrients from the food being ingested and mess up gut health. I would normally tell you to find a naturopath who can do some tests, but just assume that's the problem and go to the chemist and get something from them. It will be quicker; it could be weeks before you can get an appointment at a clinic, and it certainly can't do any harm to give him an over the counter treatment. We worm our pets all the time in Australia, but we about forget ourselves."

"That's gross Beth. Worms? Yuck."

"You do realise a great deal of the western world has parasites. I do a cleanse every six months to take care of them."

"You do?" Jill asked her sister.

"You *don't*?"

"No. I didn't know it was a thing. Where on earth would he get worms from anyway? I thought that sort of thing only happened in third world countries."

"You can get them from all sorts of places. He could have eaten undercooked food or picked up eggs if someone hadn't washed their hands properly after using the bathroom and then touched something the boy also touched."

"Well I feel sick now."

"Then get to the chemist, and make sure you're using good hygiene around the boy. You don't want to end up with them. And maybe take the medication as well. I'm surprised Matthew isn't on to this."

"Well he will be now. And you're still arriving about twelve on Christmas day?"

"Yep. Should I bring a present for your new kid? Maybe some clothes."

"That's a lovely idea, but I would try a size seven. He's eight, but that size will be too big on him."

"Got it. And I hope it all goes well. See you next week."

"See ya."

Jillian grabbed her bag and keys, and after yelling towards the kitchen that she was popping out for a few minutes she got into her car and headed towards the local shops. Trust her sister to think of an answer no one else had considered. But worms. That was just bizarre.

Chapter Nineteen

Over the crushing headache and the sound of her own heart thumping – probably as much from fear as from her rising blood pressure – Joan could hear the siren of the ambulance she had just been bundled into. She heard the paramedic call ahead to the hospital telling them that it was urgent and to be ready with Magnesium Sulphate. Joan knew what that was from last time. It was to stop seizures.

She had been all good. Until yesterday this had been a typical pregnancy. Her first clue that something might be wrong was when she noticed it was hurting her ankles to walk. Taking a look she saw that they looked a little puffier than the day before, but David, after having a look told her they were as gorgeous as ever and she was imagining it. She tried to put her fears aside but had slept poorly, a headache creeping up until it became unbearable and she gave up trying to sleep.

When she called her Doctor this morning to ask what pain killer she could safely take to help with the headache she insisted Joan come in to see her immediately. After a few Paracetamol tablets she felt the headache recede a little and told David to stay home. He could watch the children – she was capable of driving herself. Her Doctor's office was only fifteen minutes away. That was a mistake.

Joan had negotiated her way through the morning traffic badly. The roads were full of mothers who were dropping their children off at school – the worst time of the day to drive David always said. School had only been back for a few days after the Christmas holidays and the drivers on the road seemed to have forgotten … how to. Joan knew it didn't help that she was having trouble focusing and had almost gone through a red light, slamming on the break at the last second. That had been agony. The pain in her ankles intensified and when she finally pulled into the carpark of the medical centre she struggled to manoeuvre her pregnant tummy from behind the steering wheel. Holding up her own weight was excruciating.

The receptionist had seen Joan falter from her desk, barely able to walk and after yelling for help ran outside to help Joan keep her balance. Together they limped into the office and when her Doctor rushed out of her office she didn't hesitate. An ambulance was called immediately, and Doctor Williams put the blood pressure cuff on Joan. Seeing that the reading was one-forty-five over ninety-five, the Doctor swore under her breathe and asked Joan to remain calm, she was here, and help was on the way.

Doctor Williams asked her receptionist to cancel her appointments for the morning and told her to ring Joan's husband. He would need to meet them at the Monash Medical Centre as soon as possible, in the emergency ward. Joan could hear the phone call to her husband being made, but with the pounding in her head intensifying, she couldn't take it all in and only heard snippets of the conversation. She felt like she was underwater and the sound above the surface was distant and garbled. She tried to concentrate on what the doctor was saying to her about staying calm, but terror was setting in. Not so much for herself, but for the baby.

~~~

Grabbing his ringing phone from the table, David didn't recognise the number, but answered it anyway. It could be a supplier or a new client.

"Hello, David speaking," he said as he picked up the toast Will had just flung across the table. Apparently he didn't like jam anymore.

"Mister Saunders, this is Allie from Doctor William's office. I'm sorry to have to tell you this, but your wife has suffered a medical emergency. She has been taken by ambulance to Monash. The Doctor needs you to meet her at the emergency department."

David didn't answer Allie but hung up the phone and plucked Will from his booster seat at the table. He yelled at Bella – who was watching cartoons on the couch – to put her shoes on and shoved his phone in his pocket. This would have been easier if she had been tucked up safely at school, but her small private school didn't start until tomorrow. She grumbled that she didn't know where her shoes were, and when David saw that she was wearing slippers he decided that was good enough and grabbed her by her hand telling her they were going to see Mummy. David didn't realise that he too, was only wearing slippers.

Slamming his car into reverse out of the garage, he dialled Beth. He couldn't think of a time he had ever called her, and only had her number in his phone for emergencies. She picked up immediately.

"What's wrong, David?" she asked, knowing that he wasn't calling for a chat.

"Joan's been taken by ambulance to Monash. Can you meet me there?"

"I'm already on my way. Did they tell you why?"

But David had already hung up, throwing his phone on the passenger seat so he could concentrate on the traffic. The hospital was a twenty-minute drive, and while they had practiced several routes to find the quickest way, he intended on making it in fifteen. Beth lived much closer, and she would beat him to the hospital. Two minutes later his phone rang, this time through the Bluetooth system and he answered when he saw Matthew's name come up on the screen.

"Mate, what's happening?"

"I don't know," he answered as he beeped his horn at a slow driver in a minivan, before changing lanes, and cutting off a Ute, who's driver had no problem returning the favour by beeping his own horn. Will, frightened by the noise and picking up on his Fathers tension, began crying in the back seat.

"David, calm down. Driving crazy won't get you to Joan any faster, and if you have an accident you won't be any good to her. Just tell me what you need?"

"I have both kids with me. I would call Mum and Dad to come and get them, but they took their caravan up the coast to New South Wales. It will take them a few days to get back."

"That's easy. I'm on my way to the hospital now with Jill. She can drive your car home and look after the kids. She needs to be home to pick up Jay from school this afternoon, but that's hours away. We can sort something out by then. How far are you from the hospital?"

"I'm almost there."

"Good. Hang in there mate. I'll see you in half an hour," Matthew said before disconnecting the call.

A few minutes later he pulled up outside the hospital and pulled into the last fifteen-minute parking space. Beth was waiting outside for him and hurried over to the driver's side.

"Have you seen her? Is she alright?" he asked, his throat choked with panic. He'd kept it together, but now that he was at the hospital he was overwhelmed with fear. Had he killed his wife because he had been too lazy and too afraid to get a vasectomy?

"They wouldn't let me in, and they wouldn't even confirm she's here.

You go, and I'll park your car and take care of the kids. Give her my love and call me if you find out anything. I'll be here as long as you need me."

David leapt out of his car, grabbing his phone from the front seat and raced inside. There were two people already waiting at the window speaking to triage nurses. He wanted to break down the door that stood between him and his wife, but security was tight and if he made a scene chances were he would never get in.

t felt like hours, but it had only been a minute when the nurse called him over and asked how she could help him today.

"My wife came here in an ambulance," he blurted, "I need to see her."

The nurse, used to dealing with distraught family members, asked for the patient's name. She typed Joan Saunders into the computer, and then frowned.

"She's not on our system yet Mister Saunders, but let me make a call, and we'll find out what's going on, shall we?" She dialled a number and then, after asking if Joan had arrived at the hospital gave David a sympathetic glance and then, hanging up the phone, immediately pushed the security button to the door and called him through.

"Follow me please," she said, and David was taken to a large cubical near the nurse's station. The nurse pulled the curtain back to allow him to enter. What he saw was devastating.

A belt was strapped to his wife's stomach to monitor the baby. Leads were coming off her chest and leg to monitor her heart rate and a blood pressure cuff was attached to one arm and she had a drip in the other one. Doctor Williams was holding her hand and talking gently to Joan asking her to stay calm while another doctor was watching the screen as the blood pressure cuff expanded.

They gave each other a look when the reading confirmed that her blood pressure was rising, not decreasing.

"Is her husband here yet? We need to talk to him before we go ahead with the emergency caesarean."

"I'm here," David called from the opening and both doctors turned towards him, the look of concern very clear on both of their faces. Their grave expressions did nothing to alleviate his fears, and he knew then that Joan was in real trouble.

"David," Doctor Williams said, taking control of the situation. "Joan has very high blood pressure. We have administered Magnesium Sulphate to stop her having a seizure, which has worked so far, but the Labetalol isn't working to bring down her blood pressure. We don't like how high it is. Time is of the essence here and we need to get this baby out asap. With her history we don't want to wait any longer."

"Will the baby be okay? Joan has told me repeatedly to put the baby's life ahead of her own," he said, but he knew he didn't care right now. His wife was his only priority.

"The baby is doing fine David. Its heart rate is good and at thirty-four weeks it's viable. It will need a few weeks in the neonatal ICU, but that's okay. Our concern right now is Joan. We need to go to theatre now. If we don't she is at risk of having a stroke."

"Then do it. Can I be in there with her during the operation?" he asked feeling like he had been punched in the guts.

"I'm sorry, no. There is a team getting prepped now, but we can't wait for you to get gowned up," she said as an orderly appeared in the cubicle beside David.

"Am I taking this patient to theatre?" the orderly asked.

"Yes," Doctor Williams answered as the orderly checked that his paperwork and the name on Joan's wrist band matched and then disconnected the leads and attached them to a portable monitor.

As the nurses prepared Joan for transport David rushed to her side. He would only have a few seconds with her and wanted to reassure her that he was here, and she was going to be fine.

"Joanie," he said, gently pushing her hair from her face, "I'm here."

Joan who was conscious, but distressed, didn't seem to be able to focus on him and as the orderly pulled the bed backwards out of the cubicle, David realised he was completely powerless. This could be the last time he saw his wife alive. Fear, real fear, overwhelmed him. Last time there had been time for him to gown up for the surgery and he had been there when Will was born. As he followed behind Joan's bed at the doctor's suggestion people moved out of the way to let them through. Even strangers understood that this was a serious situation.

They took the lift to the surgical ward and David grabbed Joan's hand trying to let her know he was there while he told her that he loved her, but she didn't respond to him and he couldn't tell if she even knew he was there. The lift opened out to another nurse's station, and Doctor Williams pointed David to a small waiting room. She would not be performing the surgery, but she wasn't leaving until she knew the outcome. Joan was whisked away behind large double doors which closed quietly behind her. Doctor Williams tried to tell him that the surgeons were the best, but her words fell on deaf ears. David had retreated into himself and couldn't be reached. They each took a seat while they quietly waited for news.

Chapter Twenty

Jill and Matthew rushed through the hospital to the Nesso café where they'd arranged to meet Beth and the children. They heard them before they saw them – Will was crying hysterically – probably because he didn't understand what was going on. He knew Beth, but right now the only person he wanted was his mother.

"Beth have you heard anything?" Jill asked as she pulled out the last chair at the table while Matthew hovered, unsure what to do with himself.

"No," Beth shook her head after swallowing a sip of her flat white. Bella was drinking what looked like a baby chino, while Will was ignoring the juice box Beth had bought him in the hope it would calm him down if he had something else to concentrate on. It hadn't worked and he'd poured at least half of it all over himself.

"The nurses won't give me any information and I texted David, but he hasn't answered. All I know is that she came in an ambulance from her doctor's surgery. If it wasn't serious they wouldn't have taken her by ambulance, would they?"

"Maybe the doctor was just being cautious," Matthew tried to reassure her. "Let's not panic until we know what's actually happening. Jill's going to take David's car home with the kids to their house. It's better for them to be there instead of here all day. We just have to find David so we can get the car keys."

"No need," Beth said as she searched in her handbag for them. Finding them, she handed them to Jill. "The car's at the back of the parking lot. That's the closest spot I could find."

"Do you think you could come with me? It might be a struggle getting these two back to the car on my own," Jill decided. She pulled out a tissue from her bag and attempted to wipe Will's runny nose, but he shook his head from side to side, and took his crying to a whole new level. People were beginning to look at them and giving each other that 'why don't they do something about that kid' look, so Jill gave up. Right now his runny nose was the least of their problems.

"I think we should get going. Matthew please call me as soon as you hear something," Jill insisted as she stood, taking Bella's hand and helped her off the seat.

"I promise. I'm going to see if I can track David down. Are you staying at the hospital Beth?"

"I'm not going anywhere. I'll come back here once I've helped Jill with the kids," Beth confirmed. "Have either of you called Caroline and Adam?" Matthew and Jill both shook their heads. "Do you want me to do it?" Matthew asked.

"No. I'll do it," Beth replied, "we need to be careful giving Caroline bad news. As strong as she looks, news like this could bring everything back."

"We don't know it's bad news yet," Jillian reminded her sister.

"And let's hope and pray it's not. But we still need to be careful with Caroline. Now let's get these two home." Matthew leaned over and kissed Jill goodbye and then picked up a very sticky Will and handed him to Beth. He sat in Jill's vacated chair and texted David for the third time asking where he was, but it remained unread and David hadn't responded to his other messages either.

As the women walked to the car, Beth rang Sarah to see if she could relieve Jill this afternoon from watching the kids so she could pick Jay up from school at three o'clock. Sarah agreed immediately when she heard what was going on, deciding she could skip her final class for the day and extracted a promise from her mum to let her know what was happening with Joan as soon as she knew anything. She would give the kids dinner and stay the night if necessary.

When Jill arrived back at David and Joan's home twenty minutes later, she didn't need to find the house key on David's chain. She found the door ajar, and at first Jill worried there might be someone inside. After a search of all the rooms she confirmed that she and the kids were alone in the house and decided David must have been in such a hurry he forgot to lock up. She sent Bella up to her bedroom to get changed out of the pyjamas she was still wearing and took Will to the bathroom. She ran a warm bath, remembering that Joan once mentioned that letting Will play in the water was the quickest way to get him to calm down. Once she got his pyjamas off him and put him into the water he let her wipe his filthy face, a combination of tears, juice and snot. Joan was right and soon he was playing happily with his boats. The television had still been on when they arrived back at the house so she knew Bella would be entertained while she watched Will play in the water. At least the screaming had finally stopped. She sent up a quick prayer, even though it wasn't something she really believed in the way her sister did, asking God to look after her friend and her baby.

~~~

Matthew finally received a text from David telling him he was in the surgical waiting room but didn't think the staff would let Matthew in. Matthew, used to getting his way in business, decided it was worth a shot and presented himself to the nurse's station once he found the right ward on the map.

"I'm here for Joan Saunders," he told the nurse who finally looked up from her paperwork.

"And you are?"

"I'm her brother," he lied. It could be true he decided. They both had dark hair.

She typed on her keyboard and a minute later declared that her brother was not her next of kin.

"I know I'm not her next of kin, but she's my sister and my brother in law is here all alone. He's freaking out and needs a shoulder. So can you please tell me where he is?"

The nurse gave him the once over, trying to decide if he was going to be a problem and then pointed to the waiting room. Matthew rushed to the room where he found David sitting with a woman he didn't recognise. There were a few other people dotted around the room waiting, all obviously hoping for good news.

Matthew leaned over and gently touched David on the shoulder. He didn't want to scare him, but David was so far away he hadn't noticed his best friend. He looked up and it was very clear to Matthew that David had been crying. He had never seen him cry before, not when Charlie broke off their engagement weeks before the wedding, or even when Joan went through the crisis with her last pregnancy.

"Mate, have you heard something?" he asked.

"No, nothing. But it's taking too long. Something must be wrong."

"David, it's only been forty-five minutes. Sometimes it can take a bit longer," Doctor Williams repeated. She told him this every time he looked at his watch and said it was taking too long. "Until someone comes out and tells us otherwise, we have to assume everything is going well."

Matthew sat down beside David and silently waited with him. There was nothing he could say that could make this situation better. Matthew's encouraging words would do nothing to alleviate the fear radiating off David. Only the surgeon could do that.

Another fifteen minutes passed in silence, with David only moving to check his watch every few minutes, before a surgeon finally came out to talk to him, recognising Dr Williams who he consulted with occasionally.

"Mister Sanders, we have performed the caesarean, and everything went as expected during the operation."

David who had stood, bent over and exhaled in relief, and then noticed the concerned look of the surgeon.

"Please tell me something isn't wrong with the baby?" he begged.

"No. We delivered a healthy girl. She's very small, but a few weeks in the NICU should sort that out."

"Then what's wrong? Because I can see from your face that there's a problem."

"We'd hoped that when we delivered the baby your wife's blood pressure would drop. Unfortunately, it hasn't. We have moved her to an ICU bed where she will be constantly monitored until we can get it under control."

"Can I see her please?"

"You can, but she's still unconscious. There was no time for an epidural, so we did the operation under a general anaesthetic. She'll be out for a while longer, and we will be monitoring her for some time yet. With her blood pressure so high there is still a chance of stroke. The Labetalol wasn't working so we gave her Nifedipine. If there is no change they will give her another dose and see how she goes." He looked at his watch. "I'm sorry, I have another surgery to get to," he apologised as he turned to Doctor Williams. "Paula, do you mind taking Mr Saunders to ICU to see his wife and then to the NICU so he can meet his new daughter?" he asked. "And good luck Mister Saunders. I hope everything will be fine."

Doctor Williams asked David to follow her after cautioning Matthew that they would never let him into ICU. Matthew said he would track down Beth and give her the news, but he wasn't going home. He would be there for as long as he was needed. All David had to do was call or text.

When they arrived at the ICU, Doctor Williams requested to see Joan's chart and left David to have a few moments alone with his wife. A nurse took him through, and he found his wife still sleepy after the anaesthetic. Her hair was tucked under the scrub cap and her usually olive complexion was drained of all colour. Monitors were recording her heart rate and her blood pressure. A nurse assured him that for now, the medication was working, and her blood pressure had dropped. Not enough, but it was better than it had been.

David sat by her bed holding her hand and begged her in a whisper to be alright. He'd been there for ten minutes when the alarms started going off. A nurse and a doctor rushed to her side, telling David he had to leave. When he refused to go the nurse said he was endangering his wife because they needed space to work. He reluctantly stepped outside the cubicle, but he could see them inject something into her drip before the nurse turned and closed the curtain behind her.

Another nurse led him away from Joan's bed and directed him to a chair which he slumped into as he dropped his head into his hands.

It felt to David like an eternity passed before a doctor came out to talk to him. "Mr Saunders. We have your wife's blood pressure back under control for now. She's awake so you can spend a few minutes with her, but then we think it's best you go down and meet your new baby." David stood and followed the Doctor who left them alone.

"Joanie, it's me. You did it love. We have a daughter," he whispered.

"David, what happened?" Joan asked, her voice so quiet he could hardly hear her.

"You had to have an emergency caesarean."

"The baby," she cried. "Is the baby okay?"

"Yes she's fine. I hear she's small, but they think she will be able to go home in a few weeks."

"What does she look like? Is she perfect?"

"I haven't seen her yet, Joanie. I've been too worried about you."

"David," she said her voice hoarse from the intubation, struggled to focus her gaze properly on him. "You have to go and see the baby. Hold her if they let you as much as you can. She needs physical contact with her parents, and I can't do it yet."

"I'll see her soon. But I want to stay here with you."

"David, I'm begging you. You have to be me until I can." The monitors started beeping again as the blood pressure cuff started automatically measuring Joan's pressure. The nurse appeared at the curtain.

"Mr Saunders, I need you to leave now. You seem to be raising her pressure, not a lot, but we need to keep your wife as calm as possible. You can come back tomorrow, but for now I suggest you go and spend some time with your new daughter."

"What if something happens? I need to be here."

"We will call you if there is any change. I promise. But we can't do our job with you hovering over her. She's in good hands and our doctors deal with this more often than you might think. Dr Williams asked me to tell you she had to leave but she will be staying in touch with us about your wife's condition. You'll find your daughter in the maternity ward."

David – knowing that they were never going to let him spend the rest of the day by Joan's bed – left the ICU in defeat. It was his job to protect his wife, to keep her safe, but instead he had put her in this situation. This was all his fault, and now he was expected to go and meet the baby whose very existence, although through no fault of her own, had been complicit in endangering the life of the woman he loved more than anything in the world.

David was able to find the Children's Hospital easily enough, and when he got there he found both Beth and Matthew waiting for him outside the ward. They rushed over to him asking how Joan was. He explained the problems with her blood pressure and that he had been kicked out of the ICU.

"We haven't been able to see the baby," Beth informed him. "They wouldn't give us any information about her condition either. They said they will only talk to you."

"Then I better go and talk to the nurses," David said. "You two don't need to stay here. I'll be fine."

"We aren't going anywhere, David. Apart from the fact that you have no way of getting home, you need someone to look after you. This has been as traumatic for you as it has been for Joan. Go and see your baby and we'll track you down some food. And when you're ready one of us will drive you home," Matthew promised. "I doubt they'll let you stay here all night, and if you want to be any good to Joan you'll need to get some sleep."

"Oh, the kids?" he asked. "I'm sorry, I'm not thinking straight. I'd completely forgotten about them. Are they okay?"

"They're fine. Jill took them home and Sarah is staying the night, so it doesn't matter when you get home. Caroline is going to look after them tomorrow, and from there we will sort out a schedule to watch Will and Bella until Joan can come home. When it comes to the kids you have nothing to worry about."

~~~

When Sarah arrived at David and Joan's house she found Bella happily tucked up on the couch watching television. Jillian said that Will was asleep, and she'd taken some mince out of the freezer so Sarah could make a spaghetti bolognaise for dinner. She rushed off, hoping she would be at school in time to pick up Jay.

Everything was going fine until she heard Will padding down the hall. He was in a big boy bed now and had been able to get himself up after his nap. When he saw Sarah – who he'd known since he was born – he started crying. Obviously, the day had been much too much for him and yet another face in his home was enough to set him off. Sarah picked him up to comfort him, but he thrashed his entire body, trying to squirm out of her grip. Afraid he was going to injure himself, or her for that matter, she put him down on the couch with Bella, hoping that the cartoons would distract him from screaming for his mother. Bella had barely moved from the couch all day and Sarah wondered if she should try and get her to do something else. Joan was big on limiting their time in front of the telly, but Sarah had no idea what else kids did all day. And she needed to get on with cooking dinner anyway.

Eventually Will cried himself out, his screams gradually quieting until he finally fell silent in front of the television, his thumb in his mouth as he stared at the screen. While he had been screaming, Sarah had waited for a knock on the door from the police, expecting them to turn up to see why she had been murdering a child, because when he got going that's what it sounded like. How had her mother coped with three of them?

The bolognaise was ready by five o'clock and she decided to fed the kids early. She hoped that way she would be able to get both of them off to bed by six o'clock – having no idea that was much too early – so she could put something other than ABC kids on. The singing from the shows was driving her nuts. She didn't understand that Will's long, late nap would mean he wasn't going to sleep for hours. And when Bella begun asking when her Mummy was coming home and Sarah couldn't tell her, there had been a few tears from her as well. She collected both kids from the couch and put Will in his booster seat and Bella climbed into a chair. Bella was happy to eat her dinner and chatted away telling Sarah how she was going to school tomorrow in grade one. Sarah, not knowing if Will could feed himself or not picked up a spoon and tried to give him some of the pasta. He began shaking his head back and forth and yelling no, no, no.

Sarah remembered there was some sort of aeroplane trick parents did to get their kids to eat so she began making noises and flying the spoon to Will's mouth. He clamped his lips shut and smacked her hand away. Sarah tried again and again spaghetti was thrown all over the floor.

"This shouldn't be this hard Will. Please eat some?" she begged.

"No. I want Mummy," he replied and that's when he picked up the entire bowl of spaghetti and threw it straight at Sarah. She sat there in disbelief, as she looked down at her tee-shirt now covered in red sauce with bits of spaghetti hanging off her face and hair. Her phone began ringing at the same time and expecting it to be her mother she answered it, neglecting to check who was calling.

"Hi," she said as she watched Will who had picked up some of the spaghetti that had dropped onto the table and was rubbing it in his hair.

"Sarah, it's Michael. How's it going?"

"How's it going?" she answered, panic in her voice, before she had a chance to remember that she wasn't supposed to be talking to him. "I'm stuck here with a monster. Covered in spaghetti. It is *not* going well."

Michael chuckled knowing Will's reputation for being naughty. "Mum said you were babysitting tonight. I thought I might check and see if you needed a hand. I've been told I'm good with kids and I'm not far away. I could come and help till they fall asleep."

"When can you get here? I'm not cut out for this babysitting thing."

"I'm ten minutes away. I was in the area visiting a friend."

"Then what are you waiting for? I need help now!"

When Sarah opened the door minutes later, Michael took in the scene. Will was running around the family room with dinner smooshed into his hair. Bella was chasing him, and the harder she tried to grab her brother the faster he ran thinking this was the best fun he'd had all day. But the look on Sarah's face told the story. Covered in sauce with a few strands of spaghetti that she'd missed still hanging off her hair she looked defeated. She didn't say anything, just stepped aside to allow Michael entry. As Will ran past him, he scooped him up and held him tight.

"Hello little man. Are you being naughty?"

"Playing chasey," Will replied.

"And did you eat your dinner?"

"No," Will shook his head, watching Michael.

"Well I'm starving. Is there anymore Sarah?"

Sarah who was still standing in the doorway, her face grim, nodded and walked towards the kitchen.

Michael returned Will to his booster seat, and Will so intrigued with the new visitor who didn't seem afraid of him, sat watching. When Sarah put a plate of dinner in front of him, Michael took the fork she offered him and began eating.

"Mmm, yummy," he said, taking another bite, "do you want some Will?"

Will shook his head in the negative.

"Oh well, all the more for me. Are you going to have some Sarah? It's delicious ."

"Ah, sure," she replied pulling another plate out of the cupboard and made herself a small serving.

"Maybe you could bring a bowl for my friend Will here."

"Sure, why not? Let's give the maniac something else to throw around. Maybe then we'll end up with matching red tee-shirts," she replied as she

174

found another plastic bowl in the cupboard. After filling it she set it down in front of Will and took a seat further away from him this time. She was not going to be on the receiving end of another tantrum. Will didn't touch his food but watched as Michael continued to eat his dinner and made appreciative noises. Sarah picked up her fork and began eating too. At least Will wasn't throwing it this time.

"So, how have you been Sarah?" Michael asked. "I haven't seen you since that party we worked before Christmas."

"I'm good thanks," she replied. "Well not tonight maybe, but you know, fine."

"I hear you passed your exams. I sent you a text congratulating you, but you didn't respond."

"I must have missed it."

"Funny that. Because it was marked as read. And there was the one when I asked you out for a drink to celebrate. You didn't respond to that one either."

"I've been busy. Sorry. I didn't mean to be rude."

"If I didn't know better I would think you've been avoiding me. But I'm wrong ... right?"

"Of course you're wrong. Why would I avoid you Michael?"

"I don't know. I can't think of one reason why, unless you're upset with me, and I can't think why that would be." He looked over to Will who, with the attention no longer on him had started picking up strands of spaghetti and was shoving it into his mouth.

"Seems he likes it after all," Michael pointed out to Sarah.

"Should I give him a spoon? Eww, that's revolting." She scrunched up her face in disgust as Will scooped up a handful of the meat sauce and licked it into his mouth.

"Nope. Just ignore it. At least he's eating. And it's good by the way."

"Thanks. But it's not exactly the hardest meal to make."

"It's still good. And you're not off the hook you know. If I've offended you, I want to know why."

"You haven't offended me Michael," Sarah sighed. "Like I said, I've been busy." Michael knew Sarah well enough to see that she was lying. But he would tackle the subject again once the kids were in bed. He'd been hurt when Sarah ignored his texts, and considering her a friend, wanted to fix the situation.

They fell silent as they finished their dinner, and when they were done Michael promised to clean the kitchen if Sarah bathed the children. She would have preferred to wash the dishes, but Michael had already started clearing the table, so she disappeared off to the bathroom to run the water. Fifteen minutes later both kids were clean, in pyjamas and Will had even permitted her to put a nappy on him for bed. The task had been easier than she thought, the fight finally gone out of him. Michael suggested she have a shower herself and threw her a tee-shirt of Joan's that he'd found in the clean washing basket.

When she returned, having taken the time to wash the spaghetti out of her hair she found Michael sitting on the couch sandwiched between the two children. He was reading *The Hungry Caterpillar*, a book she remembered from her own childhood. After two other books Michael declared it was time for bed and both kids obediently followed him. Sarah got Bella into bed while Michael decided it was best if he tucked Will in. Bella asked for her mother again, but with no idea of what was happening, Sarah didn't know what to tell her. All she knew after receiving a short text earlier was that the baby was a girl, but there had been no details about Joan.

Once Bella was settled, Sarah found Michael on the couch flipping through the channels. She sat on the couch opposite him and sighed loudly.

"That was hard work. I don't think I want kids if this is what it's like. And I only have to be here for one day. What's a lifetime like?"

"You'll change your mind."

"Doubt it. And why are you so good with kids? I don't think I've ever seen you with any before."

"Margaux had a niece and a nephew. They were great kids and I enjoyed their company. And children pick up on our feelings. If we're stressed, they're stressed. I was calm and it rubbed off."

"Yeah," she snorted. "I was definitely stressed," she said as she settled properly into the couch, exhausted after the day she'd had. "You don't need to stay here with me, but thanks. I couldn't have done this on my own. I think Will and I matched each other in tears this evening."

"It was fun. I'll stay a bit longer though. I still want to talk to you about why you've been avoiding me." He wondered why he was suddenly so nervous to be around Sarah and to talk to her. He didn't understand why he cared so much that she was shutting him out, but her ignoring him over the past two months had really bothered him. But it seemed that was the end of the conversation for tonight. Her eyes were shut, and from the sound of her breathing it looked like she had fallen asleep.

Chapter Twenty-One

David left Matthew and Beth, promising to let them know if there was any change in Joan's condition, and walked slowly towards the front desk. A nurse looked up from her paperwork and asked if she could help him. After giving her his details and showing some identification she directed him towards the NICU. He knew he should be excited to meet his daughter, but right now he just felt numb. Bright murals all over the walls and colourful furniture did nothing to lift his spirits and he wondered if he was the only parent who found the cheery atmosphere overwhelming. But this space wasn't for the parents was it? It was for the kids who had to be here, hurt or ill, and it made sense to make it fun for them.

When he finally found the NICU he presented himself to yet another nurses station. After telling the nurse who he was, she made a phone call and told him his daughter's nurse would be with him in a few minutes. He took a seat and waited some more. The minutes turned into half an hour before finally someone sat down beside him and introduced herself.

"Hi Mr Saunders, or can I call you David? I'm Annie and I will be your daughter's nurse for the rest of the day."

"David's fine," he responded.

"Okay," she nodded. "Sorry to have kept you waiting. I got caught up with one of the patients. David, your daughter is small, but she is doing well. I'll take you through to see her now and you can stay with her for as long as you like." She stood up and motioned for him to follow her. He found himself in a large room with several incubators. There were other parents, some holding tiny infants, some gazing at their children in their incubators. There were monitors everywhere and the constant beep of machines would be enough to drive anyone crazy. Annie stopped in front of one of the incubators and smiled at him.

"David, this is your daughter. Do you have a name for her yet?" David shook his head. "We couldn't agree. I wanted to name her after my Grandmother, but Joan thought the name Katherine sounded too royal. We already have a son named Will."

Annie smiled at him. "I think your wife might have been right. We understand she is still in the ICU for now."

"She is," David confirmed, as his voice cracked. He knew he was close to breaking and he didn't want to do it here, in front of a nurse and his new baby. He finally looked into the incubator, not prepared for just how small she was. She had miniature hands and her eyes were scrunched closed like the light bothered her. He didn't blame her. She wasn't supposed to be here yet. Her skin was like fine china, almost translucent and he could see spiderweb like veins criss-cross over her body. She was wearing nothing but the tiniest nappy he had ever seen, and he wondered if she was cold.

"My wife wants me to hold her. She said it's very important, but she's so small." He held up his hands, rough from years of construction, terrified if he held her, he would hurt her.

"She *is* too small David. Right now her skin is very delicate. That's why she isn't wearing any clothes yet."

"But isn't she cold like that?"

"The bed is perfectly heated so no, she's not cold. She's being feed through that tube you see for now. It will be a while before you or your wife can feed her yourselves, but if your wife chooses to breast feed, we will give that to your baby through the tube."

"Joan did that with both our other two babies."

"That's good. If she can – but we don't pressure Mum – it is better for the baby. Mother's milk has the right nutrients and it helps develop the baby's immunity. At the moment she's at risk of infection. A baby's immune system develops in the last few weeks of gestation, so we need to be extra careful with germs around her. But her breathing is good, and at the moment we are very optimistic that you will be able to take her home in a few weeks, maybe a month.

"If I can't hold her, is there any point me staying here?"

"She doesn't know you're here," Annie told him, recognising the emotional strain he was under, "but being here can help you to bond with her. If you need to talk to someone about how you're coping I can organise a counsellor to talk to. Or a Chaplain if you prefer."

"No, I'm okay, but thanks. I guess I'll stay for a while then." He fell into a rocking chair next to the tiny bed that was helping to keep his child alive. Across the room at another incubator a mother looked up from where she was feeding her own tiny baby and smiled at him. He guessed over the next few weeks he would get to know some of these parents who were in the same situation as him. But for now he just wanted to be left alone. He barely had the energy to keep himself together, let alone make small talk.

He watched his daughter's chest rise and fall, remembering how different it had been with his other children. Bella had been born, round and healthy. And when Will was born, at thirty-six weeks, Joan had been there, asking all the right questions and taking charge of the situation. He'd followed her lead, and her absolute certainty that their baby boy was going to be fine had been enough for him. But this time he was alone. He took his phone out again, checking if there was any word from the ICU, but there were only messages from friends and family asking how things were going. It was driving him crazy that Joan was so close, but he wasn't allowed to be with her. He dragged his attention back to his daughter, watching while Annie made notes on a chart. She looked down at him and smiled.

"It all looks good. I'll bring you a bottle of water. You look like you need it. And we have sandwiches if you're hungry, but you'll have to eat them in the parents lounge."

David shook his head, mumbling that he wasn't hungry, even though he hadn't eaten for hours. Annie moved to another incubator while David continued to keep watch over his tiny child.

~~~

David jumped when he felt a hand touch his shoulder. He realised he must have fallen asleep and was horrified at himself. He was supposed to be looking out for his child, not sleeping.

"I'm so sorry," he said and then yawned. "Has something happened," he asked.

"No David. Everything's fine. I'll be handing over to another nurse soon, so I was just saying goodbye. I'll probably see you tomorrow. But maybe you should go home for today. Your baby is settled, and you look like you could do with a meal and a real bed. We will call you if there is any change in her condition."

"Have you heard anything about Joanie?"

"No, but that's good news. Go home and get some sleep. Tomorrow you can see your wife, it's late and they won't let you in now."

"Yeah," he sighed. "I need to check on my other kids too. Thanks for everything you're doing here. I'll be back in the morning." He stood up from the chair, stretching and took one last look at his daughter, taking a photo to show Joan in the morning. Once he was outside the NICU ward he realised he didn't have his keys or a car. Matthew was probably still sitting here waiting to take him home. Poor guy, it was already eight o'clock. He pulled his phone out of his pocket, ignoring the missed calls and texts. He didn't want to read them right now and have to answer people's questions, and instead called Matthew to find out where he was.

Matthew answered on the first ring, obviously he had been waiting for his call.

"David, what's happening?" he asked.

"Can we talk about this in the car? I was just wondering where you are. I'm going to head home and come back in the morning."

"There's been a change of plans. I had an emergency at work so Adam is going to take you home. He's waiting in the chapel for you."

"Oh, okay. I'll find it."

"David, how's Joan and the baby?"

"I haven't heard any more about Joan. I can only assume that means she's okay for now. And the baby is … she's so small. But the nurse seems to think she will be alright. I can come back in the morning, but they'll ring me if there is any change."

"Okay. I'll pass that along to everyone. Do you want me to call your parents? They're frantic."

"Please. Tell them I'll call them tomorrow." He thanked Matthew and then asked a passing cleaner where to find the chapel.

~~~

Adam had been praying in the chapel while he waited for David. He had unwavering faith that God was in control of this situation, but it didn't stop him for pleading for the life of Joan and her baby. He felt a tap on his shoulder and looked up to see David, unshaven, crumpled and wearing slippers, looking down at him. Adam slid across to make space for his friend and patted the space he had just vacated. David considered his invitation for a moment and then sunk into the pew.

"Matthew says you're here to take me home. Thanks."

"It's not a problem. I also wanted to come and pray for you and Joan. And the baby. Any name yet?"

David shook his head. "We couldn't decide. We thought we had a few weeks yet."

"How are they both doing?"

"Baby's okay. Small, but no complications so far. They think she'll be fine. No promises, but at the moment there's nothing to worry about. It's Joan who's having all the problems. Her blood pressure keeps spiking, and the doctor said there's still a risk of a stroke if they can't get it under control. I wanted to stay, but they said no." David checked his phone again, paranoid he was going to miss a call, but like every other time he checked his phone, there was nothing. The not knowing was killing him. He took a deep breath in that turned into a sob. Adam sat quietly as the dam broke and David let out all the built-up emotion and fear today had brought him. When he finally took in a deep cleansing breath and the crying tapered off, he looked at Adam who understood the despair David was feeling, the anger that there was nothing he could do.

"I can't help her. They won't even let me sit with her and be there if she needs me. I don't think I have ever felt this helpless."

"When I feel lost, and hopeless the only thing I know to do is pray. You don't have to do anything, just let me pray for you and your family."

"You know I don't believe in that stuff. And if it's actually true and there is a God, why would he listen to me? I haven't exactly been his biggest fan."

"No, but *I do* believe and I'm a huge fan," Adam said. "I can start, and you can say nothing, or you can jump in if you want."

"Sure," David shrugged his shoulders, exhaustion crumbling his usual defences when it came to religion. "It can't do any harm."

Adam closed his eyes and laid a hand gently on David's shoulder. "Dear God. I know that you know exactly what is happening here today. You see everything. We ask today that you consider Joan and her new baby. You created both of them. You love both of them. We ask for protection for the baby and the best nurses and doctors to take care of her. We ask that she thrives and can go home with both her parents as soon as possible. And for Joan we ask that her blood pressure drops back to a normal, healthy rate. That there is no damage to her organs or her brain, and that she recovers quickly so she can care for her children and her new baby. Father, you hold the universe in the palm of your hand, and you hold the Saunders family there too. Amen."

"Dear God," Adam heard David whisper after a few minutes of silence. "If you are real, if you care, I'm begging you. Please save my wife." They sat there for another minute after David's heartfelt but simple prayer, and then Adam rose from his seat. It was time to get David home to his children and his bed. It was almost nine o'clock and David needed some food and some sleep. They made their way out to the now empty carpark and after swinging through a fast food drive through, Adam headed towards David's Beaumaris home.

~~~

The doctor looked at the clock. Joan's blood pressure had been steadily rising for the last hour. But at eight-forty-five it had peaked, and the experienced doctor was becoming increasingly worried. None of the medication to lower her BP worked for more than a few hours, but at least the Magnesium had stopped any seizures. Joan's anaesthetic had worn off hours ago, so now she knew what was happening to her body, and he'd seen the terror in her eyes. They'd asked her to try and remain calm, but it didn't make any difference. Her blood pressure was out of her control.

"Can we try another antihypertensive drug?" the nurse, Amelia, asked. "I'm really concerned," she said after they stepped out of the cubicle. They lost patients in the ICU, but to lose a healthy woman with a new baby was not something the nurse, or the doctor, were willing to accept.

"No, not yet. If we do, there's a high chance of overdose. She's had the maximum safe amount. Right now there's nothing we can do. I just hope someone out there is praying for her." Amelia gave him a withering look. Doctor Jamison was well known for his belief in God, but many of the other staff members couldn't understand how a man who'd studied science for so many years could believe in such an outdated myth.

"I'll stay with her and try to keep her calm. She said her headache was getting worse again, and she's becoming more agitated." Amelia opened the curtain, surprised to find Joan asleep. Since she'd woken up from her operation, she had been too distraught to sleep. When she checked the monitor, she saw that Joan's heartbeat had fallen to seventy beats a minute and her oxygen level was at ninety-nine percent. She didn't want to wait until the blood pressure cuff automatically measured the patients BP and pushed a button to make it happen. After a minute, the reading came back at one-thirty over eighty-five. It had dropped significantly, back into the safe level. Amelia stuck her head out the curtain and called Doctor Jamison over.

"Her blood pressure has dropped," she informed him. He pulled back the curtain and glanced at the monitor. All her number's looked good and she was fast asleep. Even the cuff hadn't woken her. He sent up a quick prayer of thanks to God and asked that she remained out of danger.

"Looks good, Amelia. Maybe someone was praying for her after all. Let me know if there is any change," he said as he entered the next cubicle. He would pray – like he always did – for this patient too.

Chapter Twenty-Two

When David woke the next morning there had been a second where he reached over to pat his wife's pregnant tummy. When he found the other side of the bed empty he sat up with a start, remembering the horrors of yesterday and grabbed the phone that had been charging beside the bed. There were no new messages from the hospital, but he took that as a good sign. If there was something to know they would have asked him to call them back immediately. He could hear voices coming from the kitchen and decided he needed to investigate who was in his home. Last night when Adam had dropped him off, he'd found Sarah asleep on the couch and Michael watching a movie with the volume turned low. After enquiring if there was any more news, Michael left for the night, but David didn't want to disturb the sleeping Sarah, so he'd left her there.

Last night David tossed and turned for hours until he finally fell into an exhausted sleep. It was now eight o'clock and he needed to check on his kids and then get to the hospital. He found Will in his booster seat eating a piece of toast, and Caroline brushing out Bella's hair. She was dressed in her school uniform and her new backpack was by the front door. He'd completely forgotten that today was her first day of grade one.

187

"Daddy," she said, pulling away from Caroline, who had only just managed to get her dark curls into a ponytail, and ran towards him, jumping into his arms. "Where's Mummy?"

"She's at the hospital with the baby. Did Caroline tell you it's a girl?"

"No," Bella shook her head, "she said you wanted it to be a surprise."

"Well, you have a new sister. She's very little so she can't come home for a while until she grows a bit more."

"Is Mummy going to stay with her?"

"Do you know what?" he said looking over Bella's head to Caroline, understanding she hadn't said anything, knowing she should leave it to David to decide what to tell the children. "I don't know when Mummy will be home. But I promise I will ask the Doctor when I go and visit with her later."

"Can we go and visit her too?"

"I promise to ask the Doctor that too. It looks like you're all set for school today," he said putting her back down. Joan had made sure everything was ready for Bella's first day of school weeks ago, and he was grateful for her organisational skills. Today would be easier if he knew Bella was busy at school. That only left Will to deal with. They'd hired a girl from down the road who had babysat for them in the past, to come after school each day for a few hours to give Joan a chance to rest throughout her pregnancy. But Savannah was back at school, and all day with Will alone would be too much anyway.

"If it's alright with you David?" Caroline asked, "Will is going to hang out with me for the day. If we swap cars, I can take Bella to school and Will can come to mine for a bit. That way we don't have to move the car seats. When school's over, I'll pick up Bella and bring them both back here. Beth will be here, and she can feed them and get them ready for bed. That way you can stay at the hospital as long as you like. I'll swing by the hospital once Beth arrives and swap our cars over."

"Really? You don't mind a day with this ratbag?" he said as he tousled the hair on his son's head.

"I'm looking forward to it. We have plans to spend the day in the kitchen making lots of meals to fill your freezer with, don't we Will?" He answered her with a grin and a mouth full of vegemite toast.

"I just need a spare set of keys for Joan's car if you have them, and the address for her doctor. We'll sort out someone to pick her car up today and bring it back here. Probably Tom and Beth will do it before she arrives here."

Another thing he hadn't thought about, David was grateful they had such good friends in their lives.

"Now, why don't you have a quick shower while I make you some eggs for breakfast?" Caroline offered, "and then it will be time to get Bella off to school."

~~~

When David arrived at the ICU an hour later and asked to see Joan, a nurse he hadn't met before looked at the patient list and informed him she was no longer with them. Misunderstanding her, David thought she was telling him that his wife had passed away. Seeing her mistake, she rushed from behind her desk to try and grab him before he collapsed. Another nurse put a seat under him and told him that she had been moved to maternity during the night.

"You shouldn't do that to people," David complained. "I could have had a heart attack."

"Mr Saunders, trust me, if something *had* happened to your wife we would have contacted you immediately. We actually came close to calling you, but about nine o'clock last night her blood pressure dropped, and she had a restful night. Once someone is out of danger, we move them to a ward. These beds are in high demand."

"What time did you say her blood pressure dropped?" he asked.

"I can check the chart, but Amelia, Mrs Saunders nurse, said it was about nine pm."

That's exactly when we were praying, David thought. *It couldn't be.*

"Can I go and visit her in maternity?"

"It's not regular visiting hours but let me call and check with the nurses. I think they might make an exception under the circumstances."

Relief flooded David as it began to sink in that Joan was going to be alright. He needed to see her now. He jumped out of the chair the nurse had provided for him as she made a call to maternity while he paced back and forth. She asked after Joan and then put the phone down.

"Mr Saunders, if you go to the NICU they are expecting you. Joan has been there since she woke up this morning."

David gave them a hurried thank you and then took the lift to the ground floor. He was in the children's ward within minutes, thinking about how much time he would be spending here for the next few weeks. The same nurse from yesterday saw him and let him through security. She didn't have a chance to walk him to his daughter, he knew where to find her and his wife. The sight of Joan, in a wheelchair, hair messy and still in a hospital gown was the most beautiful thing he had ever seen.

"Joan," he called quietly. He didn't want to wake up the babies, and there were other parents already there, and he didn't want to disturb them either. Hearing his voice, Joan turned and beamed at him.

"Have you seen her? She's tiny, but she's perfect."

"Just like you," he said and then leaned down to kiss her. "Are you alright? Yesterday we were all so worried. But here you are, and you look wonderful."

"Well my stomach's been cut open so that hurts, I desperately need a shower and I haven't eaten yet, but yes I feel wonderful."

"Well at least I can feed you. Tell me what you want, and I'll get it for you."

"I can't eat in here. Let's just sit with our daughter for a bit longer and then we can go. I'm sorry I scared you. It was pretty scary for me too."

"Do you remember what happened?"

"No. Most of it's a blur. I got to the doctor's office, and from there I only remember bits and pieces. Even after the caesarean things are a bit fuzzy. I woke up about midnight when they were moving me into the maternity ward and I felt much better, much clearer. The doctor must have found the right drug. They still have to do some tests to make sure there has been no damage to my liver or kidneys, but the headache is gone, and I can think clearly again. David, it was much scarier than last time. This was all so uncontrolled."

"I know Joanie," he agreed, smoothing her hair back from her forehead. "I was terrified I was going to lose you. I don't know how I would have gone on. But I have to tell you something really weird, and please don't judge me. I don't think it was the doctors who saved you."

Joan looked at her husband with confusion. How else would she have been saved?

"Adam prayed for you last night, and then I prayed for you too. It was right at the time that the nurse told me your blood pressure went back to normal."

"You did not," Joan exclaimed in disbelief and then noticed other parents' glance in their direction. She lowered her voice, and then asked, "*You* prayed? To God? To Adam's God?"

"I know. I don't believe in God. But it worked. I don't know why, and I don't know how, but here you are sitting with our daughter, both of you alive. If there really is such a thing as a miracle, then this is it."

"I wouldn't tell the doctor that. He might not be impressed to know you think a fictitious character was responsible for bringing my blood pressure back to normal. Oh, and by the way, he came down to see me in the maternity ward this morning and I told him we would name the baby after him."

He raised his eyebrows and whistled. "That's brave. What if he's called Barry or I don't know – Ross. You can't call a girl that."

"His name is Alex. What about Alexandra? Alexandra Jane Saunders."

He looked into the incubator at his tiny daughter and said, "I think it's a perfect name."

Chapter Twenty-Three

"Jay be careful," Jill yelled from the park bench she was sharing with her sister. In the last month they had come here every Saturday. Once David's parents had cut their holiday short, returning to Victoria as soon as possible after Alexandra's birth, the sisters hadn't been needed as much for babysitting during the week. But until Joan was fully recovered from her surgery, Jill and Beth had been taking her kids to the park on the weekend so they could let off some steam and give Joan and David a break from the somewhat energetic Will.

Bella claimed Jay as her best friend as soon as they meet, even though there was a two-year age gap. And Jay was so sweet that her let her follow him everywhere, which was a big deal considering she was a girl. It reminded Beth of the way Sarah used to follow Michael around all those years ago.

The change in Jay's appearance was dramatic. Jill had taken her advice, and after a couple of doses of worming tablets he started putting on weight. Playing out in the sun had given him some colour and feeling safe and secure had let him relax enough for Matthew and Jill to discover that, underneath his solemn demeanour, there was a funny little boy just waiting to be discovered.

For the first few weeks he barely spoke a word to Jill and Matthew, answering any questions they asked with a simple yes or no. Zoe had been another matter. When they were home together wherever she went he would be there too. If she was watching television he was there cuddled up beside her, clinging to her like a koala, and it was Zoe who read him a story every night before he went to sleep. At first he didn't trust either Matthew or Jill and avoided spending time with them. But he hadn't give them any problems in the first few weeks of his stay.

Christmas day had been overwhelming for him, and he spent most of the day hiding in his bedroom. The Fraser clan were a boisterous lot and after a few beers Lochie had insisted on a game of back-yard cricket. Even Zoe hadn't been able to convince Jay to join them, he instead watched from the window. Jill's heart hurt watching the little boy who was so obviously afraid of adults and she wondered what else had gone on in his mother's house that the social worker hadn't told them about or had been unaware of.

But his eyes had lit up when it was time to open the presents. Between her and Matthew, and Beth's family he'd been spoilt with new clothes and toys. That had been the first, tiny step to getting him to feel like he was part of the family.

He also settled well into school, and now that his true personality was shining through, he'd made friends. Last week he'd even been invited to the birthday party of one of the boys in his class. He spent ages trying to figure out what he was going to wear to the party, and buying the gift had been excruciating. Jill wanted to purchase whatever trendy toy was at the front of Big W where they displayed their hot ticket items. Unfortunately, Jay had other ideas and wandered up and down the aisles for an hour, trying to find something perfect that fitted into the thirty dollar budget that Jill set. He finally settled on a Transformer toy – when did they come back in fashion? – and Jill had let out a sigh of relief. Maybe next time she would give him a catalogue to look through and purchase a gift online. Shopping with kids was torture.

Mandy checked on them several times a week when Jay first arrived, but she now felt comfortable that Jay was happy and mostly left them to it. His mother had applied for, but was not being granted visitation, however the situation was going to be reassessed next month. Jill had taken Jay several times to see his grandfather Tony, who turned out to be a wonderful old man. He felt guilty that his health wasn't good enough to care for his grandson, and he was embarrassed and bewildered by his only daughter's behaviour. While he understood intellectually that her actions were out of her control, he had expected her good upbringing to override her new impulses.

Jay, who had scampered up the top of the rope-climb, turned and, holding on with one hand, waved to Jill and Beth. Before Jill had a chance to tell Jay to get down Beth turned to her.

"Jill, chill. Do you remember the parks we used to hang out in? A wooden slide with splinters and a few rope swings. There was none of this mulch everywhere for a soft landing if we fell, and there were never any parents around to make sure we were safe. Mum would tell us to get out of the house with never a thought of where we were going, and we were always fine."

"I can't believe she did that. Most Saturday's, and every day it wasn't pouring with rain on school holidays she kicked us out of the house," Jill remembered. "Anything could have happened to us."

"Nah. We were with our friends. Gangs of us riding our bikes to each other's houses or the beach. I don't think we ever had more than fifty cents in our pockets for some lollies and to make a call from a phone booth if we needed to," she laughed, remember the joys of growing up in the eighties in Australia. "Now we track our kids via their mobiles, we can spy on them on social media. And that's if they even have the time to just hang out with their friends because they're in too many classes and sporting activities so they can 'get ahead'." Beth always resisted the pressure most parents felt to sign their children up for extracurricular activities that filled their nights and weekends, and her kids had turned out just fine.

"You *can't* let your ten-year-old out unsupervised the way we were anymore. You'd be accused of neglect these days. It's sad it's come to this. Especially for the kids."

"The world has changed since we were children," Beth agreed. "I dread to think what it will be like when our kids have their own."

"Yeah. Parents probably won't let them leave the home without a chip to track them at all times."

"Sounds like a great plan," Beth replied sarcastically.

The sisters fell silent for a minute as they took a sip of their coffee and looked out over the water. Black Rock Playground had the most amazing view. The silence was shattered when Will let out a piercing yell. He'd been happily digging in the mulch with his bucket and spade beside another little boy, but it appeared the friendship was over. The other little boy's mother was bearing down quickly on the pair, and by the look on her face she was not happy that her little cherub was in a tug of war over Will's shovel. Beth and Jill gave each other a look, and both said at the same time, "Time to go."

Beth scooped Will up and gently removed the stolen spade from the other lad before his mother could give Will a lecture on sharing. Jill called Bella and Jay down from the jungle gym and after calling them a few more times, she threatened to climb up and come and get them. They finally slid down the slide together and followed Jill back to the car. They'd all come in Jill's vehicle because it was next to impossible to get a park on a Saturday morning, let along two and the cost of parking near the playground was ridiculous. The drive back to David and Joan's house didn't normally take long, but today the traffic was bumper to bumper. It looked like everyone had decided to get out and enjoy the sunny Melbourne weather. Before too long it would be freezing again, and people would be moaning about the rain and the cold.

When they pulled into the driveway a few minutes later David was outside with the lawn mower. They waved to him as he pushed it back and forward over his much-loved grass and opened the front door without knocking. They didn't want to wake Alexandra, and Joan repeatedly told them if the door was unlocked to just come on in.

They found her on the rocking chair outside in the sun. Alex – as she was already being called – had developed a bit of jaundice and the doctors recommended short periods of sunlight every day. Usually Joan would place the crib by the window, but it was such a beautiful Melbourne morning and so mild, that Joan hadn't been able to resist feeding her daughter outside on the covered deck that David built them last summer.

"Hi you two," Joan greeted them. "Where are my little terrors?"

"Jay and Bella are already in the playroom. Will is still outside with David, following behind with his toy lawnmower. It's so adorable I took a picture." Beth showed Joan the picture she'd snapped a minute ago and Joan smiled at the image of her two men. Will adored his father and copied everything he did, including everything he said. It had become necessary for David to tone down his language recently, especially when he was driving because Will heard everything and repeated it at the most embarrassing moments.

"Can one of you hold Alex while I go and put the jug on?" Joan asked.

"I'll do it," Jill jumped up, but Joan waved her back down to the outdoor couch they'd plopped into when they arrived. "I've been sitting too long. It's good to get up and move about." She handed Alex carefully to Jill and then made her way through the French doors and into the kitchen. Beth could hear her moving about, pulling out mugs and putting some biscuits on a plate.

"She's still so small," Jill whispered in awe. Alex was now a month old and had been home from the hospital for ten days. Apart from the mild jaundice she'd done very well in hospital. Her due date was still two weeks away and it showed. She was now about the size she would have been if she'd been delivered full term.

Beth watched her little sister cuddling the sleeping Alex close to her and felt deeply sad that she was never going to have a baby of her own. Beth knew how badly Jill wanted to be a mother, but she was now forty-three, nearly forty-four, so it was very unlikely to happen.

When Joan returned a few minutes later with a tray containing cups and a tea pot she confirmed that Bella and Jay were happily having their own tea party in the playroom. Well, Bella was happy. Jay was going along with it.

"I've been thinking about having a party," Joan announced after she poured the tea.

"To celebrate Alex's birth, or just 'cause you can?" Jill asked.

"For both of those reasons. I never got to have the baby shower you were planning for me, and the weather has been perfect. If we have a barbeque on a Sunday afternoon we can do it outside. David's worked so hard on the garden; I'd love to show it off."

"And we can both help you. You still need to take it easy," Beth reminded her.

"I'm fine, really. It's been a month since the operation, and I'm just so thrilled to have Alex home with us. It's so much easier than pumping milk all day and visiting the hospital to be with her."

"We're still going to help you. If we make it a potluck, you'll barely have to lift a finger," Jill said.

"And I think we better include Caroline. She is, after all, an expert on parties."

"Won't she be too busy?" Joan asked.

"No. Sarah said Event's is quiet at the moment. All the Christmas parties are over, and apart from a few big celebration birthday's coming up Sarah hasn't got much work on. March is never busy for Events." Beth pulled out her phone and tapped a message to Caroline. Less than a minute later she had a response.

"Get ready girls," Beth told them. "She's on her way."

Chapter Twenty-Four

J oan dropped a kiss on Alex's forehead as she passed her husband who was showing their daughter off to the neighbours. The backyard and house were heaving with people. Originally they'd only intended inviting their closest friends, but then decided to invite the neighbours on either side because of the noise. They then had to invite the ones across the street for the same reason, and before they knew it, everyone from the small court they lived on was coming. The staff in the office of David's construction company heard about the party and it would have been rude not to include them too. Even Phil, who worked with David for years, but usually said no to parties, wanted to be here today. He had a soft spot for Joan and still claimed that it was because of him that David and Joan got together in the end, even though it wasn't strictly true. David's parents insisted on inviting their siblings so they could met the new addition to the family and David's sister Jessica had arrived with her husband and teenagers in tow.

Even Abby, Joan's half-sister drove down from Ballarat and was staying for a few days to spend some time with her niece. Most people with a new baby would not have attempted to host such a large event, especially after all the drama surrounding Alex's birth, but Joan was in her happy place. She loved hearing her friends and family laughing with one another, children shouting in the backyard to their friends and the smell of sausages cooking. Matthew and Adam had taken charge of the barbeque and told David to go and mingle with his guests. The kitchen was full of beautiful salads and desserts, each woman trying to outdo another. This was the kind of day Joan dreamed of when she was little and even into her teenage years. Surrounded by people who loved each other and wanted to spend time together. Her heart was full.

As usual Caroline took control of the kitchen. She'd been here all afternoon putting up decorations, and filling vases with lilies and roses that perfumed the air. It still surprised Joan sometimes when she saw Caroline in her house. When they were teenagers they'd loathed each other, and each had wondered what Beth saw in the other. When they were in school both girls competed for Beth's attention, but she never let either one claim the title of best friend. She loved them equally. Maturity claimed them both and their friendship had grown slowly in the past few years and now they understood each other in a way they hadn't when they were in high school. Joan understood why Caroline was the way she was. Serious and always striving for perfection. That was the expectation of her strict, albeit distant parents and her desire to please them had driven her to do whatever she could do to win their acceptance.

And Caroline understood that Joan, unwanted by her mother and with no knowledge of who her father was, needed to be the centre of attention when she was younger. She wanted people to see her and like her. When Caroline really got to know her she admired the way Joan fought to become an architect even though she was one of the disadvantaged kids who often fell into a dead-end job because they were too busy trying to survive to have any ambition. They might never be quite as relaxed with each other as they both were with Beth – who was the glue holding everyone together – but they were good friends now.

"Out," Caroline ordered when she saw Joan heading towards the kitchen. "Go and be with your guests."

"I'm just checking that everything's alright. You might have needed some help."

Caroline tipped her head to the side and raised her eyebrows in response.

"Alright, I'm going," Joan laughed. Caroline thrived on organising a party, and anyone who got in her way, or suggested she do something different, was likely to regret ever questioning her. Joan left her to it, taking a delicious mini quiche off a platter before going to check on what was happening in the playroom. Seeing that a few kids from the street were playing happily with Bella she moved outside to visit with all the people who had been so wonderful while she was in hospital.

Lochie and Michael had commandeered a couple of chairs at the end of the garden and were catching up with what was happening in each other's life. Lochie, recently finished his electrical apprenticeship, was considering going out on his own. He said he needed a few more months working for a boss and then thought he would have enough money saved up to survive for six months while he built his business.

Michael knew Lochie well enough to know that after two beers he would be able to get almost anything out of him. He was hoping his mate would spill the beans on what was going on with Sarah. Because since he'd helped her with Joan's kids that night she'd gone back to avoiding him. When he saw her at the house working with his mum she'd been polite, but distant and the two times he'd been brave enough to ask her out for that drink he'd promised her, she claimed she was too busy with TAFE or work.

He took the top off the beer he'd snagged earlier and handed it to Lochie, who dropped the empty he had been holding on the grass. "Thanks mate," he said as he lifted it and they clinked bottles.

"How's Sarah liking TAFE?" Michael asked.

"Dunno. To be honest I don't see that much of her. She's always working when I visit the old's and we don't have the kind of relationship where we're texting or calling each other all the time. You probably see her more than I do." Michael watched as Lochie took another swallow of his drink and decided to go for it. The sooner he got to the bottom of this the better.

"I do see her at the house sometimes," he started, "but she seems to be avoiding me. I was wondering if you knew why. I thought I might have offended her, but I can't think of any reason why."

"Avoiding you, really? I would have thought she would be following you around like a puppy dog now that it's over with Margaux. She was your shadow when we were kids."

"She was *our* shadow. I always assumed she just wanted to hang out with her big brother. Isabelle was always bugging me to play with her when she was little. I don't think it was me Sarah was following around."

"Me? Nah, she couldn't stand me. Not that I can blame her. I was a bit of a jerk when I was a kid. It was you she interested in." Noting the confused look on Michael's face he said, "You do know she had a massive crush on you?"

What? Lochie thought, something finally clicking into place for him. *This was news to him.*

"Are you sure? She never said anything to me."

"Oh come on, you'd have to be blind not to notice. It was obvious to everyone else.

"I had no idea," Michael said, wondering how he had missed it. It didn't explain her behaviour towards him now though.

"Trust me. She was mad about you." He took another slug of his beer and then proceeded to tell one of Sarah's secrets. "I remember the time I caught her writing Sarah Anderson over and over again, practicing her signature. She must have been fifteen," Lochie laughed. "I bribed her out of her pocket money for a month not to say anything to you. I guess I'll have to pay her back now."

You *were* a jerk, Michael decided. But he hadn't been much better. Once he'd hit his teenage years he barely noticed Sarah. She was just a kid who got in the way when he wanted to hang out with his mate. He was surprised by Lochie's admission, but he guessed it made sense. She had always been around, trying to get his attention. She wasn't doing that anymore.

"That doesn't explain why she's avoiding me now though, does it."

"What do you expect? She was probably devastated when you came home with Margaux," Lochie said in a rare insight into his sister's feelings.

"But we broke up months ago. Why would she start ignoring me after we broke up?"

Lochie shrugged his shoulders. "Maybe she got over you. Realised you were too old, or she just doesn't like you anymore. Who cares?"

"Yeah, who cares?" Michael repeated.

~~~

Several hours into the party everyone was having a good time. Well everyone except Sarah. She'd done her best to avoid Michael, hiding away with Caroline in the kitchen when she could, and so far she'd done a good job. But more than once during the afternoon she felt like someone was watching her, and every time she turned she saw Michael's eyes on her. At one point he motioned her over, but she pretended she didn't notice and went back to cooing over Alexandra who was adorable. Maybe babies weren't so bad after all. It was just a shame they turned into toddlers.

She felt a tap on her shoulder and turned to find Michael right beside her.

"Hi Sarah. How's it going?" he asked, noticing how lovely she looked today. Her hair was caught up in a bun with a few escaped tendrils grazing her cheeks.

"Oh, hi Michael. Busy, you know."

"Really? Mum said it's quiet at the moment."

"TAFE keeps me busy."

"And are you enjoying it?"

"I love it," she replied. "I'm actually learning things I want to know. And you. How's Uni going?"

"Good. Busy too, but I'm enjoying it. I was thinking I still owe you that drink. From Christmas."

"Oh. I'd forgotten all about that." She swatted her hand in dismissal. "Don't worry about it. I'm sure you have lots of friends you'd rather waste an evening on."

"Actually, I *want* to hang out with you. I never did get to celebrate your eighteenth birthday properly. Better late than never. I insist."

"Well send me a text then and maybe we can do it in the next few weeks," she tried, hoping he would forget.

"Why don't you check your diary and we can make a time now." He opened the calendar on his phone. "I'm free on Wednesday night. Say about seven?"

Sarah reluctantly pulled her phone out of her pocket and opened her own calendar, but already knew there was nothing there. She had thrown herself into TAFE and barely saw any of her other friends since school finished. She hadn't felt like socializing with the kids she'd hung out with for years. She was over how nasty the girls could be to each other, and the boys still acted like they were twelve and should be embarrassed by themselves.

Michael looked at her screen and seeing that Wednesday night was free, took her phone from her and added drinks with Michael at seven. He set a reminder for a day before and then an hour before so she couldn't claim she forgot.

"I'll pick you up from your place," he confirmed and then handed Sarah her phone back. He didn't like how things were going between them and on Wednesday night he was going to sort it out. If she was over him there was no reason they couldn't be friends again.

~~~

Beth decided she needed to find out what was bothering Tom. He'd been standing at the back of the garden near the cubby house taking a call. After watching him for a few minutes and seeing how serious he looked, she began to worry that something was wrong. When he hung up he started rubbing the back of his neck the way he did when he was feeling stressed. She walked over to him quickly, a look of concern on her face. Half an hour ago he'd been having a great time talking to David, sharing building site disaster stories. Now he looked like he was going to be sick.

"Tom, what's wrong?"

He shook his head. "Now's not the time Beth. We can talk about it when we get home."

"But you look so concerned. Something must have happened. Did someone die?" she exclaimed. "Is it my mum?"

"No Beth," he reassured her. "No one has died. But there's a good chance they are going to wish they had by the time I'm done with them."

"Who?" Beth asked, but from the disgust on her husband's face she could make a pretty good guess. Nathan.

Chapter Twenty-Five

"Sit down!" Tom yelled.

Nathan took a seat on the couch, confused and frightened. He'd never seen his father this angry. Neither had Beth. Tom was usually the most even tempered man anyone knew, and it was rare for him to raise his voice.

They'd left the party shortly after Tom took the phone call, Beth insisting she drive home. In his current mood she worried that Tom would be a danger on the road. He sighed repeatedly the whole way, and from the back-seat Nathan and Sarah exchanged glances wondering what could have happened to made their father so angry. When they arrived back at their house Tom asked Sarah if she could please leave them alone, and relieved she wasn't the target of her father's fury, she escaped to her bedroom.

"Dad, I don't know what I've done to make you so angry," Nathan pleaded.

"Are you sure? You can't think of anything you've done recently that would upset me this much."

"I promise," he said shaking his head. "I have no idea why you're so mad."

"Then let me tell you and see if this jogs your memory. I got a phone

207

call tonight from a very distraught mother. She told me you've been exchanging unsavoury photos with her daughter."

"Oh," Nate said and then looked sideways at his mother who had sat down beside him. He saw her expression change from concern at his father's mood to disappointment and she dropped her head into her hands and exhaled loudly. It had taken months for them to get their relationship back to normal and now this. He did not want to be talking about this in front of her, and from the look on her face, she didn't want to be here either.

"Dad, can we talk about this in private?"

"I tried that with you Nathan. I've spent time with you discussing your issues and I thought we were making good progress, and then you go and do this. With a girl from school. Your mother needs to know what you've been up to, and especially because we know her parents."

"Who?" Beth asked, but she wasn't sure she really wanted to know. If this got out they would be ostracized by the other parents and Nathan might even need to move to a new school. He had just started year ten, and it would be a terrible time to make a change.

"Doreen Mitchell, Amber's mother." Beth's heart sank. Doreen was a horrible gossip. She was the mother who attended every school event and signed up for every committee, but never actually did anything constructive. She was too busy pointing out everyone else's flaws. If she made it her mission, then Nathan was finished at that school. And she wouldn't put it past Doreen to ring the Police. Tom was going to have to get in line behind her to kill Nathan.

"Dad *she* sent *me* that picture. I promise you I didn't ask for it."

"Did you look at it?"

"It just came up on my phone. I couldn't help but see it."

"And you sent her one back?"

"Only because she made me."

"Oh come on Nathan. How could she do that?"

"She said if I didn't she would tell her mother I had been asking her for pictures. But I swear I didn't. I don't like her. She's not even very pretty."

"I hardly think that's the point Nathan," Beth exclaimed. "Why didn't you tell us what was going on? Or at least say something to your dad. He could have come up with a way to handle the situation. Now we have to deal with Doreen Mitchell," Beth cried. All through this whole thing with Nathan she'd felt humiliated and embarrassed because of her son's behaviour. Now she just felt defeated. He might end up with a Police record.

"I can prove it, Mum. I never asked her for anything, and the photo I sent back wasn't that bad. It was just one with my shirt off. Nothing else."

"That's bad enough, Nathan."

"Can you please just look at my phone and you'll see I'm telling the truth." He took his phone out of his back pocket and handed it to his dad.

"You know the code. Look at my texts. It came last night, and I *was* going to talk to you about it, but I thought I'd wait until after the party. Mum was so excited about it, and I didn't want to upset her."

Tom didn't take the phone, and instead asked Beth to look. He had no intention of looking at pictures of an underage girl. Nathan put the pin in and then after finding the text messages handed it to his Mum.

At first it seemed innocent. Amber had texted the usual 'hey' and then Nathan responded with a 'hey' of his own.

'Whatcha doin'

'Watching telly'

'Wanna see something interesting' she asked followed by a selfie of her in a tank top.

Beth could see that Nathan hadn't responded and ten minutes later there was another text, this time with her only in a bra. Nathan had texted back for her to 'stop it' and that's when things got nasty. She told him if he didn't send a picture of himself without his shirt on back to her, she would tell her parents that he had asked her for the pictures. Beth saw that he had indeed responded with a picture of himself without a shirt, but his face wasn't visible.

She looked up at Tom who was staring at her. She nodded that 'yes' what Nathan had told them was the truth.

"Why would she do this?" Beth asked. "I can see that you didn't instigate anything. Unless you've deleted earlier texts?"

"I promise you I didn't. I've never even given her my number. She must have got it from someone else. And why did she do it?" He shrugged his shoulders. "It's a new thing the girls at school are doing. They think it's funny to get us boys in trouble. Especially the ones they like that don't like them back. Amber's friend Chloe told me that Amber liked me last week. I wasn't interested, and I probably should have been a bit nicer, but I said there was no way I would ever go out with her. I didn't hear anything else until last night when she sent the photo. So either she thought it might make me like her, or her intention was to get me into trouble all along. I mean, she told her mother didn't she."

Tom slipped into the chair across from them. He shook his head in disbelief. He'd heard of this on the teacher's grapevine but thought it was a false rumour. He always gave girls the benefit of the doubt and assumed it was boys that were the ones that were misbehaving. It seemed he'd been wrong.

"I'm sorry, Nathan. I should have talked to you before I flew off the handle."

"It's alright, Dad. I understand why you thought it might have been me. But I promise I've been trying so hard and I do still slip up occasionally. But I'm not stupid enough to ask a girl like Amber for a photo."

"I'm glad you're finally getting it, Nathan. Something like this could stay on your record forever.

"At least all she did was send a photo," Nathan told his parents. "I've heard at some schools there are girls saying guys have touched them, when they didn't, just to get them in trouble or to get them to do stupid stuff for them like their homework. People always believe them. But not all girls are as nice as you think."

"Apparently not. But we still have to deal with Doreen. She said she was considering going to the Police."

"Why don't you leave her to me?" Beth insisted.

"Mum let it go. I made sure I didn't get my face in the photo. It could be anyone."

"So what? Next time Amber might make an accusation that gets some-one arrested. And the Police would only need to check the number to see where the photo of you came from. It's time her mother knew what her daughter has been getting up to, and it's time Amber found out you can't go around making false claims that can ruin someone's life. Because every time a woman does that it's makes it harder for people to believe the real victims."

~~~

Beth and Doreen agreed to meet at a local coffee shop the next morning once the school day started. It would mean being late for her own classes, but this was worth it. Doreen arrived ten minutes late, and threw Beth a look of disgust before she went to the counter to place her order. She took her time, and stopped to greet a few popular mums, letting Beth know she was the one with the friends and connections in school, before she finally sat down at the table with Beth. She didn't bother with any small talk or even a hello and got straight to the point.

"I want to know what you're going to do about your son? I want to go to the school and maybe even the Police, but Amber has begged me not to.

I've agreed to that for now, but if you think he's going to get away with his disgusting behaviour you have another thing coming. I *insist* that he is severely punished."

Beth stirred her coffee and then tapped the spoon on the lip of the cup. She carefully placed it on the saucer and then picked up Nathan's phone. She opened the text messages that Amber had instigated and held the phone up for Doreen to see.

"I think you'll find your answer here. The first text on Saturday night came from your daughter. Did she fail to tell you that?"

Doreen huffed and tried to grab the phone.

"I don't think so," Beth said, making sure she had a tight grip on the phone. I can't have you deleting anything. Not that it really matters. If I decide to take this matter to the Police I will give them permission to check Nathans text log. It will show that Amber sent the first photo without being asked. It will show that she sent a second photo without being asked, that one more provocative than the first. And then it will show your daughter threatening my son. He felt he didn't have a choice."

"That can't be true," Doreen spluttered. "He must have said something in an earlier text?"

"Well I'm happy to look at the phone records to see if that's true. Because Nathan is quite certain he has never had any phone communication with Amber before Saturday night, and he made it clear earlier during the week that he had no interest in your daughter. I think you'll find he's not the one to blame here."

"Why would Amber start this? She knows better than that." Doreen shook her head in confusion. "I saw the picture of Nathan by accident yesterday when I walked in on her and Cloe looking at it, but she wouldn't let me see her phone, just told me her version of what had happened. I hate these new fingerprint phones. I have no idea what she's getting up to on it.

I don't know what to say Beth," the accusatory tone gone from her voice, to be replaced by one of embarrassment. "Obviously, I need to get to the bottom of this."

"Doreen, we've known each other a long time." Beth stopped and took another sip of her coffee. "We aren't exactly friends, but I'm sure you're a good person and a good mother. You don't want your daughter to be pulled before the school principal and you certainly don't want her facing charges for distributing child pornography. I suggest you have her delete the photos off her phone, and when you confirm that she has done that I will delete them off Nathans. Not before. And in case you were wondering, no one else has seen them. Just me and Nathan. He didn't forward then to anyone, and his father refused to look." Doreen looked relieved, if Nathan had passed them to his friends this could have got out of hand and her daughter could be in serious trouble.

"When you strode in here before, you issued me a few orders," Beth continued, "I have a few of my own. I have spoken to Nathan and he has promised not to say anything to anyone at school. He doesn't want an apology from Amber. He just wants her to stay away from him. But I do expect you to go home and have a few stern words to your daughter. You know as well as I do what happens when a false accusation is made. It can ruin someone's life. Now if you'll excuse me I need to get to school. Can I assume the matter is dropped?" She waited until Doreen nodded, not making eye contact with Beth. Beth picked up the handbag she had slung over the back of her chair and left Doreen sitting at the table, noting that their exchange had been watched by the mummy mafia as she called the group of women who ran the school behind the scenes. She wondered how Doreen would explain this to them. She was one of those people who wanted everyone a little in awe and a little afraid of her. It was obvious to anyone watching that Beth was neither. She was starting to feel a little sorry for Amber though. She couldn't imagine what the girl was in for when she got home.

~~~

"Mum, guess what happened at school today?"

"I don't know. You got an A in math's."

"Doubtful," Nathan sniggered. "I found a note shoved into my locker."

"You did? Can I assume it was from Amber?"

"Yep. All it said was *sorry, Amber*, but that's something isn't it?"

"It is. And I expect you to keep your promise not to tell anyone what happened."

"Yeah, but it would make a great story. No one would ever believe snooty old Amber would do anything like that."

"Nathan, everyone makes mistakes. And remember you promised to not say anything. Let's just hope she learns from this."

"Yeah, yeah. I won't say a word. And Mum,"

"Yes Nathan."

"Thanks for standing up for me. Mrs. Mitchell is one scary old lady."

"Yeah. Well I can be a pretty scary old lady myself when I need to be."

Chapter Twenty-Six

Michael was still trying to pluck up the courage to talk to Sarah about why she'd been avoiding him for the past few months. They'd been sitting in the quiet pub for half an hour now and he still didn't know how to broach her childhood crush without embarrassing her and looking like an idiot if Lochie was wrong about the whole thing. He was the one keeping the conversation going tonight, asking her about TAFE, work, her friends. Anything to fill the silence – except the real reason he'd asked her to meet him tonight. She answered all his questions politely, but there had been none of the easy conversation that he hoped would break the ice. And boy was she being icy. He'd hoped he would be able to slip it in that he'd heard the silliest rumour about her and that he knew it couldn't be true. She could deny it and then he could tell her he hadn't believed it anyway. Or if she confirmed it, he could reassure her that everyone had crushes, especially when they were teenagers and it was no big deal. Either way he hoped it would clear the air and they could go back to being friends. He missed seeing her smiling face around the house. When he saw her now she didn't seek him out like she used to, and he hadn't realised how much he enjoyed talking with her.

Tonight Sarah had been dismissive of him, almost rude. She checked her phone regularly and told him that she needed to leave once she finished her drink. She'd insisted on meeting him in the city bar and refused his earlier offer to pick her up. He knew he was running out of time to broach the subject, and just needed to bite the bullet and ask her. It was obvious she didn't have feelings for him anymore – she could barely stand to be in his presence.

"Sarah, the reason I asked you out tonight was I wanted to ask you about something I heard. It's funny really and probably not true. Someone told me that,"

"Michael," a voice boomed across the room, "I thought it was you." He broke off his question and looked over to see Daniel Cross, an old school acquaintance pick up his drink from the bar and stride towards their table.

"G'day Daniel," Michael said, forcing himself not to sound annoyed at the interruption. He had disliked 'Dan the man', as he called himself, when they were in school together, and couldn't imagine that was likely to change. The last thing he wanted was to have to spend any of his evening with him.

"Long time no see," Daniel replied, and the two men shook hands. Daniel, acknowledging Sarah, asked the obvious question.

"Sorry, I'm not interrupting a date, am I?"

"No you're not," Sarah answered. "This is definitely not a date. Why don't you join us?"

Are you sure?" Daniel asked, sensing the tension in Sarah's voice, and getting the impression from the look on Michael's face that this was the last thing his old classmate wanted. But Sarah pushed out a chair and Daniel who had popped into the bar for a quick drink after working late was alone, so why not? If Michael wasn't on a date with this gorgeous girl then more fool him. Daniel hadn't even noticed Michael when he first walked into the pub, it was Sarah who'd caught his eye.

"Are you going to introduce me to your friend?" he asked as he took the seat Sarah offered him.

"Daniel this is Sarah, Sarah this is Daniel. We went to school together."

"Nice to meet you Sarah," he said putting out his hand for her to shake. "And how are you Michael. I don't think I've seen you since graduation. Did you ever become a doctor?" He turned to Sarah. "That's all he ever talked about at school – he did nothing but study. No matter how hard we tried, we could never get him to a party in year twelve."

"I'm good. Still working on the doctor thing. Once I finish this year, they'll let me loose on the public. And what are you doing?"

"I'm working for an importing company as an accountant. We import food from all over the world. Specialty stuff, spices, sauces, and cheeses. We track down small manufacturers and sell to high end deli's and restaurants all over Australia. And what about you Sarah? What keeps you busy all day?" he asked, using the 'I'm totally fascinated in everything you have to say' voice he'd perfected over the years.

"I'm doing my Cert IV in commercial cooking. I work for Michael's mother, but one day I hope to have my own catering company."

"So you're learning how to run a kitchen?"

"Yep. And how to deal with staff, budgets and cooking as well."

"Sound's fascinating. And we're almost in the same business. I bring the food into the country and then you cook and serve it." He moved his chair closer to Sarah's and swivelled to face her, turning his back to Michael. "I know the owners of some of the best restaurants in Melbourne. I'd love to take you out sometime and introduce you to them. You might pick up a few tips that could help you with your future plans. I'm sure I can get you a look at some of the finest kitchens in the city."

It was a good thing Daniel had his back to Michael or he would have seen him roll his eyes. Michael was about to say that Sarah was much too busy to go out with him, when she smiled – all the way to her eyes, something Michael hadn't seen her do for a long time – and said she would love to go out.

"Aren't you a bit old for Sarah?" he blurted, even though he hadn't meant to say it out loud. Daniel turned to him.

"You're in a pub together. I guess I just assumed she was over eighteen." He turned back to Sarah with a worried look on his face. Sarah nodded in confirmation.

"I am eighteen, almost nineteen. Michael's just being like an over-protective big brother."

"Oh phew," he grinned at her. "I know it's short notice, but are you free tomorrow night for dinner?"

"Turns out I am."

"Perfect. Why don't you ring my number and then I'll have yours. He rattled of his number and a few seconds later his phone rang. He immediately put her number in his contacts after asking Sarah for her surname.

"How about I make some calls and I'll get back to you in the morning with a time and place." He took a last swig of his beer and then stood up.

"Nice to see you, Michael. Let's catch up soon. I'll let you two get back to your evening."

"No need," Sarah said as she too stood. "I was just leaving. Thanks for the drink Michael."

"Ah yeah. Are you sure you need to go? We haven't finished our conversation."

"Another time okay. I need to get some homework done."

"Are you parked far?" Daniel asked. "I could walk you to your car."

"I'd like that," Sarah replied as she grabbed her handbag from the back of the chair.

"Bye, Michael," they said in unison and then Michael was left sitting alone at the table wondering what had just happened. Nothing had been resolved with Sarah, and now he was feeling something unfamiliar. He wanted to convince himself that the sick feeling he felt in the pit of his stomach was concern that Sarah was going out with Daniel, who had always been a bit of a lad. But he didn't think it was. He couldn't actually be jealous ... could he?

~~~

Sarah wasn't as excited about tonight as she would have hoped. She'd been flattered that Daniel asked her out for dinner and grateful he'd given her an out last night from her awkward meeting with Michael. And yes, she couldn't deny that he was attractive. He looked more like a surfer than an accountant with his blonde wavy hair and deep blue eyes. And he was taking her to a new restaurant in the CBD called Perry's that was booked out months in advance, so that should have been enough to have her on cloud nine. Instead she wished she could curl up in bed and watch something funny on telly.

She'd tried ignoring Michael over the last few months but was ready to admit that it wasn't working. Her feelings for him hadn't changed or even lessened a little and she hated being distant and shutting him out. It took all her energy when she was around him to give off a detached demeanour. When he had been engaged to Margaux, she understood there was no hope for her, and she tried dating other guys. But she constantly compared any date to Michael and found them immature or boring. Since Noah, she hadn't gone out with anyone a second time, unwilling to waste their time or hers. When she found out that Michael and Margaux had broken up, she momentarily flirted with the idea that one day he might notice her, but she was too practical, too sensible to let herself think about it for long. In the past every time she hoped, every time she imagined a future with him, she hurt herself and all it did was set her back. She knew she was never going to move on if she kept pining and she finally accepted nothing was ever going to happen. He would meet someone his own age, someone clever and nice and this time he would marry her. They would have a perfect life together and Sarah would be stuck watching from the side-lines. So she renewed her determination to move on and went on dates if she was asked. Surely one day she would meet someone who would replace Michael in her heart.

It had been torture last night sitting with Michael, ignoring him. She hadn't wanted to, but she thought it was the best way to protect herself. It would be easier if he would leave her alone, but he seemed determined that they would be friends, so she was going to have to change tact. She decided last night when she got home that instead of ignoring him from now on, she was going to treat him the way he treated her. If he was going to act like she was his little sister, she was going to treat him like an annoying big brother. Hopefully then he would stop asking what was wrong, and she could get on with her life. And the next time he fell in love with someone, she would be ready. And maybe by then she might even have someone of her own.

Sarah took one more look in the mirror and decided this was as good as it was going to get. She picked up her car keys and checked the directions on her phone one last time before saying goodnight to her parents on the way out the door.

When she arrived at the famous Perry's, Daniel was already waiting at the table for her. He stood and pulled out her chair after politely kissing her on the cheek. The waiter bought over the menus and she ordered a soft drink. Daniel encouraged her to have a glass of wine, but she reminded him she was eighteen. There was no way she was going to risk her license by being over the limit.

"How did you get a table here tonight? Everyone at school is going to be so jealous of me when I tell them that I had dinner at Perry's." The restaurant reminded her of an old jazz club, dark with only small lamps at every table for lighting. A pianist played in the corner and people were sitting at the bar laughing together over the sound of ice being dropped into glasses. The only thing missing was a cloud of cigarette smoke. It was a bit like being in a secret club, the entrance hidden away down a side alley with stairs leading to an underground cellar. People walking past on the street probably had no idea the restaurant was even there.

"We import a very rare prosciutto from an artisan farmer outside of Parma in Italy. It's aged for twenty-four months and costs a small fortune. Perry's is the only restaurant in Melbourne that we supply. So they find us a table anytime we want. I've ordered the grazing plate to start with, so you'll be able to try it tonight."

"You ordered already?"

"Just the starter. Don't worry," he smiled. "I'm not *that* guy. If you want, I can cancel it and you can pick something else. I just wanted to show you the sort of things we import."

"No. Don't be silly. It sounds perfect. I was hoping to try the oven roasted Barramundi with scallops in the prawn sauce, that's all. I read a review of it when Perry's first opened. It sounded delicious."

"It is. I've had it before. And I'm going to have the Fettuccine Alla Perry. He makes it with the most delicious truffles, and the veal shank is slow cooked to perfection."

The waiter came over and took their order. Daniel poured Sarah a glass of water and they chatted about her classes and his work. This was only in his second year out of university, so he was still a junior accountant. But Callahan's Imports was growing, and he hoped he had a big future with the company.

Daniel knew how to behave on a first date. He asked Sarah about her family and told her funny anecdotes about growing up the only child of his elderly parents. He had been a much-desired surprise, so his parents spoiled him rotten. He'd attended the same exclusive school as Michael and been given every opportunity to get ahead. His parents helped him buy his first apartment in the city, but he hoped to move further out to the nearby suburbs when he had a family one day. He said he wanted several kids because even though he had been given a wonderful childhood, he'd been lonely a lot of the time, and didn't want that for his own children.

This was the first time Sarah had gone on a date with anyone who even gave children a fleeting thought, and Daniel suddenly seemed so adult. Maybe Michael was right, and he was too old for her. But it was nice to be taken seriously for a change and not treated like a kid.

The prosciutto lived up to its reputation, as had the rest of the dinner. By the time the dessert menu arrived at the table, Sarah didn't think she could eat another thing, but Daniel convinced her to split a vanilla panna cotta with berry compote. It was just as delicious as the rest of the meal and Sarah promised herself she was going to try and find a recipe for it when she got home. The evening went by quickly, and there was none of the awkward silences she had experienced on other dates. When they were finished dinner Daniel asked her if it would be alright if he called her during the week. Surprising herself, she immediately agreed. She might not have the same heart wrenching attraction for him that she did for Michael, but he was funny and cute, and she would be happy to spend another evening with him.

Chapter Twenty-Seven

"So what's on your mind David? You said you had something you wanted to discuss with me," Adam said leaning back in his chair.

David looked around the café to make sure no one could overhear him. It felt completely bizarre sitting here with Adam in the middle of the day. Sort of like a weird first date. He couldn't remember a time they'd ever gone out together alone. Yes they spent a lot of time with each other's family's and he considered Adam a friend, but their friendship was instigated by the girls. If Caroline and Joan had a falling out, they would probably never see each other again.

"Do you remember the day Alex was born? When you prayed with me in the chapel? "

"Of course. I don't think I'll ever forget that night."

"I haven't stopped thinking about it. I keep telling myself the timing was a coincidence, that Joan would have got better whether you prayed or not. But it doesn't add up. At the exact time we were praying, her blood pressure dropped and never went up again. And Alex is thriving. She could have had all sorts of health issues, but she's doing so well. It's like she wasn't born premature at all."

"So what's your question? How can I help?"

223

"I want you to prove to me that God is real and that He healed Joan."

Adam exhaled and rubbed his chin. People had been debating this issue for thousands of years and even the greatest theologians couldn't definitively prove the existence of God, especially to a sceptic. Adam's belief in God came from faith and his experiences with him, he couldn't show David a photo and say, 'here He is.'

"It sounds like you already have your proof. God healed Joan; so why are you having trouble believing it?"

David thought for a minute trying to put his long held beliefs into a sentence. "Well science, for starters. You were probably taught the same things in school as I was. Evolution, Darwinism, all that stuff. My parents didn't believe in God and I've only ever been in a church for weddings or funerals. Over the past few months I've tried to imagine God, but it feels too preposterous to believe in some Being in the sky who made the universe in a week and is controlling everything. And if it's true he's not doing a very good job of it. Look at the state of the world. Murder, abuse, people starving in poor countries and the rest of us run by corrupt politicians and corporations that make billions while their employees are just getting by. If he is real, he isn't exactly up for the Nobel Peace prize, is he?"

Adam took a sip of his coffee while he thought through David's statement. He sent a quiet prayer to God and asked for wisdom.

"Okay. So the first thing you feel is that it's preposterous to believe that one being created everything in six literal days? So instead you believe that over billions of years the earth formed itself along with the stars and other planets. They somehow manage to stay spinning in space without falling. And then there's the Sun that evolved at just the right distance from Earth to provide heat and light without boiling or freezing the oceans. We also have the Moon that is exactly the right size and distance from the Earth to control our tides. Lucky it's doing such a good job considering it was made by accident. Then you think it's credible that bacteria turned into multi celled organisms that then turned into fish and birds. Then, on their own, they changed into animals that eventually evolved into humans. Please don't take offense because I promise I'm not trying to sound condescending. But you have no problem believing all of that? Now in my opinion, *that* takes a lot of faith. That accident, after accident, after accident resulted in all of this," Adam said.

"Fair enough. When you put it like that it does sound a bit farfetched. But no more than the idea of God. I bet you can't tell me where He came from. As far as I can tell, nobody can."

"You're right. I have no idea *how* He is. For me He always was and always will be. I accepted a long time ago that I won't know. That's faith. But can you explain to me where you think the building blocks of the universe came from? Where the bacteria that evolved came from? How did imperfect environments and creatures exist long enough to evolve without dying out, because they wouldn't have been evolved enough to reproduce perfectly? If things aren't working properly reproduction doesn't happen. And where are all the fossils of the in-betweens?"

"There's that Lucy fossil they found back in the seventies. She was halfway between ape and human," David said, remembering some of his year ten science.

"When I first considered that God might be real I did some research on evolution. I even wondered if both could be true. Maybe that God started the process, but he let it take billions of years. We were both told in high school science that Lucy was the missing link. What they didn't tell us was that an intact skeleton wasn't found. They found a scattering of bones. The knee joint they claim belonged to Lucy is actually from a human and was found over 800 feet away from the other bones. Almost all of the skull was missing, and they reconstructed it out of plaster and put the few bone pieces they found in so it would look the way they imagined it should. The pelvis was reconstructed after sawing parts of the bones off and the wrist bones attributed to Lucy showed that the fossil did not walk upright like a human, but on all fours like an ape. Even Darwin questioned why there weren't humanoid fossils all over the place. They just don't exist."

David considered Adam's answer for a minute. He had always believed what he had been taught in school and hadn't considered for a moment that it could be incorrect. But then they called it the *theory* of evolution, not the facts of evolution, didn't they. He was definitely going to need to look further into what Adam had just told him.

"Alright. Say for arguments sake I believe you. Lucy was faked, or at least wrongly identified and evolution is all just a big lie. Your God created the universe in six days and is in charge of the whole show. It still doesn't answer why the world is such a mess. If I was in charge, if I was God, I would want my creation to be a wonderful place to live. Nobody would get sick or die. There would be no hate or poverty. Why does he let these things exist? Why is there evil if God's supposed to be this perfect being? Where's the love Adam?"

"Simple. Free will. Let me ask you this. Did Joan choose to love you or are you forcing her to?"

"She chose to love me."

"That's right. And you chose to love Joan and your kids. But what kind of relationship would you have if she had no choice? It wouldn't be love. And think about that for a second. A human's ability to love, think, decide. We have been created with emotions and thoughts. We can create and invent. Our bodies work every day as long as we keep putting food and water into it. Yes, we can get sick and at some point, we will die. But for the most part everything just happens. We don't have to think about breathing. And amazingly, the air we breathe is perfect for us. If the chemical composition was out by a fraction, we would all die. So if evolution was true, how would it have worked with all these different systems changing independently and at different times, but still working perfectly together with nothing controlling them. And how did they all independently manage to be perfect for sustaining human life. For me it's like it was all created in unity by one master designer and in the perfect order to sustain human life."

"Maybe. I don't know. Who says these things can't these things just happen over time?"

"Let me give you an example you might relate to. If you put all the building materials of a house on a block and walked away, how many years do you think it would take for the house to build itself."

"Come on. You know a house can't build itself," David said.

"What about if you added all the tools needed. How long then."

"It would never get build. Eventually the materials would rot, and the tools would rust. Without a design and someone to build it there will never be a house," David confirmed.

"Exactly," Adam said, watching it dawn on David's face that he knew a house couldn't build itself, but he believed that the entire universe was created with a whole lot less.

"So you honestly believe your God created everything and then let us choose to reject Him if we want? And you really believe he healed Joan?" David shook his head, still unwilling to believe it was even possible, let alone probable. "Why would he do that, save Joan's life when I don't believe in him and neither does she?"

"What if He loves you? And this was His way of showing you that love and proving to you that He does exist."

David finished off his coffee before answering, thinking through Adam's statement.

"If that's true and He does exist, then He certainly has my attention."

~~~

David had been tossing and turning for over an hour. He'd thought about his conversation with Adam for the rest of the day and hadn't been able to concentrate on work. Thankfully, Phil picked up two mistakes in a quote he was working on for a block of units they were pitching for. The mistake would have cost him thousands.

Before they left the coffee shop Adam had told David to call him day or night if he had any questions. It was already eleven o'clock and it wasn't fair to ring this late, but he knew he wasn't going to sleep. He'd thought about the evolution thing all day and when he dissected it, he found very little validity in the theory. He was turning fifty next month, more than half his life over and here he was considering that he might have been misled for most of it.

He quietly slipped out of bed and then shut the door behind him, making his way silently through the house. Alex was due to wake up soon to be fed, so the last thing Joan needed was to be woken early. He grabbed his phone from the bench where it had been charging and decided to take Adam up on his offer. He switched on a lamp before sinking into a chair in his home study. The room was far enough away from the bedrooms that his voice wouldn't disturb his family. He found Adam's contact in his recent calls and dialled it. His phone only rang three times before his call was answered.

"G'day mate. You're still up?"

"I hope I'm not disturbing you. I had a few more questions and I know it's late, but I couldn't sleep."

"No problem. I was up. What did you want to ask me?"

"The whole Jesus thing. I know nothing about him except what I've heard in Christmas carols."

Adam had been waiting for the New York stock exchange to open after the weekend which was why he was still up. He'd made some great investments last year that were doing really well, and he wanted to see how they opened for the week. The US market was making gains every day and Australia's market was following quickly behind. He was making a lot of money at the moment for himself and for his clients.

He'd wondered if his chat with David had fallen on deaf ears today, but obviously something he said had hit home. He had continued to pray for David during the rest of the day and it looked like God had continued working on him.

"I'll try and keep this simple. Jesus is God's son. He entered into his own creation by being born to the virgin Mary as God in human form. He remained sinless while He was here, and when He was thirty-three, He was crucified by the Jewish leaders of the time. They did this because of His claim that He was the son of God, but His death had been God's plan all along. A blood sacrifice was needed so we could receive forgiveness for our sins. So Jesus willingly became that sacrifice. He died so we could be reconciled to God. And then three days later He rose from the dead. Anyone who believes that He died for their sins and repents will be saved. Instead of going to hell when they die, they instead go to heaven to spend eternity with God. But it's not a get out of jail free card. Repent means to turn away from sin. None of us will ever be perfect, but with God's help we can walk away from sin and become a new creation."

"But Adam, I'm a good person. If God's so loving – like you suggest – why would He let good people go to hell? I get it if He sends murderers or rapists there. But why, if this place is real, and I can tell you I find it hard to believe it is, would ordinary, good people end up there. Most of us humans are just trying to get by. I provide for my family, I don't cheat on my wife, I even pay my taxes. What have I done that's bad enough to send me to hell?"

"Have you ever lied?"

"Of course. Who hasn't?"

"Lying is a sin. So is murder, adultery and stealing. But God doesn't grade our sins from one for tiny infractions and a ten if we do something really terrible. He's perfect, so he can't look at us in our sinful state, and he judges all sin the same. But the sacrifice that Jesus made means that if we ask for forgiveness and become clean, God can see us through – let's say – a perfection filter. And He tells us that when we ask Him for forgiveness, He literally forgets our sin. And as hard as it might be for you to believe, once I asked God for forgiveness and understood what Jesus had done for me, I didn't want to do those things anymore. Don't get me wrong. I stuff up. I get angry, I have bad thoughts. I'm not always as loving towards people as I should be. But over the past six years these things have lessened."

"It sounds *exhausting* trying to be perfect all the time," David said. "I don't think I'm up for that, or even want to try."

"When you married Joan you stopped seeing other women right? Is that exhausting? No. You do it because you love her, and it's not even an effort. You know me David. I'm not perfect. But when my attitude changed so did my actions. My relationship with Jesus defines me. He created me so he knows I'm not perfect and never will be. But little by little I am changing, and He helps me to become more like Him, and I *want* to be like Him. I can't wait until the day I stand before God at the end of my life and He tells me 'well done son'. That's what I want most in my life now. To one day hear those words from God."

David fell silent. His head was spinning with all sorts of thoughts. What would people think of him if he decided this God thing wasn't a myth after all? But if it was true, then who cared what other people thought? And then he was back to worrying about having to tell his parents and his friends who would think he'd lost his mind. And then he flipped back to wondering why he cared so much. Why go to hell because of stubborn pride? And what about his children? If he never told them about God and it turned out the whole thing was true, was he making sure they would be in hell with him?

"You've given me a lot to think about. And thanks for picking up the phone. I'm not sure your answers are going to help me to get any sleep though."

"Like I said, call me any time. I'm happy to answer your questions. And David, do you have a Bible?"

"Ah, no. I don't think so."

"Then do me a favour. Google psalms chapter eight."

"Salms eight. Okay. Night Adam."

"Night David."

David was even more unsettled after the phone call and after checking on each of the children he stepped out onto the back porch. He wrapped his dressing gown tighter around himself. April was turning out to be chilly and he predicted a cold winter. As he stepped out further, the security light went on and lit up the backyard. He saw that the maple's leaves were turning a beautiful rust and soon they would fall off and highlight the amazing architecture of the tree and its branches. The azaleas were in full flower and the grass was a deep emerald after the recent rains. When he looked at his garden through Adam's eyes he could almost believe that this had all been created by a clever designer. It was getting too cold to stand outside and he decided he'd better go in and look up the reference Adam had given him before he forgot it. After a few tries at spelling psalms he pulled up chapter eight on his phone. When he read verse three he felt like it had been written just for him. The David who had penned it all those years ago was speaking to him now.

Rebecca Pater

When I consider Your heavens, the work of Your fingers. The moon and the stars, which You have ordained. What is man that You are mindful of him, and the son of man that You visit him? For You have made him a little lower than the angels,

And You have crowned him with glory and honour. You have made him to have dominion over the works of Your hands: You have put all things under his feet, All sheep and oxen —even the beasts of the field, the birds of the air, and the fish of the sea that pass through the paths of the seas. O Lord, our Lord,

How excellent is Your name in all the earth!

Chapter Twenty-Eight

“I think that's about it. Carrbridge house is booked for the fourth of May. The caterers have the menu and you did post the invitations didn't you?" Caroline asked, looking up from her list, but knew Sarah would have done it the minute they were ready to go out.

"Yes of course. A week ago. RSVP's are coming to my phone or email and we already have thirty people who responded yes. David's fiftieth is going to be the best party we throw all year."

Caroline and Sarah had been working on the event for a few weeks. Joan originally planned on throwing a surprise party for David like the one Tom threw for Beth seven years ago. But as the invite list grew, she realised there was no way she would be able to keep him from finding out. His mother, lovely as she was, had no capacity for keeping a secret from anyone and Joan quickly realised it was much easier to tell David she was planning a party. And with three young children, it didn't take long to figure out she would never be able to manage everything herself, and decided to hire Events by Caroline. They'd been given the friends and family discount and now everything was running smoothly. All Joan needed to do was turn up.

Carrbridge House, and Bridget and Alistair – the somewhat eccentric owners – were almost part of the family now. Beth's fortieth birthday had been held at the venue, as had Joan and David's wedding. It was where Matthew and Jillian first met during said wedding, and where they celebrated their own nuptials eighteen months later.

Matthew and Jillian's wedding had gone about as smoothly as Joan and David's. Except that this time instead of digging through the water pipe and leaving the property without water for a few hours, Alistair left the gate open to the paddock where the goats were kept. When Caroline arrived to put the finishing touches on the ballroom and check that the caterers were under control she found all the hard work she'd done the day before and earlier that morning undone. Being November, Jill and Matthew had decided on an outdoor ceremony. Caroline spent hours arranging all the chairs and setting up the urns of flowers that had been delivered, before racing home to get changed and have her hair done.

When she arrived back at Carrbridge three hours before the ceremony, expecting to do nothing more than tweak a few things and make sure the waiters and cooks had turned up, she found goats running amok. The flowers had all been eaten and the goats were now chewing on the crisp white bows that Caroline lovingly tied to the back of every chair. When she started yelling at the goats to get away, one of them crouched down and urinated all over the white carpet that she'd laid down the aisle. Alistair, hearing Caroline's yelling and the goats bleating at the mad woman who was trying to chase them off, tried to round up the goats and return them to their paddock. Of course the three goats scattered in different directions. It had taken Bridget with a broom and two of the wait staff to help Alistair get them back into their paddock where they belonged. But it was too late, and the damage was done. This was Events by Caroline's first official wedding and she'd planned on letting the guests know she was available to hire for parties of their own. Who would want her now?

But Caroline being Caroline, after allowing herself a minute of despair, decided she wasn't going to be defeated. She ordered Alistair to remove the runner from the isle and after he slung it over the clothesline he was able to pressure wash the stain off. After a quick towel dry, Bridget was ordered not to move until she had it completely dry, courtesy of a hairdryer. If it had been winter there would have been no hope.

While the runner was being attended to, Caroline raced into nearby Mornington and raided the flower shops. She visited every florist and scavenged just enough white flowers to replace the goat's lunch and then she made her final stop at a Fabric Box. She bought out every bolt of white organza they had, and then drove faster than she ever had back to Carrbridge House. With minutes to go before guests started arriving, she managed to replace the chewed bows on the back of the chairs. They were not as perfect as she would have liked, but it would have to do. As people milled around the rose garden with a glass of champagne in hand, Alistair and Caroline returned the now clean and dry runner to the centre aisle and no one had any idea that disaster had again been averted. They really should have learned by now and found somewhere else to hold their events, but the friends loved the place so much, and it certainly gave them funny stories to tell about their parties. Tom still grumbled occasionally about being ordered to fix the plumbing just hours before Joan and David's wedding. But he hadn't had a choice. Caroline had ordered him, and he knew it wasn't worth his life to let her down.

Caroline was hoping that this time everything would go to plan. Bridget and Alistair were much too old to be running Carrbridge house, and their great niece had emigrated from Scotland to take over the business with Bridget promising she was a very capable woman. Caroline would be meeting Shona next week to discuss how she wanted the ballroom organised, so she would get to size her up then. She couldn't be more disorganised than her Aunt and Uncle though.

Sarah's phone pinged and she saw that it was another RSVP. It was from Michael and he added that he was bringing a date. Sarah pulled out the printed page with the list of the invited guests and put a tick beside Michael's name and then added the name, Emeline Thompson, beside his. David's fiftieth was a sit-down dinner with a DJ and dancing after. She would need to account for 'plus ones' to make sure the numbers for dinner were right, but inevitably someone would bring a date at the last minute and not tell them.

"That's thirty-two now."

"Huh?" Caroline looked up from the menu she had been tweaking. These days every second person had some sort of allergy or refused to eat meat. The new vegan trend was really throwing a spanner in the works for her. It was easy to adjust a meal for a vegetarian, but the vegans couldn't eat much of anything and it was hard to come up with delicious food that looked as good as the regular meal and didn't take hours to make for only one or two people. Caroline was considering hiring a new cook who could focus on making just the specialty meals or even outsourcing these meals because it was cutting into the bottom line. But she didn't have much of a choice in the matter. If she fed someone peanuts who was allergic she could be sued.

"Michael's just RSVP'd with a guest. So now we're up to thirty-two."

"Who's he bringing?"

"Emeline Thompson. Do you know her?"

Caroline stopped before she answered, not wanting to upset Sarah. Michael had been seeing someone he referred to as Emmy for a few weeks now. Neither she or Adam had met her yet and he'd told them very little about her. All they knew was that he had met her at Uni.

Caroline shook her head. "No, I haven't met her. Probably just a friend."

"It's alright Caroline. I'm completely over him. I've been seeing Daniel for a month now, and we're having a lot of fun. I'm not going to get upset because Michael is dating someone."

"And you're happy with Daniel? He's a few years older and from what Michael has said he had a bit of a reputation in high school."

"Older is good. I'm not wasting another moment on teenage boys. And if you're worried about *my* reputation, don't worry. I've made it very clear to him that I have no intention of having sex with him. A very wise woman convinced me that nothing good comes from sleeping with someone you aren't married to, and how wonderful it is to wait."

"Well, your Mum will be very proud of you, and thrilled you took her advice," she replied, surprised at Sarah's honesty with her.

"Mum," Sarah snorted. "Doubtful. It was Joan who told me that. When I turned sixteen she took me out for a coffee and told me what she had been like when she was in her teens and twenties. And how unhappy it had made her. When she decided she was never going to sleep with someone again until she was married she said it took so much emotional pressure and expectation off her. She would know that any guy who didn't respect her decision wasn't worth her time or her love. And that when David agreed to wait until they were married she knew that he really did love her. Any guy that thinks he's going to pressure me won't last long."

"Well your mum will still be proud of your decision even if it the advice didn't come from her."

"Oh don't get me wrong," Sarah rolled her eyes. "She gave me plenty of advice. Even Dad sat me down for the 'all boys are after is sex' talk, and that was one torturous conversation I never want to repeat. I understand what they were saying and why they were saying it. And I've spent enough time in church youth groups to hear all the lectures, and I don't disagree with them. But my personal choice is based on what I've seen. People break up all the time. It's almost always the girl left with the tattered reputation, especially when they're young, while the guy looks like a hero to his mates."

"And do your friends agree with you? From what I've seen lately of kids your age, you must be a minority."

"To be honest, I haven't really discussed it with them. I brought it up once, but they teased me and said I'd change my mind the minute the right guy came along. Morals don't go down so well when you're a teenager. And yet they all have failed relationships behind them, and I saw the other day that one of my classmates is pregnant. She's all over Facebook saying how wonderful it will be to become a mother so young and that she doesn't need a man in her life. I feel sad for that baby. What kind of life will it have without a dad?"

Caroline had been in the same situation when she became pregnant with Michael. Adam could have abandoned her, and she would have been alone with a baby and have no support. Her parents would never have helped her. An unwed, pregnant daughter would have bought shame to them and they would have disowned her. She was fortunate that Adam stepped up and married her and together they had forged a wonderful life. Of course there had been up's and downs over the years, and Isabelle's death had almost destroyed them. But they loved each other, and with God at the centre of their relationship now, they would overcome any difficulties that came their way. And while she knew the way their marriage started, with her getting pregnant on purpose in the hope of holding on to Adam hadn't been the best start, she could never regret becoming pregnant. But with age she realised things could have turned out very differently. She just wished she'd had half the maturity Sarah was showing when she was her age.

"You never know. It might turn out alright. Maybe the dad will play a role in his child's life."

Sarah shrugged her shoulders, knowing the guy and understanding that the last thing he would ever do was take any responsibility. "Maybe," she said. "But I never intend to find myself in a situation like that."

Chapter Twenty-Nine

Matthew and Jillian had been dreading it all week, but they knew they had no choice. Jay's first visit with his mother was happening and there was nothing they could do to stop it. Mandy agreed to let them drive Jay to his Grandfather's house instead of taking him herself. She would collect Jay from their car and Matthew and Jill would wait down the road while the two hour visit took place. That way if there was a problem with the meeting they would be there to comfort Jay and take him back to their own home, while Mandy dealt with Jay's mum. Mandy wasn't sure about the visitation, but her boss insisted that the child should be allowed to see his mother in a supervised setting. Martha seemed to behave better when her father was around so it was decided Jay would visit with the two of them together, while Mandy observed. If it went well there would be more visits and Mandy had already warned Jill that Jay's mother intended to apply to have him returned to her.

Jay's mum had agreed that if Jay was returned to her she would give up her home and they would both live with her father. That way if any problems arose, Jay's grandfather could notify the authorities and he would be there daily to make sure Jay was being fed and properly cared for. Combined with getting herself a job in a local warehouse packing orders for delivery, and promising that she was taking her medication, Jays mum had a good shot at getting custody.

Five months had gone by since Jay had seen his mother. He'd cried for her when he first arrived at the Brook's house, but it had been a long time since he had done that. His teacher who was pleased with how Jay had settled into his class, told Jill that he was exceptionally bright, catching up to the rest of the class quickly after the weeks of school he'd missed the previous year.

Jillian did her best not to love Jay the way she had with Sam and Kelly, but he made it impossible not to. He'd transformed from shy and afraid to bubbly and confident. He loved playing tricks on them and more than once Zoe had chased him around the house after he'd hidden behind a door and jumped out at her in the dark, thinking it was hilarious fun. He no longer avoided Matthew or Jillian like he did when he first moved in and was now part of the family.

But now with talk of returning him to his mother permanently, Jill felt like her heart might break all over again. She knew it was selfish to want to keep him forever, but she couldn't help it. She didn't want to return him to his mother. Mandy told them they would need to wait and see how today's visit went before any decisions would be made, but there would probably be more contact in the future now that Jay's mother was complying with her doctor's orders and working in a stable job again. Jillian wanted the best life for Jay, but she couldn't see how living with his mother would provide that. He had been so unhappy when he arrived at their house. Now he was settled with their family – had become a part of it – and they were probably going to lose him. She couldn't keep putting herself through this.

Jillian tried to concentrate on the book she was reading while they waited for Jay's visit to finish. She read the same page over and over but still had no idea what was happening in the story, that only last night had gripped her attention. Matthew was reading emails on his phone and had taken two work calls even though it was a Saturday. Jillian checked the time again and saw that there was only five minutes left of the visit. She hoped they wouldn't be kept waiting too much longer. Zoe was at a friend's house – Jillian didn't like leaving her at home alone yet – and they were expected to collect her in about an hour.

The quiet of the afternoon was broken by the sound of a siren. At first it was distant, but very quickly it drew closer and then Jillian saw the flashing lights as an ambulance sped into the street. It passed their car and continued on down the short street, pulling into the driveway of Jay's grandfather's house. Jillian and Matthew took one look at each other and then flung open their car doors. As Jillian ran, the phone that she was still holding rang and she saw that it was Martin.

"What's happened?" she begged as she stopped, puffing wildly. Matthew who was fitter continued running, wishing they'd parked closer to the house, but they hadn't wanted to be seen by Jay's mother.

"Can you come to the house? You need to take Jay home."

"Is he alright Martin?" she yelled, panicked.

"He's okay. Just frightened. It's Martha."

"We'll be there in a minute," she confirmed but she could see Matthew had already reached the house and ran in just behind the paramedics.

Jillian doubled her efforts and arrived at the house barely able to breathe. She found Jay and Martin sitting together in a lounge room at the front of the house. Jay was crying and Martin looked shocked and pale. Jill joined them on the couch and pulled Jay into a hug, relieved they both appeared to be okay physically. Matthew was nowhere to be seen, and Jill assumed he was trying to find out what was going on.

Matthew ran into the house, not noticing Jay or Martin in the front room, and found Mandy sitting at the dining table. She had blood all over her shirt and she looked distraught. Through the door Matthew could see two paramedics working on a slight woman who was lying on the kitchen floor. Her blonde hair was fanned around her face and she too was covered in blood.

"Mandy," Matthew said gently, not wanting to frighten the young women who hadn't noticed him take a seat opposite her. She looked up at the sound of his voice, and when she saw his concerned face she began crying.

"Mandy, what happened?"

"She ... so much blood," Mandy wailed and then her steady stream of tears turned into sobs.

Matthew could see that he wasn't going to get any information out of the social worker and decided to try the paramedics. He got up from the table and walked to the kitchen door. The floor was strewn with tea towels covered in blood and the paramedics were lifting Jay's mother onto the stretcher, her lower arms wrapped in bandages.

"Can you please tell me what's happened?" he asked.

"Who are you?" the male paramedic asked.

"I'm the foster parent of this women's little boy. He was here for a visit with her."

"I'm sorry, sir. We can't give you any information. We're going to transport her to hospital." He gave Matthew the name of a nearby emergency and suggested he find a relative who could talk to the doctors after she was admitted. They began pushing the stretcher out through the kitchen and past the dining room. When they walked past the lounge room Matthew heard Jay start to cry hysterically while Jill tried to hold him back from touching his mother who appeared to be unconscious.

Matthew strode down the hall and picking up Jay, held him close, turning Jay's view away from the paramedics as they loaded his mother into the ambulance. The ambulance pulled out of the driveway and as they headed down the street they turned the sirens back on. That was obviously not a good sign if they needed to get where they were going quickly.

"Jill, I need to talk to Mandy. Can you please take Jay home?" Matthew turned to Martin. "You can stay with us for a few days. Why don't you go and quickly pack a bag."

"I don't want to put you out," he replied, but Matthew could see from they way his hands were shaking that the old man was distressed and there was no way he was going to allow Martin to stay here alone.

"Martin, Jay needs you. You will be doing us a favour. Go grab some clothes and your toiletries. And if you need any medications grab those too."

"I can't," he shook his head. "I keep them in the kitchen. I can't go in there."

"Then tell me where to find them," Matthew told him gently. "I'll get them for you. Go with Jill and I'll see you at home as soon as I can." Matthew returned Jay to the couch beside Jill while Martin directed Matthew to where he kept his medication in the kitchen.

Matthew turned back down the hall and headed to the dining room. Mandy was still sitting at the table, but she finally had her crying under control. Matthew decided to try again and pulled out the chair opposite her.

"Mandy, Jill is taking Jay and Martin back to our house. He can't stay here." Mandy nodded her consent but didn't offer any explanation for what had gone on this afternoon.

"You need to tell me what happened. I can't help Jay if I don't know. You were supervising a visit with his mum. Was it going well?"

"Yes," she replied, finally finding her voice. "I had just checked the time and said that we needed to be leaving in a few minutes. I don't normally supervise visits on the weekend, but Martha has only just started her new job and didn't want to ask her boss for time off during the week. I have a party to go to tonight and wasn't going to have enough time to get ready if the visit ran over," Mandy explained unnecessarily. "Martha asked if we would be able to do this again next week and I said it would be up to my supervisor, but that we would have to make a time during the week next time if a visit was approved. And then she asked if Jay could stay a bit longer. I told her no, the visit needed to come to an end, and that's when she started becoming agitated. Pacing around the room and mumbling to herself. I could see that Jay was becoming upset by her behaviour, so I guess he's seen it before. I was about to say goodbye and walk Jay back to your car, but then Martha went into the kitchen after telling us she was going to get a glass of water. She shut the door behind her, but I could hear the water running and didn't think anything about it. Jay was telling his grandfather about his first game of footy this morning at Auskick so I decided to wait until Martha came out of the kitchen so they could say goodbye. I guess a few more minutes went by and then we heard a thump. I ran in and found Martha on the floor."

"Did Jay see her?"

"He did. It was awful. She had blood all over her. She'd cut her wrists, there was a knife beside her. I grabbed a tea towel and Martin gave me more, and then I yelled at him to call an ambulance and get Jay out of the kitchen."

"There was a lot of blood Mandy. I could be wrong, but I wouldn't have thought someone would bleed that much that quickly."

"Her wrists were a mess. She hadn't cut once, but multiple times, crisscrossed all over her arms. I tried to stop the bleeding."

"I'm sure you did Mandy. You did the right thing, but this must be a shock for you. Is there someone I can call for you? Your boss or even a friend. I don't think you should drive right now."

"I'll call my boss. I need to report the incident to him. He's going to be furious." Mandy pulled her phone out of her handbag and after looking through her contacts, connected a call to her boss's mobile number.

Leaving her to it, Matthew went into the kitchen, stepping over discarded tea towels to get to the cupboard where Martin said he kept his meds. After finding them he surveyed the kitchen. Someone was going to need to clean up the mess before Martin could come home. He let out a heavy sigh. What a disaster. Martin was such a nice old guy, thrown into a horrible situation, along with Jay, and even Martha. No one was to blame; this was one of those things that nobody could control. He checked that the back door was locked before returning to the dining room and heard his phone ping. It was a message from Jill saying that they were about to leave, and did he want her to wait, or come back for him once she had Jay settled. He replied that he would catch a cab home once he got Mandy sorted.

She looked up when he returned from the kitchen and said that her boss had been informed and was going to meet her in the office in half an hour. Matthew suggested he drive her to work in her own car and Mandy gratefully accepted his offer. After finding a set of keys he locked the front door behind him. Now that the practicalities had been handled his thoughts turned to Jay. What would it do to him, seeing his mother like that? He had only recently started feeling safe. They were going to have to start all over again with him.

~~~

Martin hadn't moved from the couch since they arrived home. He'd called the hospital and was told that Martha was in a stable condition. They had been able to stitch up her self-inflicted injuries, which thankfully were not as serious as first thought. The doctor asked about Martha's mental state, and when he was told about Martha's history he promised to contact the doctor treating her and together they would start to make some decisions about her care. He did inform Martin that after consulting a psychiatrist who was on staff, they would be admitting her on a forty-eight hour hold for her own safety.

"Martin," Jill said, pulling him back from his daze. It's time for dinner."

"I'm not very hungry but thank you."

"I know. But it would be good for Jay to see you. He's very traumatized. I've finally got him to agree to come downstairs and eat."

"Alright love. And thank you for letting me stay here tonight. I ... I don't think I could have faced that mess. I'll go back tomorrow and sort it. I'll be out of your hair before you know it."

"Martin. It's already been taken care of. I have a friend who promised to go and clean it up tomorrow, but even then we aren't letting you go home until you're ready. Jay needs you, and you need Jay."

"But you don't even know me."

"Doesn't matter. Jay is part of our family, so that makes you part of it too. What we need to concentrate on is getting Jay back to where he was before today and making sure that Martha gets the help she needs."

Martin rose from the couch and Jill tucked her arm under his. Together they walked into the cosy kitchen where Matthew and the kids were waiting. He hadn't realised how hungry he was until he was greeted with the scent of a freshly cooked roast chicken. He also hadn't realised how lonely he'd been until he saw concerned faces looking up at him. This had been one of the worst days of his life, and yet the kindness of these people that he barely knew warmed him in a way that he hadn't felt since his wife had died all those years ago.

Chapter Thirty

S arah finished putting the last of the place cards out. She knew she should have seated Daniel and Michael on the same table so they could catch up, but she had no desire to spend the evening with Michael and instead put him and his date somewhere else. Yes, she was over him, but she didn't want to watch him fawning over a new girl. That would be too much.

She'd been dating Daniel for almost two months now and at first it had been going great. They had a lot of fun together, and he'd introduced her to restaurants all over Melbourne. She had even been allowed into some of their kitchens during the day while the apprentices and assistant chefs prepped for the night ahead, arguing good naturedly over who was faster at chopping an onion or whose sauces were better. Most people might find it boring to watch pasta being made by hand, but for her it was heaven.

The best visit by far though was the day Daniel took her to the warehouse where Callahans stored the hundreds of specialty items they imported from around the world. She had been able to taste different cheeses and cured meats inside a specially built temperature controlled room. On crusty bread she tried small batch chutney's and jams, and finished with sweet delicacies that she had never heard of before. She had eaten just one sublime chocolate from Switzerland that had made it into one of her dreams, but at one hundred dollars for a tiny box, she was going to have to stick with Dairy Milk for the time being. Caroline had been jealous when Sarah described the shelves laden with exquisite treats, and made her promise that if she was ever invited back she would sneak her in too.

Daniel had been incredibly respectful of her physically at the beginning of the relationship, but recently he'd begun dropping hints about his expectations. Sarah understood where he was coming from and what he wanted. He was nearly twenty-three with a string of girlfriends behind him and had probably slept with most of them. Sarah liked Daniel, but nowhere near enough to even consider changing her very firm rule about no sex before marriage, and she knew that this relationship was definitely *not* heading anywhere near marriage. Not for her anyway. After a date they would engage in a little kissing in the car before she thanked Daniel for the night out and went inside her house alone. It was easy for now because she still lived with her parents. Daniel could hardly expect her to walk him past Beth and Tom and into her bedroom. She'd resisted going to his apartment so far, insisting he drop her home after a date, but he said it was time she saw where he lived, and he thought it would be romantic to spend an evening alone, promising to cook dinner for her.

Sarah knew the pressure would be on then. Yes, she liked Daniel, but she didn't love him, not even close. When they first started dating she hoped her feelings would develop further, but they never moved past the initial physical attraction, and when she took the time to examine their relationship she wondered if he had been nothing more than convenient distraction. He had rescued her from whatever awkward conversation Michael planned at that awful night out months ago, and she'd been flattered by the attention from someone older and sophisticated. But if that was all it was then she was going to need to end it. It wasn't fair to him, and she had no desire to expend her energy fending him off when she had no interest in him physically. And if she was honest, listening to him drone on about himself and how popular he had been in high school was getting boring. Talk about ego.

"Sarah," Shona called out to her and Sarah snapped back to the present. She found Shona a little frightening – the stern woman in her forties never smiled – and sometimes Sarah wondered why she wanted to run a business where she had to engage with the public. Even Caroline found her daunting but had decided she would not cave into Shona's bizarre demands. Shona, it appeared was not a fan of parties. She tried to convince them that a DJ was a bad idea and a stringed quartet would be a better choice for David's party. David had laughed and laughed when they passed on the suggestion and vetoed it immediately, along with Shona's idea that all the guests should be gone by ten pm.

Caroline told Sarah the stories of the disasters that had befallen them when Bridget and Alistair were involved in an event but said she was worried that tonight's party might be even worse with Shona in charge. So far so good, but negotiating with Shona had been a nightmare. Caroline said it was like being trapped in a cross over episode of Taggart – whatever that was? – and Neighbours. It turned out Shona came to Australia expecting to make friends with everyone in the street, even though the property was several acres and you couldn't even see the neighbour's homes.

And Caroline couldn't understand a word Shona said. It turned out that when Shona said 'I cannae do it', that didn't mean yes. It meant no, and for a week Caroline had been under the impression that Shona was happy to open up the ballroom at seven this morning so they could have the flowers delivered first thing. When Caroline tried to confirm that Shona would be waiting for the delivery she had yelled, "I cannae do it' over and over, until it dawned on Caroline that she was refusing to get up early, and that cannae meant can't. Eventually Bridget intervened, insisting Shona give Caroline a key to let herself in if Shona didn't want to be up that early. But Shona had been emphatic that if she had to stay until midnight for the party – the word said with distain – then she wasn't getting up until ten. Caroline did not see a future for Shona in the hospitality business.

Sarah had to admit – if only to herself – that it had been entertaining watching the battle of wills. Caroline, perfectionist, determined and hard-working had met her match. Shona was lazy, slovenly, and stubborn. If she didn't want to do something then there was no way to get her to move. She put more effort into refusing to do something, and then finally doing it wrong when forced, than if she had just done what had been asked of her the first time. Bridget had tried to stay out of it, defending Shona at first, but even she could see that Shona wasn't going to win them any new business. In the end she had thrown her hands in the air and told Shona to let Caroline do whatever she wanted. She was like a part of the family after all. Shona had scowled throughout the rest of the meeting, and Caroline swore she would find a new venue for future events. Sarah thought that would please Shona no end.

"Yes Shona," she said with a smile. People would be arriving in an hour and the last thing she wanted was for Shona to sabotage the evening out of spite.

"Teel that ther dundeheid to haud yer wheesht. I cannae hear meeself." Sarah took her cue from Shona's hands over her ears that it meant the music was too loud.

"He has to get the levels right, so it needs to be loud. You look tired," she commiserated, "Why don't you take yourself off somewhere quiet and have a cup of tea? We'll find you if we need you."

"Aye, I'm loused. I could do with a wee nip," she said whipping of her apron and handing it to Sarah. She didn't need a translator to understand they wouldn't be seeing much more of Shona tonight.

Chapter Thirty-One

"Oh Caroline. This looks wonderful," Joan said, spinning around to take everything in. David asked for the '90's and Caroline had given it to him. The tables were covered in lime green table clothes with lolly pink runners. The flowers still horrified Caroline, bright orange and pink gerbera's with baby's breath and there were even a few inflatable chairs and couches off to the side of the room. Caroline hoped nobody actually sat on them or they might need rescuing later.

The walls were plastered with posters of '90's pop icons. U2, a favourite of David's, was there and so was Nirvana, Salt 'n' Pepa and R.E.M. A mirror ball was hanging from the ceiling, and later after dinner the coloured lights would go on and the dancing would begin. '90's music was playing quietly in the background for now, but later it was going to get loud.

Guests were already arriving in droves. They were expecting eighty people tonight with very few saying no to their invitation. David and Joan were greeting everyone at the door and soon people were milling around in groups, laughing at each other's costumes. The op shops of Melbourne had been picked clean of high wasted acid wash jeans and plaid shirts.

Caroline saw Michael come in with Emmy and headed over to say hello. They'd only met her once, but she seemed like a nice girl. She and

Adam could see straight away that she was nothing at all like Margaux and let out a collective sigh of relief after their introduction when Emmy picked Michael up one night because his car was at the mechanic's. Emmy was pretty, but quiet and she thought, much more suited to her son. She noticed that Michael was looking at the seating chart, and then saw a frown appear on his face when he saw where he was sitting. Sarah had placed him at a table with Joan's niece and nephew and a few other people in their late teens and early twenties. Caroline knew what Sarah had done, but decided she wasn't going to intervene. If Sarah didn't want to spend an evening with her son and his date then she wasn't going to force her to. She watched as Michael turned and strode over to table seven where he picked up his and Emmy's place cards and then moving to table five, picked up the cards of two others, and replaced them with his own. From memory it looked like David's cousin's kids were being bumped to table seven.

"Michael what are you doing?" she asked, rushing over to him.

"Did you do the seating plan? You put me with people I don't know. That's not like you, Mum," he growled quietly, not wanting to make a scene.

"I didn't do the chart love."

"Sarah did this? Well too bad 'cause I'm not sitting over there. I suggest you change the chart so," he looked at the cards "Paul and Meg don't get lost." Caroline held out her hand and he handed her the cards. She put them in their new spot and rushed to the chart to change it. Caroline watched from a distance as Michael theatrically pulled out a chair at his newly assigned table and dropped into it while Emmy joined him, although much more sedately with a look of alarm on her face. When the waiter brought around a tray of drinks Michael took two, one for him and one for his date. *Shona might not be the one causing trouble tonight*, Caroline thought. *I wonder what's brought on this uncharacteristic mood.*

Sarah, finished with all the things she needed to do, joined the party. She and Caroline were now officially guests and the kitchen was under the control of Greg, who'd been supervising events for several months now, so the evening was in good hands. Assuming, of course, that Shona stayed out of the way.

When Daniel arrived he made a bee-line for her, kissing her gently on the mouth. They chatted for a few minutes about their day and then decided to take a seat at their table. When they got there she was surprised to see Michael sitting beside Lochie deep in conversation. Next to him was a very pretty blonde, who looked very uncomfortable.

"Michael," Daniel said when he saw him, "I didn't know you were coming tonight. "

"Didn't Sarah mention it?" he said, looking straight at her. "That's weird seeing that we're all such old family friends."

"I guess I didn't think Daniel needed a complete list of everyone attending tonight." She turned to Daniel. "Guess what? Michael's coming to the party tonight. But you'll have to catch up later. He's sitting at a different table."

"Not anymore," he said as he threw back the last of the wine in his glass. "I did a little re-arranging and we're going to be sitting here tonight. Next to my old friend Lochie and you Sarah. And of course your new *boyfriend* Daniel," he scowled, his tone slightly aggressive, something Sarah had never heard from Michael before.

"Hi," she said turning to the girl she assumed was Emeline, embarrassed by Michael's tone and the way he was completely ignored his date. "I'm Sarah and this is Daniel." Emmy gave a little wave from across the table and introduced herself to the pair. By now the room was full of people and the volume had risen so much it was almost impossible to hear anything. Sarah noted the time and knew that any minute Joan would invite people to find their tables and welcome them before the first course was bought out.

Michael couldn't help himself watching Daniel and Sarah from the other side of the table. They seemed very comfortable together, his arm resting on the back of her chair. Every so often he would lean in and kiss her or say something that made her smile or laugh. Seeing Daniel touch Sarah was making him crazy. Not because he wished it was him, but because he knew what a sleaze Daniel was, and Sarah deserved better. He felt a touch on his arm and turned to Emmy.

"Are you alright Michael?" she asked. "You have such a fierce look on your face."

"I'm fine – sorry – I guess I'm distracted. Do you think Daniel's too old for Sarah?"

Emmy looked at the pair across from her. They looked like a happy couple. Daniel was attentive, the way she had hoped Michael would be with her tonight, but instead he'd barely spoken to her. She'd been planning on inviting Michael back to her place after the party with the intention of taking their relationship to the next level, but with him being in such a bad mood she decided tonight was not going to be *the* night, no matter how much she liked him. They had gone on a few dates, but he had made it clear early on that he wasn't looking for anything serious after his broken engagement. She was hoping she could change his mind. Emmy, who had noticed Michael their first day at Uni years ago, had been thrilled when they bumped into each other in the student union, literally, a few weeks ago. He'd been distracted and crashed into her when she stopped to check an email on her phone. His coffee had spilled down her back, drenching her. Thankfully, it hadn't been hot, but he had been mortified and insisted on making it up to her. The bravest thing she had ever done was suggest he could do that by taking her out for dinner.

They had gone out a week later and after a pleasant evening he asked if she would like to do it again sometime. His pleasant evening had been her dream come true and she said yes immediately. She'd heard rumours about Margaux from a few of his Uni friends who'd met her and didn't think she would ever be able to compete with the picture that had been painted for her. But Margaux was gone and maybe Michael was looking for someone smart and serious this time. She knew those were qualities she possessed.

"I don't know. How old is Sarah? Twenty?" I don't think that's a big age difference."

Michael turned to her and whispered, "she's only just turned nineteen. And Daniel is a real jerk. I'm worried about her. If history is anything to go by he's going to take advantage and then dump her when he gets what he wants. That's how he was in school."

"People change," she replied. "Are you the same as you were in high school?"

"Yeah, I am," he answered. "I've known Sarah her whole life and I'm concerned about her. I don't want her to get hurt."

"Isn't Lochie her brother? If anyone should be worried it's him, and he doesn't seem to be," she said noting that the two men were laughing together at something on Lochie's phone.

Their conversation was interrupted when Joan asked everyone over a microphone to find their table. Most people had already found their seats and a minute later she welcomed everyone.

"As you know, we are here tonight to celebrate my husband's 50th birthday. He will be up later to thank you all for coming but I wanted to say a few thank-yous of my own. First to Caroline and Sarah for putting this whole thing together. Without them you would be crammed into my living room eating pizza. And to Bridget and Alistair for hosting us again at Carrbridge House. Many memories have been made here and hopefully tonight we will add to those. But I especially want to thank David, who is the most wonderful husband and father, and who I love with all my heart.

Let me be the first to toast you tonight," she said raising her glass high. "Happy fiftieth darling." Everybody lifted their glasses and repeated 'happy fiftieth darling', followed by laughter around the room.

Waiters descended, serving the first course, chicken pot stickers with a chili dipping sauce. Michael who was famished and had drunk more than he usually did – already finished with his second glass of wine – inhaled them quickly. He knew he should slow down on the alcohol, but tonight he wanted to let go a little. Emmy was driving, so what did it matter?

Across the room at another table Beth and Jill were discussing Jay. Beth had seen the mess left by Martha's suicide attempt when she and Joan had cleaned the kitchen the next day. Together they'd removed all trace of what had taken place so Martin could return home when he was ready.

"He's not great Beth," Jill told her. "He's gone all quiet again. We've kept him home from school this week and let him spend his days with Martin."

"How's Martin taking it?"

"No better than Jay. And I'm worried about his health. I don't think he should go back to his home alone, but apart from staying with us a bit longer I don't know what the solution is. If it was Mum, I'd build her a granny flat so she could still have her independence. But Martin isn't Mum, and what would happen to him if they moved Jay to another home? It would be weird having some old guy, as lovely as he is, living in the backyard."

"Can he move into a retirement home? That way there will be people his own age to keep him company and help if anything goes wrong."

"We asked him if he had considered that option, but if Martha needed to come and live with him in the future, she can't if he's in a village. Most of them don't allow someone to stay permanently, so he vetoed the idea. Not that I think it's likely. Her doctor is recommending a group home for her. Carer's can make sure she takes the meds she needs, and she'll have somewhere safe to live. She can't live alone at the moment. There's a risk she'll try and self-harm again"

"It doesn't sound like she'll get Jay back any time soon then."

"No," she shook her head. "Mandy said after what happened she can't be trusted with Jay. They've asked if we will consider making his stay long term and we said yes. We can apply for permanent custody, but that takes time. They need to see that he's doing well with us. And right now he's not. I'm afraid that if his grandfather goes home he'll become even more withdrawn."

"Then let Martin stay for now. You have enough room, and I bet he's not causing you any trouble."

"Not at all. In fact I don't think the garden has ever looked better. We told him he didn't need to do it, but he said it helps keep his mind of his problems. So for now, I think you're right. Martin will stay until Jay gets back to normal, if that's even possible."

Chapter Thirty-Two

"What are you doing out here all alone in the cold David? You do know there's a party going on, and I understand you're the guest of honour.

"Hey Adam. Just taking a breather. It's so loud in there. My head was swimming."

"Well as long as you're okay, I'll leave you to it. Want me to tell Joan you'll be back in a few? She was looking for you. I think she wants to do the speeches"

"That would be great," David nodded. Thanks." Adam turned to walk back inside when David called out to him.

"Actually, do you have a minute? I was going to call you tomorrow for a chat, but now's as good a time as any."

"Sure. There's a little room off to the side of the ballroom. We can go in through the French doors and no one will bother us. It's warmer than out here. I can't believe how quickly the weather has turned this year."

David followed Adam inside and they sank opposite each other into two ancient, sagging chairs after closing the doors behind them. They could still hear the party, but it was muffled, and an open fire warmed the room. Caroline had been worried about oldies getting stuck in the inflatable chairs, but Adam thought they might need some help getting out of these relics. He sat patiently, waiting for David to start. He seemed almost distressed, rubbing the back of his neck and when he sighed loudly for the third time, Adam began to worry that something was wrong.

"Why don't you just spit it out David? Something is clearly bothering you, and if I can help I will."

"Sorry, I didn't mean to give you the impression that something was wrong. It's not. I'm just nervous I guess. Thing is, I haven't been able to stop thinking about your God. I've tried, believe me, but He keeps popping into my thoughts at the most inopportune moments. I keep seeing His creation everywhere." David paused, trying to articulate what he had been thinking for days now. He had made his decision, but if he waited any longer he was afraid he would back out – let logic take over – and the opportunity would pass.

"I don't know the right term, I tried Googling it, but the phrases sounded so silly. Born again, become a Christian, whatever. I don't want a label. I just know whatever you have, I want it too."

"You want to make God the Lord over your life. Is that what you're trying to say?"

"Yeah I guess it is. I saw prayers online, but I felt if I did it on my own it would be like it never happened. I feel like I need a witness. And I was hoping you would be that for me. And that way I have to stick to it. Mean it."

"I would love to be your witness. But I just need to ask you first. We are at a party, and this shouldn't be a flippant decision. You aren't … drunk, are you?"

"No mate. Not even a little. I'm too old for that these days. Can't stand waking up feeling like death. I had one beer at the start of the night, and I'm done."

"Okay then. And you're sure here is where you want to do this."

"I am. Don't get me wrong. I'm not going to go out there and make a big announcement, but I want to do it now. Before another day goes by. I've thought this through. I even know I'll have to go to church. I'm alright with that."

"You don't *have* to go to church. You won't get kicked out of the club, so to speak, if you don't, but church is a good idea. That's where you learn and grow."

"I know. I've already been listening to talks from people in the car when I'm alone. On the podcasts. People really seem to love this God of yours."

Adam smiled, realising that David no longer doubted that God existed. "Then let's get to it, and then He'll be your God too. Do you have something you want to say, or do you want to repeat after me?"

"No. I'm good. I've been thinking about this for weeks now." David closed his eyes and before he even had a chance to speak he was overcome with emotion.

"God," his voice cracked. "I don't know you very well. But I understand that you know me. You made me, and you made everything. I'm sorry," he stopped, needing a breath, "I'm sorry I haven't acknowledged you before. And I'm sorry for all the things I've done in my life that aren't good. My mate here, Adam, you know him, he calls them sins. So I will too. I'm sorry for my sins. Please forgive me for them. And show me a way to not do them anymore." David stopped, wondering if it was done, if he was saved now. And then he remembered the part he had left out. "And thank you for your son Jesus. I know about His death. I heard it was brutal, but that he was a willing sacrifice for me. So thank you Jesus for doing that. I look forward to getting to know you too."

Adam sealed David's prayer with an amen and then opened his eyes. Both could see that they were feeling as emotional as the other, tears on both men's cheeks. They looked at each other and grinned. If everyone could see them now they'd think they'd lost it. Lumbering out of the chairs they exchanged a quick man hug and then slapped each other on the back.

"I'm going to need a minute," David said. "Do you mind letting Joan know I'll be back soon? I just don't feel ready to be out there just yet."

"I'll tell her," Adam promised. "And mate, welcome to the family."

~~~

Michael watched from his seat as Daniel twirled Sarah across the dance floor clumsily. His mood hadn't improved as the evening went on, and even Emmy had given up trying to talk to him. Lochie had stepped in and was asking her about her classes. He would owe him one, but tonight Michael just wasn't in the mood for small talk. He should be having a fabulous time. Dinner had been delicious, and the speeches were funny. David's dad told endless stories about the naughty things his son got up to when he was a kid, and his sister spilt the beans with a few stories about what David got up to when he was a teenager. Things his parents hadn't known about. Michael had laughed along, but his heart wasn't in it. David's speech had been more serious. He thanked all his friends and family for their love and support, especially with what they had been through recently. Michael could see that he was emotional tonight. Not his usual – I'm a tough builder – banter anywhere in sight. But after all the fake that Michael had put up with last year from Margaux's family, it was nice to see someone who appreciated their family and friends.

Lochie leaned over and asked if it would be alright if he took Emmy out on the dance floor. Michael agreed immediately, embarrassed that he hadn't asked her to dance himself. He'd invited this perfectly nice girl to a party, and he had rudely ignored her for most of the evening. She deserved better than that. He decided then that he was going to tell her that he couldn't see her anymore. As pretty as she was, as funny and smart as he found her, there was no attraction. They would only ever be friends.

"Mind if I sit kid?" Michael looked up from where he had been staring at the tablecloth, drawing patterns with his finger in the sugar that someone had spilt earlier. His dad pulled out a chair and sat beside him.

"You're looking glum. Not having any fun?"

"I guess not."

"Not missing Margaux, are you?"

"Not even a little bit. Isn't that terrible? If things had gone differently I would be planning a move to America and making decisions about our wedding, but," he shook his head. "I barely think about her."

"Then why aren't you out there dancing with Emmy. She's a lovely girl."

"I know. She's perfect. Smart, pretty, and for some reason she likes me."

Adam raised his eyebrows, "but not for you?"

"I don't think so. I've decided to tell her I don't want to keep dating."

"If you aren't interested, then that's for the best. I've noticed you watching Daniel and Sarah a lot tonight. Is there something you want to tell me?"

"Like what? He's not right for her? He's not. That he's too old for her? Not sure about that one. She's more of an adult than he'll ever be." He shook his head and exhaled loudly. "He was such a jerk in school. I couldn't stand him. And if they stay together I'm going to have to spend more time with him. He'll end up coming to all our family events."

"Is this about Daniel or Sarah son? You seem very concerned about her, even though you just told me she's very mature and can probably take care of herself."

"Of course it's about Daniel. I know him better than she does. I've seen what he does to girls. Sarah shouldn't have to go through that."

"If you say so Michael," Adam said, not believing him for a minute.

"And let Emmy down gently. She doesn't deserve to be treated badly either." Adam stood up from his seat and Michael watched as he walked over to the DJ. They chatted for a minute and then Adam returned to his own table. *I wonder what that was about*, Michael thought when his dad gave him a quick glance and a nod. But he smiled, probably for the first time tonight as he saw his father take his wife's hand and pull her towards the dance floor as Bryan Adams *Everything I do* played.

Lochie and Emmy were still dancing together as Michael sat alone when he heard the opening notes to The Frames *Falling Slowly*, a few songs later. He didn't even think about what he was doing when he stood up out of his chair and strode towards the dance floor. He tapped Daniel on the shoulder and asked if he could cut in. He didn't give him a chance to answer, but took Sarah's hand as Daniel, surprised, stood aside.

Pulling Sarah towards him he gently rested his hand on her waist. He could feel her resistance at first, and then she relaxed into him, their bodies fitting perfectly together. They moved together as one, eyes locked, unaware anyone else was on the dance floor.

"What are you doing Michael?" Sarah asked, her heart expanding inside her chest as the warmth from him radiated over her.

"Why didn't you want to sit near me tonight?" he whispered in her ear.

"No reason. I thought you might like the people at the other table."

"I don't believe you. And why won't you talk to me anymore or even look at me?"

"Michael, I think you're imagining things."

"Sarah, please. I need to know why you avoid me every chance you get?"

"I'm not avoiding you. I'm just busy with Daniel these days, that's all. I'm sorry if I've offended you."

"Offended me. You haven't offended me. You're driving me crazy."

"*I'm* driving *you* crazy. How could I possible drive you crazy?"

263

"I don't know. You just are." He let go of her waist and twirled her slowly under his arm as the familiar words washed over him, *take this sinking boat, and point it home, we've still got time*. He pulled her close again, but this time she didn't resist, and he could feel her breath on his cheek as they danced.

"I heard something recently. That you had feelings for me. Is that true?" he asked.

Embarrassment flooded her, and she felt her cheeks begin to colour. Someone had let her secret out. "It was just a little crush when I was a kid," she answered, unable to lie to him. "But I'm over it now so let's just forget about it," she said, her defenses going up.

"I don't want to forget about it. And I really don't like what's happening between you and Daniel."

"Me and Daniel," Sarah pulled away from Michael slightly, even though they continued to dance, "are none of your business. I can see that you don't like him, but he's treated me with nothing but respect. If you're mad at him because of something that happened at school, then take it up with him Michael, but leave me out of it." She stopped moving to the music and dropped Michael's hand as she stepped further out of his embrace. He searched her face, hoping that she would understand how concerned he was for her, but all he saw was her face flash with anger. She walked past him, and off the dance floor. Michael turned and followed with his eyes as she walked back to the table.

Michael stood alone in a sea of people, his stomach churning. What was he doing? He had meant to clear the air with Sarah. Instead she was more angry with him than ever. And why did it bother him so much that Sarah and Daniel were together? It was true that he couldn't stand Daniel, but he hadn't been this upset when Margaux cheated on him. Whatever this was, he needed to get to the bottom of it.

He stepped off the dance floor, deciding he wasn't finished with his conversation with Sarah. The last thing he wanted was for her to go home upset with him. But as he approached the table, Sarah picked up her bag and Daniel grabbed her hand. He turned around and looked directly at Michael, giving him that smug smile, just like he had years ago and then he winked at him. Michael remembered that look, and he knew what the outcome was going to be. If only Sarah would listen to him. Daniel was going to make his move.

Chapter Thirty-Three

Daniel sped down the winding country roads, unconcerned about how dark it was with no streetlights. Sarah, worried that if an animal jumped out on the road they wouldn't have time to stop, gently laid her hand on Daniel's leg and suggested he slowed down a little. Seeing the concern on her face he reduced the pressure on the pedal and the car slowed down.

"Sorry. I didn't realise how fast I was going. I'm just so angry at him. How dare he upset you."

"Don't worry about it. Michael didn't upset me that much. But thanks for agreeing to leave early. I didn't want to have to sit through the rest of the night with him."

Daniel took another look across at her, delighted that she was finally starting to see what a waste of space Michael Anderson was.

"I couldn't stand him at school. He had no idea how to have any fun. Always whining that we weren't 'respectful' enough of the girls, even though I don't remember them complaining at the time. Do you know, I never once heard of him even having a date. Talk about pathetic. Girls were only interested in him when they needed someone to complain to if they got dumped. Then they'd be there crying on his puny shoulder. I mean, he could have tried it on, easy pickings, but even then he wasn't man enough."

Not responding to his nasty comments, Sarah was seeing, for the first time, a side of Daniel she didn't like. The wine must have loosened his tongue, because he had never talked so disrespectfully about women before, and he always told her he treated a girl like a princess. Apparently not.

"He was such a sap," Daniel continued. "And then when his sister died, man, everyone was falling over him with sympathy, and he lapped it up. The teachers let him get away with anything which was probably the only reason he got into Uni. I bet they gave him better grades than everyone else because of what happened."

"Daniel," Sarah warned. "Isabelle was a friend of mine. Her death was devastating, so I would be very careful what you say about her."

"Oh yeah … sorry babe," he said looking over at her, realising that he had gone too far. "It *was* sad that she died, I was just saying that he took advantage, that's all."

"If you hated Michael so much, then why did you come over and say hi to him that night in the pub?"

He grinned at her in a way she was beginning to hate. He probably thought he looked sexy, but she found it sleazy. "I noticed *you* babe. How could I not? And when I realised it was mopy Michael you were with I decided to come over. I couldn't believe someone as hot as you would be out on a date with him, and I was right. You weren't."

"You do know he's considered quite attractive. You make him sound like the hunchback of Notre Dame. And he was very recently engaged to a gorgeous, rich American."

"Yeah I heard about her. But he couldn't keep her, could he? She was probably dying of boredom and dumped him." Daniel merged onto the Peninsula Link at speed and, not for the first time during the drive home,

Sarah wondered how much he'd had to drink tonight. She hadn't noticed him drinking a lot, but at these events waiters filled the glasses all night, and people often didn't realise they'd had too much until they stood up.

Sarah fell silent. She wanted Daniel to concentrate on his driving, and although she wasn't in the mood to defend Michael, she knew what Daniel was saying wasn't true. She wasn't sure if he was jealous of Michael, or just being a complete jerk. It was probably a combination of the two. Sarah leaned over and turned the radio on, not wanting to hear another word Daniel had to say. Kilometres slipped by in silence and soon Sarah started recognising roads and breathed out a silent sigh of relief. She would be home soon and tomorrow she would call Daniel and end things.

They were only a few minutes from her house when Daniel turned the music down, and glanced across at her.

"I was thinking it's time we went on a weekend away. I know it's not summer, but there's heaps of places we could go. Even up to the ski fields. You ski, right?"

"No," she shook her head. "I don't know how. Never been."

"What? Everyone knows how to ski."

"Not me. We might have holidayed a bit differently Daniel. Skiing's expensive and Mum and Dad didn't have the money to spend on that sort of thing."

"Well then I'll teach you. Ski season opens in a month. I've got some mates going up to Dinner Plain for the long weekend. They own a house up there and they invited me. It'll be crowded so we'll have to share a room, but it will give us a chance to spend some time alone," he suggested with a purr in his voice.

"Sorry. That's Queens birthday right? I'm working that weekend. We have a huge sixtieth birthday on the Saturday night."

"So, tell them you can't make it. Or get mopy Michael to talk to his *mummy* for you. He was falling all over you tonight. I'm sure he'd do it if you cried a little and told him you needed his help."

"Michael was not falling all over me. We danced once and it meant nothing. We're old friends. And I *like* working Daniel. I've been looking forward to this party for months. It's for a QC and it's a big deal for Events. If we can pull this off Caroline will be booked out for the rest of the year. I'm not going to let her down, even if I wanted to."

"Come on babe. Don't be boring. At least pick a weekend when we can go away. And soon. I've been very patient with you, but it's getting beyond a joke," Daniel said as he pulled up outside Sarah's house, turning the car off so no one in the houses would see it's lights.

Sarah realised then that she didn't want to wait until tomorrow to break things off. She had never dumped somebody before, and didn't really know what to say, so she decided it would be best just to get it out and finish things tonight.

"Daniel listen. There's something we need to talk about."

He leaned over and kissed her. Sarah pulled back and said, "Daniel please. I'm trying to talk to you."

"Less talk babe. Your parents will be ages, and it's going to get cold in the car so why don't we go inside. No one will ever know. Or I could drive you to my place."

"Daniel," she said, putting her hands up in protest. "I wasn't planning on doing this tonight, but I've given it a lot of thought, and I think we should stop seeing each other. I like you, but you want more than I'm willing to give you."

"You what? You're breaking up with me?" He laughed and then seeing her serious expression, his face changed. He no longer looked like the friendly, relaxed Daniel he had been before. His expression told her he was angry and for the first time she began to feel nervous about Daniel.

"Please Daniel. Don't get upset. I just don't think we're compatible."

"Oh Sarah. I think we would be very compatible. You just have to let me show you."

"I'm going in now. It's been really nice getting to know you, but it's over." Sarah reached for the door handle, a trickle of fear running through her, but Daniel grabbed her hand and wrenched her arm back.

"You're not going anywhere. I have waited and waited. I never let a girl keep me hanging this long, but I made an exception for you. I thought you were worth the wait. But it turns out you're nothing but a little tease." He shook his head at her and narrowed his eyes. "I'm not going to put up with that anymore." He leaned over and roughly kissed her. Sarah knew she needed to get out of the car, or at least get someone's attention or she was going to be in a lot of trouble. She pulled her right hand from under his body while he was distracted, his hand's roaming where she didn't want them. She reached as far as she could until she found the steering wheel. She slammed her hand down and thankfully it hit the horn. Daniel hadn't been expecting the piecing noise and leaped back, banging his head on the window. She sat forward and hit the horn again. Lights went on at the neighbours and she saw Mr. Carlson open the door. She hit the horn again and he stepped out onto his porch, looking to see who was causing the commotion.

"You bitch," Daniel sneered, when he saw the man step off his porch and start walking to Daniels car. "This isn't over."

Sarah grabbed her bag from the foot well and opened the door. She scrambled out of the car and slammed the door behind her. She was shaking and knew it wasn't from the cold, but she didn't run. She wasn't going to let him know how frightened she was.

"Everything okay Sarah?" Mr. Carlson called out.

"It will be Mr. Carlson. Do you mind waiting until I get inside?"

"Of course. Want me to call the police?" Sarah looked back and could see Daniel taking in the six-foot-two man who worked as a tree lopper for a living. Daniel wouldn't stand a chance against him.

"No. I think I'll be okay." As she fitted the key into the front door lights lit up the court. Her parents car pulled into the driveway and it barely stopped before her dad flung his door open. She heard Daniel's car start and then the sound of tires squealing filled the quiet court. Her mum and dad ran over to her, and finally the shock of what could have happened hit her. She fell into her dad's arms crying, as her mum opened the door and they ushered her inside to the warmth that was her home.

"Are you alright love? Did he hurt you?"

"He would have," she said shaking. "I didn't give him the chance."

Her mum directed her to the couch and then pulled a blanket over her. "Tom, go and put the kettle on. She needs a hot chocolate."

When, after a few minutes of crying, her tears subsided and she'd calmed down, she realised it was much too early for her parents to be home. "What are you guys doing here? I would have thought you'd be at the party until Shona kicked everyone out," she said, taking a sip of the sweet, hot chocolate her dad had made for her.

"Michael found us and told us we needed to find you asap. We tried calling but you didn't pick up your phone. We thought we'd come here first, although we had no idea what we were going to do if you weren't home."

"Oh." Sarah remembered. "I forgot to charge my phone last night, and I've been at work all day, so I didn't get a chance. Why did Michael think I needed you?"

"He said when you left, Daniel turned around and winked at him. Something about him doing that in school right before he did something he shouldn't. Michael said he would have followed you, but he didn't have his car and he knew he wasn't fit to drive anyway. We got here as fast as we could."

"Well I'm glad you came. I hope I never see Daniel again, but I have a feeling it's not over yet."

~~~

Sarah was almost asleep when she heard her phone ping. She checked the message hoping it wasn't Daniel. It wasn't.

'Sarah I couldn't sleep until I knew you were okay.'

She sat for a minute. She had been so angry at Michael earlier, but he hadn't really done anything wrong. She was the one who had shut him out, and he was only being a good friend and asking why. She owed him an apology and a thank you for helping her out tonight. And now that he knew how she used to feel about him maybe soon they could have a laugh about it and move on.

'I'm okay' she replied.

'Phew. Not mad that I sent your parents' home?'

'No. And thanx. They arrived just in time'. She signed off with a smiley face and turned her phone off. She was over men today. She didn't want to hear from another one tonight.

Chapter Thirty-Four

Martha shoved as many clothes as she could fit into her backpack and then grabbed the blanket off the bed. She didn't know where she was going, but she wasn't living here anymore. This was Australia, and no one could force her to stay if she didn't want to. When she was released from the hospital she was told she couldn't go home alone and a placement in a group home had been arranged for her. The minute she'd walked in she'd hated it. The smell of mildew and sweat permeated the air, making her nauseous and when she was shown to her room she realised she wasn't going to have any privacy. She was introduced to her roommate Gabby, who talked to herself all day and would sometimes start screaming for no reason. They had promised she would be safe here, but she felt more frightened than she ever had. There were six other people living in the home, along with Susan, who supervised the inmates – as Martha thought of the residents – during the day. At night, either Carole or Brenda slept in a room of their own and made sure they were all locked up at night like prisoners.

She'd been here for a week now. Every day she had to help with the cleaning and the cooking. She had to follow the roster and if she didn't, Susan said she would lose her television privileges. Martha didn't care about

273

telly. All she wanted was to be at home with Jay. But Susan said her home was gone. They told Martha her dad had emptied all her things from her rental and now someone else was living there. She asked if she could live with her dad then, but they said she was a risk to herself and to him too, and she needed to be supervised at all times. He was coming to visit her next week, they promised, but it would be too late. She wasn't going to be here.

She remembered *that* day. She could see herself slashing at her wrists, feeling the pain, and watching blood flow out of her body. She knew it was wrong, but she hadn't been able to stop herself. When that girl told her she was taking Jay away again she couldn't bear it anymore, and found her emotions spinning out of control. If she couldn't live with her son then she didn't want to live at all.

She tried so hard to be a good mother. *Had* been a good mother. Before the accident life was wonderful. She'd worked in a job she loved as a receptionist in a doctor's office. The patients were interesting, and the doctors were always nice. It had been her responsibility to make the appointments and process the billings. She made sure the doctors kept on schedule and the patients loved her.

But after her accident she couldn't seem to manage anymore. She would take phone calls and then forget to put the appointment in the computer, or schedule it for the wrong time. She couldn't remember how to use the EFTPOS machine half the time and people started to ring, complaining they hadn't received their Medicare rebates. She increased her efforts to get it right, writing instructions down after Sally, the other receptionist showed her yet again how things worked, but everything became jumbled in her brain and she found herself confused a lot of the time.

She tried her best, desperately wanting a normal life and to be able to provide for her son, but when things went wrong she would have trouble controlling her emotions. The medications she took helped a little, but they made her feel so sick. Her doctor tried different drugs but each one was worse than the last. She felt nauseated all the time, one caused dizziness and they all made her extremely tired. She would oversleep which meant Jay often missed the first few hours of school and she would be late for work. She decided she did better without the meds and physically started feeling better once she stopped taking them. But that also meant she had even more difficulty controlling her moods, and outbursts at work and sometimes at Jay became her new normal.

The boss told her he was sorry, but after she yelled at an old woman who made a complaint about her bill, he couldn't keep her on anymore. They were very good to her, helping her sign up for disability payments, but not working meant she was home alone during the day when Jay was at school, so she was bored and lonely all the time. That's when the real trouble began.

Before her accident she didn't mind that it was just her and Jay. She wasn't interested in dating, Jay's wellbeing was her main focus, and the thought of a letting a man into her life when he was so young, didn't sit well with Martha. There would be time for that when Jay was older. The happy pair would visit her dad on the weekends so Jay could spend some time in the company of a male, and she thought all in all, they had a wonderful life. Her accident changed all of that. She knew she was different now, she could see it and feel it, but nothing she tried could fix it. The only thing the accident hadn't taken from her was her looks. At thirty-one she was still young, and people always told her how pretty she was. Men came up and talked to her when she was in the pub during the day – a place where she didn't feel judged – and sometimes if they were really nice she would invite them home. It felt lovely to have someone show her affection and she found herself feeling less lonely. But when her dad found out that sometimes she invited men back to the house he'd been furious with her. He told her she was putting herself in danger, but even worse, one of them could hurt Jay. She tried to tell him that they were nice, but he didn't believe her. It occurred to her, more than once, that he might have been the person who'd called the police and made them take Jay away from her.

The day that the authorities came to the house had been horrible. They took Jay away and said it would be a few weeks before she could see him again. She remembered howling for hours after he was gone, confused at what the problem was. Yes, the house wasn't as clean as it used to be, and there wasn't always food in the fridge, but she never hit her son. Those were the parents who should be losing their children. And it wasn't like she didn't try, but she got so muddled with money and there wasn't always enough left to buy food or the new clothes he needed.

When she found Jay and tried to take him home with her they told her she was making it impossible for her to see Jay at all and that's when she decided she was going to get her life together. It was the only way she would get him back. If she could keep a job then she could also care for her child. An agency found her a job packing orders in a warehouse. There were other people there with disabilities and the bosses made exceptions for them. She knew the company received incentives from the Government to hire people like her, but that was okay. She just needed to prove herself so they would at least let her see her son. But then she'd tried to hurt herself and now the job was gone, she didn't have a home of her own and everything that she owned could fit in her backpack.

She hated living in this awful place. They forced her to take her meds and wouldn't let her out alone. They were taken out once a week on supervised visits to the shops, but she couldn't hang out at the pub the way she used to, and she had no way of getting there anyway. She missed the men that liked to talk to her and sometimes gave her a nice cuddle and some affection. But most of all she missed Jay. She didn't know where he was at the moment, but she'd found him before, and she was going to find him again. He was somewhere, and she was going to keep looking. And next time she found him she was going to take him whether she was allowed to or not. But first things first, she had to get out of this place.

The doors weren't locked during the day, so she could just walk out when no one was looking. She had only had about a hundred dollars so there was no way she could afford somewhere to live, and she didn't know how she was going to pay for food once that ran out, but anywhere was better than here. Before her accident she'd seen people on the streets and wondered why they didn't take the help the government offered them. But now she got it. They were just like her. Willing to take their chances out on the street rather than being forced to take medication that made them sick and live with rules that meant they didn't have any freedom. And Martha decided she wasn't going to put up with it anymore.

~~~

"Martin, what's wrong? You look like you've seen a ghost," Jill said, concerned after hearing him talking quietly to someone on the phone.

"That was Mandy, Jay's case worker," he said. "Martha has disappeared."

"From the group home? How did she manage that?"

"She walked out. Took a bag and left two days ago. They hoped that she would return, but nobody's heard from her. As her next of kin I should have been notified, but I guess it slipped through the cracks. Mandy rang the home to see how Martha had settle in and that's when they told her she was gone. She said I need to report her as a missing person. If she doesn't show up soon then I can petition the courts to be named Jay's guardian. But you know I can't look after him on my own or I would have already done it. He's much better off here with you."

"He needs all of us," Matthew, who had been listening to the conversation, said, "He loves you, but we understand it's too much to take care of a little boy alone at your age. We've told you to stay for as long as you like, and we can care for him together."

"Thank you but I need to go home. I have more than overstayed my welcome and besides, what if Martha turns up at the house. She could be there right now, waiting for me."

"Then why don't we go together now? I'll drive you, while Jill stays here with the kids. And if she isn't there now, we can go back in a few days and check again."

"Thank you Matthew. But it's time for me to go home. It won't take me long to pack."

"But what about Jay?"

"I've asked Mandy to let him stay here. She agrees it's the best place for him. But I would love it if he could come and visit me occasionally if you have the time. "

Jill and Matthew exchanged a glance. They had loved having Martin stay. He had been no trouble and Jay did better with him around.

"Are you sure that's what you want to do?" Jill asked.

"It's what I need to do. You have both been so kind. And I know Jay is in safe hands. But if Martha needs me then I need to be there for her right now."

Chapter Thirty-Five

S arah picked up her phone from the table and looked at the screen. When she saw who the message was from she threw the phone back down in frustration. The texts had started off innocently enough.

The morning after the party Daniel called to apologize for his behaviour the night before, claiming he'd drunk more than he realised and was appalled at how he'd treated her. Sarah, wanting to diffuse the situation quickly, and without any more drama, lied, telling him she excepted his apology. But she also made it very clear she wouldn't be seeing him anymore and hung up. When he called again she ignored him, not answering her phone, and that's when the messages started. He tried sweet talking her at first, telling Sarah he was falling in love with her and thought they had a future together. She didn't answer the texts, not wanting to engage in a back and forth with him. She hoped her silence would be enough to get the message through to him, but that's when the flowers started showing up at the house. Expensive bouquets three days running, all thrown out by Sarah who felt sick every time she thought about what Daniel had tried to do to her. Her parents tried to convince her to go to the police and make a complaint, but it would be his word against hers, and she just wanted him to go away so she could forget him. When the tone of his messages changed from being contrite to angry she messaged him once, telling him she was blocking him and to leave her alone.

Now messages were coming in from different numbers, but they were all from Daniel. Whether he was using prepaid phones, or borrowing them from his friends, she didn't know, but he was bombarding her daily. He called her a tease and said she owed him. But in the last two days the messages had changed and were starting to scare her. He told her he would be seeing her again soon and how much he was looking forward to it. The messages sent chills through her, and she found herself feeling almost paranoid. For the last few days when she was walking back to her car after TAFE she felt like someone was watching her. She hadn't seen him, but she felt he was close by, so she started taking precautions – never walking alone, especially now that it was getting dark early – and she always checked her van, including the back before she got in.

"Another message?" her dad asked.

"Yep. That's three today. All the same. I'll be seeing you soon."

"I think it's time to go to the police love. I'm really concerned about your safety."

"I don't know Dad. I don't want to make a fuss. I'm sure he'll get bored soon enough and leave me alone if I keep ignoring him."

"But what if he doesn't Sarah? The more you ignore him, the worse he gets. This is stalking, and situations like this can end very badly."

"Don't you think you might be exaggerating a bit Dad?"

"Sarah you have to learn to trust your gut. You've blocked him for a reason, and he's still bothering you. And you said you feel like you're being watched." Tom shook his head in anger, deciding to take matters into his own hands, still so angry that Daniel had tried to hurt his daughter. At night he lay in bed imagining what he would do to him if Daniel showed up at the house, and couldn't understand why Sarah wouldn't involve the cops. "I can't let this go on." He picked up Sarah's phone and the message showed on the screen. He grabbed a pen and wrote the number down. He picked up his own phone and then tapping the number in wrote a text of his own.

'Daniel, this is Sarah's father. If you do not stop contacting her I will be calling the police and making a formal complaint. One more text will be all it takes.' He pressed send before Sarah could object.

"Right, that's dealt with. Anything else I can help you with? Any teachers at TAFE giving you a hard time?"

"No Dad," she smiled, grateful her dad cared so much. "But maybe you can help me out with something else." She huffed out a loud sigh. "You know I used to have a bit of a crush on Michael." Tom smiled, remembering how adorable Sarah had been following Michael around when she was little. She'd become more discreet in her teenage years, but even Tom could see it had been more than a little crush.

"I'm mostly over it, but every once and a while it pops up again. I'd like nothing more than to be done with it and just think of him as a friend, but I'm not doing very well with the moving on thing. I thought dating someone else was the answer, but you know what a disaster that's turned out to be."

"Ah … right. Sure you don't want to talk this one through with your mum?" Tom hesitated. He had no problem handling a difficult situation, but giving advice about his daughter's love life was a little out of his comfort zone. "She might have a better take on this than me."

"I have talked it through with her. She says I'll grow out of it."

"Okay. Not the advice you were looking for?" Sarah shook her head no. "Well, let's think about this. Holding all your feelings in hasn't worked, has it? So maybe you should stop doing that. Acknowledge how you feel to yourself, and if you have to, wallow a bit. Bottling everything up never helps. Realise that he doesn't feel the same, but that doesn't mean there's anything wrong with how you feel. It's not like you're stalking him and sending him crazy texts all day like Daniel's doing to you. But being honest with him might help you let it go once and for all. But what do I know? I'm just your dad."

"You're the best dad, and that's some good advice, although I can't believe I'm talking to you about it. So you think talking to him is the way to go? Because Michael asked if we could meet up so we can clear the air after what happened at the party. I'm leaning toward to saying yes, even if it's going to be totally awkward. I'm the one who was rude at David's party and I can't go on pretending nothing happened. Our families are too close for that, and I work for his mum. I'm bound to run into him, and I don't want it to be weird. I owe him an apology and I think I should just get it over and done with."

"Then you should do it. Apologize and tell him how you feel, but make it clear that you understand he doesn't reciprocate your feelings. You haven't done anything wrong, and you can't help how you feel. It might help you move on."

"Yeah, I think you're right," she nodded, "just get it out in the open."

~~~

Sarah and Michael agreed to meet two days later for lunch at a café near her TAFE. Sarah felt sick all morning, and had failed miserably at learning anything in her early classes. She'd spent years avoiding this discussion, dreaming one day he would be the one to make a move, but today she was going to bite the bullet and come clean. She was also going to apologize for her stupid behaviour on the dance floor, and for ignoring him since he'd come back from America. If he understood why she'd behaved the way she had, hopefully he would forgive her. But she would make it very clear that she got it. They would only ever be friends and she was okay with that.

He was already waiting inside for her, drinking a coffee at a table near the window. When he saw her, he jumped up and pulled her chair out after saying hello. She gave him a weak smile, embarrassed by the way she had been treating him the last few months. She answered his question on how her morning was, then busied herself checking the menu. Not that she was hungry – hadn't been for two days.

"What do you want? I'm going to have the BLT sandwich with chips."

"Sounds good. I'll have the same," she answered, glad he couldn't hear how fast her heart was thumping. Michael went to the counter and returned a few minutes later with a diet coke, knowing it was her favourite.

"Sarah," he said at the same as she said "Michael." They laughed together and then he told her to go ahead.

"Firstly please let me apologize for walking off on you at David's party. It was rude. You didn't do anything wrong; it was all me."

"You have nothing to apologize for. I was the one in the wrong. Putting you on the spot like that. I wish I'd handled it better. I just didn't like you being there with Daniel. You deserve better than him. But if I need to keep seeing him at family event's I promise to try and behave."

"You don't have to worry about that. I haven't seen him since that night. He's a complete jerk. I broke it off as soon as we got back to my place."

Michael felt a wave of happiness overwhelm him when he heard her say that. Daniel was never the right guy for Sarah, and he was thrilled she'd ended it. In school all Daniel had cared about was sleeping with as many girls as possible. Michael couldn't imagine that he'd changed much. He also knew what Daniel was like when he was rejected. He had no problem dumping a girl once he was done with her, but there had been stories of how nasty he could be if things were reversed.

"How did he take that?"

"To be honest, not great. Things got a little out of hand, but I was able to get out of the car, and then, thanks to you, Mum and Dad turned up and he took off. He was sending me some scary text messages, but Dad let him know if he continued he would be calling the cops. I haven't heard from him since."

"Good old Tom. I would expect nothing less. Did you keep the text's for the police to look at in case he shows up again? He can be very persistent from what I remember."

"Yeah I did. But hopefully I won't hear from him again." The waitress put their sandwiches down, and Michael picked his up immediately. Sarah, still not hungry, chewed on a chip.

Michael noticed she wasn't really eating and offered to order her something else if she wanted. Sarah shook her head.

"There's something I need to say to you. And it's easier if you just let me talk and don't interrupt me. Okay?"

"Okay," he replied.

Sarah took a deep breath in and then exhaled. She couldn't believe she was actually going to say this to him.

"What you said, when we were dancing, about me having feelings for you," she paused for a second, and then decided to just get it over and done with. "Like I said, it's true. Since I was six years old I've had a little crush on you. But I lied when I said I was over it. And I know, you don't feel like that about me and I'm okay with that. I am trying to get over it. I will get over it. But that's why I've been avoiding you. And probably why I went out with Daniel. I'm desperate to move on and I thought dating him would help. I just hope this doesn't ruin our friendship. You're with Emmy now, and I'll meet someone else one day."

Before he could stop himself, the words tumbled out of Michael's mouth, "I don't want you to move on."

"What?"

"I said I don't want you to move on." Michael paused, surprised that he was admitting this out loud, as much to himself as to her. "I told you that you were driving me crazy. Turns out it wasn't because I don't like Daniel, although I don't. But when I saw you with him, the way he touched you when you were dancing, and how he acted like you belonged to him, it made me jealous."

"Jealous. But, I don't understand. You're with Emmy."

"She dumped me that night after you left, but I'd already decided to end it. She said she wasn't interested in competing for my affections."

"Your affections. For who? ... for *me*?"

"It seems so. I'm not really sure how it happened. I couldn't even tell you *when* it happened. But when I was in America for my engagement party, I thought about you. Not all the time, but once in a while you would pop into my head, and I'd think 'I wonder what Sarah's doing'. Now I think about you all of the time." Michael looked up from his plate of food and held Sarah's gaze, noting the look of confusion.

"Is this a joke Michael? Because if it is it's not a very nice one."

He shook his head. "Nope, definitely not a joke. I didn't even realise I was feeling anything until you left the party with that creep. And then when Emmy said what she did, things started falling into place for me. But seriously. I wanted to punch Daniel in his smug face."

"You did? Well you might just get your chance." Michael turned toward the voice that cut into their conversation and looked up to find Daniel standing next to their table. "What are you doing, sitting here with my girlfriend?" Neither of them had noticed Daniel enter the coffee shop, so engrossed had they been with each other.

"Daniel. I am not your girlfriend. And what are you doing here?" Sarah asked, absolutely furious that he'd interrupted Michael during what could be one of the most important moments in her life. "Shouldn't you be at work? In the city?"

"I was so heartbroken after our misunderstanding that my boss gave me the week off. I thought I might catch you at TAFE so we could sort everything out, and you know, make up," he said and then raised his eyebrows suggestively. Disgust ran through Sarah at the thought of him ever touching her again.

"You have been following me, haven't you? I knew it. You need to leave now. I am not your girlfriend," she repeated slowly so there was no misunderstanding. "And I don't want to see you anymore."

"Come on Sarah. Don't be like that. We had fun together, and I know we could have even more. I don't know what you're doing with mopy Michael," he said as he grabbed her under the elbow, to pull her up, "but it's over. You are my girlfriend."

Michael had been so surprised to see Daniel that he watched the exchange without a word. But seeing Daniel touch Sarah, try and pull her out of the seat was more than enough to make him spring into action. He pushed his chair back, and stood up, his six foot one frame towering over the shorter Daniel. But Daniel was stockier, and he was angry.

"Ohh look at you. Finally going to try and be a man, are you? Give it up Anderson. You don't have a chance against me."

"Wanna find out?"

"Hey you two. Take it outside," a voice boomed across the cafe. A cook appeared from the kitchen, and with his tattoo's and a crooked nose that looked like it had seen a fight or two of its own, both men momentarily stopped.

"And if you don't I'm going to call the police."

"No need. I'm going to do it myself," Sarah called out to the very large, very intimidating man. "He's," and she pointed to Daniel, "been stalking me for weeks."

Sarah pulled out her phone – and while the cook watched on from the counter – dialled the number for the Moorabbin Police station that her dad had insisted she program into her phone the other night. She didn't break eye contact with Daniel as she told the person on the other end of the line that she wanted to make a stalking complaint. Daniel who had always been a bully had never been challenged by a girl before, and in the past his relationships usually ended on his terms and when he was ready. But Sarah had been different from the beginning, standing her ground, and he recognised her steely resolve. *Whatever,* he suddenly thought. *She wasn't worth it anyway, and if the police started sniffing around that would be it for his job. They had already warned him about all the days of work he'd missed in the last few weeks while he'd been watching Sarah's comings and goings.* He gave Michael a push in his chest, but it was nothing more than a defiant gesture, and then turned and stormed out of the café. Sarah heard his car door slam and then through the window saw him pull into traffic, nearly hitting another driver.

"Excuse me miss, are you there?" she heard down the phone line. "Are you in danger. If you are please call 000 immediately. If not you will need to come in and file an official complaint."

"Thank you Officer. No, I'm not in danger. I'll consider coming in, but for now I think everything is okay. He's left."

"Are you sure? We have a record of this call. Do you want me to follow up?"

"Leave it with me. But I think he got the point." She ended the call after thanking the officer for his time, and put her phone back down on the table. People in the café who had been watching the drama went back to their lunch, the excitement over, and after the cook gave the pair a stern look, returned to the kitchen. Michael sat back down and grinned at her.

"Wow. I guess no one should ever mess with you."

"You weren't too bad yourself Michael. Were you really going to hit him?"

"If I had to. I wasn't going to let him hurt you."

"Thank you. That's very heroic of you, but I get the feeling we won't be seeing him anymore."

"I hope not," Michael paused. "Hey, Sarah?"

"Yes Michael."

"I didn't get a chance to finish what I was saying."

"I know Michael."

"I said I couldn't stop thinking about you."

"You did. So what do you think that means?"

"I think it means I'd like to take you out sometime. Soon. On a date."

"Yeah?" she whispered.

"Would that be okay?"

"Yeah," she repeated so quietly he almost didn't catch it. But he saw the smile grow on her face, the one that reached all the way to her beautiful eyes.

Michael reached across the table and cupped her face in his hand. They were only centimetres apart, but it was still much too far. He stroked her chin gently with his thumb, and then he leaned further towards her. And when he kissed her for the first time, he finally understood why he had been so angry, so jealous. He hadn't known, hadn't realised before that he should be the only person who ever kissed Sarah again. And with that knowing, he could feel himself tumbling slowly, finally, falling for her.

Chapter Thirty-Six

A dam picked up his briefcase and was about to put his phone inside when he noticed a new text from his cop buddy Patrick. Adam, assuming that it must be time for their annual game of golf, considered reading it later. If he didn't get going he was going to be late for work. But curiosity got the better of him and he tapped on the screen. It didn't take long to realise that this wasn't about golf at all.

Hey Adam. Just thought you might like to take a look at the *Australian Financial Review* today. Page 5. Pat.

Adam knew that if he didn't leave the house in the next few minutes he would get stuck in the school traffic and considered looking at the paper tonight. But what was the point of being the boss if you couldn't be late once and a while? He usually checked the first few pages of the paper, but hadn't bothered today. He headed back to the kitchen where they always ate breakfast at the table in the cosy bay window that overlooked the garden. Picking up the paper that Caroline left for him every morning, he flipped quickly to page five, and then sat down. He was going to be late this morning, but it didn't matter. This was much more important.

Tycoon Pleads Guilty

Baltimore businessman, Emerson Thornton, plead guilty yesterday to multiple charges. A 3-year joint FBI/AFP international task-force uncovered a string of crimes, including human trafficking.

Senior partner of Thornton and Holmes Capital, Thornton negotiated a plea bargain but could face a minimum of ten years in federal prison. Additional charges were brought by the SEC and the DOJ including multiple counts of drug trafficking, bribery, extortion and hiring illegal aliens.

Thornton has been investigated numerous times by the DOJ, but charges were never laid. Australian Federal Police (AFP) were able to link Thornton to the task-force investigation when they received an anonymous tip last year. Documents received by the AFP linked illegal drug imports that were being routed from China, bound for the US, and then smuggled into Australia, hidden in plain sight as over the counter pain medication. The AFP issued a statement confirming that several entries in a secret ledger compiled by Thornton identified an Australian national who had been flagged as suspicious. The unnamed individual co-operated with the police, providing evidence of Thornton's connection to the illegal drug imports in exchange for a reduced sentence. The FBI executed search warrants for Thornton's home and office which led to the retrieval of documents that will be used as evidence in multiple bribery charges.

Thornton also plead guilty to exploiting illegal workers and paying them below the minimum wage, as well as facilitating the movement of illegals over the Mexican/US border and dispersing them throughout the USA to work in multiple operations, both legal and illegal.

The DOJ has applied to seize Thornton's assets under the Executive Order issued by President Donald Trump. Executive Order 13818 – 'Blocking the property of persons involved in serious human rights abuse or corruption', was issued on 21 December 2017. Thornton's lawyers are contesting the seizure of assets.

Further charges are expected to be brought against several other persons, including government employees who have been accused of receiving bribes from Thornton, as well as union leaders and members who were complicit in securing illegal workers and housing them in substandard accommodation, often with multiple families living in squalor.

Thornton's family has not made a public comment at this time and have requested privacy.

Adam put the paper down, genuinely shocked. He knew Emerson was a bad guy, but he couldn't have even begun to imagine how evil he really was. Human trafficking. Unbelievable. He was still sitting at the table in silence when Caroline came in to clear the dishes.

"Adam, I thought you'd left. You're going to be late for work."

Adam handed her the paper without saying anything. She read a few sentences, and then, making the connection, looked up from the page.

"But that's Margaux's father."

"Read it all. It's pretty bad." Caroline sat down and read the article all the way through before she spoke again.

"Wow. This is shocking. Can you imagine if Michael was still engaged to Margaux? It would have been a disaster."

"Absolutely. The Thornton's will be pariahs. I bet the promised internship would have disappeared as well. I can't see a prestigious hospital agreeing to employ him after this came out."

"And if the government seize all their assets, the family will be left with nothing. I can't imagine Margaux getting a job, can you?"

"I expect the kids will be alright. They had trust funds, and Thornton would have made sure they were untouchable. But they might lose Thornton Manor and all their other properties and businesses."

"I'm completely stunned. I know you didn't trust him, but this goes way beyond anything I could have imagined. I wonder who the anonymous source was. They must have been brave. And incorruptible because it sounds like Emerson was bribing people all over the place."

Adam considered for a minute not saying anything. No-one had been in touch about the evidence he provided, and it was unlikely that they ever would. But he wasn't going to start lying to his wife now.

"I'm going to tell you something, but you need to keep it a secret. It was me."

"You what?" Caroline exclaimed.

"I came across a ledger when we were staying at the manor. I took some photos of it, and then passed them on to Patrick, you know my old Uni mate who works for the Feds. I never heard from him after he thanked me for the info until this morning when he gave me a heads up about the article."

"Why didn't you tell me?"

"When months went by and I hadn't heard anything I decided I hadn't given them anything of value. Turns out I must have."

"Should we tell Michael about this?" Caroline asked.

"No, I don't think so. He doesn't need to know about Thornton and I'm certainly not going to tell him I gave information to the police. The last thing we want is him feeling sorry for Margaux and getting in touch with her. She's so manipulative, she might try and get her claws into him again. If she's looking to escape the spotlight, Australia would be a good place to do that."

"Agreed. I won't say a word, but I think you might have underestimated his relationship with Sarah. I don't think I've ever seen a man more ridiculously in love with someone before and I doubt he gives that awful girl a second thought."

"That's not true. What about me? I think I can give my son a run for his money in the love department."

"Well you're close," she smiled and then stood up from the table and kissed him gently. "My very own James Bond. Now get to work while I put the recycling out," she said as she picked up the paper and threw it in the bin. Emerson Thornton didn't deserve another minute of their time.

Chapter Thirty-Seven

"Look. I know he's tried to explain it, but I just don't get it," Joan told Beth.

Beth shrugged her shoulders. "He became a Christian. It's not that hard a concept to understand."

"Maybe not for you. You grew up going to church. But David. Uh uh," she said shaking her head. "Since I've known him he's always stayed away from serious religious types."

Beth raised her eyebrows. "Um, we spend a lot of time with you and David. And we take it pretty seriously."

"Well yeah, but you were my friend before we got married, so he didn't have a choice. And you never tried to shove it down his throat. He knew where you stood and vice versa."

"What about Adam? He and David always got along, and Adam isn't shy about sharing his faith. But I never heard David get upset with him."

"David tried to give him a break. He said he understood the Christian 'thing' Adam and Caroline had going on because it happened after Isabelle died. He called it their crutch."

Beth let out a quiet snicker. "I love you Joan, but sometimes I wonder if you have any idea what's going on in the world. I can guarantee you, following Jesus is anything but a crutch."

"Oh please. You go to your meeting once a week and have a few rules to follow. It can't be that hard."

Beth took a sip of her coffee and considered Joan's perspective for a minute. People really believe that all Christians were like that, and for some people that's all it was. Go to church and look good on the outside, while they get up to whatever they want in private. And there was a time in her life that her faith was pretty much like that. But in the last five years as she saw the transformation God had made in Adam's life, she began to wonder why she wasn't as committed to living a Godly life as he was. It had been the wakeup call she needed, and her faith and trust in God had grown. And with that so had her obedience. She believed with all her heart that it was a privilege to be accepted by God as one of his children.

"You won't hear about it on the news much Joan, but Christians all over the world are being murdered for their faith. Their churches are being torn down or burnt to ashes. Many are thrown in prison. Even here in Australia we are starting to face persecution. Granted, not the way they are in other countries, and our lives aren't at risk, but our beliefs are ridiculed constantly."

"By whom? We have freedom of religion here. You can believe in pretty much anything you want in Australia and no one bats an eyelid."

"Oh, please. A sports star puts a bible verse up on social media and he gets fired. But other sports figures drive drunk, take drugs, or get into fights and they get a slap on the wrist and maybe a fine. Christianity is being attacked by the media, big business, and government. It's free speech for all unless you're a Christian, and then when you say what you believe you're considered a bigot, hateful and not inclusive. But nobody stops to think that many of our laws came from the ten commandments or that the majority of charity in this country comes through churches or Christian organisations. This country was built on the back of Christian standards which is why it's such a great place to live, but these days those standards are being eroded and we're hated and mocked for our beliefs."

"Alright. Say that's true. Then I really don't understand why David wants to be part of that. He's always been a good person. Never hurt anyone or broke the law. Shouldn't that be enough for your God?"

"It's not about being good. How many people in the world think, hey maybe I'm *not* actually a good person? I'm thinking very few. And even the ones who know they're bad probably justify their behaviour and think what they're doing is okay. We all have different standards." She stopped for a moment, considering a situation Joan would understand without question.

"What about someone who is attracted to children? They claim they love children and aren't doing any harm if they take that attraction further than just their private feelings. Would you let your child be in a physical or even emotional relationship with that person?"

"No of course not," Joan protested. "They're my kids and anyone who even thinks about touching them better run fast and run far."

"That's right. But to that person who believes it's his right to have a physical relationship with a child, they would say you aren't considering their feelings. You're being bigoted."

"That's an extreme example Beth. Everyone knows that's evil."

"Do they? I've noticed recently that some groups are pushing to classify paedophilia as a sexual preference and not a criminal act. That's the beginning of a very slippery slope. Why do you think I left my job? I found it abhorrent what was being taught to young children about sex in school, and this curriculum was coming from our government. In society everyone has a different view on what is acceptable. God doesn't. He makes it very clear what we can and can't do. And before you point it out, yes we fail Him and ourselves all the time. But He has those standards for our own good. Like any parent, He loves us and wants to protect us from danger, and also from ourselves. You know that when you made the decision not to sleep with a man unless you were married, that it was for your own good. You decided on a standard that protected you emotionally and physically. And look at how well that turned out."

"I'm not so sure about that. I barely recognise my husband these days." Beth sat back in her chair; a questioning look on her face.

"Alright," Joan conceded. "It isn't that bad. But he is different."

"In a bad way?"

"No. He's just ... I don't know, I feel like I can't be myself anymore. I'm always worried he'll point out if I'm doing something he thinks is bad. Like the other night. I was watching a movie and this couple were ... you know. It wasn't that bad, but David got up and left the room. I asked him where he was going, and he said he didn't think it was right for him to watch it. Nothing like that ever bothered him before. Now he's all holier than thou."

"Did he tell you to turn the movie off?"

"No, but he didn't come back and watch telly until the movie was over. Our nice evening was ruined."

"So your husband doesn't want to watch other people have sex, even if it is fake. You poor thing."

"Oh shut up," Joan suggested as she gave Beth a sarcastic glare. "I mean. Where am I going to go to have fun now? All I have left now is Jill and Matthew."

"Don't be so sure," Beth grinned. "Those two are next on our list," she teased.

Chapter Thirty-Eight

Michael, who had been watching from the front window opened the door before she even had a chance to reach for the doorbell. He swooped Sarah into a hug and then kissed her.

It had only been a day since he had seen her, but it had felt like a week had gone by. It never ceased to amaze him how different this relationship was from the one he'd had with Margaux. He was no longer walking on eggshells all the time, afraid to offend or looking for signs that she loved him. He and Sarah were equally enamoured with each other and he had never been this happy in his life.

He knew eventually they would have a fight or disagree on something. Life wasn't a fairy tale, and every relationship had times where it could go either way. But from that first moment when he realised that he was falling in love, he determined that he was going to do whatever it took to cherish Sarah and make her feel like she was number one in his life. Because he knew what it felt like to not be loved properly and fully.

Michael pulled back a little, giving Sarah a chance to breath. "Hi," she exhaled. "I missed you."

"Yeah," he smiled down at her. "Me too."

"You know everyone will be watching us tonight."

"I don't care, let them. And tonight should be about Isabelle anyway. She would have almost been nineteen. I can't believe it's been seven years since she died."

"Do you still miss her?"

"Of course I do. Probably not with the same intensity as Mum and Dad, but yes I miss her. When I see other people with their siblings, fighting but happy, like you and Lochie, I wish I still had that. And I often wonder, what kind of woman she would have been if she had lived?"

"If she's anything like you, I think she would have been amazing."

"Yeah, she would have been." He untangled himself from her and slung his arm across her shoulder. "Come on. Let's get this over with."

The party was in full swing when they entered the lounge room. Jillian was sitting on the couch with Jay who was awkwardly holding baby Alex. He looked terrified, but Jill was making sure the squirming baby didn't wriggle free. At nearly four months old she was smiling and gurgling away. Caroline smiled at Michael and Sarah as she rushed back to the kitchen, used to seeing them together by now. She couldn't have been more delighted with the new romance. Even though it was early days for their relationship she was sure it was going to last. She was already planning the wedding in her head and it was going to be spectacular.

David and Matthew were huddled in the corner, heads bent, looking over some plans.

"We could have this up in no time. How long did the council tell you it will take to get a permit?"

"Months. You know how they love to drag their heels and keep people waiting. But that's okay. It gives Martin plenty of time to get used to the idea of leaving his home. He's excited to be living so close to Jay, but he's apprehensive about moving so far away from his neighbourhood. He lived in that house his whole adult life. He bought it with his wife almost fifty years ago."

"That's a long time to live somewhere so of course it'll be hard for him to leave. He must be lonely though."

"Yeah. We visit him with Jay every week, but the rest of the time he's alone, hoping Martha will show up. But the police aren't looking for her because she's an adult who left of her own free will, and no one else has seen her. He's contacted everyone he can think of that she might go to, but so far he's come up with nothing. She could be anywhere by now."

"Matthew have you thought about what happens to Martin if Jay is removed from your home? You're stuck with some old guy living in your back yard."

"Yeah we thought about it, but I don't see that happening. Martin has legal custody of Jay now, and he's told Social Services that he wants Jay to remain with us permanently. We don't know how long it will take, but we've applied for guardianship. We won't be able to adopt him without his mother's permission, and I doubt she would ever give it, even if she shows up one day. But with guardianship we make all the day-to-day decisions for him, like where he goes to school, and how he is raised. Martin lets us do that anyway, but if he passed away then social services could move him. With guardianship that won't happen."

"And you think a granny flat is the best option. Why not save a hundred thousand dollars plus, and let him live in the house with you?"

Matthew shook his head. "No. He needs his privacy, and so do we. It was fine when he stayed with us for those few weeks, but it wasn't a permanent solution. This way he lives his life, we live ours, but Jay can see him every day if he wants, and Martin has company if he gets lonely. And with his heart issues, he shouldn't be living on his own anyway. If he had a heart attack it could be days before anyone found him. We'll install those emergency buttons in the bathroom and the bedroom. That way we can be there in seconds. And the new line of food at Sustenance is doing so well that we can afford it."

"Sounds like you've thought it through. I should be able to give you an estimate by next week. Is Martin putting anything in to help pay for it?"

"He wanted to, but it gets too complicated then with who owns it. We're paying for the building, and he'll cover the running costs, power etc. The good thing is that he's decided that most of the money he gets from selling his house will go into a trust for Jay. He'll keep some so that he can do some nice things like go on holidays, but he said he doesn't need much. That way Jay gets a great start in life as an adult, and if his mother shows up at any time she can't claim any of Martin's money as next of kin. He was really worried that if she inherited it she would waste it. Her impulse control isn't good. "

"Makes sense. Is Jay doing okay after what happened with his mother?" David asked.

"He's better. He's had some bad dreams and there's been a lot of tears. But most of the time he's alright. We've decided to leave him at the public school until the end of the year. We don't want to make too many changes at once. But he's enrolled to go to Zoe's school next year. He'll get a great education there and have better opportunities."

"You're doing a lot for this kid Matthew. He's a very lucky little boy."

"Nah mate," Matthew replied, shaking his head. "We're the lucky ones. I don't think we could love him more if we were his biological parents."

~~~

Dinner was – as always – delicious. The girls had taken over the lounge room while the boys moved to the rumpus room to play pool, and they were enjoying catching up with each other. Alex was peacefully sleeping in her pram in the corner and Joan finally found herself relaxing. Her other two, along with Jay were being watched by Zoe in the theatre room where a movie played.

"So how's school going Beth?" Joan asked. "Sick of hanging out all day with the kids in your class, wishing they would pull their pants up properly?"

"You'd be surprised. At least half of the class are old ladies like me, so we keep them in line. And most of them are serious kids anyway. They're too interested in learning a better way to heal people to muck around. And I'm loving the classes. Right now we're studying about the damage a lot of pharmaceuticals do. Compared to ancient herbal remedies, a lot of the drugs doctors are prescribing are unnecessary and in some instances downright dangerous."

"Don't let Michael hear you say that Beth," Caroline warned, a cheeky smile on her face. "He's pretty anti alternative medicine, and you don't want to start off on the wrong foot with your future son-in-law."

All eyes turned to Sarah who had been quietly listening to the conversation. She felt the heat rise on her cheeks in embarrassment.

"I think it's way too soon to be suggesting anything like that," she stammered. "We've only been going out for a few weeks."

"Well I think you two are adorable together," Joan weighed in on the subject. "Watching Michael pull your chair out at dinner and bringing you drinks all night. So cute."

"We're not puppies Joan. We're adults in a private relationship, so if you don't mind, why don't we change the subject?"

The women exchanged amused glances and raised eyebrows. Kids these days were so sensitive.

"Yes, let's change the subject from how cute Michael and Sarah are together shall we?" Caroline suggested. "So, have you discussed how many children you're going to have? Because I'm going to make the best grandmother."

"Hey, what about me? I think I'm going to make a pretty awesome Gran," Beth claimed.

Sarah stood up from the couch. "I think I'll go and hang out with the boys, if you don't mind? At least I might get some sensible conversation out of them." She stormed out of the room to the sound of the four friends laughing hysterically. *Geez old people were embarrassing when they'd had a few wines*, Sarah thought.

Not watching where she was going – too annoyed by the conversation she had just been subjected to – she crashed into Michael who was coming out of the rumpus room.

"Don't go in there," he warned.

"I don't suggest you go back there," she pointed to the lounge room. "They'll eat you alive."

"Can't be as bad as that lot," he nodded towards the rumpus. "Grown men making kissing noises. Your father included. Don't they know they're embarrassing themselves?"

Sarah rolled her eyes. "Well at least they didn't ask you how many children you were planning."

"Oh yes they did. I told them to mind their own business."

"So you should. It's a long time before we need to think about things like that." And then realising what she had suggested she stuttered, "Not that I'm saying that *we* ever need to think about that, I meant, us as individuals."

"I was thinking three."

"Three what?"

"Kids. Three kids would be great. Two isn't quite enough," he answered as he slid his arms around her waist and pulled her close.

"No," she decided as she wrapped herself around his neck. "Then you end up with a middle child. I was a middle child and I wouldn't wish that on anyone. Not the first born, and not the baby either."

"Then I guess we take our chances with four," he whispered in her ear and then he kissed her, gently … slowly.

Epilogue
8th February 2020

S tanding at the open French doors that led off her family room, Jillian looked out over her backyard. It was full of friends laughing and children playing. A more perfect February evening couldn't be had.

The sun had just set, and painted the sky a dusky pink. Above the sound of people's voices she could hear crickets singing and a gentle breeze cooled the air after a sticky thirty degree day.

When they finally received word last week that they had been granted guardianship of Jay she hadn't been able to resist throwing a party to celebrate, and today had turned out perfect. Only close family and friends were invited, but that was exactly what she wanted. Martin, now part of the family had just said goodnight to her before retreating to his new granny flat in the back corner of the property where he had been living for the last month. Matthew had planted a screen of mature pittosporums to give him privacy, and so far their situation was working out well.

Matthew came up behind her and wrapped his arms around her waist.

"Happy?" he asked.

"So happy," she replied. "I don't think I could have imagined a better life."

"After losing Amelia all those years ago I never thought I would love anyone as much as I did her. I couldn't have been more wrong. Thank you for giving Zoe and I such a wonderful life."

"Back at ya babe. You know, I think 2020 is going to be the best year of our lives. A whole new decade. It's so hard to believe we're living in the roaring twenties. I'm still trying to come to terms with not being a kid in the eighties."

"Oh, I know I'm not a kid anymore. Every morning when I get out of bed and my back screams, 'what are you doing'?"

"Great. So you're telling me I'm married to an old man. Good thing I still think you look pretty hot."

"Thanks babe. You look pretty hot yourself."

"Um, excuse me you two," Caroline interrupted, but her tone was cheeky. "Can you cool it, so I get through please?" She was holding a gorgeous cake she'd made to celebrate Jay's new status as a member of the family. They stepped aside and let her through. Caroline put the cake down on the outside table and then started cutting it into slices. After sliding pieces onto plates she began passing them around. The kids swarmed around her, as did a few of the adults. She handed a plate to Michael, who was chatting to David and Tom nearby.

"It's not that big a deal is it? It's just like the flu."

"What's this?" she asked, so proud of her son who was on his way to becoming a fully-fledged doctor.

"This Coronavirus they've been talking about on the news. The virus from China," Michael answered. "We don't know that much about it yet." Michael had recently begun his internship at a Bendigo hospital and had arranged a rare night at home for the party.

"I heard people are dying of it in China," Tom said.

"I've heard that too," David confirmed. "And now we have a few cases here."

"Should we be worried Michael?" his mother asked.

Michael shrugged his shoulders. "Honestly, I don't know Mum. We don't have enough information, and China is being very quiet on the subject. We'll probably have to ride it out, the same way that we do with the flu every season. Unfortunately, some people die from these viruses. There's not much we can do about it. It's just the way it goes."

"The World Health Organisation don't seem too concerned about it, so I'm not going to worry either," Tom said. "Beth makes sure our immune systems are strong, and seriously, what else can we do? It's not like we're all going to start wearing surgical masks everywhere."

Joan walked across to the group and handed Alex to David. He reached out for his daughter. "Tag you're it," she said. "Will is causing havoc. If Matthew sees him pulling out his plants there'll be trouble." David handed Alex over to Caroline after she held her arms out in the hope she could cuddle the little girl and said, "I'll get him Joanie. You stay here and have some cake." David strode off in the direction of Will who was indeed pulling out the new annuals Matthew had planted for the party, while Caroline struggled to contain the toddler. Alex was walking already and wanted to get into everything.

"Who's the girl Nathan brought tonight?" Joan asked Tom, looking across at the pair of teenagers who were sitting together on a large swing that hung from an old oak tree that dominated the yard.

"That is Tahlia, Nathan's new girlfriend."

"Ah. From your tone I get the impression you're not too keen."

"No it's not that. She's a nice girl."

"But?"

"But Nathan's just started year eleven. I don't want him distracted."

"He'll be fine Tom. You were plenty distracted by Beth if I remember correctly, and you got through school. What about Lochie? Anyone new? Or is he still flitting from girl to girl?"

306

"Still flitting. I don't think that boy will ever settle down. Not that he has much time these days. He settles on his new house next month and every spare minute will be spent fixing it up. I don't think I've ever seen a bigger dump. And he's applying to subdivide the block and build another house on the back. Good investment, but it's going to cost him everything he's saved. I just hope the real estate market doesn't drop."

"Adam thinks the outlook is really good. The stock markets are on fire at the moment, especially in the U.S," Caroline confirmed.

"Did I hear my name?" Adam asked as he approached the group of friends.

"I was just saying you thought stocks and property would do well for the foreseeable future."

"I do. Everyone I talk to is optimistic. I tell you, I'm excited about what the next few years will bring. Did you tell them about our new acquisition?"

"I was going to wait until it was settled, but the contracts are signed, so I guess we can let the cat out of the bag. Last week we bought Carrbridge."

"You did? What on earth are you going to do with that old place?" Tom asked.

Beth, who had been finishing up some dishes joined her husband just in time to hear his question.

"What old place?"

"Caroline said she's bought Carrbridge."

Beth's mouth fell open in surprise. "You can't seriously be going into business with Alistair and Bridget. You'll kill them both."

"Don't worry Beth. They won't be there," Caroline confirmed. "After their niece went back to Scotland, they decided they were too old to run it anymore. They want to move to Queensland and retire. So we decided to buy the property. We'll give it a complete overhaul and then rent it out for weddings and parties, the same as it is now, although Events will be the only caterer allowed to operate out of it. But because we won't be living in it we'll also turn the accommodation wing into a bed and breakfast. And Sarah," she called out, gesturing for her to join them. When Sarah came over a plate of cake in her hand she continued her conversation.

"I'm hoping Sarah will run it for me."

"Run what?" Sarah asked

"My new bed and breakfast. I just bought Carrbridge House. I was hoping you'll consider moving in and managing it for me. There'll be other staff members, but you would be in charge."

"Are you serious? I have no experience. Wouldn't you want someone older?"

"No. I want you. I trust you, and I've done some research. There are hospitality courses you can do online, and I will happily pay you to do them. And there would only be four suites available, so that's no more than eight guests at a time. When it's quiet during the week you can still work on planning events that are held on the property. You could live in the cottage, so you'd have plenty of privacy."

"That would be amazing," Sarah responded delighted at the new opportunity. "I would love that."

"Well, take some time to think about it first. It will be a big change for you, living on your own."

"I don't need to think about it. I accept." Then Sarah had a thought. "Hang on, Shona won't be there will she?"

"Definitely not," Caroline smiled. Shona certainly made an impression in the short time she'd been here. "She's long gone back to Scotland. She didn't like Australia after all, and Bridget and Alistair are moving up north."

Michael watched the exchange between his mother and his girlfriend. He wished she'd spoken to him before she made her offer. He had some plans of his own, and his mother had just thrown a spanner in the works.

Sarah was going to be twenty soon and he'd decided that would be the perfect day to ask. He'd already began planning everything, and was on the hunt for a ring that Sarah would love. Because he had every intention of making sure that by the end of this year Sarah would be his wife.

Acknowledgments

Firstly, let me thank every person who has taken the time to read this, or any of my novels. It is so amazing to have someone find me on Facebook and tell me that my books helped them or entertained them. I appreciate hearing your feedback. And a special thank you to those readers who have been asking when the next novel is due. Here it is.

Thanks to my family. Without you letting me burn dinner and disappear into myself mid conversation when an idea strikes, I would just be a thoughtless woman who doesn't pay attention. I do apologize for the not-so-great dinners and the finger up in the air to stop you talking while I got a thought down before it disappeared forever. And to Wills who can't read this cause although he is the most adorable puppy in the world, he isn't very bright, thanks for keeping me company every day sitting under my desk while I pottered away on my computer.

To Monique Nicholls, my first reader of *Falling Slowly* (outside my husband who had no choice), I appreciate you so much. Just knowing you were looking forward to each new chapter kept me writing on the days when circumstances made me wish for the couch and endless episodes of *Mad About You*. Your insight made this a better story, and your love for the characters made me feel like they could be real people outside of my head. You could see them too. And for the boring details like spelling and punctuation, your attention to detail was invaluable.

I would like to say thanks to Sandra. You know who you are, and without your details about Monash Hospital I would have had to make the whole thing up. 2020 was not the year when a person could wander around a hospital getting the lay of the land.

Angela D'Alfonso was a voice on the other end of the phone (there was no meeting new people during lockdown), who talked me through her experience with Pre-eclampsia. Like all girls, we quickly found new topics to talk about, even though we were strangers, and finding out there were other people in the world who didn't believe all the hype about 'the rona' made my day. *Anne of Green Gables* would call us kindred spirits. And thank you Jen for putting us in touch, and for getting us together once we got let out of our homes for a dinner I thoroughly enjoyed.

Thank you to IndieMosh who have published this little story. You are so easy to work with, and I couldn't be more thrilled with Ally's artwork. You took a few of my ideas and brought them to life.

Writing is a solitary endeavour made possible by all the people who pop in from time to time to help, offer advice and insight and most importantly to cheer one on. Thank you.